𝕽𝔦𝔡𝔦𝔫𝔤 𝔱𝔥𝔢 𝔚𝔦𝔯𝔢

Ford Dudley

UNCLE PAUL,

BUCKLE UP AND ENJOY "THE RIDE".

— FORD

D1520097

Copyright © 2021 by Ford Dudley

All rights reserved.

No part of this book may be reproduced in any form or by any electronic or mechanical means, including information storage and retrieval systems, without written permission from the author, except for the use of brief quotations in a book review.

For Peggy

Let's keep dancing

CONTENTS

1

An icy draft washed over Franz Keller's desk. Papers fluttered under his pen. "Here you go, Sergeant. Got a letter." The mail clerk dropped an envelope in front of Keller then braced for his return to the outside. The door slammed under the wind. Delinquent snowflakes eddied in the foyer. There'd been no prediction of a storm tonight, but winter in the Netherlands was as fickle as a teenage girl.

Keller picked up the envelope. A woman's handwriting. *From Taatje?* His pulse quickened. Had she sent her answer? The envelope had no return post and was addressed precisely the way he'd told her, with his sector code—the only way it would get through the army mail room. *It must be from her.* He tucked it into his pocket. His shift was about over. He could read it later—in privacy.

Keller shuffled the last administrative forms and placed them

3

atop the never-ending stack. *Done!* His right leg was aching—the scarred area where the shrapnel had torn through his thigh. It felt like the metal was still in there. The wound had sentenced him to this assignment. *A desk job for Christ's sake.*

Keller was a damn good Wehrmacht sergeant, a noble calling. He was never meant for this—to be a secretary for a swarm of arrogant officers. On the battle line his contact with the higher ranks was rare. Orders were usually sent down to him through some flunky lieutenant, a buffer between him and the vainglorious commanders. Those lieutenants had less combat experience than Keller, and they knew it. They trusted him to cipher orders. He did it well. He'd been one of the best NCOs on the French front and he had the military record to prove it.

But this wasn't a French battlefield. It was a beehive—captains, majors, colonels—all buzzing about. And these officers were the worst kind. Most of them had never seen combat. They were businessmen when the war started and were hustled through officer training so they could become Hitler's bookkeepers. Keller didn't trust any of them.

The wound was still a hot coal buried in his thigh. He stood, flexed his hip, and massaged the needling pain. Under his pant leg was a star-shaped scar that had healed over slashed muscle. In the August battle for the Falaise Gap, a British howitzer shell exploded behind Keller's hedgerow. Now, six months later, he was sentenced to carry on the war from behind a desk. He'd trade these papers for a rifle in the blink of an eye.

He pulled on his overcoat and checked the pocket to ensure that Taatje's letter was still there. Outside, frozen wind was rolling in from the North Sea with a black storm on its heels. He flashed his identification card to the MP, turned up his collar, and walked into the Arnhem twilight.

He was *en route* to the barracks, a converted warehouse a few blocks away. The barracks were one of the structures that survived the Allied bombings. Pushing aside Dutch citizens who were left to fend for themselves, the German Army had commandeered the standing buildings in this part of Arnhem.

Wind swirled through the street and stung his face. The sidewalk was patched with ice. He searched for solid footing, but his bum leg made it tough.

A young woman, gripping a satchel over her shoulder, sprinted from an alleyway. She gasped as she spun around, looking for anything behind her. Terror in her eyes revealed the answer. A German soldier bound out of the alley. A moment later a second soldier, a fat one, huffed in his wake. The young woman dashed across the street toward a bombed-out heap of stone and mortar. Panicked, she scurried into the labyrinth of debris and rounded a toppled pillar only to run into a wall of busted concrete. The predators were upon her. The first soldier grabbed a shock of hair and jerked backward. She shrieked and stumbled backward over the rubble. Another jerk—she flipped sideways and crumpled at the feet of the fat one.

The first soldier drove his knee into her shoulder as he held her to the pavement. She flopped like a fish and her skirt flew up, exposing her white underpants. She tugged at her skirt, but the fat one pinned the skirt to the ground with his boot heel and pointed a pistol at her chest.

Fatso gulped for breath. "Haven't seen pretty legs like that in a long time." He turned to his comrade. "Those whores on the riverfront aren't sweet like this one, eh?"

Number One chuffed, "Damn nice."

Fatso pushed the fringe of her skirt up to her belly. "Bet you're hiding a sweet pussy under those knickers, aren't you girl?"

She screamed, but Number One stuffed her wool cap into her mouth. She kicked furiously until the fat one poked a pistol barrel against her forehead. She froze.

Unseen to this point, Keller came up behind them, and barked, "What's going on here, Corporal?"

Fatso whirled to see Keller standing over him. "Sergeant!" He bolted upright and thrust his shoulders back, standing to attention. "This thief was stealing food from an army supply truck, sir."

Number One still had the woman pinned. "Get her off the ground, Private," Keller ordered.

Her knee was bloody and elbows scraped. She was only a girl —*fourteen, maybe fifteen years old*. Her chest heaved and she trembled as she tried to pull her skirt down. Her eyes darted, as she prayed for a way out.

Keller said, "What's in the satchel, young lady?" She didn't understand his German words. He motioned. "Open it up."

Keller rummaged through the bag and pulled out tins of beef, German Army rations.

Fatso said, "See Sergeant, stealing right from under our eyes. What do you say you let us teach her a lesson, show her who's boss?" A note of lust was in his voice.

"I'll take it from here, Corporal. You two get back to your post."

"Come on Sarge," the fat one pleaded. "Just a few minutes for each of us—in the alleyway. What could it—"

Keller stepped into Fatso's chest. "I said I'll take it from here, Corporal."

"Yes, sir." "Yes, sir."

"Back to your post!"

"*Heil Hitler!*" Both men thrust arms outward in salute.

"*Heil Hitler!*" Keller returned salute and the two soldiers skulked back across the street. *Fuck Hitler. He's the reason everything around here has gone to hell.*

Keller grabbed the girl by the arm and roughly ushered her a half block, then pushed her down an alleyway. Behind him he heard Fatso muttering to Number One, "He just wanted the little bitch all to himself."

Keller guided the weeping girl down the alley and pulled her into an alcove. She shook from head to toe.

"Which way do you live, girl?" He spoke in Dutch.

Her sobs stifled a bit, clearly surprised to hear this German soldier speaking her language.

"I'm not going to hurt you, but you must get out of here. This area is not safe. Now, which way do you live?"

Still shaking, she swiped tears with the palm of her hand, then pointed.

"How long will it take you to get home?" asked Keller.

"F … five…five minutes."

Keller put the satchel in her hand. "Here. Hide this under your coat. Stay to the back streets, away from patrols." She stared at Keller, dumbfounded. "Go," he said.

She tucked the bag inside her coat and backed up. She pushed out the words, "You … You are Dutch?"

"My mother was Dutch," said Keller. "Now go. Get out of here."

With her eyes locked on him, the girl scuffled backward a few paces, then turned and ran.

Keller walked out of the alley and was met by a whirl of snow. The two assholes were gone. *Good.* He turned into the wind and continued toward the barracks.

He had seen this situation often while in France. The conquering Germans had crushed the French people, then enslaved them in their own country. Five years ago, when he enlisted, he did so because he was a patriot and proud to wear the *Wehrmacht* uniform. Back then, he believed what the Nazi leaders spouted. Germany would rise from the ashes of the last war and build a magnificent empire—a *Third Reich.* But Keller never imagined

Germany doing so on the backs and blood of other people. Now he was in the Netherlands, his mother's homeland. Things were worse here than in France. His conscience burned and his German uniform no longer felt majestic.

Keller arrived at the barracks and pounded the slush off his boots. It was not much warmer inside, but at least there was no wind. He stopped in the entryway and took out the envelope. Better to read it here than to have nosy bunkmates slobbering over his shoulder, which is exactly what would happen once they caught the scent of a *sweetheart letter*. He positioned himself under the bare light bulb, took off his gloves, blew warm breath into his hands, and opened it.

His eyes first went to the bottom of the page. Taatje's signature. He hadn't seen her in nine years, since the summer of 1936. They'd fallen in love when they were both seventeen years old. At that time, a German boy courting a Dutch girl didn't seem so far-fetched. After all, his German father had married his Dutch mother. But it wouldn't turn out that way for Keller.

His mother died the winter he turned eighteen. There was no longer a reason for family holidays in Holland. His father certainly wouldn't take him there. Papa neither cared for the Netherlands or the Dutch relatives. Franz Keller and Taatje Hoobinck were separated. Though only a hundred kilometers from Düsseldorf to Maarburg, the border between the two nations was gradually strangled under the grip of Hitler.

They followed different paths. Taatje helped her father on the farm. Franz went to the university. Their letters became less and less frequent.

Franz joined the army in 1940. Six weeks later, Germany invaded the Netherlands. He lost track of Taatje.

In September, he received horrible news from his sister in Germany. Their Dutch relatives who lived in the farmland outside Maarburg—aunt, uncle, and cousins—had been killed in an Allied

8

bombing raid. Also dead were Taatje's parents. Details were sketchy, but Taatje had survived.

Now, Sergeant Franz Keller had returned to the Netherlands. He was posted to a Wehrmacht administrative office in Arnhem, only a short distance down the Rhine River from Taatje's home. It was easy to trace her to an apartment where she was living in the town of Maarburg—no longer on the family farm.

He sent her a letter last week, unsure if she'd get it. He prayed she would. She had. Her reply was brief and sterile.

Dear Franz,

> *Yes, we should meet Sunday as you suggest. I'll be waiting under the DeWitt statue in the center of Maarburg. Noon. Tell no one else of this.*

Taatje

Sunday. Keller would return to Maarburg and see Taatje again. He smiled and tucked the letter deep into his pocket.

2

A coyote lurked in desert scrub, just outside the barbed wire. She paused behind a patch of prickly pear and raised her nose, sniffing for human scent on the breeze. Satisfied, she slithered through a furrow under the fence. Ears pricked high, she glided across open gravel to the garbage bins, where steel drums were sure to be chocked with tasty scraps. The coyote tipped a barrel and worked fast, gulping a stew of kitchen slop.

Camp Barlow was quiet. Prisoners-of-war were confined to barracks at 2100. Corporal Jauch and Private Fleischer were exceptions since they were working overnight detail in the mess hall. Jauch was chopping carrots in the kitchen when the front doors flew open.

He peered through the serving window. The familiar hulk of

Sergeant Müller, accompanied by two thugs, surged into the dining hall. Fleischer dropped his mop and saluted, *"Heil Hitler!"*

Müller barked back, "Leave at once, Private." Fleischer didn't hesitate.

Jauch knew they would come for him. *God, why was I so stupid? Why did I spill my guts to that asshole, Leibnitz?* He ran for the storeroom. No refuge—no place to hide behind the pallets and flour sacks. Müller's gang would swarm within seconds. Jauch dashed out the screen door and dove for the ground, then crab-crawled along the building's night shadow as he wriggled his way to the back of the building. A coyote vaulted out of a toppled trash can and flashed into the darkness.

Above Jauch, a sign hung from the gable.

Mess Hall 2A

Keep Area Clean

Trash Removal, 0845, Daily

Jauch slid into the muck among the bins. His heart pounded as he struggled to silence his gasps. Belly down, he nestled as low as he could get. *Stupid to run. Best to lie still and pray they don't see me.*

A few minutes passed. Jauch raised his head. He could hear nothing but the flit of moths around a gable lightbulb. A swath of bare earth stretched from him to the barbed wire. The guard tower was just out of view. Outside the wire were jagged silhouettes of desert mountains against a star-lit sky. A lanky yucca stood there. Its features seemed human, beckoning Jauch to sanctuary outside the prison fence.

He lay motionless. Garbage was piled high in the barrels, but afforded little cover. *Should I run for the fence? I'll be shot. Should I plead with the American guards?* It wouldn't work. The Americans would just turn him over to German officers—the *Circle*—the Nazi assholes who would bring him to reckon. That's how it worked here.

A searchlight from the guard tower passed over the sandy earth. Behind him a hinge squeaked and a door slapped. Conversation. *German.* With luck, Müller and his thugs had called off their search. More talk. Jibber-jabber English. *Müller must be chatting with the American guards. Those Nazi bastards have been given free rein in this camp. Shit! They're the ones the guards should be watching. Goddamn stupid Americans.*

Wet sludge soaked into Jauch's clothing. Maybe he could hold out until morning. By then he might come up with a way to save his skin.

Gravel crunched behind him. His heart drummed. More boots. He lay on his belly, paralyzed. The boot steps were slow, deliberate. They passed by him. Then stopped. Peering through barrels, Jauch saw the boots—big boots. Müller. They faced away from him. *They haven't seen me.*

A voice said, "Nothing. Not here."

They haven't seen me.

In one motion, Jauch's ankles were jerked backward and his face was grated through the dirt. His arms were cinched to his body by one thug, while another bridled his mouth with a loop of rope and yanked it tight. Jauch's jaw felt like it was going to pop from its sockets. He kicked recklessly until they bound his ankles. He couldn't move. The thugs stood him up, supporting him like pillars though his knees buckled. Inches in front of him was the malignant face of Müller. A thug draped a potato sack over Jauch's head. Darkness. Then a blow smashed against the side of his face as Müller's fist sent a lightning bolt through his skull. Jauch's jaw snapped and he shuddered uncontrollably. Jauch was hoisted over a thug's shoulder. He puked in successive spasms until the sack was saturated in vomit. They carried him through the clapping door. His head pounded in red waves as he was slammed into a chair.

Voices swam around like sharks. One was distinctive—Schwering, the leader of the fucking Nazi Circle. The one who controlled these apes.

"Remove his hood."

The sack was lifted from Jauch's head. Gobs of puke dripped to his shoulders. The room's bare light bulb illuminated pallets and cookery. They were in the back storeroom, one of the few places in Camp Barlow that was away from the watchful eye of the American guards. In front of Jauch was a chopping block. A tub of peeled potatoes soaked at his feet. The spare figure of Major Schwering slid into view. His square-rimmed glasses were unique, making him easy to recognize. Over the kitchen doorway behind Schwering was a poster of a cartoon pig with the English words.

WE WANT YOUR KITCHEN SCRAPS.
DON'T WASTE!
PIG FOOD

The demon pig glared down at Jauch as he struggled against the bindings.

Schwering gave a nod and Müller loosened the noose from Jauch's mouth, then dropped it around his neck. Müller pitched the other end over an overhead pipe—a makeshift gallows. Jauch attempted a plea but his mouth was wedged open by his shattered jawbone. He writhed against the constraints to no avail. They strapped his wrists behind him.

"Corporal Milo Jauch," began Schwering, "I was afraid we had missed you this evening. Now I see you had only stepped outside. It is fortunate that we may now speak." Schwering's glare fell upon Jauch. The sarcasm disappeared. "Corporal Jauch, you are viewed as an enemy of the Fatherland. You have spoken openly against the

Reich and the Führer. We are also aware that you have given military information to an American guard. Do you understand the serious nature of your traitorous acts?"

"Gnnnuhhh," Jauch tried to reply. Only gurgles came through his broken mouth. "Nunehh."

"If you had not attempted to flee, you might be able to plea your defense, eh?" Jauch struggled, only to tighten the noose. Schwering took a pack of cigarettes from his pocket—American Camels—removed one, and brought it to his lips. He flicked his lighter and drew a long puff. "Private Leibnitz came to see us. He was distressed that you had spoken to him of treasonous things."

Leibnitz is a son of a whore. I was only venting. I was mad as hell that day. But Jauch could not say what he was thinking.

"When I interviewed Leibnitz, he told me you called the Führer disparaging names, *profane* ones as a matter of fact. You told Leibnitz you hoped someone would kill Hitler. Do you deny this, Corporal?"

"Nghnnn." *What I said to that bastard I said in confidence. But I meant every word of it.* "Gngnnhgh." Blood was streaming from his mouth and nose.

"You told an American guard you'd served in Italy as an artillery gunner. Leibnitz was a witness to this discussion. He says you've had several conversations with this particular guard. One can only wonder what else you might have told him. Perhaps of your gun's capabilities? Maybe you described artillery tactics of the German Army? Certainly Corporal, you know the consequences for providing classified information to the enemy?"

Jauch could only manage an empty stare. *That was idle conversation. I spoke of no specifics. The Americans could have easily found my assignment in their records. I told him nothing. I am no traitor.*

Schwering produced a letter from his shirt pocket. "Corporal Jauch, when we became aware of these transgressions, we began intercepting your mail. In this letter, addressed to a Miss Marta

Pröehl of Furstenberg, you wrote—," Schwering adjusted his glasses. "Darling, the war will end soon. You must travel west, as far as you can. There, you will be under the control of the Americans or British, not the barbaric Russians." Schwering placed the letter in his pocket. "Rather fatalistic I would say, Corporal. Your mind is that of a deserter."

A deserter? The pain from his jaw was monstrous. *I'm not a deserter. I serve my country proudly. I am a realist. The war is lost. It's you Nazi bastards who wouldn't know the truth if it flew up your asses.* Jauch's eyes steeled against Schwering. It was all he had left in his defense.

Schwering tossed his cigarette butt into the tub of potatoes. As he left the kitchen, he said to Müller, "Guilty of treason against the Fatherland. Sergeant, carry on."

The noose tightened from above. Jauch couldn't breathe. Müller grasped the gallows line as Jauch's feet rose off the floor. He writhed. His chest convulsed for air. Nothing. His legs whipped and kicked the tub in front of him, sending it sideways. Potatoes bounced across the plywood floor in a flood. He thrashed in an effort to twist around and face Müller, his executioner. Müller heaved on the hangman's rope as if he was setting a hook in a large fish. Milo Jauch's head smashed into the overhead pipe. His neck snapped.

3

Maarburg, The Netherlands

"What are you doing, Keller?"

"Changing my clothes. What does it look like?"

"Here? In the truck?"

"Got a better place?" asked Keller. He was down to his skivvies and undershirt, having doffed his Army uniform.

"Civilian clothes?" said Hofmann, the driver. "You get permission for this?"

Keller winked.

"Crap, you going to get me in trouble, too? Just because you get one day of liberty doesn't mean you should get yourself thrown in the stockade—along with your buddy," said Hofmann, pointing a finger at himself. "They've got military police here in Maarburg, too."

"MPs won't be looking for a tall, good-looker like me. More likely to be on the lookout for a beady-eyed NCO like you." Keller chuckled, then imitated a gruff MP. "Whatcha hiding in the back of this truck, Sergeant? Whiskey? Morphine? Women?"

"Very funny. Just don't take me down with you, goddamnit."

"Nothing to worry about, Hofmann." Keller tied his shoe and tucked his uniform into a duffel. "Pull over here."

"You know where you are?"

"I know this town like the back of my hand," said Keller. "You can pick me up later, right here."

"It will take me about three hours to drop this load in Zelhem and get back. Be here at 1400, or you'll be walking back to Arnhem. Got it, buddy?"

"Loud and clear," said Keller. He grabbed the small bag of chocolates he'd stowed at his feet. "Don't want to forget this." He'd paid a premium for the black-market sweets. He zipped up the duffle, slung it over his shoulder, and got out of the truck.

Maarburg was a welcome sight to Keller. The sun had broken through and gnawed at frozen patches on the cobbled streets. This town—*his town*— hadn't been smashed as badly as Arnhem. The stone buildings, the high-peaked roofs, the granite chimneys, were as he remembered. Wonderful memories were here. Yet, some things weren't the same. Color was missing. He remembered a town with bright awnings and flower boxes. They weren't here anymore. In their absence were German banners—swastikas.

As he walked, water dripped from melting icicles along store fronts. It pooled on the paving stones and reflected the midday sun. Keller passed shops and cafes. Most were boarded, shut down— victims of war. He passed a long queue of people standing with empty bowls, waiting for a ladle of thin soup. The people were different too—clothing threadbare and faces gaunt. He'd seen the same in Arnhem. Keller slipped the bag of chocolates deep into his duffel.

He walked toward the Marktplein, the town square. His leg was rebelling. Hot barbs shot from hip to knee. He pushed through the pain, easing his limp. The more he loosened the muscle, the less severe the sting. Five months had passed since army surgeons had removed the shrapnel. The wound hadn't healed properly, likely the result of an overworked field hospital. Doctors told him his leg would never be right again, that he should plan on using a cane for the rest of his life. He took that as a challenge. He chucked the cane a month ago—next, this goddamn limp.

The people on the street looked drained, yet he was greeted with courteous smiles from the passersby. Keller returned their gestures with a *"Hallo"* or *"Goedemorgen."*

The street opened into the Marktplein. The square was lined by the grandest buildings in Maarburg. A grassy park stood inside the traffic circle. Tall elms, dormant now, formed a canopy over walk-ways and benches. The sun reflected off the steeple of Saint Maarten's Church, which stood over the city like a mother protecting her children. Across the square, the city hall hadn't fared as well. Its roof had been bombed out, a black cauldron gaping open to the sky.

Keller crossed the street toward the statue of Johan de Witt, where he would meet Taatje. An old man walked past, tipped his hat and wished Keller a nice day. The warmth of the Maarburgers was welcome. They didn't know he was a German soldier.

Taatje stood at the foot of the statue. Keller would recognize her anywhere. Chocolate brown locks fell from under a cocked beret. She wore an overcoat, tightened at the waist. "Taatje, you look beautiful."

Taatje turned on him. "Don't speak, Franz!"

Keller was surprised. "Why?"

"You are German—your accent." She was severe. "Follow behind me, not too closely." She began a quick pace. No greeting.

No embrace. Not even a peck on the cheek. No choice, Keller followed her, taking a wide girth around rubble that was piled on the sidewalk.

Their reunion was off to an odd start. *Taatje Hoobinck and Franz Keller*—best friends as kids—sweethearts as teenagers. *Now?* He admired her as he followed. Taatje had been gangly as a teenager, but she'd outgrown that. *Quite a woman.* She walked with a purpose. He lengthened his stride to keep up.

Keller tried to lighten the mood. He leaned toward her shoulder and said in a forced whisper, "I may have a German accent, but my Dutch is good, is it not?"

"Your Dutch was always good, Franz. Your mother saw to that. No talking now. There will be time for that soon. Please, shut up." He backed off a few paces, trailing Taatje through the familiar streets.

Franz's mother, Carin de Zoute, grew up on a farm about ten kilometers outside of Maarburg. She married Heinrich Keller, a German. They lived in Düsseldorf, not far up the Rhine River, on the German side. Every summer, Carin took her kids to stay on the family farm. Usually, Heinrich stayed home and worked. The de Zoute clan welcomed Carin, Franz, and his younger sister, Laila, with open arms.

Franz's best friend in those days was his cousin, Balthasar. Balt and Franz never lacked for exciting things to do—fishing in a canal, playing tag in a wheat field, or jumping on the backs of yearling cows (forbidden, not that it mattered). The Dutch countryside brought new adventure every day.

In 1932, Franz was thirteen years old. That summer, Balt introduced him to Taatje Hoobinck. She was the same age as the boys. Her father owned a neighboring farm and raised horses. Keller had never been on a horse. The Hoobincks taught him to ride and he took to it quickly. "You're a natural," Taatje once declared. Franz loved everything about horses, even the dirty chores that came with them. Many times he pleaded with Balt to get up early and go riding. Balt would rather sleep. Most often, it was just Franz and Taatje on those morning rides.

Young Franz found another reason to love his Dutch summers—Taatje.

She was carefree, opinionated, and fearless. It was Taatje that convinced Balt and Franz to pilfer a bottle of Uncle Gerolf's peach schnapps. The three bandits passed it among themselves in the hay loft on a hot afternoon. A puking Balt brought that escapade to an end. Each day was a gift from Taatje, whether it was galloping bare-back, driving the tractor, or hitchhiking to town to see an American movie. Every day was perfect with Taatje. Franz was intoxicated.

He returned each of the next four summers. Balt, Taatje, and Franz stayed fast friends throughout. Since Balt had little interest in horses, Taatje and Franz spent more time together, riding the pastures and trails of the Maarburg countryside. They shared secrets and chatted for hours on those dazzling summer days. In the summer of 1936, his last in Maarburg, they declared their love for each other.

Keller labored to keep up. Taatje rounded a corner onto a narrow street—no one around. "Taatje, slow down." He kept his voice low. "I have a bad leg."

She looked back at him, observing his limp. "Sorry Franz, but we must keep moving." She kept up the pace. "When we get to this corner, you must stop and wait there. Five minutes. I'll continue on the street to the right, Kuiperstraat. My flat is number 131, on the left side, up the stairs. There is a red flower box outside my window. You'll see it. Walk up the stairs and come right in. Don't knock. Remember, number 131."

Franz did as he was told. He feigned interest in a tobacconist window and a meerschaum pipe carved in the shape of the god, Neptune. He thought about Taatje. She was always so happy. Nothing ever dragged her down. *But today—she's sitting on needles.* After five minutes he walked up Kuiperstraat.

He found the red flower box. An old lady peered at him through a downstairs apartment window. As he turned toward her, the drapes slapped shut.

Keller went up the stairs. The doorway to number 131 was cracked. He went in. The apartment was dark, curtains drawn. Taatje shut the door behind him.

He presented her with the bag. *Maybe this will break the ice?*

"What's this?"

"Chocolate. For you. Not easy to find around—"

Th … Thank you." She gulped down three in succession, devouring them like a starving animal. Her eyes met his, then she turned away.

"Taatje, what's going on?" said Keller.

She finished another chocolate. "I need to trust you."

"Of course you can trust me. It's me, Franz! Best friends. Remember?"

Taatje pivoted. Her face turned to iron. "Best friends? Best friends? You're a German soldier—a fucking German soldier! How can you be my best friend?"

She might as well have smashed him with a club.

"I'm not your enemy." He realized the inherent lie. "I love this country as much as I ever did. I've been posted to duty here because I speak the language—been here for only three weeks."

"Then you've been here long enough to see what's happened. Your fucking Germans have spent five years murdering us, stealing

21

from us, starving us—you've destroyed our lives." Tears of rage cascaded down her cheeks.

Keller knew she was right. The Dutch had been kicked out of their homes and businesses. They were subjected to curfews, travel restrictions, and a brutal police force. Those who were suspected of anti-Hitler sentiment were murdered. All the Jews were gone. For Dutch citizens, finding food was often impossible. The Germans took their share first—and the Dutch settled for what was left, if there was anything.

Keller said, "I wish to hell this hadn't happened. You may not believe me, but I love this country." Taatje said nothing, only shook her head in disbelief.

Her silence was suffocating. Keller finally spoke. "Tell me then, if you feel that way, why did you answer my letter? Why did you agree to meet me?"

"It wasn't for the reasons you think."

"I don't get it."

"I was afraid to meet with you, Franz. You are my enemy. But I've been praying that you're still the good man that I once knew—that you haven't been brainwashed by those Nazi bastards—and that you will do the right thing." She wiped away the tears and squared her shoulders, now composed, businesslike. "I am going to tell you something—something you may not want to believe—though you will have *no choice* but to believe it. Then, I'm going to ask you to help me. It will be dangerous, Franz. But if you believe what I tell you, you *will* do it. Not for me. Not for the Netherlands. You'll do it for yourself."

4

Camp Barlow, Arizona

Major Schwering appraised the scene in front of him. Two thousand prisoners-of-war gathered on the quad—a well-trodden pitch of desert hardpan—in the middle of the camp. The morning soccer match was suspended for this important assembly.

The ten o'clock muster was set by the Germans, not the Americans. By 0955, every soldier was in tight rank and file. Uniforms pressed. Boots shined. Silence.

Schwering was perched atop a plywood stage erected that morning. Though only two steps above ground level, it elevated the officers over the enlisted masses. When he was satisfied, Schwering stepped to Hoefer. "Colonel, everything is in order."

"Yes, Major. You've organized things splendidly. I congratulate you."

Schwering saluted, heel clacking against the wood pulpit. He'd crafted this ceremony to evoke patriotism, to make these soldiers forget they were prisoners on some distant corner of the earth. He buffed his square-rimmed glasses with a tidy handkerchief. Squinting, he privately cursed his awful vision—a weakness. In all other ways, he was strong. He read Goethe and Schopenhauer, worshipped the music of Wagner, and could recite passages from *Mein Kampf*. He was fit and sharp in his tailored uniform.

Colonel Hoefer was the highest ranking German in camp, but Schwering was the most feared.

Today, not a single soldier wore their work togs. Schwering made sure of it. Guaranteed by the Geneva Convention, they were permitted to wear military dress at a funeral rather than their everyday PW-emblazoned coveralls. Uniforms of the *Wehrmacht*, the *Luftwaffe*, and the *Kriegsmarine* lined the procession. The coffin of Corporal Milo Jauch, carried shoulder-high by pallbearers, moved in precise cadence past ranks of the *Third Reich*.

Schwering moved to the center of the platform—Moses standing before the Red Sea.

In 1942, shortly after they'd arrived at Camp Barlow, Hoefer charged Schwering with the formation of a secret conclave—a committee with a single purpose—to ensure all Camp Barlow Germans march in lockstep with Hitler's doctrine. This committee would be sculpted of the most ardent Nazis—*the Circle*. The organization was quickly and finely tuned—an overlord with an iron fist. Any POW who bucked their fascist principles would be brought to heel.

Schwering nodded toward the prison orchestra. With a sweep of the conductor's hand, the low brass began the somber pulse of a dirge. A lone violin added the haunting melody of Beethoven's *Funeral March*.

Soldiers were positioned according to their tenure. The longest serving prisoners were honored by occupying the front ranks while recent arrivals stood to the rear. Most front-rank soldiers wore the tan-khaki of the North African theater. Like Schwering, these were troops of the *Afrika Korps* who were captured in an earlier stage of the war. By Schwering's gauge, these men were true National Socialists—patriots from the beginning. They had witnessed the Nazi resurrection of the Fatherland, had studied Hitler's doctrine, and swore to avenge the treason of Versailles. These were the heroes of glorious victories in Poland, France, the Netherlands, and North Africa. They were defenders of the *Reich*—men who knew that *only* military strength could break their shackles and enable Germany to assume its rightful place as the greatest nation on earth. *Yes, these gallant men understood!*

Schwering glared toward the rear. Most uniforms were darker colors—green and gray. This group was different. In the past year, POWs arrived at Camp Barlow from recent battles in Normandy, Belgium, and the Netherlands. Many of the *greens* had been trained on a short schedule and thrown onto the front line. Shoddy discipline was evident and their patriotism was questionable. *These new soldiers have no spine. They lack the zeal of victory. They may know how to shoot a rifle, but many have forsaken the cause of our struggle.*

A smattering of American guards lined the quad perimeter. Until last summer, Schwering regarded the Americans as a mere nuisance. But after the Normandy invasion—*D-Day* the Americans called it—the Yanks boasted with giddy pride about America's recent victories in glorified exaggeration. They goaded the Germans by proclaiming Allied victory to be "just around the corner." *Just around the corner.* And now the guards were bragging of another great triumph in a Belgian forest they called the "the Bulge." *Just around the corner. Allied propaganda—but poison to German morale.* Yet, in this American twaddle was one truth that stabbed Schwering. German military power, once irrefutable, was giving way to an inferior enemy.

The American guards were ignorant of the Circle, but all Germans had guessed the fate of Corporal Jauch. *Compliance through fear*—a concept tapped from the *Führer*. Schwering was

Hitler's agent at Camp Barlow. Every German knew it. They also knew this funeral was not really a memorial to Corporal Jauch—rather it was a reminder to the troops that Naziism survives on this distant strip in the American desert.

Jauch's casket was draped with a German flag—a bold swastika. As the procession passed, each soldier snapped his heels and thrust forward a Nazi salute. The pallbearers elevated the coffin to arm's length as it glided over the Teutonic brethren.

The procession inched up the platform steps in slow rhythm. The casket was placed on a front pedestal and the flag bearer raised a Nazi standard high overhead. On cue, the congregation hailed victory in booming unison.

"Sieg heil!"

"Sieg heil!"

"Sieg heil!"

Colonel Hoefer moved to center stage. He extolled Corporal Jauch's undying love for the Fatherland. Then he spoke of the unfortunate accident, how Jauch had been standing under a warehouse hoist when it broke away from its moorings and the heavily laden pallets crushed their unfortunate comrade. Jauch lost his life while serving his nation. A hero.

Hoefer's eulogy was a bag of lies—but that didn't matter. Aryan soldiers stood at rigid attention. Alert. Proud. They honored their nation whose flag was draped over the coffin—on the dais of a righteous creed. Never mind that Jauch, a traitor to the *Reich*, was being committed to the earth with honors befitting a hero. This demonstration wasn't about Milo Jauch. It served a higher purpose.

Hoefer completed his tribute and the orchestra played the *Königgrätzer March*, known to be one of the Führer's favorites. A light breeze drifted from the valley floor, carrying the fragrance of creosote blossoms and mesquite. Hoefer saluted Schwering. Everything was in order.

5

Maarburg

Keller's eyes adjusted to the dark. Taatje's flat was spartan—a table and two chairs—a mattress on a bare floor with a few boxes next to it.

Taatje said, "Franz, you know about your cousins, Balt and Jana? Your aunt and uncle? My parents? You know they are dead?"

"I was in a hospital bed when I heard about it. I wished I could have gotten back home to Düsseldorf to help my sister through it. It was very difficult for Laila." He paused. "Me too. Balt was my best friend."

"Do you know how they died, Franz?"

"American bombs. An army chaplain told me about it."

Taatje balked, "An army chaplain?"

"At the hospital. I asked him to find out what happened. He said American P-47s crossed over the Rhine and bombed the countryside. They were all killed. September 20th.

27

"That was a lie, the same lie we were told here in Maarburg. There were no American planes that day." She reached behind the pot-bellied stove and loosened a hearth stone. She removed a leather folder from a void under the stone and placed it on the table.

Taatje fanned out some photographs in front of Keller. Each had a number written on it, one through seven. "Franz, look at these photos. What do you see in them?"

Keller scrutinized each one. He took two of the pictures to the window where streams of light filtered in. Taatje said nothing. She studied Franz as he assembled the puzzle. She remembered him as compassionate and smart. Was this the old Franz Keller—or a brainwashed version? Taatje was gambling.

Keller swallowed hard. His voice wavered. "This is your father's barn in all the photographs, isn't it?"

Taatje nodded.

He said, "The photos must have been taken from quite a distance. They're fuzzy—hard to make out everything. But it's clear what was happening." The seven photographs, taken in succession, showed German soldiers with rifles pointed at civilians. Dutch farmers, their wives, and children were being herded into the barn. Photograph #7 showed the arrival of a military staff car.

"Taatje, is this you?" he said, pointing to a figure in a white coat.

"Yes, it is." She appeared in three of the photographs.

He moved his finger to another grainy image. "This fellow? Balt?"

"Yes, Franz."

"Who else?"

Taatje took photo #1 from the stack. It showed about thirty people, at gunpoint, being herded into the barn. She pointed, "These two are your aunt and uncle. This little girl is your cousin, Jana. These two…" She choked, "This is my mother and father."

"Who are the others?"

"Neighbors, friends. You knew most of these folks when we were kids. The Germans rounded them all up. They believed someone had been helping the Allies by ferrying reconnaissance squads across the river."

"How do you know that?"

"Because that's what they told us. They said that if we didn't tell them who was helping the Allies, they would kill us."

Taatje reached into the leather bag and removed another photograph, the last one. She placed it in front of Franz. The image was taken from the same distant location as the others. It showed the barn on fire, swallowed in flames. On the right side of the photograph, German soldiers were gathered around the staff car, watching the fire. One of the soldiers in the picture appeared to be taking photographs with a tripod camera. There were no townsfolk in this photo. "My God," said Keller. "The people? They were inside?"

"All of them, Franz." She was riveted on the picture.

"And you? Where were you?"

Her eyes went to a white speck on the hillside, to the far side of the photograph.

"Move inside. Quickly! Move!"

Taatje stared into the muzzle of a rifle. German soldiers were shouting as they herded everyone into the barn. Taatje was among the last ones pushed into the building. The officer at the head of the line—the one in charge—stood by the barn door, and appraised each captive as they filed by. As Taatje passed, he thrust out his arm and steadied his hand against her belly. She froze. His lips curled like an angry wolf. His face could have been that of the Devil. A smirk left no doubt that he had captured his prize.

An army vehicle pulled near the barn. All soldiers snapped to attention, including the Devil. "General, sir!" he offered. A bull of a man stepped down from the staff car. The Devil continued, "General. Sir! We were not expecting you from Arnhem today." Taatje stood motionless. She understood the German language, as did most Dutch.

"Captain Gerber, I sent *you* here to do this job, rather than rely on the infantry. I assumed you would have matters in hand by now, but I see that you have *not* completed the task. The crime that has occurred here is quite serious. Therefore, I have personally come to make certain we find the guilty parties." One of the general's minions assembled a camera and tripod, and then hurried into the barn with it. "Have you uncovered the identities of the insurgents, Captain Gerber?"

"Not yet, General. We have gathered the locals. No doubt some of them know who's behind it."

"Let's waste no more time then. Take all of them inside, now." Soldiers pushed the rest of the townsfolk into the barn.

Gerber—the Devil—clutched the sleeve of Taatje's white coat. "You stay close to me," he whispered, then moved his hand inside her coat to the small of her back. They were the last to enter the barn. His large hand clamped her waist. All the villagers, except Taatje, were driven to the far wall. Her eyes met her father's across the barn. They might as well have been separated by an ocean. The soldiers trained their weapons on the villagers.

The camera was placed next to Taatje. Horses, in their stalls, clopped at the tension. Sunlight beamed through gaps in the planks. The general moved toward the middle of the barn.

"Ladies and gentlemen, you have been brought here for one simple reason. There are persons among you who have been helping the enemy—the Americans and British who are entrenched on the other side of the Rhine. Criminals among you have been bringing enemy commandos across the river, and have given them sanctuary. For all I know, you may be hiding them as we speak. My purpose here is simple. I must know who the guilty parties are. Tell me what I need to know, and the innocent among you will return to your homes. But, mark my words, I will not leave here until I have what I came for." The general's voice was calm, even amiable. Taatje watched him carefully. He paced in front of his captives, with hopes of engaging at least one of them with his mock-friendliness. His foot scudded through scattered straw into a hidden mound of manure. His anger flashed, but he quickly recaptured his benevolent tone. "Now, who will tell me what I need to know? I must have names."

The villagers huddled together. No one spoke. The general motioned to two of his sentries. "Bring that one forward." He pointed to a middle-aged man standing near the front of the huddle. The soldiers hustled the man to front-and-center. "What is your name, man?"

He rasped, "Bickel, Walterus Bickel."

"Mr. Bickel, please tell me the names of the conspirators. Do it for your sake and that of your friends." Bickel stared at the ground. The general drew his Luger and poked the muzzle behind Bickel's ear. The general's voice gained force. "Again Mr. Bickel, the names please." Bickel looked toward heaven.

A deafening blast crashed through the barn as the general pulled the trigger. Horses bayed and banged against their stalls. The captives screamed and cowered in a mass. Bickel's blood sprayed outward, showering a few guards. His corpse sprawled in the dusty hay. "Captain Gerber, bring me that little girl." The general pointed toward Jana. Gerber released his grip on Taatje and obeyed the general. He pulled Jana from her screaming mother. "Captain, hold your pistol on this little girl."

Balt sprang forward. "Let her go. I'll tell you what you need to know. I am the one who helped the Americans. The only one. Shoot me. Leave my sister alone. Let the others go."

The general again summoned his amicable voice. "Nice try

young man, but I've done some gambling in my day. I know the odds of randomly selecting the sister of the *one-and-only conspirator*. You are willing to sacrifice yourself for your sister. Noble, but not good enough. I still won't have the true criminals." He placed the nose of his pistol on Balt's forehead. "Now, young man, give me the real names."

Balt threw his arm upward in an attempt to knock away the pistol. A shot rang out. Balt's chest was smashed by a rifle bullet. Another shot. Taatje screamed as the small body of Jana lurched away from Gerber's gun and tumbled like a rag doll. Gun smoke swirled as women wailed. Horses shrieked and kicked.

Taatje was desperate. There was no way to help the others who were jumbled against the far wall. She watched her father crouching over her mother, shielding her, her face in his shirt as she screamed. Taatje was the only captive on this side of the barn—the *door* side. Her instinct took over. As soldiers recoiled in the smoky haze, she lunged for the doorway, tumbling through dirt and surging outward, her legs pumping wildly before they found firm ground in the daylight. She stumbled and clawed until righting herself, then dashed to the hill behind the barn. She saw trees and thick bushes on top of the hill—maybe a place to hide? A glimpse behind. No one there. Maybe she hadn't been seen? She churned up the steep hill, grasping and pulling at anything that might help.

As if it was a nightmare, she couldn't move fast enough. Her shoes kept slipping. Desperate to make it to the crest, she kicked them off and scrambled barefoot. As she neared the top she heard gasping and boots digging behind her. She glanced backward. He was climbing after her. The Devil. Taatje pumped her legs as if pedaling a bicycle. She clutched at anything ahead of her. Two more gunshots came from the barn—and endless screaming.

She surged higher, but the heaving gasps were closing in. She reached for the next handhold, a bush at the top, but the Devil grabbed her ankle and pulled. Taatje clung to the hillside with her fingernails digging into the scree. Her teeth plowed the earth as she was dragged downward. She fought to keep her feet under her as she slid—back to the Devil. He grabbed her coattail. She flung her arms backward and pulled away, sliding out of the coat. She was freed of his grasp for the moment. Taatje turned and saw the Devil, who was slipping and off balance. But she was sliding too—toward him.

The situation was clear. He could have shot her, but hadn't. He intended to rape her. He'd told her as much. Then, she was certain, he would murder her.

As Gerber tottered for footing, Taatje gathered her legs underneath her and thrust outward. She shrieked as she slammed into his gut. The Devil gasped as they both lurched into the air and plunged downward. She tumbled behind Gerber then caromed off the hillside, head-over-heels, pitching and chucking until she flopped to a halt at the bottom of the hill, face-up. Gerber was next to her, writhing and gulping for air.

Her head whirled, fuddled as a drunk. A haze of screaming voices enveloped her. She tried to focus on their source, the barn. Her attention was quickly drawn to something closer. Still flailing on the ground, the Devil sucked in a deep breath. Then another.

"You whore!" He gulped again. "You fucking bitch. I'll kill you, whore!" He slapped for his holster. Taatje lay on the ground only a few feet from him. She struggled for balance and tried to stand up but floundered on the ground. She needed a weapon. A rock. A stick. There was nothing. And no time. She pivoted her shoulder into the dirt and thrust her foot into him like a harpoon. It smashed into Gerber's face. She heard his nose crunch, and felt her toe sink into something soft. Gerber shrieked like a banshee. "Aieeehhh! My eye. My eye!"

As the Devil thrashed, Taatje struggled to her feet. In a dizzy zigzag, she clambered for the hill and climbed again. Upward was her only salvation. Up! Desperate, she snatched and pulled while coaxing her wobbly legs. Up! She clawed past her coat and shoes that flagged the hillside. She reached the top, grabbed two handfuls of thick brambles and with a final heave, yanked herself over the top into a sanctuary of brush. Her lungs pulsed, searching for air. She shimmied on her belly until positioning herself at the crest, where she could peer downhill. No one had followed her but she was terrified by what was happening below. Rapid gunfire. Screeching horses. Shards of the barn blasted outward. Human cries, that had been constant, were snuffed in the hail of gunfire. The whither of bullets stopped. A final anguished cry was silenced with the crack of a single gunshot. The horses were silent too. Taatje screamed into the dirt.

From behind the weedy blind she watched the German soldiers as they poured out of the barn. The large one, the general, bellowed orders. Cans of gasoline were produced as they doused the barn. Her heart wailed for the nightmare to end. At the base of the hill, another soldier attended to Gerber, who was still in agony—bloodied hands gripping his face.

Crackling flames lashed up the barn walls. People she knew, people she loved—*her parents*—were inside the barn. Fire lapped at the sky. Taatje was helpless. She trembled and fixed her gaze on the barn, now consumed in a blaze.

Her nightmare trance was broken when Gerber staggered to his feet. This wasn't over. They would come after her. She scutted like a crab, away from the horror, pushing through thorny brambles that scratched at her arms and legs. When she was deep in the thicket she stood and ran faster than she ever had in her life.

Taatje stared into the photograph. Above the burning barn was the white speck—her coat. Her tears dripped against the table top.

"I left them behind. I left them all to die."

"If you hadn't, you'd be dead too," said Franz.

Taatje was silent. She shrugged as if to say, *That might have been for the best.*

Keller wanted to hold her, to comfort her. He extended an arm but she turned away. He nodded and sat at the table, studying the horror in the photos.

After a couple of minutes, Taatje blotted at her eyes and sat across from him. She waited until he looked up. "Speak to me, Franz."

His voice was low and raspy. "So, everything was a lie. No bombs. No American planes. They were all murdered?"

"Yes, Franz, slaughtered by Germans. *That* is the truth. The lies you heard were the same ones printed in the newspapers—the Nazi-controlled newspapers."

"How did you get these photographs?"

She hemmed as she measured an answer. "I can't tell you … only that I am associated with … a group that cares about things like this. The truth must be known when the war is over."

"You belong to the resistance?"

"Call it what you want, Franz. I've been part of it for five years, since our country was stolen from us."

"The photographs?"

Taatje didn't answer.

Keller said, "You said you need my help. If you need me, then I need the truth."

She considered Keller's conditions. "I'll tell you what I can. My *people* were alerted that day, when the German vehicles drove into our farmland—not a usual pattern for their patrols. Unfortunately for us, the Germans acted very quickly—not enough time to get word to me. If there had been time, we might have been able to scatter. At the least, it would have saved some of us. My *associate* followed behind the convoy at a distance. He got as close as he could, then climbed to the top of a neighbor's silo. He took the pictures from there."

"Your associate? What is going on, Taatje? Where are the others? Your resistance comrades? Why aren't they here, too? We could all have a lovely cup of tea, then they could kill me and have their German trophy."

Taatje wouldn't tell Franz that her associate, Willem, was waiting under the stairwell, ready, should things go wrong. "That's not why you're here, Franz. I had to convince them that it was worth it to involve you. I told them because you are half Dutch, you'd seek justice for your family's murder. The others wouldn't meet with you. They would never trust you—a German soldier. But I know you. I hope I know you …"

Keller stood and walked to the window. He opened the curtain.

Taatje warned, "Don't stand in the window, Franz."

"I suppose I need to see the world for what it is." He slid the curtain shut. "Where do I come in? Why would you want me to see these pictures? I'm the enemy. What makes me different from the soldiers in those photographs?"

"You work in Arnhem, at Van Sloten House."

Van Sloten House was a well-known landmark in Arnhem, a beautiful mansion in the center of town. The German Army commandeered it and converted it to an administrative head-quarters.

"So? I'm a file clerk. Just a goddamned file clerk."

"Franz, do you recognize this officer?" She pointed to the large man in photograph #6, the commanding officer getting out of the staff car. "This is the one who gave the orders that day. He is responsible for the slaughter of thirty-four people."

Keller looked over the grainy photograph. "The picture's not clear. Should I know him?"

"He is General Martin Uhlemann. You are under his command, Franz. He is the murderer."

Keller made the connection. Uhlemann was the military over-seer of non-tactical operations. He managed all the record-keeping in Arnhem District. The general's office was on the top floor of the mansion where a sergeant rarely had reason to go. Keller had seen the general a few times, walking the stairs with adjutants in tow. Uhlemann had the body of a heavyweight wrestler, his size as imposing as his rank. Keller studied the photo again. Yes, that was Uhlemann.

"What do your friends want me to do? Kill a general? You think I can simply walk up to his office, pull out a pistol, and shoot him? I'd never get that close. Even if I could, it would be suicide."

"That's not what we—not what *I* am asking you to do, Franz. You work in the building. You have access to military records. All army documents for this district are stored in the basement of Van Sloten House. I am asking you to steal one. There must be a report that was signed by the general. It will be dated September 20, 1944, the date he murdered these people. The paper will detail his lies about those people dying under a rain of Allied bombs. The report will contradict these photographs."

Keller shot back, "What you're asking me to do is treason and probably impossible. How do you even know where the records are kept?"

"There are Dutch civilians who work in the building—meager, insignificant jobs. But they keep their eyes open. Some of them report to us."

"Why don't you have *one of them* steal this report?"

"They don't have access to the records. You do. With your help, Franz, we can prove the lie."

Keller shook his head in in disbelief. "Prove it to whom?"

"The end of this war is coming. Soon. The only ones who refuse to believe it are you Germans. Everyone but Hitler realizes that Belgium was his last chance. When it ends, the criminals will be brought to justice. Uhlemann must not be allowed to walk away. He must pay for this."

Keller paused and slowly nodded. "You are right. This war is lost. It should have ended a long time ago." He lifted the stack. "But do you think these photographs and a falsified record will be enough to hang him?"

"That—plus my testimony as an eyewitness."

Keller shuffled through the photographs. "I don't think it will be enough. These photos were taken from such a distance. They're not clear at all. It may come down to your word against his."

"Yes, it may," said Taatje. "That is why we must gather as much evidence as possible." Her eyes welled. "Franz, this man is a butcher. He murdered my mother and father. He murdered your aunt and uncle … Balt … and little Jana. And others. All dead! I was there, Franz. I saw him pull the trigger and blow apart Mr. Bickel's head. I saw him give the order to set the fire. I heard the gunshots."

Taatje buried her face in Franz's chest and sobbed. Keller cradled her in his arms. She shuddered as he soothed his hand along her back.

Taatje lifted her head. In a diluted voice, she said, "There's another thing you must know, Franz. They were *all* innocent. None of *them* were helping the Allies. There was only one person in that barn who did."

She looked up at Franz.

"Me," she said.

6

Arnhem

Keller tossed in his bunk. Sleep wasn't coming. Three days had passed since he'd met Taatje, since he learned the horror of Maarburg. Now he carried a burden with no clear answers.

Can I believe her, or am I being played for a pawn?

The photographs don't lie.

Act against a Wehrmacht general? That would be insanity.

Uhlemann is a murderer. He should hang.

Can I even get to the documents without suspicion?

My duty is to the Fatherland— "Blood and Iron".

This would be treason.

What about Balt, Jana, and all the others? Don't they deserve justice?

Sometime after midnight, while watching shadows waltz across the ceiling, he made his decision.

39

Keller arrived for work early the next morning. His desk was near the grand entrance of the former mansion.

Van Sloten House was the most elegant residence in Arnhem, certainly the nicest to survive last autumn's battle. It was a neo-gothic jewel that stood in contrast to the city center, less than a mile away. That neighborhood was a blackened scar of twisted iron and rubble. Van Sloten House had been fortunate, spared from artillery shells and bombers.

The building's dormers were peaked with stone carvings. The interior had finely detailed woodwork and glossy oak floors. Each of the twenty-seven rooms still had elegant carpets and much of the original furniture. However, the paintings and heirlooms had disappeared when the Germans took over, replaced by Nazi banners. Keller's desk hugged a wall near the spacious entry, once used to greet aristocratic guests. Other austere desks and cabinets were spaced under crystal chandeliers and an elaborately gilt ceiling. On the wall adjacent to Keller's desk, under a hand-carved maple cornice, was a large painting of the Führer—Adolf Hitler's imperious eyes watching over his world.

Keller sat at his desk and shuffled through his paperwork, just as he would on any other day. But today would not be ordinary.

He'd been in dangerous situations before. He'd hunkered down under a rain of American naval guns at Anzio. He fought through the hedgerows of Normandy and survived the Allied steamroller. He'd had his leg torn open at the Falaise Gap. However, he had not tasted dread like he did now. A soldier knew how to prepare for battle, but this was different.

Keller grabbed a stack of papers given to him yesterday by Major Grossfeld. He slid them into a folder and titled it *Major E. Grossfeld, Maarburg Damage Estimates*. He scratched some notes on a lined pad. The notes read *Major Grossfeld / Dates of incidents / railroad destruction near Maarburg / repair estimates*. Keller's note pad was a lie. The documents from Major Grossfeld were not about Maarburg, but were inconsequential communiqués with Berlin regarding freight costs. Today Major Grossfeld was in transit to Amsterdam. This was Keller's day to act.

Geli Obenaus was across the room from Keller, typing at a rapid pace. Geli was one of five German women working at Van Sloten House. She was a member of the *Helferin*, the women's auxiliary corps. Her job was to aid the ground-floor clerks, including Keller.

Geli and Franz had become quick friends. Each had a sharp wit and delighted in teasing the other—friendly high jinx. Their office gags brightened otherwise tedious days.

"Geli," said Franz, impersonating the voice of a movie star, "be a dear and fetch me one of Major Grossfeld's reports. I need it to check some figures on a repair estimate."

Geli swiveled toward Franz. Her field-gray skirt inched up slightly above her knee—no accident—just pure Geli. She wore the *Helferin* uniform that mirrored the army uniform, right down to the neck tie. The black-buck shoes and starched collars minimized most women's femininity—but not Geli Obenaus. Only Geli could pose that ponderous shoe in such a way as to catch a man's eye. Keller had seen several men try to gain favor, only to be spurned. But she treated Keller differently. She flirted jokingly with him. "What Franz, not even a *Good Morning*?" she cooed in a Marlene Dietrich impression.

"Any morning is wonderful when it begins with you, Geli." Franz loved playing along. "Please accept my apology, Miss Obenaus."

Geli pushed off with the sole of her shoe. Her office chair whirred over the wood floor. The wheels halted in flawless position at the side of Keller's desk, as if it was a shuffleboard puck landing on the *10*. She placed her elbows on his desk, resting her chin in woven fingers. *Perfect Dietrich.* Her eyes were a foot away and settled on him like a cat at a birdcage. She purred, "Now what is it that you want of me, darling?"

Keller grinned. He reckoned she was probably a decade older than him. Little doubt she drew on a storied life. He was *almost* certain her flirtation was fiction. They played each other like a tennis match, each volley harder than the last. Her eyes batted—his turn to return serve. Geli was a master of the game.

"My angel—" Keller really hammed it up. "Would you be so good as to fetch me Major Grossfeld's report on the damaged rail line south of Maarburg?" He leaned in, closing the distance between them by half.

Dietrich disappeared. "I'm afraid you're on your own there, Luv. Those files are in the basement. I don't have clearance." Pointing, she said, "You do." Her finger tapped the end of his nose. She pushed her chair back to her own desk. *Game over.*

"Geli, you used to work upstairs as General Uhlemann's secretary, right?" This was a tender subject. Geli had been demoted to the first floor a few months before Keller's arrival. Rumor had it that the general didn't care for her cheeky nature.

"Yes, so—?"

"Tell me how you organized his files before they were sent to the records room. By name? Date?"

"There will be a clerk in the records room who can help you find it."

"Yes, but... those guys are dunderheads. I don't want to spend two hours on a five minute job."

She nodded. He had a point. "Before I sent anything to the basement I was required to paste a tag on it. It was headed with the *geographic sector*. Underneath that was the *date of submission* for filing, and *the officer* that originated it. I'm sure it's still done that way. Just find the files for *Maarburg Sector*, then the *date* and *officer*."

Keller bowed, hamming it up one last time. "Miss Obenaus, I'm indebted."

Geli had given Keller what he needed. He'd been in the records basement once before, long enough to experience the vast array of cabinets that housed documents for the entire Arnhem district—a confounding jungle of army red tape. He picked up his pen, pad, and a folder—a place to hide the incriminating document, *if he could find it*. As Keller turned from his desk, his eyes met Adolf Hitler's. Five years ago, when he joined the army, that painting would have been a source of pride. Now it was chilling.

7

It was an especially dark night with the clouds drowning the moonlight. Taatje dropped a burning roll of newsprint into the pit. The gasoline jumped with a *WHOOSH* as the dry tinder came to life. She and Willem had dug three pits at the corners of a fallow field. Each hole was four feet deep, making the fires easy to spot from the air, but less visible from ground level. Thick trees outlined the field. This was a perfect site for a parachute drop.

In two minutes, an American plane was due to fly overhead. The flaming triangle marked the drop zone. Willem and Taatje were the only resistance fighters at the field, though other comrades were not far away. As soon as the paratroopers were on the ground, Taatje's job was to take the commandos to safe hiding. Willem would cover the pits. If everything worked, the Germans wouldn't know anything.

"Come on Blondi," said Willem. "Stand under the trees until

44

they've landed."

Taatje was christened with the nickname *Blondi* in her early days with the underground. Most who heard it assumed it was a joke because of her dark hair. In fact, she'd been tabbed by Willem, who had called her tenacious, like a police dog—like Hitler's famous dog, Blondi. It was good for a laugh at the time. Now the nickname was inexorable.

Partisan Action Netherlands, PAN, was one of several resistance groups that formed after the 1940 invasion. Different chapters had different specialties, such as providing reconnaissance for the Allies, protecting downed airmen, raising funds, stockpiling weapons, and protecting Jews. In recent months, Taatje's chapter assisted Allied commandos who infiltrated Nazi territory north of the Rhine. They also set up weapon caches in the countryside. Working with the Belgian resistance, they smuggled contraband across the Rhine. Sometimes the cargo was human. They observed German military movement and transmitted the information to the Allies, serving as forward eyes for the British, Canadians, Poles, and Americans. On this night, a unit of United States Army Rangers was dropping in.

A thrumming pulse droned through the clouds. Taatje couldn't see the airplanes, but the pitch was certain. The thick night should hide the planes from German notice, at least long enough. To her right, she heard a thud, then another in front of her. Dark silhouettes floated onto the field like ash settling from a doused fire. Soldiers scrambled as they hit the ground, immediately bunching their parachutes and locating the equipment that descended alongside them.

"Mickey Mouse," Taatje said to the soldier nearest to her.

"Popeye," responded the soldier as he wrapped his chute cords. He whistled three short bursts.

Taatje said, "When you're ready, I'm the one who will lead you out of here." The soldier raised an index finger, motioned her to wait, not understand her language. Two seconds later, another soldier appeared out of the dark.

"Popeye," said the second soldier.

"Mickey Mouse."

He spoke to Taatje in Dutch. "We're combing the area for anything missing. So far, it looks like a clean drop. We're mustering under those trees. I'm Corporal Veldhuis. You're our guide?"

Taatje nodded. "You're Dutch?"

"From Rotterdam. Been training with these Yanks in Scotland since '43."

"Glad you're back," said Taatje.

She followed Veldhuis to the trees where the Rangers were gathering. The Americans were speaking in guarded voices. Taatje was fluent in French and German, but understood little English. She'd helped several British soldiers in the last year. Their tongue was difficult, but if she listened carefully, she could make out enough for basic communication. The Americans, on the other hand, spoke a very strange sort of English. They used peculiar words in a twisty accent. When the Yanks talked with each other, it sounded like dogs growling.

The American leader was Lieutenant McCampbell. He noticed Taatje, but ignored her while he orchestrated the exit from the drop zone. He was well-rehearsed, directing men and equipment into an organized unit, getting ready to move out. He used hand and arm signals—little talk. When everything was to his liking, he turned to Taatje. "Popeye?" he questioned.

"Mickey Mouse." Now that the fires were out, her eyes adjusted to the dark. Lieutenant McCampbell was young, younger than her, but had the worn look of a hardened soldier. "If you're ready, follow me," she said to McCampbell. Veldhuis translated. Taatje led the fourteen American Rangers along the forest path.

Willem completed filling the second fire pit. He spread leaves and grass over his handiwork.

8

Arnhem

The basement was cold with cave-like air. Two guards flanked the entry to the records room. Keller was ready. He flashed his identification and walked to the authorization table. He was in luck. The clerk was a lowly private.

"Sergeant!" The private saluted.

"Private, please point me toward Major Grossfeld's records. I need his figures on railway damage near Maarburg." Keller pointed to the title on the folder he had falsified.

"The Maarburg files are in the back, Sergeant. I'll show you."

"That won't be necessary. Just point me in the right direction." He didn't want an ambitious clerk dogging him.

Two officers entered through an inner doorway. Keller snapped to attention. The officers took their time while Keller awaited release from his salute. *Damn. My luck just changed. This lieutenant is in charge down here, not the private.*

Lieutenant Zeigler said to the other officer. "I'll have an assistant find those munitions lists and get them to you directly, Captain." Then he turned to Keller and the private. "As you were."

The private picked up where he left off. "Sergeant, you'll find Major Grossfeld's reports on Maarburg in the nook to the back left." He pointed toward an alcove. "Anything about rail lines or bomb damage should be there. Those files will be in the black cabinets. None of those documents may leave the room."

"Thank you, private." Before Keller could leave, the Captain interrupted.

"Maarburg, eh? Why will you need access to the major's reports, Sergeant—?"

"Keller, sir. Sergeant Keller."

The captain's face was peculiar. His nose was an angled crook. More strange was his left eye. It didn't follow the direction of his right, and the color was different. *Glass?*

"Sergeant Keller, why do you need access to files about buildings that were destroyed in Maarburg? That area was hit by bombs a long time ago. I should know. I was there." The captain cocked his head and scrutinized Keller with his working eye. "It seems a rather late request."

"Sir, I am revising a cost-and-repair estimate for Major Grossfeld. If you'll pardon my saying so sir, Major Grossfeld's handwriting can be difficult to read. Some of his data is illegible, but I should be able to lift the figures from earlier reports." Keller had passed the point of no-return.

Lieutenant Zeigler stepped in. "Captain Gerber, it's quite common for the editing clerks to check their copies against the documents down here. Sergeant Keller isn't the first to complain of an officer's handwriting." Both officers chuckled.

"Carry on, Sergeant," said Gerber.

Keller walked toward the alcove. *Gerber? My God! Gerber!* Taatje's nightmare had sprung to life. Keller boiled. Instinct bade him to turn around and tear into Gerber. *That would be stupid.* He wouldn't get more than one good punch before guards would be all over him. *No. Stay with the plan and Gerber will get what's coming to him.*

Keller worked quickly through the files. The Maarburg section occupied four tall cabinets. The second cabinet contained Major Grossfeld's records. The bottom two drawers in the cabinet furthest right held General Uhlemann's. Keller shuffled through the Uhlemann folders. Just as Geli told him, they were organized chronologically. The September, 1944 documents were in the bottom drawer. September 18...19...20. He lifted the September 20, 1944 folder. It contained only three papers. He placed them in the dummy folder—then replaced them with blank papers and set it down flat on top of the standing files. His fingers trembled as he manipulated each sheet. *Why am I able to steady a rifle at an enemy and my hands are rock solid? Now, I can hardly separate sheets of paper?* He scanned down the page. This was the correct document. Most of the report detailed Uhlemann's personal observances of destruction outside of Maarburg. The cause of the destruction was listed as low altitude bombardment by American P-47's and British Typhoons. *Lies.*

On the third sheet, above Uhlemann's signature, something caught Keller's eye. It was a list of the subordinates who were with the general that day. Noted were his adjutants, his driver, and Captain Jürgen Gerber, head of Van Sloten House Security. Also on the list was Corporal Oskar Brill, photographer. *A photographer? Did they really take pictures of this massacre?* Taatje's photos were taken from a distance and had no detail. *But if Brill's photos could be found, they may—.*

"Sergeant." The voice came from behind the kneeling Keller. "May I help you find what you're looking for?" Keller's heart skipped a beat. He stood and found himself toe-to-toe with Lieutenant Zeigler. As he did so, he deftly closed the Uhlemann folder.

"Lieutenant, I'm afraid I'm a bit lost in these files. I'm trying to find Major Grossfeld's recent reports on the Maarburg sector repations."

"You're looking in the wrong place Sergeant." Zeigler bent to the open file drawer and picked up the folder that Keller had left on top. "These are last year's records. This file isn't even Major Grossfeld's. It's General Uhlemann's." The lieutenant held the folder that contained the dummy blanks. He pointed to the label tag on the outside, showing the date and officer's name.

Acting dumbfounded, Keller pulled the folder from Zeigler's hand, "How stupid of me. I was trying to find the information by looking at the dates on the documents themselves." Keller stooped and slid the Uhlemann folder into its rightful niche and pushed the drawer shut.

Opening a top drawer, Zeigler said, "Here is where you will find the recent reports on the Maarburg sector. Use the tags and you'll locate what you need." Zeigler turned and walked back to the desk.

Keller had what he came for—Uhlemann's report. *In the hands of a prosecutor, would this be seen as strong evidence?* A bigger question dogged him. *What about Oskar Brill, the photographer? What did he get on film?*

9

"Park the Jeep under the shade of that tree. Otherwise, these seats will be hotter 'n hell when we come out," said Colonel Riley. Davenport, his XO, cut the steering wheel in a tight arc until the Jeep crunched to a stop under the shade of a mesquite.

"Will this do, sir?" asked Davenport.

"Suits me fine, Jim. So, this is the Cattlemen's Club. Looks like a spiffy joint. Nice to beat tracks away from that camp. Sure hope they're going to offer us a cold beer. Maybe two."

Chet Riley was a veteran of the First World War. He remained in the Army until 1934 when he retired with a full pension. Living his dream. He and Lynn moved back to their native Ohio where they bought a small bungalow in Westerville, just outside of Columbus. He became a part-time handyman. That income, added to his pension, was enough to get by. At least, they were better off than most folks during the Depression. Pearl Harbor changed all that. The Army needed officers with experience. Chet re-enlisted, assuming his previous rank. "If my country wants me, they can have me. Hell, I'm fifty-four years old. They use old guys like me for one of two things, to train the new guys or to push around a pencil. They're not going to make me fight against the Japs," he assured Lynn. After two years of doing exactly what he'd predicted, Colonel Chet Riley was assigned to command a prisoner-of-war camp in Arizona.

Riley and Davenport walked up to the veranda of the Cattlemen's Club. Compared to any other place around here, this was high-class. Nestled on a slope, it had an impressive vista of the San Miguel Valley, overlooking the town of Barlow from a high altar. Ranches and farms checkered the desert floor. The officers stepped into the entryway and admired the décor. "Jesus, Mary, and Joseph! Look at this place will ya?" said Riley. "Who the hell are these people, anyway?"

"All ranch owners, sir. You've got to have a registered brand to be a member."

"How the hell do you know that?"

"Just doing my homework," Davenport lowered his voice. "The ranchers are the ones with the money around here, Colonel. The bigger the ranch—the more money. The more money—the more important you are. I'd be willing to bet the decisions made in this place hold more water than the ones made down at the town hall."

"You seem to know a heck of a lot about this town," said Riley.

"I grew up in Montana cattle country, sir. It ain't any different."

Their boots clopped over a pine floor into the main hall. The walls were paneled in rich cherry wood. Trophies of deer and elk encircled the coffered ceiling. One wall was covered by a mural featuring Arizona cowboys at full gallop chasing a thunderous herd of cattle through a desert wash. Riley and Davenport walked over to the bar, where high-back leather stools were set under a glossy marble bar. Liquor shelves were stocked with ten times the variety of booze they'd ever seen at an officers' club.

Riley took it all in. "Holy shit. The Elks Lodge back in Westerville has nothing on this place."

A fellow emerged from the back hallway wearing a broad smile. "Hi there," he said, thrusting his hand forward. "I'm Mason Johnson, owner of the Circle-J Ranch and president of the Cattlemen's Association. Just call me Mason. Everybody does." He was dressed the part in a snap-button shirt and bolo tie. His blue jeans fell over the tops of snake-skin boots.

"I'm Colonel Riley. Call me Chet. This is Major Jim Davenport." They shook hands. "This is quite a play house you have here."

"Ain't it? Name your poison, Colonel. Scotch or Bourbon?"

"Scotch, I suppose."

"You got it." Mason walked behind the bar and grabbed a new bottle. He put it on a tray along with four glasses. "C'mon, follow me. Let's take this into the board-room." Riley and Davenport followed Mason Johnson through the back corridor and to a door posted,

Cattlemen's Association
Executive Board Members Only

The board-room was even fancier than the main hall, complete with hand-carved woodwork. Framed photographs of prize bulls dotted the walls, each one named and labeled with a brass placard. Mason took the high-back seat at the head of the table—an Arizona version of King Arthur. Already seated to Mason's right was another fellow wearing a beige shirt with a silver badge.

He stood, "Hello gentlemen. I'm Gene Kirby, deputy sheriff. Mason asked me to join you all today."

Mason said, "I figured that if we can work out a deal here, the local law ought to know what's goin' on."

Mason poured each man a shot from the bottle.

Riley read the label. "Fifteen-year-old Scotch? Hell, this ain't the cheap stuff!"

"Cheers," proclaimed Mason. Davenport passed the shot glass under his nose and took a sip. It warmed the back of his palate as he savored the vapors of the fine whisky. The other three men threw back their shots and blew out a collective *Haaaa...* Mason started to refill the empty glasses.

Deputy Kirby placed his hand over his glass. "That's all for me, Mason. I'm workin' today."

Davenport chimed in. "I'll just nurse this one if you don't mind, Mr. Johnson," and took another sip.

"Suit yourself, Jim. What'ya say Chet?"

"I ain't going to be a wallflower. Keep pourin'."

Both men tossed back the second shot.

Mason Johnson swiveled upon his throne. "I'll get right to the point, gentlemen." Although he addressed both officers, he looked at Riley. "The war has played hell with the work force around here. It's been more than three years since Pearl Harbor. In that time, we've lost most of our workers. Our ranch hands have headed off to the war. Nobody in these parts is surprised that Arizona cowboys make the best fightin' men. Hell, Teddy Roosevelt knew that fifty years ago when he put together the Rough Riders. Half of them boys were cowpokes. Bet you didn't know that." Mason stared into his empty glass. "My own son joined the Army right after Pearl Harbor. Tank cavalry. Damn good soldier too, until he was killed in Morocco by them fuckin' Krauts." Mason's voice cracked.

"I'm sorry to hear that, Mr. Johnson," said Riley.

"Well, that ain't the half of it, Colonel. I helped my son buy his own ranch before the war. Now, his wife's runnin' it, and she don't know shit from Shinola when it comes to cattle ranching. This war is hurting all of us." Mason took a deep breath and poured himself and Riley another one. "Anyway, all the young men around here are off fightin' in Europe or against the Japs. Even the Mexicans are gone. They all joined up too. Used to be you couldn't spit around here without hittin' about three of 'em. One thing I'll say though, those Mexicans make good cowboys. It's in their blood." Deputy Kirby nodded in agreement.

Mason emptied half his glass, dabbed his lips with his sleeve, and continued. "But that still ain't the all of it. Even the men who are too old to fight have headed off to Phoenix or Albuquerque or *God-knows-where* to work in the factories. They're makin' bombs and fighter planes and such. Uncle Sam may say he needs all those men, but goddamnit, we need 'em too. Where the hell does Franklin *Dumb-ass* Roosevelt think he's going to get the beef to feed all them soldiers? I'll tell you where. Right here! I sure as hell wish Franklin *Dumb-ass* had half the brains as his Uncle Teddy."

"How do we fit in, Mr. Johnson?" asked Davenport, although he'd already guessed the answer.

"You've got a bunch of manpower just sittin' on their asses up there at Camp Kraut. I know you've already got hundreds of them prisoners workin' for the farmers down along the San Miguel. What we're askin'—what the Cattlemen's Association is askin'—is to use some of them German boys to work on our ranches. I'd be willin' to bet that lots of them boys grew up on farms. Those fellas'll know their way around livestock. Heck, even better, if you can find me some that can ride a horse. We know we'd have to pay for 'em, but I figured we wouldn't have to pay as much as we pay the Mexicans. The way we heard it, we'd pay their wages to the government, then you issue camp scrip to the prisoners."

Riley nodded in agreement. "You're right, Mr. Johnson. We have a few hundred prisoners working at different farms in the valley. But there's a lot of paperwork to fill out."

"We've already filled out all the goddamn forms. Our secretary sent it in about three months ago. Haven't heard a damn thing back. With all them goddamn Democrats runnin' the show in Washington, I ain't too surprised. They probably think they need to invent a whole new government agency just to deal with makin' Germans into cowboys." Riley chuckled. Mason was winning him over. He added, "Franky Fuckin' Roosevelt will probably give it a name, the German Cowpokes Administration, The GCA, and fund it with millions of goddamned tax dollars!" Chet Riley laughed aloud.

"The Army has given consideration to using POWs for ranch work, Mr. Johnson," added Davenport, "but the problem is supervision. We can use guards to keep an eye on field workers. That's not hard to do. But how can we watch the prisoners when they're riding around on horseback, chasing cattle?"

"Aw Hell," said Mason, standing up, "You fellas know as well as I do that your Krauts are being guarded pretty loosely nowadays. We all know the war is just about over and they're going to lose. They'd be damn fools to try runnin' away now. They'd be givin' up a free boat ride back to Kraut-land. Heck, Colonel, just yesterday I saw a couple of your young guards park their truck in front of Esther's Mercantile. While your boys went into the bar across the street to get a beer, they left their Krauts sittin' under the sycamore next to Esther's, drinkin' Coca-Colas. Them German boys just lollygagged in the shade until your guards came out of the bar and took 'em back to your camp. Nobody's going to try to escape, now."

Mason had it right, and Davenport knew it. Laxness had seeped into Camp Barlow. Although Davenport would never say it aloud, he believed the problem started at the top, from Colonel Riley. Riley didn't have the wherewithal to run a large camp like Barlow. His nonchalance would never be tolerated if he was on the front lines, but here on a far outpost of the war, it was overlooked.

Gene Kirby spoke up, "Colonel. Major. Mason asked me to come by today to set your minds at ease. The fact is we've never had any problem with any of your POWs working in this valley. The U.S. Army seems to have it all under control. Your guards and the MPs get the job done. But I can assure you that if anything did happen, like let's say a prisoner did try to escape, we've got deputies who know this desert like the back of their hands. An escaped prisoner wouldn't get very far before we'd track 'em down."

Mason jumped in. "I'm a businessman, Colonel. Spring round-up is comin' up fast. If the ranchers in this valley don't get some cowboys up into the hills over the next few months, we'll all lose money and the Army won't get its beef. Frankly, Colonel, we don't care if those cowboys are American, German, or Eskimos. We've got work to do. The Cattlemen's Association has already handed in the paperwork to the War Manpower Commission, but it's dyin' a slow death on some government asshole's desk. We need some help to get it movin', some Army help. That's where you come in Colonel. We're willin' to make it worth your while if you can convince those dumb-shits in Washington that we need this done right away." Riley was nodding his agreement. "You gentlemen don't mind if I show the Colonel my office do ya'? Are you a hunter, Colonel? Let me show you the six-point white tail I shot last fall."

Riley stood, uneasy on his feet. He'd already downed three shots and Mason was pouring him another. The two men made their way out of the board room. Riley weaved behind Mason like a trailer with a flat tire.

"Welcome to Barlow, Major," said Kirby, "where cattle is king." There was a distinct hint of sarcasm in Kirby's voice, acknowledgement that he and Davenport were bystanders in the big scheme. Davenport had little doubt that Mason Johnson was going to offer

Colonel Riley something *under the table*—to expedite matters. He suspected the colonel would probably accept it.

Davenport's glass still contained a bit of whisky. He raised it toward the deputy sheriff. "If cattle is king," he toasted, "then here's to the pawns."

10

Arnhem

Keller fidgeted with the ink bottle on his desk. He kept an eye on Geli, waiting for her to step outside for her morning break. He trusted her as much as anyone, but he didn't want any questions, not even from her. She wrapped herself in a coat and scarf, grabbed her tea, and headed for the back door of the mansion. No one but Keller remained in the room.

He took out the papers he'd nabbed from Uhlemann's file, folded them lengthwise, and tucked them inside his uniform jacket. Using a typing eraser and fountain pen, he altered an old travel pass. His *new* orders were valid for this evening. He slid it in his pocket alongside the stolen records.

Everything was in order. The dangerous part was behind him. There was, however, something eating at Keller and he didn't want to leave it on the table. He needed to talk to Geli. He grabbed his overcoat and a brown bag from inside his desk. He knew where to find her.

"It's freezing out here," said Keller. "I don't get it."

"It's peaceful," said Geli. Every morning on her break, Geli took a cup of hot tea to the garden. She sat at her favorite bench under a wide alder. The plants and flowers had been long neglected, but the war hadn't stolen the garden's tranquility. "This is my haven."

"I brought you something." He sat next to her and produced two cherry pastries.

"Where did you get that?"

"Sometimes it pays to be an NCO."

Geli lifted an eyebrow. "Since when?"

"Actually, they're two days old, left over from a meeting on the third floor. But, if you don't want—"

"Too late!" She snatched a tart from his hand. "Haven't seen one of these in months. Scrumptious!" She winked and savored the bite.

"I have a question for you, Geli."

"Hmmm. Sounds serious, Franz. What's on your mind?"

"When you were on the third floor, did you know a photographer? A corporal by the name of Brill?"

"Oskar? Sure I know him. He follows the general around like a puppy."

"Why would he do that?"

Geli paused and set down her teacup. "I guess you don't know much about the general, do you?"

He knew a very dark side of the general, but Geli was about to tell him more.

She continued, "General Uhlemann is an extremely vain man." She grinned. "It's no secret to anyone on the third floor that he plans to go into politics when the war is over. Rumor has it he has his eyes on the Reich Ministry."

"Lofty goal. Where does Brill come into it?"

"The general is a self-promoter. Oskar was a professional photographer before the war. So, Uhlemann brought in Oskar to take photographs that will *glorify* his military legacy. The general takes him everywhere. Oskar's photographs will come into play when the general begins his political career—you know, documenting him as some sort of war hero." She laughed. "Some hero—"

"Brill? You call him Oskar. Do you know him well?"

"Too well. He's a son of a bitch."

Keller smiled. He loved the way she spoke her mind. "Is there a place where he might keep his photographs?"

"I can tell you exactly where—a dark room on the second floor. He calls it his *studio*. I know *all too well* where he keeps his photographs. *I've seen them.*"

"Do you think you could get me in there, into the dark room? You have connections. You know everyone."

"Franz, I've been in trouble before, you know. Demoted. They said I have a big mouth. Next time, they'll kick me out of the Corps."

"I shouldn't have asked."

Geli cocked her head. "You have me interested, Franz. Do you have something on Oskar Brill? Some dirt?"

"Maybe. The only way I will know is to get to his photographs without him knowing."

Geli finished her tart, all the while measuring Keller. "Frieda works on the third floor. She has all the keys. We're good friends. But what's up, Franz? Sounds like you're going to find some trouble."

Keller shook his head. He could say no more.

"Just tell me this. These photos—this thing that's so important—is this for your job or is it something personal?"

"It's personal, Geli."

Lieutenant Zeigler was buried in a stack of requisitions and didn't notice Gerber's approach. Startled, Zeigler bolted upright, *"Heil Hitler!"*

"Heil Hitler, Lieutenant."

"Sir, how may I be of assistance?"

"Stand easy, Lieutenant. Something's been gnawing at me since I left here earlier."

"Sir?"

Gerber cocked his head so his good eye cast upon Zeigler. His glass eye wandered. Zeigler had heard the rumors about Gerber's eye. There were several versions. Something had happened to him in Maarburg. But was it the result of a bomb, a fire, a bullet, or a whore who poked his eye out? No one was sure. No one dared ask.

Gerber said, "That sergeant who was in this basement earlier was looking through the Maarburg records, correct?"

"Yes, that was Sergeant Keller. He was doing some editing for Major Grossfeld. Something about repair estimates on a rail line."

"You understand, Lieutenant, I was in Maarburg during the Allied bombings. It seems strange to me that Major Grossfeld would be working up repair estimates on a project that was started five months ago."

"It is a bit odd, now that you mention it," said Zeigler. "The sergeant was searching through the wrong files, until I straightened him out."

Gerber's attention piqued. "Which files?"

"He was thumbing through General Uhlemann's reports, looking in the wrong place."

"Lieutenant Zeigler," said Gerber, his eye bearing down, "show me exactly which files he was looking through."

11

Netherlands Countryside

Taatje led the American Rangers to an empty grain silo. The Resistance had used it before to hide smugglers and patriots.

McCampbell told Taatje, "We'll wait here for a couple hours. We move out an hour before first light." Veldhuis translated.

She said to Veldhuis, "Tell him my instructions are to stay here until daybreak. I'm less likely to appear suspicious in the daylight, in case I cross any German patrols."

Some Rangers were hunched against the walls while others crammed in the loft. Taatje watched the Americans check and recheck their weapons—rifles, machine guns, plastique explosives, and countless rounds of ammunition. They assembled two bazookas.

Taatje felt awkward, a lone woman crowded into this silo with a bunch of foreign men. Normally, she and Willem were paired for this type of assignment, but circumstances required them to separate after the drop. She listened to the garbling Americans but couldn't fathom what they were saying. One of the Rangers looked at her, said something, and winked. She turned away and moved next to Veldhuis.

"Will the war end soon?" she asked him. "What will happen now that Hitler has lost in the Ardennes?"

"No one knows, really," said Veldhuis. "The Allies are celebrating the great victory—the *Battle of the Bulge* the Americans call it. The *Hun is on the Run* they like to say. But, heaven knows, there's still plenty of punch left in the Germans. Impossible to say how long they will hold out. We might have to fight them all the way to Berlin."

"What about the Netherlands? Now that France and Belgium are liberated, will we be next?"

Veldhuis's hesitation made Taatje's heart sink. "I suppose only Roosevelt and Churchill know the answer to that one. All we get is rumors. What we've been hearing is that the Netherlands will have to wait, perhaps until the war is over. That might be a good thing, though. If there's another invasion, our people are the ones who will suffer the most. Remember what happened in September, the last time the Allies tried to liberate us? How many thousands of our countrymen were caught up in the middle of that—and lost their lives?"

"So, we just wait? We already have no food. No heat," said Taatje.

"The new line of thinking seems to be to take the fighting right into Germany. That's what we're hearing, anyway."

"And leave us forgotten?"

"No, not forgotten, just postponed. The Netherlands is still of strategic importance. That's why these Rangers are here right now."

"Am I allowed to know the mission?" asked Taatje.

"Actually, more than that. Lieutenant McCampbell wants to know if you will come with us. He could use some local eyes. He also wants me to tell you it will be dangerous. The decision is yours."

"What, precisely, will we do?"

Veldhuis explained, "A couple miles from here is a German radar station. Near it is a battery of German eighty-eights, anti-aircraft guns. We will attack both sites simultaneously. If we're successful, one big piece of the German's coastal air defense will be disabled. We must get it done at dawn—not any earlier and definitely not any later. An armada of American B-17s is scheduled to fly directly overhead in the early morning light on their way to Germany. If these Rangers are successful, those bombers will have a better chance of getting to Germany—and back—without being swarmed by Messerschmitts or flak."

Taatje said, "So, we are clearing a path for the American bombers to get through to Germany and blow the hell out of Berlin?"

"Or Hamburg, or Cologne, or Bremerhaven. They never tell us."

Taatje said, "I'm in. Of course. Count me in."

McCampbell looked at his watch. "It's time, gents. Grab and go." Like clockwork, the Rangers slung haversacks, attached bandoleers, and clipped canteens. Taatje also performed a final check. Underneath her overcoat, she wore a shoulder-sling holster that held an old Danish Schouboe pistol, a relic of the Great War. Six rounds, ready to fire. In less than a minute the group was ready to move out.

Taatje tugged at McCampbell's shoulder strap. "Follow me," she said. "I know the safest way through the woods."

McCampbell said to Veldhuis, "No translation needed. It's pretty damn obvious she knows what the hell she's doing." He signaled Taatje. "Lead on."

1 2

Arnhem

No one was looking, so Frieda passed the skeleton key to Geli. Both women were *Helferin*, a small sorority at Van Sloten House.

"Do you have something on that pig, Oskar Brill?" whispered Frieda.

Geli said, "I'm not sure what I've got. I won't know until we get into his dark room."

"We?"

"Don't ask, Luv. I'll tell you what I can later."

"I hope you find enough to pinch his balls off." Frieda pulled Geli close. "If you find his stash of … ahem—you know … please destroy any of mine. Burn them. That bastard."

Geli nodded.

"Bring my key right back," said Frieda.

The dark room was on the second floor—no special clearance needed. Geli turned the key. She and Keller entered Brill's dark room. An acrid tinge hung in the air, chemicals. The room was cluttered with photo equipment, trays, and paper shavings. They ducked under a string of hanging photos.

"You weren't kidding," said Keller. "This guy really is a pig."

"We have only a short time in here, Franz. I assume you're looking for his *girlie* photos?"

"*Girlie photos*? Why would I—?"

"I just figured he took some pictures of somebody you know. A girlfriend maybe?"

"Wha ... What are you talking about?"

Geli knelt and reached under a work bench. "Oskar has a ledge between the rails under this table top." She reached between the table's upper slats and took out a flat box. "This is where he keeps the photos he doesn't want anyone to see."

"How do you know this?"

"Because that son-of-a-bitch brought me here, once! He wanted me to pose for him." She spread the contents over the bench top. "He paraded these pictures in front of me so I could see how *artistically tasteful* his work was."

The photographs depicted women in seductive poses. Each subject wore little, if any, clothing. *Nudie* shots.

"In case you're wondering, Franz. You won't find any pictures of me. He offered me twenty-five marks to meet him at his friend's place and pose. He said that the pictures would only be used by art students who were learning oil painting. Artistic! Look at this trash. I told him to go to hell. I'll bet he sells them on the street corner, or to some raunchy magazine. Probably makes good money off of them." Geli took one of the photographs from the middle of the table and turned it face down. "I doubt Frieda wants me showing you this one."

"Frieda? From the third floor?"

"Unfortunately, she fell for his scheme. I'm doing her a favor." Geli tore the photo into small pieces and put them in her pocket.

"But you said 'no'?"

"I certainly did, but that wasn't the end of it. When he realized I wouldn't take my clothes off for him, he came on to me, right here in this room. Started running his filthy hands all over me. I slapped him and got out of here as fast as I could. The pig."

"So, you are showing me these because—?"

"I'd assumed there is something you're looking for—photos of someone in particular, a girlfriend? Isn't that what you meant when you said you needed to get in here because of *something personal*?"

Keller grinned at the mix-up. "No. I'm looking for photographs of a different sort. But, they are just as likely to be hidden." He began looking under the work bench.

"We must hurry," said Geli as she put the bawdy shots back in their hiding place. Keller was on hands and knees, searching under the equipment tables.

"What *are* you looking for?" asked Geli as she watched him crawling around.

"I'd rather not say. I don't want to involve you more than I already have." He guessed that if this photographer had pictures of the massacre, he would realize their value and keep copies. Now that he knew something of Brill's personality and greed, he was certain of it.

Keller's fingers found an envelope tacked under a photo-enlarger and worked it free. Using a trimming knife, he slit open the envelope.

He took a photograph from the envelope. Immediately, he knew he had what he was looking for. He motioned Geli to step back. "Not for your eyes." He thumbed through the photos. Keller's jaw clenched—muscles danced under the tension. Silently, he studied each picture. The story in the photographs unfolded exactly as Taatje had described. But, this was even worse than hearing about it. Now he could *see* it. Each photo was clear. He saw terror in the faces—some of them people he had known. He saw the victims as they faced their execution. He saw the murderers—Uhlemann, Gerber, and others. He saw *his* people being slaughtered. The barn ablaze. A hideous funeral pyre.

"Franz, we must go now."

Geli's words shattered his trance. He nodded and slipped the envelope inside his jacket and followed her out the door. He said to her quietly, "I need a minute. Excuse me."

"You're as white as a ghost, Franz." He didn't reply. "I'll return the key to Frieda." She watched as he drifted, in a stupor, toward the men's washroom. She waited in the hall until he made it through the door.

Keller buried his head in the sink. He wanted to vomit, but nothing came up. He ran water over the back of his neck and splashed his face. He looked toward the reflection in the mirror, but all he could see were the gruesome images swimming in his head.

13

Arnhem

The secretary was away. A clerk pointed Captain Gerber to Keller's vacant desk. Gerber scoured the drawers, rummaging through the contents. His wrath grew. The clerk pretended not to notice, no need to draw Gerber's notorious ire.

Gerber produced a folder, the Grossfeld file. He had what he was looking for, but was perplexed. Nothing inside. *Why not?* Zeigler had been specific, Sergeant Keller was seeking Grossfeld's Maarburg reports. *This should be it! Why would this guy want information on Maarburg—and why was he snooping in Uhlemann's files?* Gerber crossed the room to the secretary's desk, picked up the telephone and clicked the cradle. "Connect me with General Uhlemann's secretary please."

Geli rounded the corner on her return from the third floor, having dropped off Frieda's key. An officer stood at her desk, using her telephone. He was angry. She stood back, trying to blend in with the wall. She knew about this captain, the one with the mangled face. The scuttle among the *Helferin* was to steer clear of him. This fellow was wicked.

The telephone connected. "Good Day. This is Captain Gerber. I would like to speak with General Uhlemann, please. It is a matter of urgency—. When do you expect him to return—? Then I'll come upstairs and wait for him."

Gerber stormed to Keller's desk and rifled through the top drawer. He pulled out Keller's firearm, a pistol. Like most clerks, Keller did not carry his weapon but kept his pistol in his desk. Gerber also snatched a folder. He blew past Geli and clipped up the stairs.

Geli was panicked. This must be connected to Brill's photographs, that were now in Franz's possession. *The general was about to be involved?* They were coming after Franz. At this moment she was the only one who knew where he was.

Keller doused his head under the faucet. His world had turned upside down. When he joined the army, he was a believer. *Deutsch-land über alles!* Germany above all! His faith had wavered during the war, but he blamed that on a few bad leaders. *That will happen in any army, any government. Serving my country is still the right thing to do.* That's what he used to tell himself. In the past year, when it became obvious Germany could not win the war, his patriotism crumbled. He knew what most soldiers knew—*Hitler and his cronies are blinded by this Nazi claptrap. Everyone is suffering because of it, including Germans.* Yet, he told himself, that too would go away once a truce was reached. Now Taatje had sent him on an odyssey that was shattering all his convictions and was sucking him down a whirlpool. *Is it all a lie?* Keller stared at his reflection. *Am I a lie also?*

The door swung open. From the corner of his eye, Keller caught the image of a large fellow. Through the mirror he saw the officer's uniform. Keller's reaction was automatic. He turned with a rigid salute. The officer wore silver-braided epaulettes, a general.

"At ease." The general chuckled at Keller's soggy face. "You're not supposed to take a bath in here, sergeant."

"No, sir."

"The officers' WC is out of order. The pipes are backed up. Shit all over the floor. I'm sure you non-coms won't mind if we use yours for now. Who says shit flows downhill?" He laughed as he unzipped his fly.

Uhlemann! This is Uhlemann!

Keller ran his fingers through his hair, acting busy. At the urinal, three feet away from him, was the man he had come to loath, the coward who hid behind an army uniform and massacred innocent people. *I could kill him right now.* His rage welled as he listened to the buzz of the general's piss tattering against porcelain. He thought of using a knife or a pistol to the back of Uhlemann's head. *It would be so easy. Right now.* But Keller no longer carried a weapon.

Uhlemann zipped his fly. "You look a little green, sergeant. Too much to drink last night? Maybe you should step outside and get some fresh air." The general moved close to Keller and dabbed his hands under the only faucet. Their shoulders brushed together. Keller froze, side-by-side with Uhlemann. Keller grabbed a towel from the bar in front of him. His hands clenched as he brought it to his face and covered his eyes. The darkness was a relief. He heard the door open and dropped the towel to see the general's back disappear. As quickly as he had appeared, Uhlemann was gone.

14

Netherlands Countryside

The American Rangers followed Taatje through the darkness, passing the ruins of a burnt-out farmhouse. A breeze carried the dank odor of charred wood. Taatje knew the stories of many families, other victims of Uhlemann's inquisition. The crusade to purge the area of Dutch resistance had been an utter failure. Not a single member of the Maarburg PAN had been captured or killed. But many innocents had been victims of Uhlemann's witch hunt.

Taatje guided the Americans through the countryside, undetected by the Germans. She was proud she had done well.

The target was in sight, a black silhouette against the pre-dawn horizon. The Rangers hunched down in a thicket. A low haze had settled in the clearing, masking the field between themselves and the radar station. The contraption was a large mesh bowl about 10 meters across. In the gloaming, the steel supports resembled spider legs. The unit slowly rotated, searching the heavens for intruders from Great Britain. A cubicle was fixed to the back side of the structure. That's where the operators would be. In a swath around the station, the stubble field had been cleared of trees and brush. No guards could be seen, but no doubt, they'd be out there.

McCampbell signaled his marauders. Five of them moved out toward the anti-aircraft battery over the hill. Other Rangers spread out independently to take up positions surrounding the radar station. The actions were well rehearsed. McCampbell signaled Taatje to stay close. She followed him and two other soldiers down the hill until they came to a wire fence along the station's perimeter. Corporal Norton, wire clippers in hand, made short work of the fence. Within seconds, he cut an opening large enough to crawl through. McCampbell motioned for them to wait. Sergeant Sandoz appeared. With rapid hand signals, he indicated there were three Germans patrolling the perimeter. Sandoz pointed out their locations. McCampbell signaled, *"Ignore the two on the far side of the enclosure and target the one nearest."* They pulled their knives. McCampbell's Ka-Bar had a black blade about eight inches long. He rubbed his thumb perpendicular to its arced edge. This was to be a silent kill. McCampbell and Sandoz crawled through the hole in the fence and disappeared into the mist. Norton and Wiesnewski remained behind with Taatje.

The two Rangers prepared for the task ahead. Wiesnewski set up a wire coil, equipping it for the RDX plastique explosive from his haversack. Norton readied ammunition for his bazooka. He looked up at Taatje, smiled wryly and gestured for her to cover her ears. She nodded in understanding. Norton smiled at her and held up three fingers while inaudibly mouthing the words, "Three minutes. Three minutes. Boom." He pointed over the hill in the direction of the anti-aircraft battery and repeated, "Boom." He winked at Taatje. His grin beamed larger. She couldn't believe it. He was flirting with her! She'd heard about oversexed American soldiers, but this exceeded the rumors. Hell's fire was about to be unleashed and this fellow was making a pass. She rolled her eyes and turned her gaze.

McCampbell and Sandoz returned as silently as they had left. McCampbell held the bloodied Ka-Bar, indicating the kill was successful. He wiped the blade on his trouser leg and slipped it in the sheath. He gave two quick fist pumps and Wiesnewski hurried through the opening with a rifle in one hand and the wire coil in the other. Sandoz picked up the satchel and charges of RDX, then followed Wiesnewski toward the radar station.

McCampbell crawled through the fence. He grabbed Taatje's arm and pulled her with him until they got within 15 meters of Norton's bazooka. They ducked behind a rooted berm. McCampbell lay prone and readied his M1 rifle. He motioned her *down* and to move *next to* him. As she did, she steadied her pistol and took a deep breath. McCampbell grinned when he saw the short-barreled sidearm. "That thing's as old as my granddad," he whispered. "You've got guts little lady." The three minutes were almost up.

"C'mon, hurry," McCampbell muttered under his breath. From over the hill in the direction of the anti-aircraft battery, there was a ground-shaking thump. A half-mile away, a fireball unwound and lit up the landscape. "Goddamnit," said McCampbell. "Sandy and Wizz should have been back by now." German voices barked through the blind mist. McCampbell and Taatje lay frozen. Guns ready. They could hear the Germans spreading out. Probably only two or three of them, but it wouldn't be long before they were joined by more.

Sandoz and Wiesnewski emerged in front of McCampbell and Taatje. Two fist pumps. The explosives were set. The timer was ticking. Rifle shots pealed—flames from a muzzle—visible and close. Wiesnewski's chest erupted as he was hurled against the fence. Sandoz was writhing on the ground, screaming for Jesus. Two more bursts were fired from the same location. Sandoz lurched with each shot and fell silent. McCampbell took a bead on the muzzle flares and opened fire. Three rapid bursts. The German soldier dithered like a marionette, then crumpled.

McCampbell hollered to his flank, "Now Norton, now!"

Faaarrumph. Norton unleashed the bazooka. The rocket streaked toward its mark and exploded into the radar unit's stanchion. A second bazooka, from the far side of the enclosure, followed with another volley. That shell missed and shattered trees on the opposite hillside. Norton signaled for help reloading.

McCampbell slapped Taatje on the back saying, "Stay here." He would help Norton. Another German appeared and shot twice in Norton's direction, then dove to the ground about twenty meters in front of Taatje—and shot again. McCampbell and Norton scrambled for cover. The German hadn't seen Taatje. He fired two more rounds at the Americans. The first bullet ricocheted. The second rang off metal.

Taatje had practiced shooting her pistol many times, though usually without ammunition—and had never pointed it toward a person. She supported the weapon with both hands, exhaled, and squeezed the trigger. The bullet blazed forward as the pistol recoiled. She tamed it and squeezed another. And another. The dark shape of the German soldier flailed upward, then thrashed on the ground. She shot again. And again—until her quarry was a lifeless twist.

The center of the field erupted in an ear-shattering explosion. A giant ball of flame roiled into the sky. The concussive wave hurled debris over Taatje. Fiery shards shot everywhere. Husks of metal rained in the surrounding forest. The massive radar bowl leaped from its moorings and collapsed into the inferno. Taatje buried her face in the dirt.

Within seconds the din subsided. In one motion, someone lifted Taatje off the ground by her collar. McCampbell held her upright. "You OK? That was some damn fine shooting." She caught his meaning and allowed herself a small smile. "C'mon," he said. "We ain't stickin' around."

Flames illuminated the site. The American soldiers, weapons ready, merged into the clearing. A lone German soldier ran from the burning wreckage. He saw the Americans move toward him—stopped and spun. He was surrounded. He dropped his rifle, raised his hands over his head, facing the Americans who circled him like a wolf pack. "I surrender! Prisoner! I surrender." A few of the Americans on one side of the circle shouted curses at the trapped German. They moved in closer. He turned toward those voices and begged, "I surrender. I surr—." One shot tolled from behind the German. His head exploded and his body lurched to the ground, shuddering in nervous reflexes.

Taatje swung toward McCampbell. She screamed, *"Waarom?"*

He turned to face her. "You want to know why? Why? We don't take any prisoners. We can't. What would we do with him?" He motioned toward the burning radar station. "It's a shitty war." She glared at him. "Let's go," he said. "The Krauts will be swarming this place in no time." Two of the commandos stripped the belts and packs from their slain comrades, Sandoz and Wiesnewski. Their bodies were hoisted over the shoulders of two Rangers. The squad moved out fast, leaving the flaming wreckage behind. The rest of the Americans, those who had destroyed the anti-aircraft guns, were already waiting at the ridge path.

They moved overland for about a half hour. Taatje led them down a small canal road where two covered hay trucks were waiting. The trucks would take them to a boat house where they would wait out the day. After dark, they would cross the Rhine.

Taatje climbed into the back of one a truck. She huddled off to a corner by herself. The morning's events repeated over and over in her mind. She was surprised at herself. She wasn't bothered by the fact that she'd killed someone. He was the enemy, kill or be killed. No remorse. Yet, the death of that last German, the boy who tried to surrender, horrified her. It reminded her of that afternoon in her father's barn as she watched helpless Mr. Bickel get murdered by Uhlemann. She envisioned both incidents until she could no longer separate them. She stared blankly out the back of the truck. Morning light was cleansing the valley. Above, white streaks scratched the blue sky—contrails of high altitude airplanes. There were a few hundred scratches heading east. The American B-17's. Taatje closed her eyes.

15

Arnhem

Keller wished he could have killed the man. Uhlemann was vermin—filthy spume worthy of a blade or a bullet. His uniform made no difference. Not anymore.

"Franz, are you in there?" Geli's head appeared through the men's room doorway. She saw him by the sink and rushed in. "Franz, what's going on? I just passed General Uhlemann in the hallway. He came out of this washroom. What in the name of God are you up to?" Keller's head was in a different world. She grabbed him by the shoulders. "Listen to me. I don't know what you're doing, but you're in serious trouble. Captain Gerber was just rifling through your desk. He found some papers, and he took your gun. He was mad as hell and on his way up to see Uhlemann with what-ever he found. They'll be searching for you any minute. What is happening, Franz? What about me? Will they be coming for me too?"

"When did Gerber leave my desk?"

"A minute ago. Maybe two. He ran up to Uhlemann's office, telling the secretary he needed to talk to the general right away. Why would a captain need to talk to a general about you?"

"They're in it together. They need to cover each other's tracks."

"Why? In what together, Franz?"

Keller felt like he was on the front line again. In France, the battlefield was always changing. On two occasions, his unit was cut off from command—on an *island*. As a sergeant, he was in charge, responsible for making good decisions and responsible for the men under him. He passed those tests because his training paid off. *A sergeant shall: (A) Recognize conditions (B) Evaluate options (C) Adjust objectives (D) Take action.*

"Geli, listen to me. Gerber will have his security goons searching for me within minutes. They don't know you helped me. Leave here right now. Go back to your desk and start typing something, anything. Act like this day is no different than any other. You know nothing about this. Understand?"

"But I really *don't know* what it's about."

"You're better off."

"And you? What will you do, Franz?"

"I'm working on it. Now go."

As she opened the door, an officer was in front of her on his way in. She stopped him in his tracks. "Major! So glad you're here," Geli improvised. "The ladies room is occupied and I can't wait any longer. Be a dear, would you, and guard the door for me? I won't be but a minute." She tickled the major's chin while pushing him back into the hall and shut the door before he had a chance to reply. Geli turned to Franz and whispered, "What now? He'll stay there until I come out."

Franz stuck his head out the window. He was about five meters above the sidewalk. There were a few pedestrians walking about—but no men in uniform. He whispered to Geli, "Thank you." He leaned forward to kiss her cheek. As he did, she turned his head so their lips met. He accepted the brief kiss. "I must go. Now."

Keller climbed through the window, feet first, and in one motion, pushed outward. He dropped at an angle, hit the ground and rolled. Just like basic training. One thing was different—he didn't have this bum leg back then. Pain shot through him like he'd been hit with another mortar blast. He rolled upright, staggered to right himself, and immediately walked, hobbled, away from Van Sloten House. A few passersby gawked. Keller didn't look up. He kept walking. Stinging volleys ricocheted through his leg with every step. He was a block away when he heard three short bursts from a whistle, the signal for the guards. Within a minute, they would be searching for him. Within a half hour, all of Arnhem district would be alerted. He couldn't slow down now.

He was probably a dead man, but they hadn't caught him yet. He reached inside his jacket. The papers were there, as were the photographs. The next objective was to deliver them. He could worry about saving his own skin after that.

The rail station was only a few blocks ahead. He controlled his limp by imagining a march cadence. His mind sang *Panzerlied*, a favorite marching song of the Wehrmacht. Keller smirked at his self-created irony. With his forged pass he could board a train and ride out of Arnhem before an arrest bulletin was circulated. But could he get to Maarburg before news of his warrant? If not, the military police would be watching the station. Forget the train, too risky. *Adjust objectives.* He had another idea.

He turned down a side street toward the Waterfront, about a half mile away. The new route took him through the ravaged center of Arnhem. The area looked like a giant had stepped on the buildings and ground them under his foot. It took him ten minutes to make it to the river. The Waterfront was a tattered phoenix that had risen from the ashes—a seedy, red light district. Prostitutes and extortionists were hustling the quay the way a barker works a circus. Even at midday the spectacle was a steady flow. The breeze carried a pungent scent, a concoction of fish, fried lard, and boat exhaust. Keller pushed through the throng of people. Music and boisterous voices were coming from the Wilde Kat Cabaret. He paid five guilders and entered the dark club. Though it was midday, the Wilde Kat was pulsing. Men hovered around the bar. Liquor was flowing. Cigarette smoke hovered like a fog. On stage, a bare breasted dancer flounced to clanging tempos from an out-of-tune piano. Her admirers whooped as she dragged a boa across sotted faces in the front row. Most of the men in the Wilde Kat were German soldiers. This was Keller's best chance.

16

Camp Barlow

Hoefer crossed the quadrangle from the officers' barracks. Schwering, who'd been waiting on the opposite side, walked out to meet him.

"Colonel Hoefer. Sir!" Schwering saluted.

"Major!" Hoefer returned salute. "Punctual as always, I see."

Hoefer and Schwering often met in the middle of the quadrangle. Here, the two highest-ranking German officers in the POW camp discussed confidential matters. The wide open quad was the perfect spot. No eavesdropping.

Hoefer laughed as they converged. "Reminds me of that silly movie the Americans showed us last month, yes? You remember, the one in which the cowboys walk into the middle of the town, pull pistols, and shoot each other. What was it called?"

"I believe that was *The Sheriff of Tombstone*. You're not going to shoot me, are you sir?"

Hoefer chuckled. "No, no, Major. I'm afraid the Americans have taken away my six-shooter pistol. You know, Colonel Riley was telling me they film those American cowboy movies not far from here."

"So I've heard," replied Schwering. "May I ask about your meeting with the American colonel?"

"Yes, certainly. Rather funny, but my discussion with Colonel Riley had to do with cowboys also."

"Sir?"

"Colonel Riley wants us to supply the neighboring cattle ranches with workers and select them from among our enlisted ranks. Our German soldiers have proven to be superb cotton pickers on the local farms. Now the cattlemen want to use our men to do their cattle chores."

"What did you say, sir?"

"There wasn't much I could say, Major. The Geneva Convention requires it. If the Americans say they want German cowboys, they get German cowboys. The same sort of thing is going on back in the Fatherland. American prisoners-of-war are tending German fields and repairing German railroads."

"You're right of course, Colonel. Yet, I find it worrisome. The Americans have been indoctrinating our men with their propaganda—trying to turn them away from National Socialism—and debauch them with American-style democracy. A failed system for weaklings if you ask me. Now the damned Americans hope to make cowboys out of Aryan men? Ludicrous!"

"Which is precisely why we keep *the list*, eh Major?"

"Yes, Colonel. Certainly."

The *list* was a common reason for these private meetings between Hoefer and Schwering. By casting his web, Schwering kept track of the Germans at Camp Barlow. He knew each soldier's devotion to Naziism. The secret list was comprised of names, men who had shown signs of rejecting Hitler. Those men were under the watchful eye of *the Circle*, Schwering's Nazi lackeys. Those on the list were denied privileges in the camp and were not assigned duties that had them working closely with Americans. Their names were never submitted for labor outside the camp. If a *listed prisoner* failed to heed mild warnings, he'd be visited by Sergeant Müller and his *enforcement* squad. Smashed fingers and broken noses had a way of bringing most transgressors to heel. All prisoners knew of the Circle's existence. They were being watched. The evidence was sometimes subtle, sometimes not.

Schwering kept the list in his locked desk and updated it when necessary. There was but one draft and Colonel Hoefer was the only other person to see it. Rarely, an individual's name was underlined in red ink. Schwering and Hoefer referred to this as a *red man*, a prisoner who was of particular concern. The last *red man* was Corporal Milo Jauch.

"How many cowboys do they want, Colonel?"

"They're asking for twenty-five. They want us to provide them with German boys who've had experience around farm animals. They especially want men who can ride horses."

"Maybe they also want us to find some men who can have a shootout with the Sheriff of Tombstone?" Schwering sniggered.

"Just be sure that none of our cowboys come from the list, Major. By the way, are there any men with whom I need to be particularly concerned—any *red* men?"

"No Colonel, not at the present. But we're keeping our eyes on a few."

17

On the Rhine River

The US Army Rangers piled out of the trucks. Willem was waiting for them at the boat house. Veldhuis interpreted as Willem explained the plan to McCampbell, "You'll remain here until night-fall. When the sun is down, you'll take that boat across the river." Willem pointed toward a skiff that was tied to the dock. "The Germans will be looking for you once they figure out what happened to their radar station. You have not been followed, but they will be looking everywhere. You'll hide inside the boat house until nightfall."

McCampbell walked inside. The small building was crammed with oars, nets, and fishing tackle. He said, "It's a good enough hiding place, but if the Germans find us we'll be sitting ducks. I'm going to put two look-outs on the road and on the bank of the river. Maybe put one in the boat, too."

"No," said Willem. "You Americans need to stay out of sight. We'll watch the road. We'll give you warning."

McCampbell cocked his head toward Willem, sizing him up. "With all due respect, my men are trained to protect each other and I'm not going to turn that responsibility over to somebody else."

Willem balked, "Very well. I'll have people up and down the road. We'll give you warning if the Germans approach, but you're on your own if there's to be a fight."

"That works," said McCampbell.

Willem said, "It will be dark by 2100. Leave then. Take the skiff. Its motor has been overhauled and it moves fairly fast, but God help you if you're spotted by a German boat. Head directly across the river. We'll radio our people on the opposite bank. They'll flash an amber light. Follow that light right up onto land. Be ready to run like hell as soon as you hit the opposite bank. If the boat makes it across unseen, our people will hide it.

McCampbell hated the idea of waiting out the day but this Dutch partisan was right. They didn't dare move across the Rhine until nightfall. Even then, it would be treacherous. He divided up the look-out shifts and prepared his men to settle in for a long day.

Taatje walked over to Willem. "I'm going to leave now. I haven't slept in a day and half and I need to get back to my place."

"Blondi, don't go to town. You stay close by. I need you here."

"No, Willem. I am going back to my own flat. Don't tell me otherwise. I'll be back here before midnight to help erase any sign the Americans have been here."

"Why are you being such a bitch? What is so important back at your place?" He stepped toward her and grasped her chin in his hand. "You're meeting that German soldier of yours again, are you?" She pulled away. "You're making a mistake, Blondi. You think you can trust a German? Forget about him, he won't help you. You're playing with poison." She backed away. "Stay here. You take orders from me."

Her eyes steeled. "I used to be your lap dog. Not anymore."

When Taatje was new to the resistance, she fell for Willem. He was twenty years older and held an important post with PAN. He wooed her and eventually got her into bed. At first, she put up with his arrogance but when he flaunted her like a trophy, she told him to go to hell and shunned all his advances after that. Her rejection didn't sit well with Willem and sent him into several tirades. During one of his fits he backhanded her, launching her into a wall. She pulled a knife before he could punch her again. "One step closer and I'll kill you." Her resolve seemed to hit its mark. He hadn't hit her since and seemed to give up on her sexually, although she was never quite sure. Unfortunately for Taatje, they remained resistance *partners* due to necessity. Both of them knew the Maarburg area and were well-versed in the needed skills. He was still domineering and tried to control her in other ways. At least he hadn't hit her again—but she always kept the knife ready.

She crossed the knoll to Willem's motorbike.

"I said stay here, bitch!"

She stamped the kick-starter and revved the motor. Black smoke chortled from the exhaust pipe. Willem ran toward her as she wheeled a wide circle, spraying gravel.

"Damn you!" He grabbed for the scooter as she passed, but she dipped the handlebar and dodged him. He missed his mark and stumbled to the ground. "Dirty slut!"

Taatje gave full throttle and whirred up the gravel road. She disappeared over the hill toward Maarburg.

18

Arnhem

Keller's instincts had been right. This might be his ticket out of Arnhem. He knew the reputation of the waterfront. After the last battle, squalid enterprises sprang from the bombed-out quay, transforming the area into a bawdy skid row. Gambling halls, peep shows, whorehouses, and the black market were nurtured by a seamy underground. Important to Keller was the fact that the waterfront teemed with off-duty German soldiers.

He pushed his way into the Wilde Kat Cabaret. Once an ancient warehouse, the plank floors were rotten and splintered. Timber joists sagged like a swayback horse with beams water-stained from a long-neglected roof. A horde of men jostled for space.

He worked through the crowd, questioning soldiers, the most sober ones, to find anyone who might be driving south. He was pointed toward two privates who were seated next to the stage. Keller weaved through a mob of drunks to get to them. The privates were entranced by Bibi, the headline dancer, who was making her third appearance on stage since Keller's arrival. She was the only dancer that afternoon.

"Private Tauber?" Keller tried to get his attention over the din. He tapped his shoulder. "Private Tauber?"

Tauber caught sight of Keller and stood. "Yes, Sergeant," he shouted. "You're not going to take my front-row seat are you?"

"No, no, Private. Sit down. I want to ask you a favor. I understand you are heading south this afternoon."

Tauber seemed perturbed that Bibi's jiggling routine was being interrupted. "That's right, Sergeant. Voss and I are driving a Kübelwagen that way. We have to deliver it to the motor pool in Gendringen. Doesn't have to be there until 1900."

"Can I get a lift to Maarburg? It's on your way."

Tauber and Voss jumped up, whistling and hooting as Bibi removed her lacy corset and flung it behind her. It was the same strip tease she'd performed ten minutes earlier, but this crowd had a short memory. They chanted for her to take off her lacey brassiere. The two privates settled back in their seats and gave only cursory attention to Keller. "Sure Sergeant, we can take you there. Why don't you go get yourself a beer and come back in an hour or two?"

"Actually, Private, I was hoping we could leave soon. I need to get there in a hurry. I'll make it worth your while."

Tauber rolled his eyes as if nothing could be worth sacrificing an hour in Bibi's paradise. "How much?"

"Twenty five guilders."

"Dutch money is worthless. Pay me in German marks and you've got a deal. We'll leave after I finish this beer, eh?"

"I'll give you fifty marks if we leave right now."

Bibi tossed her brassiere toward the rafters. The crowd jumped to their feet, roaring approval. A drunk soldier climbed onto the stage, raising his glass toward the dancer. *Prosit! Prosit!* The crowd joined his merriment and toasted Bibi. The drunk onstage began singing *You Run Through all my Dreams,* the popular Lizzi Waldmüller song. Soon all the Germans joined in. Bibi completed her routine by parading to the beat of her off-key admirers. As the song ended, she curtsied and her breasts wobbled to the most raucous cheer of the day. Then she fluttered off stage.

Tauber gave a final, piercing whistle, then turned his attention to Keller. He tipped his beer glass and drained it. "Fifty marks, you say? What are we waiting for? The Kübelwagen is parked on the next street."

"There are no signs of his whereabouts, General. He has disappeared."

"Have you issued a bulletin to all checkpoints—to the Army Patrol Service—the train stations?"

"Yes, sir. He won't get far." Gerber was trying to foster assurance, but it wasn't working.

Uhlemann said, "He must be captured soon. Those documents he pilfered are very damning—*damning to you and to me.* Is there any indication as to what this sergeant … what's his name?"

"Keller, sir."

"Keller. Is there any indication as to what this son-of-a-bitch may be planning to do with the Maarburg papers? Do you have a theory?"

"We've scoured his personnel file and his military records. One thing arouses suspicion. He is half-Dutch. His mother grew up on a farm outside Maarburg. We're checking to see if he still has relatives in the area."

"Was he stationed here in September, on the day that we … restored discipline in the Maarburg countryside?"

"No, General. He arrived only three and a half weeks ago. Before that, he spent six months in military hospitals."

Uhlemann's temper was rising. "Captain Gerber, I am holding you responsible for his capture. You're in charge of the goddamned security detail here, and that security was breached. Find him!"

"Yes, General sir," Gerber barked and his heels clicked.

"Heil Hitler!"

"Heil Hitler!" Gerber hurried down the stairs. Preoccupied, he didn't notice Corporal Oskar Brill as he passed him on the second floor landing.

Brill was heading toward his dark room. He'd been out all day, having been called away that morning to take photographs of a destroyed radar station outside Maarburg.

Brill turned the key to the dark room, his private kingdom. He immediately noticed things out of place. On the enlargement table were small slices of paper and his trimming knife, unsheathed. Brown strips from one of his photo envelopes littered the table top. He dropped to his knees and searched the underside of the table top. The envelope was gone, along with the photographs he had considered destroying, *many times*, but did not. Dread washed over him. Blackmail was a dangerous game. The photographs might have brought him fortune one day. Now someone else had them. Brill wrapped his head in his arms. "God in Heaven. No! God in Heaven!"

The Kübelwagen sputtered along the country roads that connected Arnhem to Maarburg. Tauber drove. Keller rode in the passenger seat much to the dismay of Voss. The small, general-purpose vehicle was stuffed with auto components to be delivered to the motor pool in Gendringen. Voss crammed into what little space was left. He sulked, not happy to leave the Wilde Kat early or to give up his seat to this hitchhiking sergeant. Furthermore, Tauber had given no indication he intended to share the fifty mark fee.

They arrived in Maarburg as sunlight was fading. Keller directed Tauber to the corner of Brouwerstraat and Kuiperstraat. "There's a tobacconist there that carries my favorite tobacco," Keller said. "Just drop me off here, please."

The brakes squeaked as the Kübelwagen stopped in front of the tobacco shop. "Here are the fifty marks, as promised," said Keller as he removed the cash from his billfold.

Tauber snatched the bills from Keller's hand. "I'll take care of it, Sergeant." Tauber had it in his shirt pocket before Voss could say anything.

As Keller left the vehicle, Voss popped into the front seat, reclaiming his status. "Thanks for the lift, fellows," said Keller.

"A pleasure, Sergeant," said Tauber as he patted the treasure in his pocket.

Keller hobbled to the sidewalk. His leg had stiffened during the ride from Arnhem. He approached the window display at the tobacco shop and gazed at the same meerschaum pipe as he had a few days earlier. He waited until the Kübelwagen rounded the corner and disappeared. Then he walked toward Taatje's flat.

Tauber drove a block then hit the brake. "Why are you stopping," asked Voss.

"Didn't you notice anything strange?"

"Yeah. You haven't given me my twenty-five marks?"

Tauber grinned. The cash remained in his pocket. "Didn't you notice that the tobacco shop was closed? Also, Keller said he was going to pick up some of his favorite tobacco. He doesn't smoke. If he was a smoker, he would have smoked when he was with us."

"So?" said Voss, uninterested.

"Listen! Why in the hell would he pay fifty marks to buy tobacco in Maarburg? Why wouldn't he just get it in Arnhem?"

"Who cares?" said Voss.

"So he's lying to us. He's hiding something." Tauber turned the vehicle around.

Voss said, "You're joking, right? Who gives a shit?"

Tauber ignored his buddy and drove back to the tobacco shop. The Kübelwagen pulled up to the intersection where they'd dropped off Keller. "That's him," said Voss. He recognized the uneven gait of Keller, a half-block down Kuiperstraat, walking away. Tauber eased the vehicle onto Kuiperstraat and crawled forward. They watched Keller from a distance. Keller crossed to the opposite sidewalk to a recessed stairwell. "He went in there, the building with the red flower box."

"What's that son-of-a-bitch up to?" said Tauber. He edged closer and stopped on the opposite side of the street. The window curtain above the red flower box opened. Keller stood in the window with his back to it. A candle flickered inside the room. A woman stepped toward Keller. Then, Keller shut the curtain.

"Must be his whore," said Voss.

"Maybe," replied Tauber, "but why did he go to such trouble to hide it from us? It doesn't add up." Tauber noted the address, 131 on Kuiperstraat, and then he pulled away. "We don't have to be in Gendringen for a couple of hours. Let's see if we can find a beer hall in this town."

19

Arnhem

Captain Gerber stormed into his office, which was situated across the carriageway, behind the Van Sloten mansion. When the German army took over the property, they put the security detail in the decrepit carriage house. It was an afterthought and Gerber resented it, indignant that his security detail was relegated to a space once used for horses and oily machines—stains of both still evident on the bare stone floor. "Shit and grease," he sneered. His office was the only place in the building with heat, but the pot-bellied stove was useless when wind whistled through the rotting window sills. The situation was worse for his men who bunked in the stables. *Why are men of lower rank given desks in the luxurious mansion? Here I am—a captain of the Reich—fingers frozen in this stinking horse shed.*

Gerber knew the scuttle. Others called him Uhlemann's *lackey,* and he was afraid they were right. Orders came down that required him to do things outside the bounds of a security detail. And he wasn't the only one. Uhlemann had others who served his will, a secretary who acted as a party hostess and a photographer who was his publicity agent. Gerber slammed another scoop of coal into the stove.

He thought about Maarburg. *Why did the general send a security unit to roust the peasants that day? My unit! For God's sake, there are goddam infantry patrols in Maarburg who should have done the job. Why? Because Uhlemann can control me. It was a damned publicity stunt that went bad. I've been covering his ass since—and now I'm fucked, unless I can stop this bastard, Keller.*

Lieutenant Zeigler entered Gerber's office. "My, it gets awfully cold in here, Captain. Forgot to requisition coal?" Gerber was in no mood for the thin joke. Zeigler's grin disappeared. "I have a copy of the list you requested, Captain. It shows all the civilian casualties from the Maarburg sector in September '44."

Gerber snatched the report out of Zeigler's hands.

"That runaway sergeant has caused quite a stir," said Zeigler, prodding for information. "My guess is that all this fuss has some-thing to do with his visit to the records room this morning, eh?"

Gerber trained his eye on Zeigler. "That will be all, Lieutenant."

"Yes sir! *Heil Hitler!*" Zeigler quickly left.

Gerber put on his overcoat and sat down. *Why in hell did I end up under this fucking general?* Uhlemann was a political appointment. He wasn't academy trained. Not a true Wehrmacht officer. There was no evidence of Prussian military tradition about the man. Uhlemann was an industrialist. *He's a bootlicking businessman. He ate Nazi shit and said it tasted like chocolate pudding. Probably sucked Göring's cock to get his commission.*

Gerber looked over the new document. His comparison between the list of *Maarburg Deceased* and Keller's personnel file produced a result. Keller's mother was noted in the latter

98

file—*Carin Keller*, Maiden Name: *Carin de Zoute*. Among the civilian casualties listed in the first file were *Balthasar de Zoute, Jana de Zoute*, and *Malena De Zoute*. The *Date of Death* for all three was September 20, 1944.

20

Maarburg

Taatje fell into bed. She dozed intermittently through the afternoon and into evening. Sleep was uneasy. Haunting visions jolted her slumber—the faces of Sandoz and Wiesnewski—the enemy's body thrashing as she pulled the trigger—and the pitiful face of the German boy who tried to surrender. His terror-cries transformed into her mother's screams, swallowed in flames. A pounding noise turned Taatje's dream to another vision—the young soldier's brain exploding as a bullet ripped through his head. The pounding grew louder. She jerked awake, sopped with sweat. The room was nearly dark. *Is the sun down? Is someone knocking?* She stumbled to the door and answered in a raspy voice. "Who is it? Who's there?"

"It's Franz. Let me in."

"Franz?" She opened the door. "What time is it? You're early."

"Things have changed. I had no choice." He flipped a lamp switch but it didn't work.

She said, "The electricity has been out for a couple of days. It happens all the time. I'll light a candle." As she did, Keller opened the curtain to let the twilight filter in. The candle cast a diluted glow. The dim flicker illuminated Taatje as she set the candle on the table. The vision stopped him in his tracks. She wore a rumpled slip that loosely fell from her shoulders. Her dark hair was tousled and her eyes were heavy from sleep. The soft image reminded Keller of a Vermeer painting—a complex woman set against a dim, uncertain background. She captured his heart as she always had. He still loved her.

"Franz, please close the curtain." She wrapped herself in a blanket.

"I brought everything you asked." Keller placed the papers and envelope on the table. He removed three pages. Unfolding them, he said, "These records show Uhlemann's activities on September 20th. They prove he was not in Maarburg that day. They contradict your photographs. Local records show the fire to be September 20th. This proves Uhlemann's story is a lie."

Taatje plunged into the documents, studying each word under the candlelight. Keller paced silently and watched her expression as she took in each one. She looked up. "This is excellent, Franz. There are lawyers in our group, who are dedicated to crucifying bastards like Uhlemann. In a court, these papers will prove his lies. Then it will be up to me, my testimony. I am the only witness, the only one still alive. The only non-German. Maybe it will be enough to make that bastard hang."

Keller pointed to the tattered envelope under his hand. "There's more here. Not easy to look at."

"What is it?"

"More photographs," he said. "They were taken inside the barn that day. These pictures are proof. Uhlemann is a murderer. So is Gerber, the one who tried to rape you." Her eyes riveted on the envelope. "You won't need to testify. These pictures tell the whole story. Uhlemann will hang."

"Let me see them, please."

He slid the photographs from the envelope. He took the bottom one from the stack and kept it, face down. He placed the others in front of her and gave her some space. She studied them one at a time but spent only a few seconds on each. The photos were large and clear. Taatje's face was stone as she witnessed the butchery of that day. Most of the pictures were taken after she fled the barn, while she fought with Gerber, and while she hid in the bushes watching flames swallow the barn and all who were inside. The photographs told the truth—innocent people were murdered by Uhlemann and his jackals. Tears streamed from her eyes but her expression remained granite. The last photo showed Franz's Aunt Malena, clubbed by a rifle butt as she rushed to her dying child, Jana.

Taatje looked toward Franz and registered his anguish. "It seems my destiny is to witness death." Her voice scraped like a rusty blade, eyes boring into the candle flame. "Death follows me."

Franz held one photograph in his hand. "What about that one?" she said.

"This one is for me," he said.

"Why? Is there anything left that could surprise me?"

He moved to her and lightly touched her hand, "Please."

She considered his odd request for a moment, "Very well."

Franz took a paring knife from the counter and sliced the photograph down the middle. Half of it, he placed inside his jacket pocket. He crumbled the other half and held it over the candle. Once alight, he tossed it into the stove.

Keller gathered the documents and photographs and slid them into the envelope. "You must put these away. Keep them safe until the war is over."

Taatje lifted the loose stone behind the stove. "You and I are the only ones who know where these things are hidden. If something happens to me, then it's up to you." Her voice seemed resigned, as if she didn't expect to live that long. She put the items in the hidden void and replaced the top stone.

"And your friends? The resistance? Don't they know about this hiding place?"

"No, and I'm not going to tell them. They would take these things out of my hands and I won't let anyone do that. I'll keep them until the time is right. This is my crusade."

In central Maarburg, Tauber found what he was looking for. The beer hall had been christened with a German spelling, *Rheinhaus*, sure to cater to Wehrmacht soldiers. Tauber parked the Kübelwagen on the street. "Come on," he said to Voss, "we have plenty of time for a beer."

Voss said, "I can see the wheels turning in your head. What are you thinking?"

"I think if that asshole sergeant was willing to pay fifty marks to drive him to Maarburg, he might be willing to pay a lot more—."

"For us to keep our mouths shut about his whore?"

"Exactly!"

They chuckled as they walked along the busy sidewalk toward the Rheinhaus. A forearm smacked into Tauber's chest, stopping him in his tracks. "Identification please." The soldier wore a metal chest plate that hung from a chain around his neck. On the plate was a green swastika clutched in the talons of an eagle. He was *Feldjäger*, military police. These guys were known as *Hitler's chained dogs*, an earned reputation of ruthless brutality. Tauber bit his lip. His quick mouth tended to get him in trouble. This time, he knew better.

"Yes, sir." They produced their travel papers.

"You're coming from Arnhem?"

"Yes, sir. We're delivering that vehicle to Gendringen," said Voss, pointing toward the Kübelwagen.

The Feldjäger studied their faces. Two other *dogs* arrived out of nowhere and hovered over Tauber and Voss like vultures on carrion. "We're looking for a Wehrmacht sergeant who was last seen in Arnhem. Taller than you. Walks with a limp. Seen him, Private?"

Tauber swallowed hard. He'd given Keller a lift without authorization and taken a bribe for it. That could mean a week in the stockade, or worse, especially if Keller turned out to be a criminal. Tauber looked over to Voss, masking a glare that implored silence.

The *chained dogs* smelled fear. The leader moved to within an inch of Tauber's ear. "Answer me, Private. One more time. Have you seen this man?"

"Yes, sir!" exploded Voss.

21

Banks of the Rhine

"How you coming along in there, Thud?" McCampbell was standing on the boat deck and yelling through a small hatch into the engine compartment.

Thud's answer was muffled. "Just about done, Lieutenant. Carburetor's cleaned out. Just gotta check this fuel line. But daggonnit, there ain't much wiggle room in here."

"This thing going to run?"

"Slicker 'n snot, sir."

"That's all we need. Just has to get across the river. How much longer?"

"Should be done in ten minutes, sir. Just gotta git to this dad-gummed hose clamp."

McCampbell said, "Finish up quick. It's almost dark and we don't want your flashlight drawing any attention. As soon as you're done, get your butt in the boat shack with everybody else."

"Yes, sir."

Corporal Thad Allen grew up in West Virginia coal country. His dad was a mechanic in the mines and Thad was a chip off the old block. There *wasn't nuthin'* the Allen boys couldn't fix. Lieutenant McCampbell knew it too and he insisted "Thud" Allen be part of this mission. The last phase of the plan involved crossing the Rhine in a motorboat provided by the Dutch resistance. McCampbell shunned the idea of counting on anybody but his own men, US Army Rangers. He admitted to himself the Dutch had done a good job so far, especially that pretty gal who was damn handy with a pistol. But he wasn't going to take any chance of stranding his men on shore, or worse, in the middle of the Rhine River. Thud Allen was insurance.

Twenty minutes later, the job was done. Thud shimmied out of the engine compartment and crawled over two rolled tarpaulins. The bodies of Sandoz and Wiesnewski were wrapped in those tarps and had been placed low in the hull. He gestured a sign-of-the-Cross as he passed over them. The sky was dark. Thud doused the flashlight.

He heard a triple-whistle from the lookout on the jetty. Tucking himself under the deck and against the hull, he grabbed his M-1 off the transom and double-checked the clip. Lieutenant McCampbell had been very clear—no one was to engage the enemy. *Only as a last resort and it'll probably be suicide. One shot and there'll be Krauts swarming on us like flies on bear shit.*

Allen was still. The night was silent except for the waters lapping against the shore. He heard a droning murmur in the distance. His finger tapped on the trigger-guard as the hum gradually grew louder. Thud wasn't an expert on boats, but he knew motors. The thrumming was from a large engine. He peeked over the gunwale and was blinded by a bright spotlight that lit up the interior of the skiff. The light moved away, then returned. The engine was loud. The big boat was close. The searchlight bore down. Light beams pierced through openings on the thin deck. Thud teased the trigger. This must be the German patrol boat they'd seen cruising the shore earlier in the day. That time, however, it hadn't entered the cove. The light's sweep halted. The beacon shined through the hatch onto the white tarpaulins. Allen heard loud conversation from the boat. German. He snugged the rifle to his shoulder. If one jackboot stepped on deck, he'd open fire. Better to be the first than the last. His buddies would join the fight once they heard shots. If they could wipe out these Krauts, he'd fire up the skiff and they'd race for the other shore. Maybe they'd make it.

There was a banging against the hull. The German boat was so close that the two crafts were slapping against each other in the swells. Each thump jarred Allen as he did his best to steady his rifle from his cramped slot. There was a clatter above him. Were the Germans using poles to push against the skiff? To separate the boats? The poles were only inches above him.

Allen cradled the rifle stock in his left hand and stretched the fingers of his right. He fought his tendency to tense up when firing a weapon, a bad habit for a soldier. He exhaled and loosely positioned his index finger over the trigger. Ready.

The knocking stopped. His eyes and muzzle were fixed on the gunwale.

The light beam moved off the boat and across to the bank. Allen blinked rapidly, adjusting his eyes to the new darkness. The large engine revved and drubbed slowly away. They were leaving. He began breathing again.

Five minutes passed before he heard a voice. "Allen? Thud? You OK?" He crawled out from his hiding place.

"Dang near pissed my pants, but I'm OK, Lieutenant."

"That was close," said McCampbell.

"This boat's ready to go right now," said Thud. "Just say the word."

McCampbell spoke to Norton. "Corporal, you glassed this patrol when they came through here this afternoon, right?"

"Yes, sir."

"What was their pattern?"

"They zigzagged, sir. Every time they moved upstream they'd go about a half mile, then they'd double back. They could be back here in a few minutes."

"Listen up," McCampbell said to the squad. "We're not gonna take a chance of being in this little motorboat if the big boy comes back. We'll take up positions in the bushes around this cove. Stay out of the boathouse. We'd be sittin' ducks in there if the Krauts decided to open up on us. It's twenty-hundred hours right now. We'll wait as long as it takes. Give that big Kraut fucker a chance to move out of here. Then we're gonna get the hell across this goddamn river."

22

Maarburg

Taatje carried the basin to her nightstand. She dropped the blanket next to her and sat on the bed. Wearing only a slip, she lathered the washcloth with a cake of soap. "I have to leave in a few hours. Something I must do."

"In the middle of the night?" asked Franz.

She shrugged her shoulders. It was clear she wasn't going to tell him why. There's some food in the sack there. Are you hungry?"

"Starving. I haven't eaten since this morning." He emptied the sack to find three hard tack biscuits and two square tins, one of them already opened. In the dim light he read the label, *SPAM*. "What is this?" said Keller.

"American soldiers gave it to me this morning. I've already eaten some."

Keller bit into the hard biscuit, not unlike the *Panzerplatten* he was accustomed to on the French front. The meat brick tasted peculiar. "Americans could learn about sausage-making from us," he said.

"True, true. But beggars can't be choosers. That's a feast compared to what we've been living on these days." She worked the washcloth over her neck, shoulders, and arms. "Turn around."

"Sorry?"

"Face the other way. I need some privacy."

"Oh. Of course." He turned away and slid the unfinished food back into the sack. He'd leave it for Taatje.

"You haven't told me why you're here *now*," said Taatje. "We were supposed to meet tomorrow morning by the statue. Coming here in your uniform could create trouble."

With his back to her, he took off his Wehrmacht jacket and set it on the table with the swastika pin face-down. He told a short version of the day's events—the files, the dark room, his escape from Van Sloten House, and hitching a ride to Maarburg. Water splashed in the basin as Taatje wrung out the washcloth. He didn't mention his encounters with Gerber or Uhlemann, sparing her mention of her demons.

"So, what will you do now, Franz? You can't go back."

"I don't know. The plan blew up in my face. I had to survive. The first thing was to get out of Arnhem. Next was getting these things to you. I haven't figured out the next step."

Taatje touched his shoulder and turned him around. She cupped his chin and pulled his lips to hers, shuddering as she kissed him. Was she weeping? Her arms slipped around his shoulders. She held tight, lips moving desperately against his. Her tears smeared against his cheeks. She dropped her head and sobbed.

He held her gently as she buried her face in his shirt. Her chest trembled as she wracked with convulsive sobs, intermittently surfacing for breath.

She smacked her fist against his chest a couple of times, yet continued to nestle her cheek into his shoulder. He wished he knew her mind. She was in pain. That was obvious. Her family's murder kept coming back to haunt her, and he'd been part of that. There was something else too, but he couldn't pinpoint it—something to do with her life in the resistance—but it was unlikely she'd confide that to him. And where did he fit? She wasn't making it easy to figure out.

"Hold me tight, Franz."

He smoothed his hand along her back, her slip flowing easily in his hand. She clung to him, with muscles knotted. "I don't want to let go. I want to be here forever."

As they stood, he cradled her, running his fingers through her hair and stroking her back. He was beginning to understand. Her embrace felt safe for him too. The world around them was on fire, but they were finding peace in each other. It took him back to their last summer together. Things were good then, when they were in love.

Gradually, her weeping slowed, her grasp loosened, and she began breathing steadily. They swayed gently to an unheard tempo, moving with each other for a long, long dance. It felt as if she was falling asleep in his arms.

He whispered, "I've imagined this for years, holding you again. I think of you every day."

"Are the memories good?"

"Do you remember that day your parents went to town. We came back from a ride, put the horses away, and discovered we had the house to ourselves. We spent the whole day in your bedroom. Remember?"

He felt her snicker. "Of course I remember. We were naked." Another snicker. "We were naked *all day*. That would be hard to forget."

"And we made love. What? A dozen times or so?"

"I think you might be exaggerating." She squeezed his waist the same way she used to.

"That was the best day of my life," he said.

She paused to consider. "Yes. I think mine too."

Their swaying dance continued to the silent music.

Taatje looked up. Their lips met again, this time softly. No desperation. The kiss was long and easy.

"You are still absolutely beautiful to me," he said.

Taatje stepped back. She pulled the slip over her head and let it fall to the floor. "Let's imagine that day did not end." She took his hand and pulled him toward the bed.

23

Only four German women worked in Van Sloten House. All were members of the *Wehrmacht Helferin*, the Army Women's Auxiliary. Their dormitory was a spare, single room, the former maids' quarters. Each had a bed and an armoire. The lavatory was across the hallway.

Geli was in bed, reading a magazine. Two security guards burst in. She pulled the sheet to her neck. The other pajama-clad women scrambled for robes and covers.

"Attention!" barked the lead guard. Geli dropped the magazine, jumped out of bed and assumed a rigid stance at the foot of her bed. The other women did likewise. The Helferin were support staff, yet they were a trained component of the army and were expected to comport with military discipline.

"Which one of you is *Haupthelferin* Raubel?"

"I am *Haupthelferin* Raubel," replied Geli—eyes forward, shoulders back. Captain Gerber walked in the room.

The guard pointed out Geli. "Captain, this is Raubel."

"Thank you, Corporal. Please escort the other ladies outside. Allow them to put on their shoes and coats. It's very cold outside, ladies. Raubel, you will remain."

Anna and Mathilde slipped on their shoes and woolen greatcoats. Each glanced toward Geli with grievous concern. Frieda turned her back while she buttoned up. As she left, she didn't look toward Geli. Her eyes were red. Gerber passed her as he crossed the room and gave a slight nod. Frieda burst into tears and hurried out the door.

Geli's heart jumped. *My God, Frieda has told him.*

One of Gerber's guards remained by the doorway. The other went outside with the women. Gerber hovered next to Geli. She remained *at attention*, eyes forward.

Gerber began, "*Fräulein* Raubel."

"*Haupthelferin* Raubel, *Herr* Captain." She inserted her rank, as she was wearing pajamas, no insignia. Maybe Gerber didn't know her level. A Helferin rank did not carry the weight as those of the army. Yet, the Helferin were normally addressed by their rank as a form of army protocol.

Gerber, perturbed by the interruption, raised his voice. "*Fräulein* Raubel, I will decide if you are worthy of respect. That will depend upon my determination as to whether you have broken your covenant with the army."

"Yes, sir."

"You realize there was an inquiry today at the administrative complex, a search for Sergeant Keller, whom you appear to know well. You and he work in the same office, correct?"

"Yes, sir."

I've spoken to others. They tell me, you and he are friendly. True?"

"Yes, sir."

"—and you spent time with him today? Time away from your duties? You were seen with him in the garden during your morning break. Yes?"

"Yes, sir."

"You were also seen together on the second floor corridor. At the same time, you had procured a key to the photography room. Did you and Sergeant Keller enter that room?"

"Yes, sir." *My God, Frieda told him everything. I'm done for.*

Up to this point, Geli had answered truthfully. There was no way around it. But more truths would damn her. Rumors flew around Van Sloten House all afternoon. *The missing sergeant, Keller, had stolen classified papers—papers he would sell to the enemy. The traitor must be captured.* She had not seen the photographs Keller pilfered. She didn't know if Captain Gerber even knew of any missing photographs. *If Gerber finds out I helped Franz steal anything, this day could be my last. Frieda told Gerber she gave me the dark room key, but she did not know why I needed it.* Geli had only one card to play.

"Why were the two of you in the dark room, *Fräulein*?

Geli realized this must be her best performance—better than any *Marlene Dietrich* parody. "Captain, must you really ask?"

"Damn it, *Fräulein*, answer the question!"

"Sir, Sergeant Keller and I used the photography room for *romantic* purposes."

"You had a sexual liaison?"

"Yes, sir."

"You realize *Helferin* are not permitted intimacy with army personnel? This would be a breach of the conduct code, a serious infraction."

"Yes, sir." *I pray, not nearly as serious as aiding in treason.*

"Did you or Sergeant Keller disturb or take anything from that dark room?" demanded Gerber.

Does he know the photos are missing? "Sir, I did not touch anything. When I was getting ... ahem ... my clothes resituated, Sergeant Keller was rummaging through some of the things on the table. He found some obscene pictures in an envelope. He showed me a couple of them. Rather lewd, but he liked them, so he slipped them in his jacket." *No sense in protecting Franz now.*

"Was there anything else? Anything he *found*?"

"I don't think so, sir, but I can't be certain."

"Why not?" Gerber's temper was growing short.

"Because ... I stepped behind a cabinet momentarily to ... um ... rearrange my brassiere."

"Quite a time to be modest?"

"Sir, my brassiere has a vexing clasp. A lady doesn't like to be seen as *awkward* by a gentleman."

"Lady? You? No, Raubel. You're a tramp." He turned to the guard. "Corporal, I'm placing this woman under arrest. Take her to the detention cell."

Geli pleaded, "May I have time to change clothes?"

Gerber replied, "Into your uniform? You may *not*. You have defiled your uniform." Geli was manhandled out of the building into the courtyard. Frigid wind fluttered through her thin pajamas. The other three women were standing outside with the second guard. Mathilde forced a supportive smile. Anna put her hands together, as if in prayer for Geli. Frieda turned away. Geli was pushed toward the old carriage house—Gerber's security building. The other three women were ushered back into the dorm.

Geli spent the night in a small holding cell adjacent to Gerber's office. A guard was posted outside her door. She had been provided a canteen, a sheet, and a chamber pot. Nothing else. Most of the night, she huddled on the floor, shivering.

Gerber arrived shortly after sun-up. She watched him as he arranged things on his desk and shuffled through papers. His nonchalance was a show of power. After his things were in order, he stepped toward the cell. *"Fräulein,* if you value your life, you will cooperate with me."

"Am I allowed a blanket and something to eat?" Her teeth rattled.

"You have water. The rest will come after you have satisfactorily answered my questions."

He sat comfortably behind his desk while interrogating her through the iron grate. He grilled her for two hours, repeating the same questions. *What was in the envelope?* She'd already told him – lewd photos. *What about the other envelope?* She hadn't seen another envelope. *What were the other photographs? Surely she saw them?* No, she hadn't. *What was Keller planning to do with them?* She didn't know. *What about Brill? Did she know anything about other Brill-photographs?*

Gerber wanted to know as much about Brill as he did about Keller. Gerber mentioned blackmail in connection to the photographer. They were on to Brill now. They figured out he was a hustler. He might be locked in a cell somewhere too. Geli told Gerber about Brill's methods of attaining nudie photos, and his attempt to get her to pose. She had no qualms about spilling Brill's secrets. He was a bastard anyway, so let him get what's coming to him. Besides, if she could spit out some truth, he'd be more likely to believe the rest of it.

She stuck with her story throughout. She'd gone with Keller to the dark room to have sex. It was dubious ground, painting herself as a tramp—but it was necessary. Her story unleashed the lecher in Gerber. When he questioned her about sex, he entered her cell. He lingered over her as she sat, huddled against the wall. He questioned her repeatedly about her exploits with Keller and required intimate details about her with other sex partners. As he pried, his eye rolled over her. She knew of Gerber's reputation as a perverse creep. Last year, he had a shine for Mathilde. Mathilde had fended him off by never showing interest in him, but confided in Geli that she dreaded the day she might end up somewhere alone with him.

Here, in this cold cell, Geli was afraid Gerber would dismiss the guard, leaving her at his mercy. But he never did that. Someone was tracking Gerber too. No doubt he had a personal stake in this affair.

By midmorning, Gerber halted the interrogation. He told the guard, "Give *Fräulein* Raubel her things." The guard placed Geli's suitcase in the cell. It contained her personal belongings—underclothes, hair brush, tooth brush, and her only civilian outfit.

"What about my uniform?" asked Geli.

"You're no longer fit to wear the uniform. Your membership in the *Helferin* is terminated."

"You can't do that. I should have a hearing. It's my right as an auxiliary of the Wehrmacht."

"If you make a fuss, we can do it that way. The army will call for an investigation. Because this is a matter of moral charges and conspiracy with a traitor, the investigation will be turned over to the Gestapo. They will gain much more information from you than I have been able. The investigation will be followed by your court martial, which will easily prove you aided an enemy of the Reich. You'd face a firing squad that day. Do things my way and you will leave with your life."

Geli knew how things worked. Gerber was right. Even if she could present the truth, it wouldn't matter. The verdict would be predetermined. The only way to save her skin was to accept Gerber's plan, a dishonorable discharge. "What will become of me now?"

"You'll be kicked to the curb, just like any other Dutch whore."

"But I am German!"

"Be happy to be alive. You have five minutes to change clothes. Then you'll be escorted out the front gate."

"What then?"

"That is not my concern."

24

Maarburg

Franz and Taatje were motionless under the sheets, taking a respite from their last round of lovemaking. He twirled a lock of her hair. "What's on your mind?" he whispered. "It feels like you're in another world."

"I've been thinking about you."

"I've been thinking about you, too." Grinning, he moved his hand between her thighs.

"That's not what I meant." She snickered and pushed his hand away.

"Just as well. I think you've worn me out."

Taatje slid from under the covers. She kissed him. "It's nearly ten o'clock. I need to get moving." She fumbled in the dark, finding a match. The soft candlelight cast an aura around her naked body.

"My God, I wish we had the rest of the night," he said.

"Get up. I'm going to take you with me."

"And … where are we going?"

"There is a person I am meeting tonight. I believe he will help you." She slipped on her underpants.

"So, who is this fellow? Resistance?"

"Yes … he is. He'll be there, where we're going." She rummaged on the floor for her clothes.

"Why would the resistance help me, a German?"

"When they know what you've done, they won't hesitate. We've hidden other people, some of them for months. Your information will be helpful after the war," she said, buttoning her blouse. "Besides, I'll bet they already know what you did today. We have our ears to the ground."

"I don't know—"

"Do you have another idea? The *Feldjäger* will be looking for you on every street corner."

Keller had always been a planner, a creator, and a leader. As a boy, he was football captain and youth-club president. In the infantry, he quickly rose to the rank of sergeant. He had a knack for problem-solving and others counted on him for solutions. But now? He had no strategy for this—and his situation was dire. He'd face one or the other, the *Feldjäger* or Dutch resistance. "You're right. What's next?" he said.

She slapped him on the thigh. "Get dressed. We must go."

"My only clothes are my uniform."

"We'll leave through the back alley. I have a motorbike."

"Won't that raise suspicion? A Dutch woman and a German soldier on a motorbike?"

"When the sun goes down, nothing is surprising on the streets of Maarburg. It's been that way since the occupation. A German soldier with a Dutch girl? Not odd at all, unfortunately."

He dressed quickly. Taatje threw on an overcoat and grabbed her beret. They hurried down the steps to the rear of the building and into a narrow alley. Willem's motorbike was propped against the wall. She straddled the seat. "Hop on the back," she said and kicked the starter. Keller squeezed tightly to her as she revved the throttle. The little motorcycle labored under their weight as it sputtered out of the alley.

They rode through Maarburg in the darkness of the city-wide blackout. A military truck sped toward them. Taatje veered onto the sidewalk as it passed in the opposite direction. Another vehicle careened through the next intersection. Stenciled on its doors were white letters, *FELDJÄGER.* "Something's happening, Franz. We may be too late." The little motorcycle whirred through the center of town. They turned toward the square and found the traffic gnarled, at a standstill.

"Damn," said Keller, "They've set up a checkpoint. They'll stop everyone." Armed soldiers were working the spaces between vehicles and bicycles, shining lights and asking questions. Only after each one passed inspection were they permitted through the square. One of the military policemen was working his way up through the stalled traffic, anchoring the leash of an anxious Alsatian dog. He would reach their motorbike in a minute, maybe two.

"They are looking for *you*, Franz," said Taatje. "Hold on. We'll turn back."

"No!" Franz reached forward and grasped her right hand, keeping the throttle idle. "That will only get their attention. Now, slowly ease forward so you're right behind that truck."

"Why? If we stay here—."

"Do it. Time for *you* to trust *me*." said Franz. She eased the motorbike forward until it nestled behind the truck—out of the sentry's sight. Franz stood, straightened his uniform jacket, and adjusted his cap. "If you want to catch a snake, stare it straight in the eye. Then grab it!"

"That's your plan?" said Taatje.

He gave her a confident grin. "Watch me. Be ready. You're going take me out of here—in plain sight."

Keller walked toward the military policeman, doing his best not to limp. They'd be looking for that. During months of rehabilitation, he practiced walking with an even gait. If he kept his stride short, he could almost do it. He narrowed the gap between himself and the MP. The dog's ears pricked and hackles rose. From a car's length, Keller shouted, "Private, a word with you!" Keller was caustic. His rage gained the attention of everyone in the vicinity. "Get that fucking light out of my eyes or I'll jam it up your ass!"

The Alsatian lunged toward Keller, its teeth gnashing in a *primordial* snarl. The MP winched the leash as the dog's jaws clipped and frothed. Keller didn't back away. "Control that damn dog, Private!"

Keller's charade depended on him maintaining the offensive, a *blitzkrieg* waged on this unfortunate private. "Who the hell organized this checkpoint? Some shit-brained Austrian? Shut that dog up, Private!" The MP backed away, reeling in the leash. Keller stepped forward to occupy the new space between them, just like a drill instructor. "Private, I've walked from the back of this line, where my vehicle is at a goddamned standstill. Apparently, you pox-brained morons set up this roadblock without taking into account that military personnel would need to pass through? Private, I have a briefing with Colonel Immelmann in ten minutes. My balls will be nailed to a wall if I'm late, and you can wager that your nuts will be hanging right next to mine. How the hell am I going to get through this mess?" The MP was slack jawed. The dog had settled into a plaintive whine, appearing to be ready to take his next command from Keller. Other MPs had already broken from their duties, awed by the spectacle. The theatrics were working. It was time for the *coup de grâce*.

Keller pointed to a young lady in the snarled traffic. "You. Miss. Bring your motorcycle up here." He whipped his arm like a traffic cop. On cue, Taatje rolled the motorbike between the vehicles. "Now, Miss. Hurry up!"

Taatje eased forward until she was close to Keller. "What, sir? I have ... not ... wrong done, please?" Taatje joined the drama with halting German grammar—an act, as she was actually fluent in the language.

"To the contrary, *Fräulein*. You may be of great help. You have the only vehicle that can slip through this traffic. I'll pay you five guilders if you will give me a ride through this mess."

"Five guilder? Yes. You with me ... ride."

Everyone in the vicinity, civilian and military, had paused to watch the unhinged sergeant. From the back of the motorbike seat, Keller pointed his finger at the hapless private. "Alert those assholes up ahead to wave us through."

The private waved his rifle, though it was hardly necessary. They'd all witnessed the scene. Taatje knitted her way through the traffic jam. In less than a minute, they'd cleared the barricade and were on their way out of town.

2 5

Maarburg

The landlady stood at the door of the small apartment clutching the key in her clammy palm. Her eyes were cemented on the painted number beside the door frame, *131*, a meaningless thing to stare at, but she was afraid to look at the men—terrified to watch what they were doing—lest they be nettled by her curiosity. She dared not look in the eyes of any of the four German brutes who'd rousted her from her slumber and ordered her to open the upstairs apartment, the flat that she rented to that strange, young woman. These soldiers had guns. How could she refuse them? They might have shot her if she'd even dared ask why. *One thirty-one. One thirty-one.* She didn't move—like a rabbit huddled under a bush while a hawk soars overhead. *One thirty-one. Whatever they want, it's not me. It can't be. Please Lord. It's that tramp who lives in this flat. The one that comes and goes like a phantom. The one that's too pretty for her own good. God knows what she does when she's out all night? She deserves what she's going to get. They didn't find her. She's not here. Good. They're coming out. Don't look at me. Don't look at me. Please, Lord. One thirty-one. Please Lord.*

26

Netherlands Countryside

The motorbike weaved out of town. Taatje shouted over the strain of the engine, "I know a little road that goes into the countryside. It's rarely patrolled."

Keller leaned forward and propped his chin on her shoulder. The chilly night numbed his face. "Where are we going?"

"Up the river. My friend will know a way to hide you."

Again he found himself in the vexing position of trusting his fate to someone else. "What happens when he sees me, a German soldier?"

"He already knows about you. He'll listen to me. I'll make sure he does."

"How can you be sure he won't just shoot me? One less Prussian invader."

"I'm sure he would if it was up to him. He'd probably make you suffer before he finished you off."

"Sounds like a nice guy. Does he have a name?"

"Willem. He goes by Willem, but that's not his real name. No one uses real names."

The slapping of cobblestones beneath the motorbike gave way to the smooth glide of a gravel roadbed. The moonless night revealed only scattered features of farmland. A flat sheen was visible to their right, the Rhine River. Gusts buffeted against them as the little machine swerved along an invisible road.

Taatje kept the motorbike at a low speed as they buzzed down the path. The trek took them along a canal trail among fallow fields, still awaiting spring thaw. The corrugated furrows were hypnotizing as their charcoal reflections slipped past. At the end of the ditches, Taatje spurred the bike up a berm and lifted them onto a new road that paralleled the Rhine. "Willem will be just ahead," she said. Taatje flashed her headlamp three times. From the crest of the hill another light beam signaled a response. The motorbike topped the hill and Taatje turned onto a rutted trail. The bouncing headlamp guided them down an embankment toward a cove. Ahead was a dock with a single boat moored to its pier. Taatje wielded the bike through dips and potholes until she reached the flats along the river's edge. They rolled to a stop as she revved the throttle and let it sputter to extinction. The headlamp shined on the boathouse.

"Willem?" Taatje shouted. "Willem, are you here?" She leaned the motorbike against a piling. "Stay close to me, Franz. We don't want that German uniform to be the first thing Willem sees."

A flashlight beam was jittering along the rutted trail, coming their way. "Here he comes," she said.

The bounding light stopped about half way down the hill, "Blondi, stay where you are." The voice was Willem's.

"Blondi?" asked Keller.

"My code name. I told you no one uses their own name."

"But Blondi?" Keller snickered as he stroked her dark hair with his forefinger. "Why—?"

"Don't ask."

Willem's light beam bounded toward them again. He shouted, "Stay where you are. Don't move."

"It's alright, Willem. He's a friend."

Willem reached the flats about fifty meters from Taatje and Franz. He stopped in his tracks and raised his palm upward, imploring, "Blondi. Don't move!"

From the corner of his eye, Keller saw movement. Emerging from the dark was a figure with a rifle—trained on him. Then another, about ten meters from the first. He spun around. Two more silhouettes creeped up from the opposite side. Another, and another. Keller and Taatje were surrounded and the circle was closing in like a wolf pack. He moved in front of Taatje to shield her. As the ring crept closer, questions fired through Keller's mind. How did they know he was here? Had the military police followed him? Had the ruse at the checkpoint failed? Had they run into a Wehrmacht patrol?

Voices began hurling at them from one side of the surrounding pack, shouting orders, but not in German ... or Dutch. It was English. *British Army?* "Get away from the girl!" "Git yer fuckin' hands up, you Nazi prick!" "Hands over your head, mother fuck-er!" Keller turned toward the last voice as the soldier moved through the headlight's beam. He saw the uniform. *American!*

Taatje saw the uniform too. The American commandos should have been long gone! Her heart was in her throat. The Rangers were using the same tactic they had earlier when they killed the young German who was trying to surrender. As the circle constricted, Rangers from one side lured their victim's attention, while one from his backside moved in for the kill. The pack was closing in. Franz was the prey.

Taatje moved to Franz's back. She yelled at the Americans in Dutch, "Stop! Don't kill him! He's a friend! He's helped us." She beckoned toward Willem, who was still at the base of the hill. "Willem! Make them stop. Say something!" Willem was silent and didn't budge.

"Move away from the girl, asshole!" "Keep your hands in the air, you fuckin' Kraut!"

To Keller, the words weren't familiar, but their intent was clear. "Walk away from me," he said to Taatje. Keller held his hands high. "It's me they want."

"They'll kill you." She kept her back tight to Keller. "Don't shoot him. He helped us!" The Americans didn't understand her. "Veldhuis. Where's Veldhuis?" she yelled.

"Step away from the girl, asshole!" "Hands high, Kraut fucker!" The Americans on the near side continued their chatter while the far side stalked silently.

Keller rousted his memory for English vocabulary he'd learned as a school boy. "Not shoot. I not have … *Waffe* …*Waf*… weapon. Not have. I have not a weapon."

Keller's use of English quieted the taunts, but Taatje could see they were still moving in, no matter that Franz was trying to surrender. McCampbell had told her they don't take prisoners. *In a moment one of them will put a bullet through Franz's head.* She screamed at the dark, faceless pack that surrounded her. "Veldhuis! Tell the Lieutenant that this man is an ally. He has helped the resistance."

She heard Veldhuis's voice. He was using English as he called across the circle in an incomprehensible babble. The wolves' circle parted into an arc, leaving a clear line of fire beyond Keller. Taatje recognized the maneuver, the one they used right before the assassin pulled the trigger.

Taatje shrieked and threw her arms around Keller, shielding him with her body.

McCampbell's voice peeled from another point on the circle. "Don't shoot. Keep him covered. Taylor. Richey. Disarm that

Kraut." Veldhuis shouted the translation to Taatje. She loosened her grip.

The two commandos moved on Keller. Taylor pushed the muzzle of his M-1 into Keller's temple. Richey worked from Keller's front, pantomiming instructions. In a moment, Keller was on his knees. His hands were tied behind his back with his own belt.

Taatje ran to McCampbell, screaming for Franz's life. Willem emerged from the darkness. When Taatje saw Willem she lunged at him, pounding her open hands at the sides of his head. "You bastard! You bastard! You would have let us die!" Willem backed away, attempting to block the assault of flying fists and finger-nails—but she dug into him like a cat on a curtain. It took two Rangers to pull her off. They separated Taatje and Willem as if they were two schoolchildren in a playground brawl. "Now, tell me what in the hell is going on?" barked McCampbell.

He listened to Veldhuis interpret Taatje's huffing discourse. Then he questioned Willem, who was stemming a bloody nose with his shirt sleeve. "Shit!" said McCampbell. "I've been through every kind of army training you can imagine but this is a new one—breaking up a fist fight between a man and a woman." He chuckled at the sight of Willem's blood-smeared face. "She was kicking your ass, too, fella! That's what I love about being a Ranger, you just never know what's going to come your way." He said to his interpreter, "So Blondi says this guy helped steal German secrets?"

"That's right," said Veldhuis. "From General Martin Uhlemann, at that."

"Uhlemann, huh? I've heard of that guy. Walk with me." McCampbell and Veldhuis stepped out of earshot. "So what do you think, Veldhuis? Is she telling the truth?"

"Her story rang true with the other guy, Willem. He knew she'd been setting up this Kraut to steal papers for her."

"Who has the papers now?"

"PAN, I suppose. They'll use them to go after Uhlemann when the war ends."

"So let me get this straight. This Kraut-sergeant turned traitor so he could frame his general? Why in the hell would he do that?"

"According to the girl, he's half Dutch. Uhlemann killed his family."

McCampbell shook his head. "This is some fuckin' fairy tale."

"Would you like me to get more details, Lieutenant?"

"No. I've heard enough."

McCampbell held a pistol in his hand. He stepped in front of the kneeling Keller. "You're a damned crazy son-of-a-bitch." Keller cocked his head toward the American lieutenant. "I said you're one crazy Nazi bastard."

Keller steeled his eyes on McCampbell. "I am not Nazi!"

McCampbell fiddled with the safety latch on his pistol. "I guess you're not." McCampbell studied Keller. This German was vanquished, on his knees, hands tied behind his back—yet he gave no quarter. McCampbell released his ammunition clip, inspected it, then reinserted it, making sure Keller watched every move. This tough Kraut-sergeant showed no fear. A real soldier. "Do you speak Dutch? *Sprechen sie* Holland?"

"*Ja.* Yes."

"Veldhuis, come over here. Bring the girl too." Willem followed, but kept some distance from Taatje. They gathered around Keller. McCampbell holstered his pistol and said, "Interpret for me." McCampbell said to Taatje. "You're hoping that I'll let this guy go. Sounds like he's done some good things. Maybe he deserves to be set free, but I won't do that. He's still a German soldier." He waited for Veldhuis to interpret. "And, we don't take prisoners. Commandos don't do that—American commandos, British commandos, or *German* commandos. We're behind enemy lines. We can't deal with prisoners."

McCampbell allowed time for Veldhuis to catch up. Taatje stepped toward McCampbell to argue, but McCampbell held up his hand and said, "I'm going to make an exception, not because this guy is a hero. For all I know, you may be feeding me a line of bull-shit." He looked squarely at Taatje. "I'll do it because I owe you one. I'll never forget you, Blondi—poundin' bullets into that Nazi with that old pistol of yours. You saved my ass. So look, here's what's gonna happen. We'll take your German buddy across the river and make sure he's processed as a POW. That's the best I can do."

Veldhuis translated the decree. Taylor's rifle was leveled at Keller. McCampbell turned to his squad. "Grab and go men. We're movin' out in three minutes. Move it." The Rangers wasted no time. Thud Allen was the first in the boat and stood at the helm.

"Lieutenant, what about the Kraut?" said Norton as he hoisted his rucksack and ammo boxes.

"We're taking him with us. Prisoner of Uncle Sam."

"You've gotta be kiddin,' Lieutenant. I'll take care of him for ya'. One round right behind the ear—"

"Shut up, Corporal."

"Yes, sir."

"Taylor, take the prisoner into the boat."

"Yes, sir."

Taatje stood aside and watched as Franz, arms bound, was escorted onto the boat. Her tears came in a torrent. "I'm sorry, Franz. I'm so sorry." She followed behind and watched from the bank as Keller was positioned on a seat across from Taylor who trained his rifle on Keller's chest. The skiff was laden with soldiers and gear. The lines were cast from the pilings and the motor fired up. The boat chugged into the Rhine channel and disappeared into the night. Taatje staggered from the dock, her fingers tangled in her hair, and cried, "I'm so sorry, Franz. I'm so sorry."

Part Two

Part Two

27

Arizona High Desert

Four riders pressed up the foothills trail. Their horses plodded single file along a well-worn cattle track through waves of prickly pear. They were heading into the high country, known as the *Bosque Verde*. Deuce, the black and white sheepdog, followed the train of horses and stayed tight to the trail. As a pup, he'd tangled with cactus—and learned the first lesson of the desert. He'd have his chance to run free once they climbed out of the low country.

Abbie Johnson rode at the back of the line with Deuce. She loved the ride to *the Bosque* and its gradual transition from rolling desert to pine forest. In the summertime, the Bosque was a cool retreat from the blazing Arizona sun. This was March though. It could get down-right cold up there, especially if the wind whipped up.

It took most of the morning to reach the top of the rim. The riders crossed the last switchback into a grassy meadow. Abbie yelled up to Hector. "Time to stop for a break." She reined her horse in order to dismount on the uphill side. With her stature, she'd take any advantage she could. Abbie was smaller than most riders—smaller than most women at five-foot-three. *Skinny little Abbie,* she was called as a kid. The name still fit. She swung down off her horse and felt the firm ground under foot. It was a welcomed pleasure after being in the saddle for four hours. She hanked her ponytail in a rubber band and tucked it behind her hat. A cool breeze lapped through the piñons. She untied her leather jacket from the latigo straps and slipped it on. "Will, tie up Daisy and come on over here." Her nine-year-old son joined her on a flat rock at the rim's edge. "Beautiful view from here, isn't it?"

"Yeah, I guess so."

"You're not a man of many words. Just like your dad."

Abbie and Hank always stopped at this spot when they rode into the Bosque. The first time they came up here, they sat on this rock, ate sandwiches, and admired their land in the valley below. That was seven years ago when they became owners of a ranch—the *Jackrabbit-J.* Hank was excited that day. They had their future laid out before them, cattle ranchers. "Abbie, it's gonna be a great life—you, me, and Will—and any more babies that come along. It's a small ranch now, but we'll get more cattle. Breed 'em. Buy 'em. My father'll help us. We'll be big someday. You wait and see." Hank cradled Abbie and kissed her with the kind of passion they loved giving in to—and would have—if not for their toddler son pulling up wildflowers a few feet behind them. The memory took Abbie back to a time before the war, when things were clear—when she still had Hank.

Abbie gazed over the checkerboard farms that hugged the San Miguel River. On the near side of the valley was the town of Barlow, looking like a hop-scotch grid. The townsfolk—the *white* townsfolk—lived in the houses clustered between the town and the railroad tracks. West of the tracks was San Ignacio, where the

Mexicans lived. The white steeple of the Catholic Church of San Ignacio reached above all things. About two miles north of town were the stockyards, the business hub of the valley. The stockyards were out of town for good reason. Hot summer breezes swept up the valley from the south, blowing the stench away from town. Less fortunate was Camp Barlow, situated on a rise a half mile north of the stockyards. From Abbie's perch, the prisoner-of-war camp looked like toy wooden blocks spaced evenly on the scraped desert floor.

"Put your jacket on, Will," said Abbie. Will and Deuce were playing catch-me-if-you-can, a simple contest that always ended with Deuce nabbing the gleeful boy and lathering his face with a lapping tongue. Umberto grabbed Will's jacket from the saddle and tossed it to the boy. "Come here," said Abbie. "It's cold and we're going to be up here for a few days. Don't want you to catch a chill." She buttoned Will's jacket.

Hector emerged through the piñóns. "There's about forty or fifty head over the hill. They're strung down in the draw. Ready to get to work, ma'am?"

"How far to Rosado Tank? About three miles?"

"Yes ma'am. We'd better water the horses before we get started. There's run-off flowing. We'll let 'em drink downstream, then pick up the cows in the draw and push 'em toward the tank."

Abbie said to Will, "Get on your horse, young man. You heard Hector."

Hector Cruz was the ranch foreman, *El Capataz*. He'd stuck with Abbie since Hank died. Thank goodness for that. As far as she could tell, Hector knew everything there was to know about cattle. He liked to say that his Spanish ancestors were running cows on this land since before *"you white folks got off the Mayflower."* He'd always shown great respect for Abbie—*Doña Johnson*—his boss. Others in the valley didn't regard her as well. After all, she wasn't a man, and she didn't grow up on a ranch. She *married into* the cattle business. She was now twenty-eight years old and had been the ranch owner for over two years. She'd learned quickly. She had to.

This spring was going to be tougher than usual. Abbie only had two cowhands this year, Hector and Umberto, and Umberto wasn't one of the best she'd ever hired. He crossed the border a few years earlier, a *peón*, and hadn't spent much time on horseback before he came to the Jackrabbit-J. The last two years, the ranch had six cowboys. Hector had brought in some good ones. In 1943 and 1944, by the time round-up was over and the cattle were sold, the Jackrabbit-J had turned a small profit. This year, there were no cowboys to be had. All young men were off fighting the Germans or the Japanese. Hector's son, Manny, was among those who shipped out last year, a Navy man in the Pacific. There weren't even many *peóns* like Umberto around. The Jackrabbit-J was starting spring round-up on shaky footing.

The creek spilled out into a sloggy *ciénega*. The riders gave their horses time to slurp some water. Abbie said, "What do you think, Hector? Can we push these cows up the draw?"

"It might be tough, *Patrona*. If we can keep them bottled up along the creek, we can do it—push them straight on through to Rosado Tank. But if any of them bust out on the ridge, they'll be harder 'n hell to get back. That's rough country."

"I'll take that flank then," said Abbie.

"You sure, *Patrona*? I can do it."

"No, Hector, I want you on point. That way, if they spook, you're the best to handle it. Put Umberto on the right side."

"You got it, *Señora*." Hector yelled to the other two. "Umberto, *muchacho, estás en el lado derecho*. Will, little buddy, you take drag."

The cattle had been grazing up here all winter. They were scattered. Abbie figured they could pull in a small herd each week, no more than fifty head. They'd move those cattle to the corral at Rosado Tank, where they'd be branded, doctored, and separated. From there, they'd drive the marketable steers down to the stockyards. Normally, steers weren't sent to market until after fall round-up when they reached full size and brought a higher dollar. This plan wasn't ideal, but with the lack of cowboys, the cattle had to be worked in increments.

It took an hour. They were able to gather a small herd at the base of the draw and get them moving. Their aim was to keep the herd compressed and heading upstream, parallel to the creek. The hardest part would be the first mile, when they drove the cattle through a ravine, a gauntlet of manzanita and boulders, sloped steeply on both sides. The hillsides were slippery and choked with deadfall. They had to keep the cattle from traipsing through the stream bed where rocks and underbrush would block the way—best to push them onto the flattest bank as they worked through the draw. Crossing the trickling stream would be alright, but using it as the highway would be a mistake.

Hector rode at the point, ahead of the lead cattle, and spurred his horse back and forth in short bursts. He whistled, shouted, and flagged his hat, coaxing the lead steers in the right direction. Hector was a seasoned *vaquero* and could read the minds of the whiteface Herefords. He used to tell Hank, "When I was a baby, *mi Mamá* put me in a crib, but *mi Papá* put me in a saddle."

Will rode at the back of the herd and kept stragglers from falling away or stopping upon a pleasing clump of tall grass. It was the safest job and didn't carry the danger of *cutting-in* an ornery thousand-pounder. Will had pleaded for a job that was more fun, but Abbie wouldn't hear of it. Deuce stayed in the back with Will, darting back and forth across the rear arc of the herd. With low growls, he pounced at the hindquarters of stragglers and clipped at their heels. Cows' eyes bulged when the dervish came after them. Deuce was a natural herder. There was nothing that dog liked to do —*had to do*—more than push cattle.

Umberto and Abbie rode opposite flanks. Normally, there would be at least two cowboys on each side of the churning mob.

Not possible this year. Abbie and Umberto did double-duty and by day's end their horses would be lathered and spent. Today the distance was only three miles but the terrain was rugged. Abbie pushed her pony tail under her hat. She was riding Chief, a bay gelding that had been Hank's favorite horse. Abbie like him best too. He was a seasoned cow pony with long experience in cutting cattle, responsive to the rein and rolling spur. The best thing about Chief was he didn't have that stubborn streak found in other horses. Chief was content to let her be boss. No shenanigans.

A young whiteface bolted out of the herd. Abbie tugged the reins. Chief responded in a circular pivot. With a tickle of her spurs the horse dashed to cut off the renegade. Abbie and Chief worked as one, becoming a threatening two-headed monster to the reeling steer.

"Yaaw! Yaww!" Abbie cried, swinging her arm, working the horse to and fro. Each time the steer bolted for freedom it was stopped in its tracks. The fury of Chief's clattering hooves and Abbie's whoops forced the animal back toward the rumbling mob. A few more zig-zags and the obstinate creature gave up and fell back in line.

They trotted alongside the herd. Abbie felt a tingle of pride. She was pretty good on a horse, though she didn't start riding until a year after Will was born. At that time, she wasn't so sure and felt overmatched by the large beasts. But Hank started her out gently— on Daisy, an easy-going mare. Daisy was now Will's horse. Abbie fell in love with riding. When they got the deed to the Jackrabbit-J, Abbie was on horseback every day, not for fun but for the sake of the business. She rode with Hank, mending fences, checking on stock and water tanks, or doing any other job that popped up. Sometimes that included moving cattle, the most rigorous duty on the ranch. She was *pretty darn good*—not nearly as good as Hector. But she was every bit as good on a horse as most of the cowpokes that came through here.

The herd was moving at a steady pace now. The cattle were settling in and accepting the command of four busy cowboys and a tireless dog. They'd soon be out of the rugged draw and onto rolling green flats.

Abbie was riding near the front. From behind she heard the snap of breaking tinder and the roll of hooves. Her head spun to see a renegade break from the herd. A few others followed. Within seconds, more cattle changed course, following the new leader. *They're running up the hill. If they make it over the top, we'll lose them.* Abbie spurred Chief into full gallop. They hurtled in a diagonal line toward the runaways, pounding up the slope. *Move Chief, move. Got to get to the top before they do.* "Yaw! Yaw! Up Chief. Up!" pleaded Abbie. Chief thundered up the bank. Abbie tucked in low over the horse's withers, ducking from flying branches. Her boots pressed into the stirrup. Her knees gripped behind Chief's shoulders. She reined the galloping horse in a traversing slalom through pines and squat piñóns. "Hyup Chief. Hyup. Hyup!" They were gaining, nearing the crest where they could make a level run. Abbie's spur rolled. Chief charged. Branches blew aside. Beneath the horse's hooves was a blur of rocks and roots. As Chief thrust forward, Abbie rocked weight to her knees—her legs absorbing the shock of the horse's plunges and heaves. They were spanning a low ridge. Abbie could see the cattle below. The runaways hadn't climbed as quickly as she had. *We can do it, Chief. Keep movin' fella.* The horse hurtled onward, battering along the ridge.

As horse and rider charged over a ledge, a twisted old juniper rose in their path. Abbie reined to the high side. Chief cut hard and lunged for footing. His rear hooves scuttled on the granite shelf—a slick face hidden under pine needles. Chief stumbled, dipped, and surged. The momentum spun his rear quarters underneath him and he bucked skyward. Horse and rider separated, sailing backward into the gnarly tree. Its silver arms snatched Abbie as if Jonah's whale had risen to swallow her. Jagged branches clawed her neck as her shoulder smashed backward into the trunk, blasting a rainbow of shattered alligator bark. At the same time, Chief's massive thigh slammed the lower trunk with a loud crack, snapping an arm off the sturdy tree. Abbie rebounded forward and met Chief's rump. Her chest hit hard on the horse's tailbone as he recoiled. She bounced off him like a rag doll in slow flight until she smacked down on the hard hillside. She tumbled head … over feet … over arms, careening downslope until she skidded into a patch of buckthorn.

Dust clouds scattered into the breeze. Abbie tried to focus. Thorny branches poked her back. She rolled into a ball and clinched tight. Her shoulder shot with pain. She rocked on her hip and heaved, trying to gulp air—but the blow had knocked the wind out of her. Finally, gasps came in flutters. She sucked hard to fill her lungs, blowing dust as her cheek nuzzled the ground. Gradually, her breathing steadied. The terror ended.

She cradled there, unmoving, letting the cobwebs lift. The electric pain in her shoulder was starting to throb. Abbie stared at blue sky through the thorny spindles. *I think I'll just lay here a bit.* Clouds whispered by. The lacerations burned, but her breathing settled, steady now. She heard Chief's hoofs patting the earth not far away. *The big brute probably didn't even get hurt.* She stayed put, tucked up like a baby. Things were feeling better, but still stung. She was starting to believe she was whole, that she hadn't left part of herself hanging on the tree, or that she'd been run-through by one of its wicked branches. The green boughs of a ponderosa swayed high above her. *I'll be OK. I'll just stay here a little longer.*

She heard Hector. He was calling her name as he came over the hill. She didn't have the voice to holler back. Deuce was the first to arrive. He scurried in a circle around the broken juniper, on to Abbie's scent. With nose to the ground, he homed in, forty feet downhill, and dashed for his master in the thicket of buckthorn.

Deuce buried his wet nose in Abbie's neck with whimpers and snorts, his rear end gyrating in elation.

"Deuce, no. Deuuuuce." The excited dog forced a laugh from her that rallied tears. Deuce's slobber mixed with Abbie's tears and soaked up the cindery dust, caking Abbie's face with powdery muck. "Deuce. Stop it!" The dog pulled up continuing his anxious wiggle-dance.

Hector rode toward Abbie. "*Patrona*?" He dismounted while his horse slowed. "You OK ma'am?" he asked, looping his reins over a sapling. "What happened?"

"I just thought I'd stop for a picnic," she croaked, staring skyward toward Hector whose hat brimmed the sun.

"Are you laughing or crying *Señora*?"

"Both, I guess."

"What happened?" he said, surveying the uphill juniper. It bore a fresh yellow wound and a dangling arm. Abbie's trampled hat lay at its roots, like roadkill.

"The tree won."

"You gonna be OK?"

"Yeah. I think so. We lost them, didn't we?"

"Half of them ran over the hill. We won't get 'em back today. Umberto's got the rest bottled up in the draw."

"How's my horse?"

"Looks better than you, ma'am."

"Thanks a lot, Hector. Help me up. Nice and easy."

2 8

Camp Barlow

"Sergeant Müller, please shut the door. Take a seat." The sergeant stepped into the hallowed domain of Major Schwering. It was a *coup* that Schwering had his own office. After all, he was a POW. The Geneva Convention made no provision regarding private space for prisoner-officers, yet Schwering and Hoefer convinced the American Colonel, Riley, they each needed private offices. They argued it would maintain the integrity of their position, secure record keeping, and assure discretion when reprimanding soldiers. Riley liked the idea and ordered it done over objections of his XO, Jim Davenport. Riley believed the German officers had done a bang-up job in keeping camp discipline. It made *his job* so much easier. No locks on the doors! That's where Riley drew the line, although Schwering had a turn-latch fixed to the inside of his door jamb. No one ever questioned it.

"You asked to see me, sir?" said Müller.

"Yes. I'm in need of your assistance, Sergeant." Müller ran Schwering's *protocol detail*, a crew of a half-dozen enforcers. They were the strong arm of Schwering's Circle and rabidly loyal to the Führer. Schwering unleashed this Doberman pack when circumstances proved necessary.

Schwering continued, "We have a new group of soldiers coming in two days. A large group."

"How many, Major?"

"About a hundred twenty."

Müller whistled. "That's a lot."

"Indeed. That's where you come in. It will take some time to get their backgrounds through our usual sources. The Americans have *interrupted* our communications in other camps. Here at Camp Barlow, they've been snooping around the mail room and the Red Cross deliveries. So far, they've dug up nothing. But they've made it difficult to get a flow of information from the Fatherland. As you know Sergeant, I like to know everything about everybody."

"I understand, Major."

"Sergeant Müller, I expect you to have ears everywhere, particularly around the new prisoners. Understand?"

"Certainly sir."

"Another thing. The American Colonel is pressing us to provide more laborers. We're not in a position to deny him that. But I don't want any Germans assigned to work *outside the wire* if we have reason to question their *allegiance*. It's too difficult to control their mouths out there. If you have reason to doubt the patriotism of any of these neophytes, give me their names, and I'll make sure they don't leave the camp. Any questions?"

"No sir."

"Good. Set everything in place. Report back in two days. Shut the door as you leave. *Heil Hitler!*"

2 9

Bremen

Geli was lucky to get out of Arnhem. A German woman—a civilian now—wouldn't last long there. She decided it would be best to go home to Bremen, only 80 kilometers from the Dutch border. The problem was *how to get there?* No trains ran from the Netherlands to Germany anymore. The Allies had crippled the rail lines and destroyed the roadways. She had no travel papers. She would have to rely on what had always worked for her—ingenuity and charm. She used both to hitch a ride on a cargo truck. A couple of old gents from Hamburg hauled non-martial freight on a government contract. She chose well, as these fellows knew the way to get into Germany via backroads, the few that were still intact. She sat between them. *It helps to be a pretty girl.* She was nearly forty-years-old, but she still *had it.*

The truck wormed its way into Bremen, dodging burned-out

vehicles and bomb craters. She hadn't been home in almost two years. She'd read accounts of what had happened to her hometown. The Nazi newspapers made it sound as if the bumbling Allied bombers were off-target in nearly all their missions. According to the German government, the Allies couldn't hit a cow's ass with a shovel. But people who had actually seen the destruction told another story.

Bremen was a factory town. In the 1930's, Hitler's government converted its industry to the manufacture of war materiel. Steel mills, aircraft factories, and oil refineries brought Bremen an economic boon. But starting early in the war, those factories were targets of terror from on high. British and American bombers flew dozens of missions over the small city, raining an inferno. Bremen crumbled and burned under the onslaught.

The truckers dropped Geli off on a corner about a block from her old flat. It was as close as they could get. She'd have to walk the rest of the way. She headed toward her old place. Every building was either a burned-out husk or a pile of rubble. There were few people about. Some survivors scrounged amid the ruins. Others were holed-up in make-shift shelters in the shadows of former buildings.

An old woman sat under a dirty tarp. Geli asked, "Where is everyone?"

The woman said, "Some have left. Most are dead. A few of us stay here. We have nowhere else to go."

Geli found her way around piles of stone and scree. She followed a jagged path, carved out by survivors of this apocalypse. Tears rolled down her cheeks as she foundered through the carcass that was once her hometown. *How can Bremen ever rise from this hell? How can Germany ever rebuild? When the war ends—as it soon must—soldiers will not have a home to come back to. How will they find their loved ones?*

She clambered to the top of a gravel pile that covered the street corner across from her old flat. She'd already guessed what she would see. The apartment building, once her home, was gone. In its place was a 15 meter-tall mound of brick, twisted metal, and broken glass.

My God, what have we done?

30

Arizona Desert

"This train ride is pure American propaganda. I'd bet on it."

"What do you mean?" said Keller, barely interested. He nodded sleepily against the window. Unfortunately, the fellow next to him, Corporal Niklas Weber, was a loudmouth.

"We've been on this train for almost three days, right?" Weber blathered. "Well, the entire journey has taken us through some beautiful places, right? Think about it. They took us though those pretty forests when we started out on the Atlantic side. Then, they took us through green hills and farms that stretched as far as the eye could see. For the last day we've gone through this long, long desert..."

"Why is that propaganda?" asked Keller, only a little more interested.

"Think about it. Have we seen any bomb damage? No. Have we seen American cities in ruins? No. You've heard the reports. You know as well as I do that our Navy has destroyed American ship-yards and naval bases. Göring's Air Force has bombed their big cities—destroyed them! New York and Boston have been pounded into powder. Chicago too—twice as bad as what we did to London. But the Americans are afraid to show us that. Instead, they take us on a journey through countryside we have spared."

Keller shrugged and looked out the window, hoping his lack of enthusiasm would make Weber shut up. It didn't.

"It's the richest part too. I'd bet on it. Did you see those giant farm house palaces we passed a couple of days ago? That province is called Miss Sippy, I heard one of the guards say. Remember that train station we stopped at last night? El Paso? Did you see all those automobiles? That's a rich town, I tell you. They're just taking us this way because they want us to believe that America is a perfect place—and hasn't been touched by our bombs! They're not fooling anyone."

"Hmmph," Keller nodded. He'd heard exaggerations before—from Nazi leaders. *Exaggerations? Hell. They were lies.* Past July, in a morale-boosting speech, his brigade was told how the German Army had obliterated the Allies when they landed on the Normandy beaches. Keller had been part of that fight and knew the opposite to be true. In fact, the German Army was in retreat from France when the speech was given. Weber swallowed their lies. But Keller wouldn't take him to task on it. He was on a precarious perch given the circumstances surrounding his capture. The last thing he could afford to do was bring attention to himself.

"These rail cars are too nice also," continued Weber. "Why do you think they let us ride in luxury like this? In passenger cars? Hell, back in Europe, every time the army moved, we rode in freezing boxcars. These fucking Yanks are trying to brainwash us. I tell you that's a fact, Sergeant. And it's not going to work. Before this war is over, we'll take their red striped flag and cram it up their asses."

There was a piece of truth in Weber's rant—the part about being treated unexpectedly well by the Americans. Keller had been a prisoner for five weeks. He spent the first fortnight in a barbed wire pen in Belgium. He was cramped-in with other German prisoners, but they were fed and slept in tents, not much different than his infantry days. And the food was better! Maybe for Keller, an American POW camp would be the best place to wait out the war, far away from the Netherlands where the *chained dogs* were certainly looking for him.

An argument broke out a few rows ahead.

One of the antagonists popped into the aisle and cursed his nemesis. "Stand up and fight, you hairy cunt!"

Keller had seen this hothead in action during the Atlantic passage, Private Beckmann. Beckmann hoisted his fists and reeled off a string of insults. Immediately, two American MPs converged on him while two other MPs stood by the portals, weapons ready. The car echoed with profanity, German and English.

Beckmann turned his fury toward the MPs on either side of him. Veins bulging from his neck, he charged an MP, cursing as spittle flew. That was all it took. The second MP hammered down on the back of Beckmann's head with a leather blackjack. Beckmann slumped in the aisle. From the back seat, a German officer stood. Lieutenant Axel Fischer was the officer assigned to this car. Voices silenced. Keller sensed early-on this was a man to steer away from.

Fischer held his palms toward the American MPs. He pointed to his epaulette insignia—an officer, the ranking German. Fischer motioned calmly that he would take control of his men. The Americans approved the gesture and allowed Fischer up the aisle to the dazed Beckmann.

"Sergeant, assist me please," Fischer said to Keller as he walked past. Officers always look to non-coms to bid their dirty work. Keller looked toward the American MP and got a nod of approval.

Keller followed the lieutenant. Fischer ordered, "Remove this man's belt and bind his hands behind his back."

Beckmann was conscious, but groggy. Keller met no resistance binding the man's wrists.

"Now, give me your belt, Private," said Fischer, addressing the soldier who'd been the target of Beckmann's wrath. "Your name?"

"Private Ehrlich sir."

Ehrlich slipped off his belt and handed it to Fischer. Fischer calmly halved the belt, then without warning, back-handed it across Ehrlich's face. The buckle lashed his cheek, sending his head sideways. Blood bubbled down his face and streamed onto his shirt. "So much for your innocence in this matter," said Fischer. He looked back to Keller, "Hoist that asshole off the floor and get him on his knees."

Keller guessed the direction this was going. As ordered, he grabbed the woozy Beckmann by his collar, hoisted him off the deck, and pushed him to a kneeling position. Fischer took the second belt and looped it through the one that bound Beckmann's wrists, then he threaded the other end through the chrome bar above the seat. Fischer pulled the belt like a pulley until Beckmann's arms were suspended behind his back and carried most of his weight. Beckmann yelped. Fischer buckled the belt. Beckmann was in agony—immobile, kneeling with his arms yanked upward, from behind. He yowled and contorted, but his movement only tightened the hold.

The MPs had backed off, glad to let the German officer take over.

Keller slithered back to his seat, hoping to end his role in the affair.

"Damn, that fellow paid for it," whispered Weber.

"Shut up," said Keller under his breath.

"How long is he going to hang there?"

"Shut…Up."

Fischer stood over Private Beckmann, grabbed a shock of his hair, and levered his face until their eyes met. "You're an embarrassment to your uniform," said Fischer, and kicked his boot into Beckmann's gut. The private coiled inward, but the belt was taut. His eyes bugged. His veins looked ready to burst as he gagged and pissed himself. Slobber streamed from his lip. Fischer strolled to the front of the car and stood tall as if he was at the pulpit. He waited until all eyes were on him, including the MPs. The car was mute, save for the clacking iron wheels and Beckmann's groans.

Lieutenant Fischer spoke with calm diction. "You are soldiers of the Reich and must understand this army will continue its adherence to military principles. The fact you are prisoners is irrelevant. You will continue to conduct yourselves by the maxims set forth in the military code of conduct. Duty until death! If any of you fail to follow standard protocols, you will be disciplined like this pathetic shit pile. Let this be fair warning." He nodded to the American MPs —a signal he had returned their authority. Fischer sat down. Private Beckmann dangled from the seat frame.

For the next two hours, the passenger car was subdued, save for low conversation. Out the window, the dry desert moved by— scraggly trees, dry grass, and thorny cactus. The distant mountains had a dry, sandy tint.

The train slowed as it approached the next town. "I wonder why we're stopping here?" said Weber. "We just took on water a few hours ago at that little station. What was that last town called?"

"Lordsburg. This town is where we get off the train—called Vwielcoch." Keller said, tripping over the pronunciation of Willcox.

"How do you know that?" asked Weber.

"I listen to the American guards whenever I can. They talk a lot. They don't think any of us understand them."

"You speak English?"

"I learned some in school. But I've picked up twice as much since I've been a prisoner. After a while, it starts to come together."

"I don't pay much attention to them. Stupid Americans."

"Maybe you should start," said Keller.

A porter pushed a caddy up the aisle, collecting the breakfast trays. The POWs had filled themselves on oatmeal, buttered biscuits, and coffee. The journey had been an enigma. The cushioned seats, food, and service were as good as any rail line in Europe. They were prisoners of war, yet were treated like paying customers with only a few exceptions. They weren't allowed to move about the coaches and had to be accompanied to the lavatory. But the strangest absurdity had to do with the porters. They were all dark Africans—American Africans—and they served the enemy prisoners as if they were patrons. *America is a strange place.*

When the train stopped, Lieutenant Fischer told Keller to untie Beckmann's straps. Beckmann tumbled to the floor.

Fischer addressed the Germans. "We will disembark here and board another train that will take us to our destination. Form a single file when you are between the trains. No talking. The American guards will assign you to a new car when you are outside."

Keller looked out the windows to either side of the train. This wasn't a passenger station. It was a rail yard. The breeze through the open windows carried the stink of cattle. He saw POWs being transferred to the adjacent train—not passenger cars—stock cars. *We're being loaded into cattle cars!* Keller's mind flashed. He'd heard rumors about Jews being loaded into cattle cars in Europe. The SS kept their operations hush-hush, but stories spread like wildfire through the ranks of the regular army. Every Wehrmacht soldier had heard tales of mass murders and horrors in the concentration camps.

Outside Keller's window, one of the American yard workers yelled ahead to another fellow standing at the locomotive. "Ready, set, go, Bobby? We gotta git these goddamned Kraut Cars to Barlow by one o'clock."

Keller couldn't follow the American chatter, but he caught the train's destination, Barlow. *They're taking us to a place called Barlow, in cattle cars.* Keller wondered whether Barlow might be the American equivalent of Auschwitz or Buchenwald. *It can't be. There are strict international rules about treatment of prisoners. But why the cattle cars?* Maybe the loudmouth, Weber, had been right all along—the Americans had made the journey pleasant only to placate them. *Too far-fetched?* They would soon be in Barlow. Then they'd know.

31

The Bosque Verde

Abbie hurt. She'd been thrown off her horse, smashed into a tree, and caromed down a hillside. The ordeal hadn't ended. They were back in the saddle and moving the cattle—what was left of them. She'd ridden two rugged miles. Every time Chief dipped or lurched, pain rocked her battered ribs. Finally, they pushed the little herd over the ridge and onto a meadow. The corral was in view. Abbie would never be so glad to be *anywhere*—and to get off her horse.

They rode onto *Cienega Rosada*— Christened Rosada by early vaqueros for the pink rock shelf that envelopes the valley, and Cienega, an Apache word for a lush valley. Here a small creek, fed by snow and rocky springs, meandered into a bowl-shaped swale. The cienega formed a natural pasture, fringed by regal ponderosas. In warm months, the little valley would be carpeted by tall grasses, thistle, and wild raspberries. This was Abbie's favorite place on the ranch, though technically it wasn't her property.

In 1938, Hank and Abbie Johnson bought the *Ol' Jackrabbit Ranch*. They renamed it the *Jackrabbit-J*—the *J* was for *Johnson*. The ranch covered only 960 acres, all of it in the desert foothills, below the Bosque. With his father's influence, Hank secured a lease agreement with the US Grazing Service, granting him rights to the high, pasture land of the Bosque Verde, an expanse about fifty times larger than Jackrabbit-J. They could run their cattle on this federal land. Hank chose this place, *Cienega Rosada*, to build a corral in the high country. Grass and water were abundant. Hank had one of the best lease deals in southern Arizona—envied by other cattlemen.

By law, a rancher could make modest improvements on government land, so long as it didn't divert the natural watershed. Hank and Hector built the pole corral that first summer, stringing pine posts with barbed wire. One side of the corral was for horses, the other for cattle. Here the cattle would be branded, castrated, doctored, and separated. The unfortunate ones—those anointed *ready for market*—were driven downhill to the stockyards.

After the second year's round-up, Hank kept his cowboys on the payroll for an extra month. They swapped lariats for shovels and reconstructed the old earthen dam, once used by Mexican ranchers a century ago. The *Tanque Rosado*, Rosado Tank, could hold an acre of water. The reservoir was as near as an Arizona rancher could get to a *water guarantee*. Hank also built a primitive cabin of pine logs and a tin roof. It served as a shelter from winter snow and summer hailstorms, and a dry place to stow tack and supplies. Abbie called it her *palace*.

Abbie and her three cowboys drove the *half-herd* onto *Cienega Rosado* in late afternoon. Hector rode ahead and opened the corral gate. The cook, Ol' Javier, was waiting by the hut. His tent was pitched. He'd set up his kitchen on weathered boards. Ol' Javier had started the trek before sunrise, leading Benny and Tojo, the ranch mules, up to the Bosque. The stalwart beasts carried all the supplies on sawbuck packs. Everything needed for the next three days—food, bed rolls, pots and pans—was waiting for them courtesy of the mules.

The cattle tramped into the corral without complaint. Abbie dismounted with a grunt. "Here, Will, take Chief, please. Hitch 'm up."

"You OK, Mom?"

"Sure, I just need to sit down for a second." She handed her son the reins and grimaced as she perched on a stump.

Her body hurt from top to bottom, but something inside felt even worse. Ever since she lost Hank, her quest had been to keep the Jackrabbit-J on track. One day it would belong to her son. Until then, she was its caretaker. She'd done well so far. But now she had doubts. Today was a disaster. Any more like this and spring round-up would be a loss, possibly the ranch too. Worse, she might fail to deliver her son his birthright, a promise she made to herself at Hank's funeral.

She murmured to herself, "Well, this work's not going to do itself." She took a deep breath and ambled to the hitching rail. While Hector and Umberto minded the cattle, Abbie and Will tended the horses. They removed the saddles, blankets, and reins and stowed them in the hut. Will brushed out the sweaty horses with a curry-comb, while Abbie hobbled their front legs. She sent the tired ponies to join the mules, munching grass in the field. They wouldn't get far with the hobbles. She patted Chief on the rump. "Go on boy, you've earned it."

Abbie watched the two vaqueros work in the corral. Hector

released two more steers, quirting their flanks with a stiff rope, sending them running for the trees, back to freedom. Those were *Circle-J* cattle—*Mason's cattle.* Legally, they weren't supposed to be run on this land. There were federal restrictions—how many cattle could occupy any given tract, and which rancher was allowed to use it. Mason's Circle-J Ranch was south of the Jackrabbit-J by about ten miles, and *not* adjacent to the Bosque Verde. That law was clear. Government grazing land was *only available* to ranches that *bordered* it. Mason was never able to finagle rights to the high country. He'd overpopulated his government tract in the desert, so he used Hank's claim in the Bosque for his overflow. It wasn't legal, but Mason was president of the Cattlemen's Association. No one questioned him.

The whole situation rankled Abbie. From her view, Mason helped Hank buy their small ranch for the sole purpose of running *Circle-J* cattle in the Bosque. Hank was strong in most ways, but he would never say *no* to his dad. On Hank's death, Abbie inherited this arrangement, and she hated it. Each time her cowboys rounded up cattle, half the herd had to be cut loose because they had Mason's brand. They were Mason's property and were left for his crew. Today's mess stewed her wrath. If Circle-J cattle hadn't been mixed with Jackrabbit-J's, there'd have been only half as many in that draw. Much easier. No runaways. She despised that circle-brand whenever she saw it on a steer's flank.

In spring, the sun sets early in the high country and the nights turn frigid. The weary crew sat on sawed stumps around the fire and ate a supper of salt hocks and beans that had simmered for hours. Ol' Javier's Dutch oven cornbread was hot from the coals. They ate like gluttons. Umberto went off to catch some sleep. He'd be awakened later for his night-shift. Will was half asleep and wandered toward the cabin that he shared with his mom.

Abbie returned to the campfire with a blanket wrapped around her. Deuce curled at her feet. She said to Hector, "Hate to ask. How'd we do today?"

"Not too good, ma'am. Got only seventeen head in the corral, not counting mommas and babies."

"So how many can we can take down the hill?"

Hector yelled toward Umberto in the tent. "*¿Muchacho, cuántas vacas quedan en el corral? Y cuántas irán al rastro*"

Umberto's answered. "*Once, quizás doce.*"

"Eleven or twelve," said Hector.

Abbie shook her head. "We're not going to make it, are we Hector? We can't do this without a full crew?"

"Not if you keep falling off your horse."

"Funny man, Hector." She feigned a mean fist. Hector smiled and pulled out a silver flask—one Abbie had given to him after Hank's death, engraved with the initials *H.J.* He waggled it in front of her.

"I think I will." She tilted the flask to her lips. The rum felt warm. Her nostrils flared. She took another swig, savored the vapors, and passed it back to Hector. "I'm not sure what I'm going to do Hector, but I'll be damned if I'm going to give up. Damned if I'm going to let Mason take over my ranch."

Hector took a swallow and said nothing. She knew he'd stay out of the family battle. He'd worked for Mason in the past and he may have to work for him again—if the Jackrabbit-J folded. He passed the flask to Abbie.

She took a small sip this time. "Any ideas?"

"Umm. Yeah, but you ain't going to want to hear it, ma'am."

"Try me."

"The *Rocking W* hired on some prisoners from the camp. Been using 'em for about a week. The Cattlemen's Association set it up."

Abbie stiffened. "Yeah...I know about it. I got a letter. They're Germans, Hector. I threw the letter in the trash."

"Um-hmm."

"I couldn't do that, Hector. Germans? Working on my ranch?"

"You don't have to like 'em. Just put 'em to work?"

She sipped the rum, letting it swirl over her tongue. "It was Germans that killed Hank."

"I know *Patrona*. I know. But they'll have a guard with them all the time. That's part of the deal."

Abbie stood and walked around the fire. It was unthinkable. *Germans.* Bad enough having them nearby at Camp Barlow, but this would be like letting them in your back door. On the other hand, times were tough for the Jackrabbit. She needed ranch hands, needed them badly. *But Germans?* "No. I don't think so. I couldn't do that." She handed the flask back to Hector. "No, Hector. No Germans. I'm going to bed." She snugged the blanket around her shoulders and shuffled toward the hut. *"Buenas noches, Hector."*

"G'night, ma'am." Hector buttoned up his fleece jacket—three lonely hours before Umberto took over the watch.

Abbie went into the cabin and latched the door that dangled on rawhide hinges. The kerosene lamp was still glowing. Will was tucked inside his bedding, fast asleep. He'd spread out his mother's bedroll against the opposite wall. Will's slumber gave Abbie a little privacy. She took off her shirt, painfully sliding her arms out of the sleeves. Her chest ached and her shoulder would barely move. Maybe she should have drunk more of Hector's painkilling rum? She prodded her ribs. Tender, but no sharp pain—a good sign. She moved the lantern and craned her neck, attempting to see over her shoulder. It was too much of a stretch for a clear view but she glimpsed her shoulder blade, raw and scraped. It would take a few weeks to heal. She glanced at her son, sleeping soundly. Abbie worked the catch on her bra with awkward left fingers. Her left breast had slammed against Chief's tailbone and was a mottled bruise of purple, swollen, and it smarted at her touch. She was glad she wasn't built like her older sister. If she had bosoms like Susan, she might have popped one. Hank used to joke that anything more than a handful was wasted. *Amen*. She smiled at the memory.

She'd be hurting for awhile, but she was intact. Abbie freed her ponytail and found the large undershirt she'd tucked in her bed roll. She eased it over her head. The undershirt had been Hank's. She dowsed the lamp, slipped off her jeans, and crouched to the floor over objections from her aching body. Fumbling in the dark, she found her son's tussled hair. She kissed him on the forehead. "Goodnight Will."

"Mmmphh."

Abbie eased into her bedroll. "Ohhh," she gasped as she edged between the blankets. The wood planks beneath her were unforgiving. "Owww ..."

The Bosque Verde

Sun peeked through the ponderosas, causing frosted pine needles to glimmer in the little corral. "Good morning," said Abbie. Vapor puffed with each breath. Her ribs smarted as she lifted the saddle.

"Here, let me give you a hand with that." Hector hoisted Abbie's saddle onto Chief's back.

"Thanks," Abbie grimaced as she reached under the horse's belly, grabbing the cinch.

"You look a little sore today, *Patrona*. That ol' tree beat you up pretty good, huh?"

Abbie gritted her teeth. "Yeah, you could say that."

"That tree wasn't looking too good either, ma'am."

"Ouch. Don't make me laugh. It hurts!" Hector laughed while Abbie fought the urge, alternating between giggles and groans.

"You going to be able to ride today, ma'am?"

She glowered. "Sure, I can ride."

"Whatever you say, *Señora.*"

Abbie took a deep breath. "We have a decision to make today. We can take this small herd down the hill or we can go after the ones that got away yesterday."

"They scattered pretty good. Don't know how many we'll find out there."

"I know. What do you think?"

"I'll go with whatever you say, *Patrona.* You're the boss."

The boss. It hadn't always been like this. When Hank was alive he made the tough decisions. And that was okay with her. Maybe this was when she missed him most. Was she running the ranch the right way—the way Hank would have done it? God, she missed him.

Two and a half years earlier

A ranch hand escorted an Army liaison to the barn where Abbie was tending to a newborn colt. The liaison handed Abbie a telegram and began to speak to her—but he might as well have been speaking Chinese as her eyes were drawn to the telegram.

THE ARMY DEPARTMENT DEEPLY REGRETS TO
INFORM YOU THAT YOUR HUSBAND HENRY PHILLIP
JOHNSON PRIVATE FIRST CLASS U.S. ARMY WAS
KILLED IN ACTION IN THE PERFORMANCE OF HIS
DUTY AND IN THE SERVICE OF HIS COUNTRY. THE
DEPARTMENT EXTENDS TO YOU ITS SINCEREST
SYMPATHY IN YOUR GREAT LOSS.

Abbie staggered to the stall rail. Her knees buckled.

Details filtered in over the next few weeks. Hank had served with Patton's Army. He was killed by Germans during an amphibious landing, somewhere near Casablanca. The newspapers said the mission had been a success. Our boys had given Rommel a thrashing.

But that wouldn't bring Hank back.

Abbie was a widow at twenty-five. Her son, Will, was six. She explained to him what happened to his dad. He was too young to get the whole picture but old enough to feel the hurt.

"You're the man of the house now," she told Will. Of course, that wasn't true. *She* was now *the man of the house.*

Mason, her father-in-law, had a different plan and flexed his muscle. He would take over the Jackrabbit-J—*Hank's* Ranch. *He'd* run the business. *He'd* play the brokers' game. *He'd* manage the books. Abbie needn't worry. Of course she and Will should continue to live in the house. Mason declared, "This ranch will belong to the boy one day, for Christ's sake!" Until then, Mason would see things through. And Abbie? She should keep house and cook meals—just like Ellie—Mason's dutiful wife and Hank's wonderful mom.

Mason hadn't figured on one thing. The United States Army required all troops to make out their last will and testament before heading off to war. Hank's will was clear as spring water. Abigail Munro Johnson was the sole beneficiary of the Jackrabbit-J.

It was a bad day when Mason found out. It still smoldered in Abbie's memory.

"Ranching is a goddamn, tough business. Too tough for a woman. Git your head out of the clouds, girl!"

"Exactly what do you think we've been doing the last six years, Mason? We worked our fingers to the bone making something out of this place."

Abbie was right. She and Hank had fixed the old ramshackle ranch from the ground up. The barn got a new roof and tack room.

Barbed wire now fenced the pastures. The *barracon*—the cowboys' bunkhouse—was repaired with new timbers from the Bosque. And to Abbie's joy, they'd built a red brick addition onto their little adobe house. Abbie worked all the chores—swinging hammers, digging post holes, shoeing horses, and branding calves. Just like her husband, she covered the whole ranch, usually with young Will in tow.

Mason steamed. "Well, Hank's gone. My boy is dead! Ain't no way you can handle this place now."

Abbie clenched. "Maybe *you* think I can't run it, but that's exactly what I intend to do." Abbie grasped the will and waved it before Mason's eyes. "It's my legal right."

Mason raged. "Goddamnit! You wouldn't have any rights to this place if you hadn't got knocked-up right out of high school!"

That set Abbie off a cliff. "I loved Hank and he loved me. That's all that mattered!"

"And that's why you had to get married at the Justice of the Peace? No sense boasting of your sinful act in God's house."

She reeled off a round-house swing, targeting her father-in-law's chin, but he caught her arm before the punch landed. Mason wasn't tall, but he was stocky and strong. Abbie wrenched her arm from his grip and pulled away, huffing. "You son-of-a-bitch."

They locked eyes, each waiting for the other's next move. Mason broke the standoff. "Hank left you the house so you could stay here and take care of your boy. So, be it! Keep house. Cook for the hands. But the ranch?" He growled, "Hell no! I'm the one that put up the goddamn money in the first place. Those are *my* cattle up in those hills! You are bein' crazy. Goddamn crazy! You don't really believe you can run this place, do you girl?"

Damn right I do.

Abbie cradled Chief's mane under her armpit as she bridled him. The big horse bobbed his head a couple of times, making Abbie grimace as pain shot through her shoulder.

"Let's get movin' Hector," she said. "You check on Will and Umberto. See if they're about ready. Tell them we'll be taking these steers down to the valley. Maybe Ol' Javier can whip up some food to take along."

"So *Patrona*, we're going to leave those runaways up here in the Bosque?"

"Don't see where we have much choice. Even if we could find them, I'm not sure the four of us could get that big of a herd down the hill without a repeat of yesterday."

"Might be right," said Hector. "We need more hands. Sure you don't want to get us a few of those Germans? Cheap labor, *Patrona*."

Abbie grabbed the horn and winced as she pulled herself into the saddle. "I just can't do that, Hector." She trotted away.

33

Barlow

Hector grew up around cattle. Like any cowboy, he'd developed immunity to the stink of manure. Lord knows how many times he'd stepped in it, fallen in it, and ridden behind a churning production of it. But all his experience could never get him used to the stench of stockyards. Today was warm for early April. Flies hovered over the stock pens like smoke from a grass fire. Hector walked out of the small clapboard office. The shingle over the door read, AUGUST L. COOPER - BROKER. Hector wondered how Augie Cooper could stand it, plopping his business smack in the middle of all this cow shit.

Umberto was waiting outside, leaning against a fence rail. He always kept some distance when Hector talked with Anglos. Umberto didn't speak much English and knew he was easily marked as an illegal Mexican, but he'd learned how to blend into the background.

Inside the pen were twenty-three Herefords with the Jackrabbit-J brand. Twelve they'd brought down from the Bosque and eleven from the feed lot on the ranch. That was all they could muster. Hardly worth the effort.

"How did you do?" asked Umberto.

"Not too good. Only eight thirty-five," said Hector.

Augie's best offer was $8.35 per hundredweight. Last fall, the Jackrabbit had done a dollar better than that. This year was different. It was still early in the year and Augie was the only broker open for business. The others, most of them representing giant slaughterhouses in St. Louis or Los Angeles, wouldn't arrive in Barlow until fall round-up when most business was done. Augie told Hector, "Them spring cows don't have much meat on their bones. Eight thirty-five is my best price. Take it or leave it." Hector took it.

Brakes hissed as a train slowed into the stockyard siding. Hector and Umberto paid little attention. Cattle cars pulled in and out every day. But this time, a bustle of activity broke out around the train. Army trucks churned up the road and ground to a stop next to the tracks. Soldiers with rifles piled out and positioned along its length. The gate of the first stock car opened next to the cattle chute. To Hector's surprise, cattle didn't come out of the car. Men did. Soldiers—not Americans. They were German POWs and they were being herded down the cattle ramp. One of the American guards was shouting instructions at the prisoners.

"What's he saying?" asked Umberto.

"I don't know. He's hollering at them in German."

The two vaqueros watched the strange scene. About a hundred POWs were directed through one of the cattle pens and out the gates. They marched past Hector and Umberto who were entertained by the spectacle.

When the tromping prisoners got to the dirt road, they were herded up the hill toward Camp Barlow. "That looks easier than driving cattle," said Umberto. "If they try running away, you just shoot them."

Hector chuckled. "I think you're right. Maybe we should use guns too?"

"You think Mrs. Johnson would mind if we shot a few of her steers—just so the others didn't get any bad ideas?"

"Not a good idea, my friend. Cattle are a lot more valuable than Germans." They both laughed.

Hector watched until the ragged files of prisoners disappeared over the hill. "Umberto, wouldn't you think that at least a few of those Germans would know how to run cattle?"

3 4

Amsterdam

"You can't quit. You're in this until it's over. We all are," snarled Willem.

"I can't do this anymore," said Taatje. "Who's right? Who's wrong?"

"It's simple Blondi. If they wear a German uniform, they're the bad guys."

"You make it sound so easy. It's not."

"—So they captured your German boy. That was over a month ago. The bastard should feel lucky he's still alive."

"What makes you think he's alive?" she shot back. "For all we know, the Americans killed him before they crossed the river. You should have trusted me from the beginning. Franz was helping us."

"If you ask me, the Americans should have just shot him."

Taatje's impulse was to clobber him. But she'd done that once before, back when she first started with PAN. She was barely out of her teens. On that occasion, it transformed him into a beast. She succumbed to his strength—underneath his sweating body—on a filthy rug. She learned from that mistake. She slid away from him on the bench. Silence was her weapon now.

She gazed over the pond. Wild ducks had returned to the Netherlands now that the ice had thawed. Two eiders skied to a stop in the middle of the pond, joining a dozen others. *Why can simple minded birds instinctively tell friend from foe, yet with people it's never easy?*

Willem's tone ebbed. "You and he were childhood friends. I understand that. But he made a decision when he put on that uniform. You made a decision too, when you joined us. You can't quit, Blondi. It doesn't work that way."

"Why not?"

"You know how we operate. You know how the resistance works. If you're a true Netherlander, you can't quit."

"How dare you! You think if I leave your organization I'm no longer a patriot? I love my country more than I ever have and I'll continue to fight for our freedom. But I'll do it my way. I know who our real enemies are." She pointed her finger at Willem. "You've lost sight of that. With you, it's all about your pride. I won't be a part of that anymore."

His face reddened. "And I won't allow a rogue bitch out there fucking it up for the rest of us." He seized her arm. "You're not leaving. I won't let you."

Taatje jerked away. "You don't have any choice." She reached in her coat pocket, pulled out the key to Willem's motorbike, and slapped it against his chest. "Here this is yours. Cram it up your asshole!"

She jumped up from the bench. Willem grabbed at her, grazing her hip but getting a firm grip on the hem of her coat, and wrenched her toward him.

She went on instinct and swung like a cat, knuckles and nails, and caught him square on the cheek. "Don't ever touch me again."

He recoiled and wiped at the slash on his face. She feared her impulsiveness might have cost her again. Holding her round, she stood ready to swing. Surprisingly, he slid away from her on the bench. "Shit," he muttered as he looked at the crimson smear on the back of his glove.

With Willem, she always felt violated. There was only one man who'd ever made her feel safe and he was gone now. "Bastard!" She turned and marched toward the pond.

"If you walk away, you become a liability," he yelled.

She knew what that meant and began running. As Taatje skirted the edge of the pond, lounging ducks flapped madly to get out of her way.

Over the pond, on the second hill, stood an oak. A thin man sat at its base. He wore civilian clothes though he was a German soldier on duty. From his vantage point, he saw what he needed.

This was an odd assignment he told himself. After all, he, Corporal Weisner, was a trained soldier, not a detective. He'd suggested to Captain Gerber that the Gestapo would do a better job of trailing this gal. Gerber exploded, screaming that he did not want to involve the Gestapo. This matter would be handled from within, by *his* security detail! Weisner shut up and did what he was ordered. He followed the woman and reported to Gerber directly. He snapped a few photographs through a telescopic lens and jotted an entry in his notebook.

Weisner would travel back to Arnhem in the evening with nothing to report. Gerber would be outraged and piss fire at him, but what more could he do? He'd been tailing the Hoobinck woman for two weeks and there was no sign of the target. *Male. Brown hair. Taller than average. Twenty six-years-old. Severe limp.* The limp would be the telling sign. But that man never appeared. Weisner would suggest to Captain Gerber that the surveillance wasn't working—maybe a new approach should be in order. He would expect another tirade.

35

Netherlands Countryside, outside Arnhem

Lars van de Smet loved playing along the irrigation ditch that ran through the farm. Adventure was always found along its banks by this eleven-year-old boy. Today, Lars's solitary game was simple—loft a stick upstream and throw rocks at it as it drifts by. His record was seventeen strikes. That was on a large *battleship* stick, a *Bismarck*. The smaller sticks, *U-boats*, were harder to hit. His record for U-boat strikes was only six. Lars was in high spirits. It was a treat to be outside playing on a Sunday afternoon. Since the Arnhem battle last autumn, his mom rarely let him play outside. In the distance was the crumpled skeleton of Arnhem Bridge, a reminder of how close the war had come to the Van de Smet farm. But things had been quiet lately. Opa, Lars's Grandfather, said the war had moved on to Germany. The boy was quick to take advantage of this windfall and play outside before Mama and Opa changed their minds.

The sky was a blanket of gray clouds. Rain began to drizzle. Lars looked toward the house. The grown-ups weren't calling him in. *Good.* He threw another big stick in the irrigation ditch. Smack! —another *Bismarck*. miss… miss… two… miss… three… The water ran a little swifter in this part as the level dropped to the next field. Lars chased the Bismarck downstream with continuous automatic fire from his handful of stones. Four… miss… miss…five…miss… miss. The Bismarck stopped, lodged against something in the ditch. Lars pushed his way through tall weeds and edged down the gooey bank. By the time he got there, the stick had worked free and was off with the current. Lars let it go. The thing in the water was more interesting. He inched toward it and pushed it with his muddy shoe. "Haw!" he gasped and lurched backward against the bank, burying his rear end into the cold muck. The thing was a person—a *dead* person—face down in the water.

The rain was coming down harder now. Lars stared at the thing. Gradually, curiosity got the better of him. He slid closer. Was it really dead? If it jumped out of the water he'd scream as loud as he could. It wasn't moving. He tapped it again with the sole of his shoe. Nothing. He pushed it harder. The body bobbed up and down. An arm emerged from the dark water, a sleeve with insignias. A soldier! Lars had seen that sort of uniform many times. A German soldier! He sat motionless against the slick bank.

He heard Opa calling him to come in out of the rain. He ignored it. This was too important.

Lars waded in, up to his knees, and reached for the dead man's collar. He pulled it toward him. The current pushed the corpse over. Its face slid to the surface. Pale gray. Mouth gaping. Lars stared at it and contorted his own mouth to mimic the shape, then shuddered. There was a small, dark hole on one side of its head. On the other side was an opened gash of black ooze and flesh. Tiny minnows nibbled at the stringy wound. Lars was fascinated. He pulled at the body as hard as he could, dragging it, trying to work

178

the thing onto the bank. All he could manage was to get its head and shoulders onto the muddy reeds, legs still dangling in the cold murk.

Lars stood over the corpse. He wondered what a Dutch soldier would do next—a soldier like his father had been—a hero who killed Germans. Lars hadn't shot this German. Someone else had. But it was his claim now.

Opa's voice again. Yelling for him.

In a minute. In a minute.

Lars inspected his prize. Oval tags hung around its neck. The tags had punch holes around them and some numbers and letters stamped in them, but they didn't make sense. He searched inside the pockets and found a little brown booklet—soggy, but still intact. Its cover was titled *SOLDBUCH,* with an insignia of an eagle and swastika. Lars opened the booklet. Inside was a photograph of a soldier. *The same guy as the dead man?* Lars compared the picture to the corpse's face. He didn't look much like the photograph, not anymore anyway. On the facing page was information about him. The ink was blurry but Lars made out the soldier's name, *Oskar Brill.* Lars clenched the book. He had what he wanted, a trophy of his kill.

He scurried up the slick bank, digging in with knees and fingers. "Opa! Here I am. Over here. Guess what? Guess what?"

36

Camp Barlow

"Colonel, we're making a mistake giving the German officers free rein. We have an obligation to protect—"

Riley stopped Davenport in his tracks and shot back, "Hell, why should I mess up something that works? Those Krauts do such a damn good job of keeping their boys in line. Let 'em deal with their own. They'll handle all the penny ante shit that we don't need to touch. Why would I want to screw with that?"

Davenport said, "Sir, there's a gang of Nazi nut-cases inside the wire. Yesterday, a German lieutenant named Dreisenmann—he works as a medic in the camp infirmary—confided to one of our guards about these strong-arm Nazis that patrol the camp. They're called *the Circle*. They control the non-Nazis with kangaroo courts, knives, and clubs."

"Circle gangs? Courts? Horse shit Major! Haven't you been paying attention? We've been fighting a war for the last four years because *all* Krauts are Nazis. They all believe in Hitler. *Sieg*-fuckin'-*heil*, and all that shit."

"Sir, I interviewed Dreisenmann. He got into an argument with one of his buddies over the idea of a German surrender. He made the mistake of being in favor of it. The *Circle* found out and now they consider him a traitor. He's scared and I think he has good reason to be. He asked to be transferred to another camp."

"Another camp? If I start granting transfers to every prisoner with a loaded diaper, there'll be no goddamn end to it. Let the Krauts sort it out among themselves."

The new prisoners marched toward Camp Barlow. Their boots churned up bleached dust that drifted in the dry breeze. Keller had never seen such a place. Yellow, dead grass lined the roadway, nestling around pear-shaped cactus. Rugged mountains lined the valley. Their bare, rock surfaces reflected the mid-day sun. The sky was the same light-blue from one horizon to the other, and not a single cloud.

Keller considered his situation. The Americans had not shipped him halfway around the world to kill him. Camp Barlow would not be a concentration camp—not an *Auschwitz* conjured up by demented zealots. It was a prisoner-of-war camp. He didn't know what was ahead, but he decided he needn't fear the Americans.

A different angst sucked at Keller. Ever since he got his hands on Brill's photographs, he feared those who wore the same uniform as him. He thought of the savage general, Uhlemann. He'd brushed shoulders with him. Wanted to kill him right then. Wished he had. That was five weeks ago. How far could Uhlemann's tentacles stretch? To the American desert? He might not be any safer here than if Uhlemann stood in front of him with a loaded pistol. Keller's plan for survival was fluid. Stay out of the mainstream.

Don't draw attention for any reason. Watch everything that goes on in the camp. Learn from it. Use that knowledge to stay a step ahead of your enemies—whoever they might be.

He hoped his time here, as a prisoner-of-war, would be short-lived. The war should end soon. That was obvious before his capture. On the train journey, the Americans let the prisoners have newspapers, American newspapers. The annoying Corporal Weber jabbered about how the news was all Yankee propaganda. American lies. Keller didn't buy Weber's theory. Weber was loaded with opinions, but he was a harmless blowhard. There was plenty of truth in those articles that Weber hadn't picked up. For instance, Germany couldn't hang on much longer. The Americans and British had already crossed the Rhine from the west. The Russians were closing in on Berlin from the east. Bombs rained on German cities around the clock. This war *had* to end soon. *Thank God for that.* Could he survive in this remote camp until then? Could he protect his past?

They marched through the prison gate. The new POWs were turned over to the camp guards to be processed. Keller was pushed into a single-file line. Each man waited until he was motioned inside. It took an hour before Keller got his turn.

He filled out papers and was assigned a new camp identification number. Then he moved to the next station. On the counter was a placard, printed in German.

PLACE YOUR PERSONAL ITEMS ON THE COUNTER.

Keller set his only possession face-up—a tattered half-photograph. The picture was of Taatje. It was one of Brill's photos that had been taken before the horror in the barn. Keller had kept it. The picture captured Taatje's gentle beauty and her firm expression. That look in her eyes defined what he loved about her.

"Is this all you have buddy?" said the American corporal, working behind the counter.

"Pardon, please?" said Keller.

"Is this all you've got? Most of you guys have lots of knick-knacks. You know, shaving kits, cigarette-cases, things like that. Don't worry, you'll get 'em right back, as long it's not money or a weapon. Don't you have anything else?"

"No, this photograph only."

The American studied the picture and whistled. "She's a looker, a real dreamboat. Is she your wife? Girlfriend?"

Keller liked the sound of the American word *girlfriend*, especially the way the corporal pronounced it, *girrrlfriend*. Maybe he did feel that way. Why else would he have taken such care to bring the picture with him? It was the only thing he owned. The American guards in Belgium had taken his belt buckle and fountain pen. Those Yanks hungered for any souvenir with a swastika on it. Keller replied, "Yes. *Mein* girlfriend."

The corporal looked down at the photograph again and cocked his head with a friendly smirk. "I'd like to have *that* waiting for me when I get home. I'd say you're a pretty lucky guy." Keller smiled as he picked up Taatje's picture and moved to the next station.

After being prodded and probed for a medical exam, his third since becoming a prisoner, Keller moved to the room where they were assigning prison clothing. The workers behind this counter were German POWs. They eyeballed Keller and guessed his sizes. A stack of dark blue clothes accumulated on the table in front of him—trousers, shirts, shoes, socks, belt, drawers, coat, and gloves. Each of the shirts had a white *PW* branded on the back and sleeves. The trousers had the stamp on the seat of the pants.

"What about this?" asked Keller, tugging at his shirt collar.

"Keep your uniform. We wear them when the workday is done. The Americans don't object."

Keller lifted his stack of clothes and toiletries and was ushered out the back door. The new POWs milled about until all of them had come through. The newcomers were led to the far side of the compound by a veteran prisoner. They passed row upon row of identical barracks until they came to the end of the line. Theirs was a brand new building of yellow-white lumber and black tarpaper, not yet faded by the sun. A sign hung above the entry.

COMPOUND 4 - BARRACK 19.

As each soldier entered the building, they were assigned a bunk and foot locker. The privates were nearest the door, the corporals beyond them, and the sergeants had the area beyond a partial partition. Keller was pointed to that privileged section. The sergeants were allotted a bit more space than the lower ranks, and a small amount of separation. There was another fellow across the aisle from Keller, sitting on his bunk, reading a magazine.

"Welcome, Sergeant. I'm Dieter Jung, Master Sergeant, the supervisor of Barrack 19. You might say that I just became mother to a hundred and twenty new arrivals."

"You've been here awhile?" asked Keller.

"About two years. Captured at El Alamein. What about you?"

"Belgium, about a month ago." Keller claimed he'd been captured in Belgium. It was somewhat true—and erased his tracks from Arnhem.

They shook hands. "That's your bunk. Make yourself at home like I have. The Americans don't care." Jung, though he had just moved into the new barrack, already had a cozy space. He'd built a bookshelf of planks and cinder block, upon which he'd spread out his treasures and a two-shelf magazine library. Above Jung's pillow were pin-ups of sexy girls in swim suits and slinky gowns. The pin-ups formed a halo-arc over the head of his bed. "You like my girls?" said Jung. "Mostly American movie stars out of Yank Magazine. American men are imbeciles, but the women are gorgeous. Take a look." Keller stepped toward the pictures. Each had the name of the American movie star over the banner, *Yank Pin-up Girl*. Keller didn't recognize the names—*Deanna Durbin, Lucille Ball, Dorothy Malone*—they all had that ivory smile of an American Hollywood starlet. "I've got some tacks if you have pictures of your own," said Jung holding a ceramic bowl toward Keller.

Keller took two thumb tacks. "Just one," he said. He pinned the photograph of Taatje on the wood clapboard over the head of his bed.

A hundred new soldiers bustled about the barracks. Jung turned from Keller to watch his plebes. He caught sight of someone approaching the door. "Shit! I didn't expect that bastard so soon," he said to Keller.

"Who?"

"Müller—*Sergeant Major* Müller. Hitler's angel in America. Haven't heard of *the Circle* yet, have you?"

"No."

"You will." Jung stepped to the center of the aisle with voice booming. "*Achtung!*" Men scrambled. Within seconds, each stood at the aisle, facing center, shoulders back and heels together. The room fell silent.

Müller entered the barrack. "Men, I am Sergeant Major Klaus Müller. I am the senior non-commissioned officer in this camp." Müller seemed pleased with the degree of discipline among the neophytes. "A meeting is scheduled to welcome you to Camp Barlow. It will be held in Compound 4, Mess Hall 3 at sixteen-hundred. That gives you thirty-five minutes. Sergeant Jung?"

"Yes, Sergeant Major!" Jung stepped up.

"You will brief these men on proper etiquette and dress for the meeting?"

"Yes, Sergeant Major!"

"Another point of order," continued Müller. "I'm looking for Sergeant First Class Franz Keller."

Keller's heart banged. Had Uhlemann found him? He stepped forward. "Reporting, Sergeant Major!"

Müller sauntered toward Keller with eyes burning. Everyone's attention was on Keller. This was not how Keller hoped to *stay out of the mainstream.* "Sergeant Keller. I need to speak with you. Please see me after today's meeting."

"Yes, Sergeant Major!"

"That will be all!" barked Müller. He left Barrack 19.

The new prisoners assembled in the mess hall. A temporary platform with a podium had been set at the front of the center aisle. The soldiers sat on benches. Sergeants and corporals were seated on the inside of each row. At precisely four o'clock the back doors swung open.

"*Achtung!*"

Conversation stopped. The POWs popped to their feet. Two officers in Wehrmacht uniforms paced up the aisle, a colonel and a major. The officers stepped onto the platform and faced the new prisoners. As they did, twenty men of enlisted rank marched through the doorway, led by Sergeant Müller. Müller's squad lined the outside walls, hovering over the assembly.

The colonel took the platform. "At ease! Be seated. Good afternoon gentlemen. I am Colonel Erich Hoefer, the ranking German officer at Camp Barlow. Perhaps you were expecting to be briefed by the Americans. You'll get a chance to meet Colonel Riley at tomorrow's roll call. He will tell you about the American expectations at Camp Barlow. I am pleased to say that we have an understanding with our American hosts. As long as we *run a tight ship*, as the Americans say, they leave camp life and discipline to us. Let me assure you that our expectations are of *a higher standard* than that of the Americans. Our ship runs *tighter* than theirs." Hoefer chuckled.

"Colonel Riley has told me several times how pleased he is with our *stringent decorum*. We have gained the Americans' trust in these matters. Look around the room. Notice there are no American guards present during this meeting—evidence of the influence my senior staff has garnered. You are hereby given notice; you are answerable first and foremost to the Reich uniform!" Hoefer paused. The neophytes were uneasy. He had them where he wanted them. "Now gentleman, I will turn the rostrum over to my executive officer, Major Horst Schwering."

Keller thought it odd that Colonel Hoefer was so brief, quick to turn over the platform to a subordinate officer. He observed Schwering. There was a cocksure arrogance about the man. Schwering lowered the podium stand as he surveyed the crowd. He was evaluating his audience. Schwering's head pivoted slowly like an eagle perched atop its lair. He was feeding off the anxiety in the room. Schwering's gaze fell on Sergeant Müller who gave a slight nod. Schwering's eyes ignited. He cleared his throat.

"Prisoner of war. Captive. Detainee. Convict. Culprit. Prisoner. Undoubtedly, these are words you have struggled with since your capture. These are labels that have been thrust upon you. They are terminologies that you have—perhaps—wrapped around yourselves, like a disgusting flea-ridden shirt, trying to see if it fits. Trying to determine if it should fit. You might blame yourself for this predicament. You may question your own worth, your value to the nation you love. You may be asking yourself—at this very moment—if you have failed in your duty to your beloved Germany? To the uniform you wear? You may wonder if you have betrayed the German people, and your loving family back home...

Keller was seated near the back of the hall. He saw heads bobbing in agreement. The man in front of him let out a slight gasp and swayed his head, affirming relief in the realization that others shared his shame. Keller could see what was happening. Schwering was a skilled speaker, his elocution even and precise. His words were soothing and massaged many souls in the room. The cadence of the speech seemed eerily familiar.

...There is no need for despair. Despair is wasted. You are sons of the Fatherland. There is still much to be done. Yes, there is much to be done at this lone outpost in the desert. Germany calls you even from a great distance. Germany needs you — needs you to be prepared. Germany needs your bodies strong, your minds clear, and your purpose resolute. Despair? Despair? The Fatherland will call on you — and it will call soon. Despair not!

The pace of Schwering's speech was quickening. Intonation of key words was emphasized with increased volume. Keller felt someone's eyes on him. He met the frightened stare of the young soldier seated next to him, Private Schatz. Schatz appeared to be about seventeen or eighteen years old. The boy was scared as hell. Keller gave a small smile of assurance, though he shared Schatz's foreboding. *This fucking Nazi claptrap should have been ended long ago.* He wished he could promise Schatz all this Nazi fanaticism would soon be brought to an end, but he couldn't play his hand to anyone, not even the frightened lad sitting next to him.

...As I speak, Germany is resurgent. Our Air Force is winning the battles over European skies. Our missiles are pummeling London, Moscow, Washington. After a brief setback, our Army is retaking Belgium and France. Our Navy has decimated the British and American fleets who can't hang on much longer. Yes, we are prevailing. We will win this strug-

gle! Fellow sons of the Fatherland, you must be ready. One day soon our countrymen will break onto American soil. These camps will be liberated. At that point, we will take up arms and support our brothers. We will bring America to its knees!

At that prescribed point in the speech, Müller's men thrust their arms forward in salute and shouted, *"Heil Hitler! Heil Hitler!"* The congregation rose. Some individuals popped right up, others more reticent. But within seconds, everyone was standing, arms straightened toward the dais. Men's voices vibrated in piercing unison. *"Heil Hitler! Heil Hitler! Heil Hitler!"* Keller was among them. There was no choice. He loathed his actions, but *there was no choice.* *"Heil Hitler! Heil Hitler!"* Schwering raised his arms and motioned the masses to be seated. His grin was thinly veiled. He had these men in the palm of his hand.

...Sons of the Fatherland. Germany will prevail. The time will come soon when we will throw off the shackles of our oppressors. You will breathe freely again...

Franz Keller knew what he was watching. He was witnessing *the Führer*—Adolf Hitler. He'd heard Hitler on radio broadcasts and he'd seen countless newsreels of his speeches. There was no doubt. Major Schwering was an actor on this small stage, emulating the *Führer.* The articulate speech had begun calmly and gripped the heart of his audience. Just like Hitler, it gradually built by varying volume, tone, and eye contact. It was enhanced by strong, animated gestures. Yes, Schwering had studied his model well. The patterns in this spectacle were all familiar. And now Major Schwering was building to the crescendo. His arms reached upward, his fingers gripped at the heavens on the words *breathe freely again*.

...Our enemies will be vanquished. The Jews who have long controlled the world's financial pillars will be stripped of their ill-gained power. Nations who have fallen under the dark shroud of vile Jewry will soon be defeated by our armies and will be restructured under our design—the plan of National Socialism. Yes, OUR design—as hard as steel! The design of our infallible leader and of the proud Aryan people. The German people! The National Socialist Party will rule the day. That is the holy order. The Nazi struggle is the foundation upon which our great empire will be built—our empire that will last a thousand years! You will be part of it, every one of you. You are part of it now! So I ask you again. Do you despair? Do you despair? No! Through the Party you will find your strength and YOU – WILL – BE – READY! Long live Germany! Germany above all!

The assembly rose to its feet on Schwering's last phrase, a cue that modern Germans knew well. The rigid salute and incantation were instantaneous. *"Sieg Heil! Sieg Heil! Sieg Heil! Sieg Heil!—"* Through the corner of his eye Keller watched Müller's sentries. They were no longer leading the chant, but were examining the audience. No doubt, they were noting which new arrivals did not display the required zeal. Keller's salute was crisp and his recitation was not to be outdone by anyone. He could act too. Private Schatz followed Keller's lead. The chanting changed on Schwering's cue—to another Nazi Party standard—*One People! One Empire! One Leader!*

"Ein Völk! Ein Reich! Ein Führer!"
"Ein Völk! Ein Reich! Ein Führer!"
"Ein Völk! Ein Reich! Ein Führer!"

Jim Davenport leaned against the outside of a barrack, kitty-corner from the mess hall where the Germans were meeting. He tapped out a fresh cigarette from his pack of Winstons and listened to the furious chanting that rang through the walls. He'd argued with Riley again today. Allowing German officers to run meetings without American supervision was bad policy, pure and simple. He struck a match against the clapboard and drew in a long puff. Riley was always so cocksure he had the Germans pegged and under control. He was just plain wrong.

Davenport took a puff and let the sweet smoke drift through his nostrils. The *party* was breaking up. The new POWs filtered out of the mess hall and traipsed toward Barrack 19.

Several memoranda had come across Davenport's desk recently. They reported Nazi problems at other camps. The Provost Marshall's office developed a program to identify the zealous Nazis in all camps. They'd set up a few specialized compounds in Oklahoma and Louisiana that handled the extremists. But each camp commander had the power to determine how to implement the weeding-out process. That was the rub. Riley thought the program was just another case of *"government desk-jockeys getting their twat in a knot."*

The last Germans to come out of the mess hall were Hoefer and Schwering, smiling broadly. Davenport crushed the cigarette butt under his boot. He didn't know exactly what had taken place at their assembly but he was sure of two things. First, that hadn't been a run-of-the-mill welcome speech. Second, there was a big Nazi problem inside Camp Barlow.

Keller took his time leaving the mess hall. Schwering's speech was a punch to the gut. Watching frenzied soldiers conform to this diatribe carried a personal sting.

When Keller was a teenager he belonged to the *Hitler Jugend*, the Hitler Youth Organization. He recalled the annual HJ athletic tournament in Düsseldorf. Despite being a lanky fifteen-year-old, Keller was a good wrestler and represented his HJ chapter at the contest. He wrestled five matches that day and won all of them. He was the champion of his weight class. At the end of the day, all HJ athletes packed the gymnasium seats. The champions of boxing, fencing, running, and other sports took their places on the floor—the arena of honor. Keller stood with the other champions, swaggering roosters cheered on by the spectators. They stood tall and proudly listened as the Düsseldorf *Hitler-Jugend* director address the massed athletes. He spoke of pride and how their athletic determination represented what was great about Germany—how an Aryan athlete was superior to all others on earth because the German people were without rival. The director's speech gushed with the same patriotic ardor as the address just delivered by Major Schwering. On the facing wall of the gymnasium were red banners—swastikas and lightning bolts. At the center was a giant portrait of Adolf Hitler. After the medals were passed out—Franz's was gold—the gymnasium joined in singing the anthem, *Die Fahne Hoch*, The Flag Up High. Salutes and chants followed, praising Hitler and Nazi Germany. He was so proud that day. Back then, he believed all of it. Today, he felt shame.

A gray hulk eclipsed his vision. "Sergeant Keller." Müller was standing over him.

"Sergeant Major?" Keller jumped to his feet as the words cleared his lips.

"Sergeant Keller, we perused your paperwork and something came to light."

"Sir?" *What have I written that would interest this Nazi strongman?*

192

"Apparently you have some experience around horses?"

"Sir?"

"You ride horses? You listed *horseback riding* under *Sports and Hobbies.*"

Why in God's name does he ask if I ride horses? "Yes sir. That's correct."

"We've been under some pressure to come up with a few prisoners who ride horses," said Müller. "You see, we're required to provide labor for the local community when the American Army asks for it. Supplying them with farm hands hasn't been a problem, but now they want horsemen for local cattle ranches. We haven't had many to give them. And Sergeant Keller?" Müller paused until Keller's eyes met his. "By order of the Geneva Convention, enlisted men are required to be part of a labor detail if so ordered. Non-commissioned officers, such as yourself, are not required to do so. However, speaking as the one who oversees all work assignments, I suggest you take this one."

No doubt Müller had the power to make his life miserable, if he refused. But he wouldn't turn it down anyway. Working outside the camp would be the best way to stay far *from the mainstream* and away from *One People! One Empire! One Führer!* "Certainly, Sergeant Major. You've just drafted one horseman."

"Actually, Sergeant Keller, I've just drafted three. Now that you've volunteered, it's up to you to find two more horsemen from among the new troops in Barrack 19. Report to the Labor Dispatch Office at 0630 tomorrow morning. Bring your two conscripts with you."

Major Schwering bolted his door latch, then unlocked his desk drawer. He took out a leather-backed notebook and opened it. There were two pages of listed names clipped on the inside cover.

Schwering took a note out of his breast pocket. It was in Sergeant Müller's handwriting. Schwering added two names to the lists and scratched three others off. Then he searched his top drawer for something he hadn't used in a while. At first he couldn't find it. Then with fumbling fingers, he snagged it in the back of the drawer. His seldom-used red pen. He underlined one of the names in red ink, then closed the notebook and locked it in the desk. He turned off his desk lamp. It was time to retire for the night.

37

Jackrabbit-J Ranch

Hector leaned on the corral gate. Next to him was Private First Class, Charlie Brooks, from Camp Barlow. The two men observed the three POWs at work around the stables. Hector had given them simple jobs—shoveling manure, spreading hay, and currying horses. He wanted to see if these guys would work. *So far, so good.* The Germans buckled right down. But these were chores any school boy could do. The real test would come when he put them on the back of a horse.

Hector convinced his boss the Jackrabbit-J needed these Germans. *Señora* Johnson hated the idea, but when they returned from the Bosque last week with a pitifully small herd, she relented. The following day she went to the Cattlemen's Association to pick up a labor permit. That meant asking for something from her father-in-law, and she hated that more than the idea of German cowhands. Hector knew it.

Mason Johnson was the king of the valley. All the rancher-Army labor contracts came across his desk. When *Señora* Johnson returned from his office, she'd been allotted three German POW laborers. She'd pay the War Manpower Commission eighty cents per day for each of them. That was twenty cents less than she was paying Umberto.

Hector realized things would be different with the Germans. He would supervise them, the same as any other ranch hands. But he was more concerned with his boss than he was with the German greenhorns. With Spanish-speaking cowboys, *Señora* Johnson was amiable. There was always a two-way respect that flowed between her and her hired *vaqueros*. That wasn't likely to be the case with the Germans.

Private Brooks explained the daily schedule to Hector. "The prisoners will be here every morning by 0730, except Sunday. You don't have to feed 'em breakfast because they'll have already eaten at the camp. You don't have to feed 'em lunch either. The camp mess hall packs one for each of 'em every day. The truck'll be back here at 1700 to pick 'em up and take 'em back to the camp."

"So is there any work we can't have them do?" asked Hector.

"No," said Brooks. "Whatever you want them to do, so long as you don't torture or kill 'em."

"Do saddle sores count as torture?" said Hector.

Brooks laughed.

"Will you be watching them all the time?" came a woman's voice. They turned to see Abbie.

Hector introduced them. "Private Brooks, this is Mrs. Johnson. She owns the ranch."

Brooks tipped his hat with his left hand. He didn't have a right hand. His khaki shirt sleeve was pinned at the wrist. "A pleasure ma'am."

Abbie asked again. "Will you be guarding them at all times, Private Brooks?"

"Not likely ma'am. There are two of us who have to keep an eye on this group plus two field crews on the Stevenson farm. We'll be goin' back and forth. But don't worry. I'll be around a lot for the first few days."

"What if there's trouble? Will you be here? Who will handle it?" Abbie regarded his pinned sleeve. "Pardon my saying so, but you only have one hand, Mr. Brooks."

Brooks smiled. "You noticed that, huh? Yeah, I lost it in the Philippines. Shell fragment. That's why I'm not over there now, fightin' the Japs."

Abbie pursed her lips. Hector had seen this expression before—quiet anger. He jumped in. "Private Brooks says that they won't escape."

One of the prisoners approached from the stable. Abbie stepped back.

The POW addressed Hector in a heavy German accent. "Pardon, please. This horse…" He pointed to the black gelding named Pay Day, tied to the hitching post. "This horse has shoe not…not… fit. Shall I repair?"

"Pay Day's shoe falling off?" said Hector to the prisoner. "You know how to fix it?"

"Yes," the prisoner said.

"Sure, go ahead. The tack room's right through that door. Get what you need."

The German nodded in understanding and walked to the tack room, favoring a bum leg. "That fella is Sergeant Keller," said Brooks. "He speaks some English. He's actually the supervisor of the other two. He doesn't *have to work* because he's a sergeant… according to the Geneva Convention. But he says he wants to. That's true of a lot of those Krauts. Darn good workers. You think you'd better show him how to shoe that horse?"

"No, let's see if he really knows what he's doing," said Hector.

Abbie stepped back up to the rail. "What makes you think he

won't go right through the tack room and run away? What's to stop him?"

Brooks said, "These fellas never try to escape. They know it won't do 'em no good. Where would they go? Mexico? Even if they could get there, how would they get back to Germany?" Brooks could see Abbie wasn't convinced. "Besides, ma'am, we've got something else going for us. Heck, the war's almost over. We know it. They know it. They'll be going back to Germany soon enough. They don't have no reason to escape."

"Have you ever had one escape? Or attack anyone?" asked Abbie.

"From Camp Barlow? No ma'am." Brooks chuckled. "The closest we ever came was when a few of them tried to spend the night at the Red Caboose whorehou ... 'Scuse me ma'am...brothel. They traded cigarettes for cash so they could pay for it. We picked 'em up in the middle of the night in their underwear. That's the biggest manhunt we've ever had." His attempt to lighten Abbie's mood wasn't working. "No ma'am, they've never hurt any farmers or anything like that. They like workin' here. It's better than spendin' their days in the camp. We treat 'em better than their own officers do. Some of the prisoners have even told us they wish they could live here when the war's over. Crazy, huh?"

Hector watched Sergeant Keller as he worked on the black gelding. Keller seemed to know what he was doing. He wore the leather apron he'd found in the tack room. He crossed behind Pay Day, his arm pivoting on the gelding's rump, then sidled into the horse's flank to unweight its side. Keller made clicking noises and bid a few foreign words, coaxing the horse's leg off the ground. Hector didn't understand Keller's commands, but the horse seemed to get it. Keller cradled Pay Day's fetlock between his knees and removed the old shoe, using the iron tongs with a deft hand.

Abbie said, "Private Brooks, how can I be sure everything's going to be safe with those Germans?"

"Don't worry, Mrs. Johnson. I'll make sure that everything's under control. That's my job. Besides, you've got the U.S. Army on your side. You've got nothing to worry about."

"I've heard that before," muttered Abbie.

"Pardon, ma'am?" said Brooks.

"Nothing. Nothing. Hector will show you whatever you need."

Hector was glued on Keller. The German had trimmed and rasped the horse's hoof, and was in the process of nailing the new shoe in place, angling and nipping each hoof with precision. Not only was he accurate, he was fast. Hector turned to see if Mrs. Johnson was seeing this, but she was already halfway up the hill to the ranch house.

3 8

Camp Barlow

Jim Davenport was jolted awake. He staggered to the phone. The nurse at the camp infirmary insisted he come right away. One of the prisoners had died during the night. Davenport threw on his uniform, not bothering with shirt tails, and hurried out the door. It was 4 AM.

Prisoner deaths were infrequent in American camps. The War Department pressured camp commanders to diligently oversee the health and safety of Axis prisoners. In some opinions, the prisoners were downright pampered. They ate as well—if not better—than American servicemen. Their health was monitored and attended by US Army doctors and nurses. They were provided many opportunities for recreation. As a result, the Americans had the smallest POW attrition rate, by far, of any combatant throughout the war.

Colonel Riley once commented to Davenport, "Over in Europe, we do our damndest to kill the sons-of-bitches, but once we get them over here we do everything we can to keep 'em fat and healthy. Make some sense out of that, will ya'?" Behind his bluster, Riley knew the reasons were pragmatic. American POWs were being held in Axis camps. If the German hierarchy found out their soldiers in American camps were maltreated, they would retaliate. Swiss intermediaries monitored conditions in the camps, using the guidelines of the Geneva Convention. They regularly filed reports. There were also clandestine communications—called spider lines— through which crafty German POWs found ways to communicate information back to Europe, usually by finagling the prisoner mail system.

Davenport was concerned. He took an MP with him. The dead German was Lieutenant Dreisenmann. This was the medic who had reported his fear to an American guard just a few days ago. Dreisenmann told that guard he was being stalked by *the Circle.*

When Davenport got to the infirmary three people were in the room with the dead man, the American nurse and two German orderlies. Dreisenmann's corpse was face-up on a cot. Speaking to the MP, Davenport said, "Get the Germans out of the room and guard the door. I don't want anyone else in this ward."

Lieutenant Betty McCarthy, one of four nurses at Camp Barlow, remained in the room. College-trained, she was among the few officers at the desert outpost. "Betty, what happened?"

"He must've died real suddenly, like he had a coronary, Jim. Signs point to a heart attack…but I don't think it was."

"How so?"

"He'd been acting strange lately," said Betty. "Real peculiar. Afraid of his own shadow."

"What do you make of that?"

"I have no idea, but I can tell you this. Johann … Lieutenant Dreisenmann …was a healthy young man. He's worked as an orderly in this hospital for over a year, never even complained of a hangnail. He was in great shape. Look at him. Got the body of Joe

DiMaggio. I just can't believe he would *up-and-die* from a heart attack. Dr. Gibbons will be here in a few hours. He'll examine the body. Then maybe we'll know more." As she spoke, something caught her eye. "That's strange. Look at this."

Davenport moved around the cot. Betty showed him a purplish dot on Dreisenmann's neck. A small bit of blood had oozed and was smeared against the inside of his shirt collar. "That's from a puncture. A hypodermic."

"In the neck?"

"It's not right, Jim. There's something rotten going on." She paused. "There's another reason I insisted you come here."

"Go on—"

"Johann was a pretty good guy. I know I shouldn't say that with him being the enemy and all. But in a hospital you don't think of people that way. He helped the patients the same as the rest of us here. Anyway, I think he thought of me as his friend." She took an envelope out of her smock. "He must have, because he gave me this at the beginning of tonight's shift. He told me to give it to the Red Cross or the Swiss consul—whoever I could get it to first. I know I should have turned it over to Colonel Riley as soon as I got it, but..."

"No, Betty. You're doing the right thing now." Davenport opened the envelope and removed a lone sheet of paper. It was a short paragraph, hand written. "I need to get a German translator."

"You don't have to look too hard. There's plenty of those around," said Betty.

"No. I need an American to translate this."

39

Jackrabbit-J Ranch

Keller took a risk. When Sergeant Müller ordered him to find two horsemen, he weighed his options. He could probably find a few experienced riders in Barrack 19. But he wouldn't know anything else about them. He couldn't risk working alongside a Hitler-spouting Nazi. Instead he selected two soldiers who wouldn't pose that threat, even though neither knew the first thing about horses. First, he took Private Elias Schatz, that frightened boy who sat next to him during Schwering's speech. Schatz was more unnerved by Schwering's diatribe than he was. Schatz was no fascist. As a bonus, the young man grew up on a small family farm outside Wiesbaden. Though they used a tractor instead of draft horses, Schatz knew his way around chickens and milk cows. He was eighteen years old. He'd learn quickly. Keller took a bigger chance with his other selection. Corporal Niklas Weber was the loudmouth that partnered with him on the train journey across America. He was annoying, but he was not a threat. Weber preferred to listen to himself, rather than to others. During his endless ramblings on the journey, he'd never extolled the virtues of Nazism. Weber grew up in central Hamburg, the son of an accountant. The closest he'd ever been to livestock was a family cat named *Schneeball*. He might be a burden, but he'd be a safe one.

The horses were tied to the hitching post. The foreman, Hector Cruz, was supervising the process. He and the other ranch hand, Umberto, showed the Germans how to outfit an Arizona horse. For Keller, it was much the same as with Taatje's horses. Some things were different, however, such as the type of reins and the shape of the bit that went in the horse's mouth. Then there was the strange saddle. The Americans' saddle was huge compared to the European style. And it had a strange knob, a horn, sticking up from the front.

"O.K., who wants to go first? Let me see how you can ride."

"I will ride first, Mr. Cruz," said Keller, knowing he had the best chance of making a favorable impression. If Weber was first to ride, they might all be sent back to the camp.

"Knock off that *Mr. Cruz* shit. My name's Hector. *Me llamo Hector.* Get it?" The three Germans were bewildered by this multi-lingual concoction. "Aw forget it. *Mierda!*" cursed Hector. Umberto was on the other side of the corral, laughing.

Keller mounted Pay Day and circled the corral. As he rode he canted up and down in the saddle, pumping his legs like springs—the *European* style.

"What the hell are you doing?" yelled Hector. "Where'd they teach you to ride like that?" Keller reined in the horse.

Umberto was laughing boisterously. "*Se ve como está jodiendola silla,*" he roared.

Keller shot a look to Hector for translation.

"He said it looks like you're fucking your saddle. Let me fix those stirrups, *amigo*." With Keller still on horseback, Hector lengthened the stirrup buckles. "There. Now keep your butt down flat against the seat. Hold the reins in your left hand. No more of that two-fisted crap. Umberto, show him how to ride without getting his horse pregnant. *Enséñale caminar, muchacho*."

Still laughing, Umberto mounted his horse and circled the ring. He hammed it up like he was leading a parade, blowing kisses. The laughter bolstered Umberto. The big crowd-pleaser came when he mimicked Keller by humping against the saddle horn. Weber and Schatz were howling when Umberto smoothly stroked and seduced the pommel. Private Brooks put down his copy of *Stars and Stripes* and joined the carnival.

Hector told Umberto to circle the corral at a walking pace, followed by a trot, then at a canter. While Umberto acted as the model, Hector explained the proper techniques to his pupils. The language difference was like hitting a wall, so Hector used gestures and slapped at different parts of the horse, saddle, and Keller—who was still on horseback. Hector emphasized keeping their butts against the back of the saddle, positioning the toe, *not the heel*, over the stirrups, and how to move their bodies with the flow of the horse. This also resembled sexual motion and evoked more sniggering. When the lesson ended, Umberto dismounted and took a bow to exuberant applause. "Now it's your turn," said Hector, pointing to Keller.

Keller followed Umberto's pattern. He started the gelding at a walk. The American style was unnatural to him, but he converted easily enough. Hector told him to trot Pay Day. "*Hü*," Keller coaxed and tapped with his heel. "*Hü*, Pay Day." Pay Day stepped into a trot. Keller fought his instinct for the up-down cant. He was getting the feel of the western saddle and noticed something good. His leg felt fine when he rode. "*Hü*, Pay Day." He rolled his heel against the horse's ribs the way Hector instructed. Pay Day broke into an easy canter. Keller moved with the smooth flow, horse and rider were one. *"Brrrr."* He reined Pay Day to a stop. Feeling confident, Keller moved the horse through a series of quick turns, starts, and stops. He coolly synchronized reins, heel and balance into each maneuver. Pay Day answered each command with quick response. The onlookers gathered along the corral rail, watching the cool display of horsemanship.

"Brrrr, Pay Day. *Halt."* The horse dug in as Keller reined back. *"Zurück!"* commanded Keller. By manipulating the reins upward and by rolling his heels behind the horse's foreleg, Keller enticed the horse to back up. *"Zurück! Zurück!"* To his audience's amazement, the horse backpedaled slowly, heeding Keller. *"Halt,* Pay Day!" Keller patted the horse's neck and gave him praise as the other men hooted their delight in three languages. Keller dismounted and walked the horse toward the fanfare.

"Bravo. Qué bueno," praised Umberto.

"Damn, I gotta learn some of them German words," said Hector.

"He is a good horse," said Keller.

"Yeah, but I never thought he was that good!" said Hector. "You can really work him *amigo.* How about these other guys? Can they ride like you?"

"I will teach them."

"What?" said Hector, surprised.

"I will teach them. By end of day, they be riders ... Hector."

Hector locked eyes with Keller, sizing him up. "OK *amigo.* You've got a deal. That'll give me and Umberto a chance to bring up some hay. I gotta get into town too. So you're telling me by the end of the day, you'll have these guys riding horses—just like you?"

"Just like John Wayne," said Keller.

Hector chuckled. "What about him?" said Hector pointing at Brooks. "Can you teach him to ride too?"

"What?" cried Brooks. "I'm only supposed to watch these guys!" Brooks looked at his pinned sleeve, where his hand used to be.

"You only need one hand to ride, *Señor*. Besides, how are you going to watch these guys when they're riding up into the hills?" said Hector. Brooks had no reply. "Unless you plan on running behind us, you'd better be able to ride a damn horse. Have you ever ridden one?"

"A couple of times when I was a kid, at the county fair in Rochester."

"I think you're gonna need a lesson, *amigo*." Hector looked at Brooks with wide eyes, then at Keller—indicating the prisoner should teach the guard. An awkward request. Silence scorched the triangle of men.

Brooks finally broke in. "Awright. Sure. What the hell?"

"You'll teach him to ride like John Wayne, too?" Hector said to Keller.

"Yes," said Keller. "Sure. What ze hell?"

Hector returned from town in late afternoon. The bed of the old Chevrolet truck was piled high with sacks of animal feed and spools of wire. He parked next to the barn. From there, he had a vantage point to watch the new cowhands. The four of them were on horseback in the pasture, outside the corral. Keller shouted instructions as he rode alongside his pupils. Hector wondered about this experiment. Sure, these guys could do some chores around the ranch. That would help for sure, but it didn't answer the big question. Could they ride? More important, could they ride well enough to run cattle? If they couldn't, the Jackrabbit would lose money—*lots of money* that *Señora* Johnson didn't have.

He had a good eye for talent. Hector had seen dozens of cowboys come and go. He watched the new recruits through the spattered windshield. *Keller, the main guy, is a damn good rider. He's ready now. The young guy—he's still wet-behind-the-ears but he's getting the hang of it. He'll be O.K. with some more work. The other German guy though—the bigmouth—that guy is a sorry son-of-a-bitch. Shit. He's holding on to his saddle horn with both hands. The dumb shit needs to shut his mouth and listen to his teacher. Brooks is doing a little better than Weber. Hell, at least he's starting to get it right. But if he doesn't stop bouncing in his saddle his butt is going to feel like it's been dragged over asphalt.*

Hector got out of the truck, hoisted a wire roll and took it into the barn. The barn and stables were immaculate. The stalls were clean. Horses were curried with manes and tails combed. The new hay bales were stacked in the loft, in perfect rows. *Hell. I didn't even ask them to do that.* In the tack room he found all the tools hanging in their places on the wall. The bench top was clear and the pine floor swept. *No fue mal.* Not bad. Hector returned to the truck. Up the hill, he saw Abbie and her son standing on the veranda. She was also watching the riding lesson in the pasture below.

Hector whistled, calling the novices to the corral. While they unsaddled their horses, he praised their work. They'd done the chores well. He even told them they were looking like good riders, though he was more convincing than convinced. The recruits were bushed. They were wearing hang-dog faces and walked a little bowlegged. When the tack was hung and the horses put to pasture, Hector said, "Come on *hombres*, follow me."

The weary men trudged up the hill behind Hector, chattering in their own language. German had a harsh sound. Hector tried to make out what they were saying. It sounded like Weber was belly-aching about something and the other two were telling him he was full of shit. That seemed to be the tone of it anyway.

The top of the rise was a flat oasis. This was the hub of the Jackrabbit-J. Mrs. Johnson's adobe house sat on one side, and the *barracon*, the bunkhouse, was on the other. In the middle were two giant sycamores and splotches of grass. A beat-up picnic table rested under the trees—a shady little park in the desert.

The sheepdog, Deuce, raced from the main house to greet them but dug in when he saw the unfamiliar men. *Hruff – Hruff-ruff.*

"*Cállate!*" commanded Hector. Deuce stopped barking but vigilantly skirted the strangers with shoulders low. Still wary, Deuce persisted with a low growl.

Hector led the bedraggled hands to the pump next to the picnic table. "Here you go guys. This is where we knock off the trail dust after a long day." Hector took off his shirt and demonstrated the ranch custom. He primed the pump and worked its lever until cool water gushed into the trough. He doused his brown skin, sopped his head, and tapped some soap powder from a grimy can of *Boraxo*. "Come on, *amigos*. Don't be shy." The Germans pulled their PW shirts over their heads revealing alabaster-white chests. "Whew! You're blinding me," said Hector, pretending to block the reflection from their white skin. They followed Hector's example. Hector threw his shirt back on. "Wait here. I'll be right back." He walked to the *barracon*.

Hector returned with a citrus crate and set it next to the picnic table. It was full of boots—*cowboy* boots. "Here you go fellas. These are old boots that have been left behind. They're old and beat up, but maybe you can find some good ones in there. If you're gonna work in a saddle, you need a real boot, not those dog shit army boots. You need a good boot with a heel on it so your foot can't slip through the stirrup. If that happens, your horse'll drag you through the desert with your head bouncing off cactus. Believe me, you don't want that. Here pick out some boots."

Keller said, "Private Brooks. You are first."

"Thanks," said Brooks, pleased to have his authority restored. He found a pair with a reasonable fit, then the three Germans dug into the crate until they each had a pair of *cowboy boots*. They paraded under the sycamores, laughing at their clashing outfits, cowboy boots and PW breeches. Schatz and Weber started play-acting a movie western gunfight, complete with a fast-draw shootout. Weber mugged a corny death scene that climaxed the melodrama. Hector, Brooks, and Keller roared. Deuce skittered at the odd behavior. *Hruff-ruff*. But after Weber's death knell, Deuce wiggled up to Keller with ears folded and tongue wagging. Keller scratched behind Deuce's ears. The dog flopped over for a belly-rub.

"Hector. Here you go," called Abbie from the porch. She set a pail down and went back in the house.

"*Gracias, Señora*." He trotted up to the porch and got the bucket. Abbie usually brought the pail out to the picnic table after the day's work and spent a few minutes talking with the hired hands. That wouldn't happen today, but it was still a good sign. She must have seen some value in the new men.

"Here you go fellas," said Hector as he brought the pail over. "*Cerveza*."

The Germans were puzzled.

Hector smiled, "Beer."

40

Arnhem

"Close the door behind you, Captain," said General Uhlemann from behind his grand mahogany desk. When the German Army appropriated Van Sloten House from its rightful owners, they divvied the nicest furnishings to the highest ranking officers. Uhlemann's office had been the drawing room of generations of Van Sloten plutocrats. The room was replete with some of the finest carpets and draperies in the Netherlands.

Gerber and the general had been in daily communication for the past six weeks. Their conversations were normally office-to-office telephone calls. Today, however, General Uhlemann had been specific. He wanted to see Gerber in person. "Captain, I'm sure you know why you're here?"

"Yes sir."

"Well?"

"Sir, I have not procured the missing documents or photographs yet. Keller has disappeared. As you know, he is from Düsseldorf. I have sent two of my men there to track him down. If he surfaces, I'll know it. Also I have been keeping surveillance on the girl in Maarburg."

"Have you learned anything more about her?"

"She grew up on a farm near Keller's Dutch cousins. Now she lives in an apartment in the town of Maarburg. Her neighbors haven't been much help. She keeps to herself—comes and goes— sometimes for days. One of my men followed her to a rendezvous in a park. We were able to identify the man she met there, someone long suspected of being with the resistance."

"Resistance? So perhaps the partisans are hiding Keller?"

"It's possible, sir. But up to this point, she hasn't led us to him, nor has he come to her. And there's something else."

"Yes, Captain."

"Keller's mother grew up near Maarburg. We've poured through the town's records to find his connections, relatives, friends—"

"And?"

"His aunt and cousins lived on a farm in the same area."

"Lived? Where are they now?"

"Dead, sir. They all died in the barn on the day of *the incident*."

"The picture becomes clearer, doesn't it? Now we know why he wanted Corporal Brill's photographs. This makes it crucial that we stop him. Gerber, do you know why I had Corporal Brill follow me around like a puppy, taking pictures at every available opportunity?"

"No sir." Gerber lied. All officers at Van Sloten House suspected Uhlemann's political ambitions.

Uhlemann unlocked his file drawer and grabbed a folder. "Captain Gerber, I had a plan. When the war ended, I intended to begin a career in government. My eye was on Berlin. I have what it takes to be a cabinet minister, or perhaps an ambassador. But to get there

I needed to build my reputation. To get one of those lofty government posts I would be in competition with other generals, admirals, and SS bootlickers—those who had been leaders in battle. I needed to demonstrate that I was as good as any of them—not just an officer who spent the war looking out his office window. So I had Brill, a photographer, document my excursions *out in the field*. The photos show me to be an officer of action rather than a bureaucrat." Uhlemann spread the photographs across his desk, a set of the same photographs Keller had hi-jacked. He picked up a photo of himself putting a bullet through a peasant's head. "My plans were made on the assumption that we would win this war. Now that doesn't appear likely. The same photographs that could have boosted me to the highest level of the Reich could now spell my doom. Captain Gerber, do you realize how these photographs will be used if they find their way into the hands of our enemies—or worse, in the possession of an independent Dutch government?"

"Sir?"

"War crimes, Captain. The evidence will be damning. I have only one card left in my hand—"

"Sir."

Uhlemann thumbed through the photos and produced a picture of Gerber murdering a young girl. The child was Jana De Zoute, Keller's cousin. "You and I are in bed together, Captain Gerber. You share my fate. I'd say you are in it a bit deeper. You see, I have records showing the Maarburg incident was under your leadership. I will argue, if necessary, that I arrived on the scene to clean up the mess you began. It's a thin defense I admit, but with skillful legal counsel, it may just save my skin."

Gerber wiped his brow with a handkerchief. He'd felt Uhlemann's grip tightening every day since Keller's escape. Now the general had him by the balls.

"Captain Gerber, there is only one happy ending to this story, and it works for both of us."

Gerber swallowed, "We must find Keller, sir."

"Precisely. Our time is quite limited. The Allies are massing south of the Rhine. Their reconnaissance planes have been flying overhead with frequency. They're getting ready to move. We will not be able to stop them this time. Captain, we must have this matter resolved before we evacuate Arnhem. I suggest you change your strategy with the girl. If we can't lure the wolf with the hare, we must force the hare to lead us to the wolf. I've seen you in action, Captain. I have confidence in your methods."

"Yes sir."

41

Maarburg

In the dark, early morning of April 10th, Allied planes flew over the town of Maarburg. The drone of the low-altitude aircraft awakened most of the anxious citizens. In the previous week, sections of western Netherlands had been liberated. Was Maarburg next? Some people huddled low in basements, preparing for the worst, bombing runs by the Allies to loosen the German defenses. Others hunched in windows and doorways hoping to witness the spectacle that would lead to their freedom. Scattered cheering could be heard over an otherwise still night.

Taatje sat upright, her slumber stifled. It took a few moments for it to sink in—the joyous shouts of neighbors—the hum of the planes. She recognized the thrumming beat. This wasn't the shrill whine of single-engine Typhoon dive bombers. These planes droned with the calmer hum of level flight, the same hum as airplanes that made drops to the resistance. She realized what was going on.

Through PAN, she knew about the Allied plan to drop food and supplies to the starving Dutch people. The race was on. The people must get their hands on it before the Germans show up. The townsfolk didn't realize what was happening. They cheered because they thought the planes meant liberation, not food. She dressed in seconds and flew into the street. At the top of her voice she yelled, "Food! Food!" Dark parachutes dropped out of the blackness.

Sirens sounded. The Germans were on to it.

People descended into the street, ripping at the bundles and slicing them with kitchen knives. Boxes and cans spilled onto the cobbles. Two women cursed each other and argued over a single package. Others tried to drag bundles still attached to parachutes. In the frenzy, many filled their pockets and cradled as much as they could. This anarchy would accomplish little.

Taatje took charge. "Quickly, cut the pallets free of the parachute cords. Carry the food to the church. We'll hide them in the cellar. Hurry!" She ran to the largest men, slapped their backs, and yelled to do as she bid. "Move quickly! Two men to each bundle! We must get them to the church before the Germans arrive. To the church. Run!" Taatje sprinted up *Kuiperstraat*, repeating the commands to everyone she saw. Soon, others followed her lead. *Chaos* was transforming into *order*. Women worked the pallets by dividing the payloads into manageable size bundles. Some cut the parachutes into makeshift gunny-sacks. The men shuttled the bundles away. The makeshift system gained momentum. Everyone found their role and carried it out.

Within minutes, the task was complete. Every parcel of manna was off the street and safely stowed in the basement of Saint Galo's, the small church at the end of the block. Even the parachute cords were gone. But people still milled in the street. "Go back to your homes," she told them. "Don't let the Germans catch us out on the street. Come to the church service in the morning. We'll distribute the food then. Go back home."

Through the dark hours, Taatje and a dozen others toiled in the basement of Saint Galo's, packaging troves of food into satchels cut from parachute silk. The food boxes were labeled in English. Some were the olive color of the American Army. Others were colorfully packaged as if they had been taken off a market shelf. Cans of milk, beans and bully beef, boxes of Ritz crackers, and Hershey's chocolate bars were stuffed into the silk satchels.

At eight o'clock, the morning bells tolled from Saint Galo's steeple. Parishioners crowded inside for the morning service. The pews filled quickly. Others stood tightly packed along the walls. The minister praised the record attendance—for a Tuesday morning, no less. When worship ended, the congregation left, bundled in bulging winter coats, which was a bit odd for a spring day. The Germans didn't notice.

By midmorning, the task was complete. The food had been doled out. In the basement of Saint Galo's, the last remnant of parachute fabric was burned in the furnace. All evidence had been erased.

Taatje was weary, but the stroll home felt good. A few days earlier, she'd quit the resistance. Since then, she'd been second-guessing herself. Had she abandoned her duty? But she had no more appetite for the inherent violence, nor would she continue to answer to the Napoleonic Willem. Last night's enterprise was more rewarding than anything she'd done since the war began. It was bloodless and the benefit was clear. She liked being with people, rather than being a phantom. Perhaps this could be her immediate destiny—helping folks survive the end of this cruel war. The thought was warm.

She passed under the red flower box of her apartment and rounded to the stairs. She was startled by someone in the shadows. The landlady skulked at the base of the stairwell. Her eyes were severe. Maybe the old witch was angry because she'd been awakened by Taatje in the middle of the night. The old hag threatened eviction before. Taatje expected a tongue-lashing, but the landlady said nothing. The woman's lip quivered as she stepped back into her apartment and shut the door, then Taatje heard the scrape of a sliding bolt.

Taatje trod up the stairs. Her apartment door wasn't locked. Odd. Had she neglected it when she dashed out in the middle of the night? She pushed the door open. The room was dark. She took two steps inside and was startled by a silhouette in front of the window. She jumped and the food satchel dropped from under her coat and burst apart. A green can rolled along the floor until it hit the wall. Taatje froze. A man was sitting in the chair, facing away from her, looking out the window.

Her eyes were adjusting to the dark space. The man in the chair was Willem. He'd helped himself into her apartment. *Probably jimmied the lock?* She was afraid this might happen. Willem hated being trumped by anyone, particularly a woman. Now he was back. *Why? To reclaim me?* She'd stay close to the door and run, if necessary. She waited. He didn't speak. He didn't turn. He just stared out the window.

"Why are you here, Willem?" Her voice cracked. "What do you want?"

Her knee shook. If he turned on her, she'd bolt. "I told you I was finished. I'm not working for you anymore. Leave." No response. "Please leave." Still, nothing.

The dim room was becoming clearer. Willem's arms were peculiarly folded behind the chair. He didn't move. She stepped closer. His wrists were bound with an electric cord. "My God! Willem, what's going on?" She stepped next to him. Her foot slipped as she planted it beside his chair. She was standing in a dark slick of blood. Willem's throat gaped open in a jagged crescent. Blood had cascaded from the wound onto his lap and onto the floor. His face was pale and lifeless. A red trickle dripped into the pool. *This just happened.*

The door hinge squeaked. Out of its shadow appeared a uniform—German. The man stepped slowly toward Taatje, pistol in his hand. She backed against the window jamb. The man stopped a few feet short and lifted the pistol toward her chest. His face was hideous, an angled nose and a cleft through his eyebrow. His eyes didn't move in unison. She recognized him. The Devil. Gerber.

The Devil whistled, two short bursts. Another soldier came through the door and latched it.

Gerber kicked a chair toward her. "Sit down, Miss Hoobinck." His voice was horribly familiar. Terrifying images stormed through her mind as he pointed his pistol at her head. "I'll say it once more. Sit down." Taatje moved unsteadily—two steps—to the chair and sat. "Bind her hands and legs, Corporal Weisner. Use the cords from the other fellow."

Taatje watched as the skinny corporal untied Willem's binding. The cord was then tightly re-tied around her wrists and ankles. Willem's body slumped to the floor.

"You're wondering what he's doing here, Miss Hoobinck?" Gerber said, regarding the dead man. "This wasn't his lucky day. He came around looking for you. Unfortunately for him, he found us instead." Gerber snickered. "We asked him about you, but as you can see, he wasn't forthcoming. I hope you don't make the same mistake." Weisner finished securing the cords. Taatje was girded to the chair slats. The lashes bit into her flesh. "And, oh yes, we know he was with the partisans. We know the same about you. Are you hiding any weapons?"

"Corporal Weisner, train your pistol on her. If she moves, blow her brains out."

Weisner responded, "Sir, that won't be necessary. She's constrained—"

"Shut up, Corporal. Do as I say!"

Weisner pushed his gun against Taatje's temple. Gerber set his pistol on the table. Taatje's eyes darted. She wanted to scream. This was the monster who tried to rape her. Only by a stroke of luck—if it could be called that—did his lechery lead to her escape. Images of that struggle raced in her mind—her panic as Gerber chased her up the hill—the flurry as they tumbled downward—her barefoot kick into his face that sent him reeling. *His eye! I blinded him? My God, does he know who I am?*

Gerber removed his gloves and arranged them on the table next to his pistol. He stepped toward Taatje and dropped a knee to the ground. "I must check for hidden weapons," he said. But that wasn't it. He caressed and squeezed as he worked his way up her hips and thighs. Her impulse was to fight and grab the pistol, but she couldn't budge. Gerber's face moved close to hers. His stale breath hovered as he took liberty with his wiry hands, kneading her breasts. His twisted nose moved next to her ear, his breath drafting her cheek. His hand inched like a spider, down her belly. He pressed his nose against her ear as his fingers slipped between her legs. His hand clamped upward like pincers and squeezed painfully. She whipped her face toward his—her eyes burning.

Gerber grinned. "No weapons, Corporal." He snickered and walked across the room. The cold muzzle of Weisner's gun again pushed at her temple. In Taatje's line of vision was Willem's blood-soaked body, the table that held Gerber's gloves and gun, and Gerber himself, who was standing on the opposite side of the room next to the stove.

"Miss Hoobinck, I'll get right to the point," said Gerber. "I know you are acquainted with Sergeant Franz Keller. You were with him the day he escaped. That, in itself, is enough to warrant your death. As I'm sure you know, other partisans have been executed for less serious offenses. However, I am going to give you a chance to reclaim your life—which I now hold in my hands. Miss Hoobinck, I need to know the whereabouts of Sergeant Keller."

So Gerber doesn't know where Franz is? Doesn't know the Americans took him as a prisoner? It made sense. Gerber wouldn't have had a reason to look into the rosters of German POWs. No Germans witnessed Franz's capture. The other possibility was grim, that Franz had never become a prisoner-of-war. The Americans might have killed him before they were across the Rhine.

"Where is he?" demanded Gerber.

She didn't answer.

"Miss Hoobinck, he stole something from us, some important documents. I suspect you are aware of this. I will settle for those documents. Give me either Keller or those documents and you will be free." Gerber leaned against the wall, nonchalantly folding his arms. "That's not a bad deal for you, is it? Certainly better than your unfortunate friend here."

Taatje kept silent. These were lies. Her slim hope depended on the fact that Gerber believed she knew something. If she gave him that, she would be of no more use, and he would kill her.

Gerber leaned his hand on the capstone that hid the documents. "Miss Hoobinck, if you fail to cooperate with me, you will experience unthinkable agony until you tell me what I want to know. So if you know the whereabouts of Sergeant Keller, or of the documents, I suggest you speak up. Either one will win your freedom. Miss Hoobinck?"

Taatje focused on Gerber's hand, casually bracing his stance against the capstone. Only a few inches below that hand, in the wall's void, were the damning photographs and papers. The stone rocked slightly as Gerber leaned into it. *I must get his hand off the stone.* Gerber's thumb moved downward. His hand gripped the capstone. *If he pulls at it, it will slide off.*

"You can fuck yourself!" yelled Taatje.

Gerber clenched. His hand came off the stone.

"While you're at it, grab your little pencil prick and fuck your friend here too."

Gerber balled his fist and hammered Taatje's cheek. The impact knocked her chair sideways and she crashed onto the floor.

Her head was spinning. Consciousness wavered. She felt her body being hoisted upright. Gerber shouted at the other fellow. Her brain was addled and she couldn't string the words together. They were saying something about taking her out of here, taking her somewhere else. They were untying her bindings. She fought to clear her head. Her hands were unbound. *This might be my chance, my only one.* Cool blood streamed over her cheek. She struggled for steady vision. The table was a few feet away. Gerber's pistol was still on the table. She remained limp as Weisner fiddled with the lashings on her feet until they were undone. Her head was still whirling, but she had her bearings. She swung her elbow backward into Gerber's chin. The power of the blow propelled her forward—toward the pistol. It was right there, but she wobbled and staggered like a drunkard. She tripped into the other chair and tumbled over it in a half-somersault as both she and Willem's corpse tumbled to the floor. She landed on Willem with her full weight, sending a red spray from the slash on his throat. Taatje struggled for vertical and hoisted herself to the table. She grabbed the gun as the full weight of Weisner tackled her. The back of her head bounced off the wood planking, but she hadn't lost hold of the pistol. Weisner was prone and scrambling, partially on top of her. Gerber appeared over her. The wicked face swirled through her vision. *I will destroy that hideous face now.* She lifted the pistol upward, arm swaying. As the pistol barrel neared its mark, Weisner slammed it downward. The gun rang out. The bullet thudded into Willem's body. Then, Gerber's boot smashed down on her hand. Bones crunched. She screamed as Gerber took the pistol and moved over the top of her. He backhanded her with the pistol-butt. All went black.

42

Camp Barlow

Colonel Riley's daily routine began in the officers' mess, 6 AM. Two eggs, sunny-side up—slathered with catsup, buttered toast, and black coffee. He usually had breakfast alone, but Major Davenport slid into the opposite chair.

"Looks like someone crapped in your mess kit. What's goin' on, Jim?" said Riley.

Davenport caught his breath. "Sir, do you remember last year when that POW was murdered at Camp Papago Park?"

"Sure, I remember. The Kraut was a U-boat sailor. Shit, I had to drive up to Phoenix for the briefing. All the area commanders had to go to that one."

Davenport said, "He was killed by fellow Germans—Nazis."

"Damn right. Seven of 'em were caught. Said they were proud of what they did." Riley plowed a piece of toast across his plate, sopping up runny eggs. He munched as he talked. "Guilty as hell.

224

They're gonna be executed. The army's just waitin' for the war to end before they string 'em up."

"Sir, they weren't just murderers, they were an organization of Nazis inside the camp. The same damn thing has been going on in other camps all around the country."

"Get to the point, Jim?"

"It's going on right here, right now."

"Shit, Jim. I've heard this song before. Go ahead, let's hear it."

Davenport continued, "A soldier died last night in the infirmary. Murdered. This is the guy I told you about, Dreisenmann. Remember, he told us two days ago that he was being threatened by a group called *the Circle*. He asked to be transferred. You denied his request, Colonel."

Riley set down his fork. "What the hell makes you think he was murdered, Major?"

"He had a puncture from a hypodermic *in his neck*—and he'd written this letter." Davenport produced a couple sheets of paper.

"Where'd you get this?" asked Colonel Riley.

"Dreisenmann gave it to Betty McCarthy. She was working the graveyard shift. Gave it to her a few hours before he was found dead in the hospital storeroom. He asked her to give this letter to the Red Cross or the Swiss."

Riley looked over the two sheets, each quite different. "What is this, Major?"

"The one in your left hand is the note that Dreisenmann gave to Betty. The other one is my transcription of it. I just spent an hour in the camp library with a German dictionary."

"You couldn't get a German to do it for ya'? If there's one thing we've got around here it's a shit-load of Kraut translators."

"Sir, because of the nature of this murder, I didn't think it wise to involve any prisoners. We share our only American translator with Fort Bayard and he's in New Mexico right now. If you look at my translation Colonel, you'll see I wrote it down word-for-word.

The blanks are for the words I couldn't find or make out…you can only do so much with a dictionary. But I think the message is clear."

Riley read the translated page.

Dear esteem sir

    The prisoner-soldiers of this Camp Barlow are terror being from — — our — — German group. A — — organization of National Socialist devotees is for strikings and murders responsible of — — patriotic German soldiers. They called the Circle are. The — — attack anyone they think National Socialist beliefs follows not. I think certain that I next target be. The Americans have not me helped. I am desperate. I seek for sanctuary. Please me help.

Yours — —
Lieutenant Anders Dreisenmann
Serial 6WG – 12045

Riley stared at the letter. "Okay, we've got a problem." He pushed his plate aside. He stood and paced, wringing his hands.

Davenport waited. He had little faith in Riley's leadership. There was a limit to how much advice Riley would take. He was a proud man who covered his incompetence with the aplomb of traveling salesman.

Riley finally spoke. "Damn it Jim. I haven't told you this, but I've already got the Army on my back. Command's telling me I need to run a tighter ship around here. If I report this thing to them, they're gonna ream me for not havin' my nose further up the Krauts' assholes. Next thing you know, we'll have a boat load of those uppity federal legal monkeys buzzin' around here like flies on shit. I'd rather we just handle this whole thing ourselves."

"Sir, with all due respect, we're really not set up for this size of an investigation. I strongly suggest we notify the Provost Marshall."

Riley snarled, "Goddamnit Jim. If we bring them in, it's going to be a king-size pain in the ass. They'll call in those Swiss assholes too. It'll be a three-ring circus." Riley checked his temper, paused, then worked up a smile. Davenport had witnessed this Hyde-to-Jekyll transformation before. "We can handle this thing, Jim. How big can the problem be?"

Davenport chose his words carefully. "I've been keepin' my ear to the ground ever since Jauch was found dead. That thing never added up. Jauch's death was too similar to this thing that happened last night. These Nazis have a sophisticated system in place. This will be a tough nut to crack."

Riley shook his head. "How sophisticated can it be? We watch them day and night. You know, I talked to Colonel Means when I was up there at Papago Park. He handled most of his own investigation. He didn't call in the Provost SOBs until he caught the guilty ones. I think that's what we've gotta do here, Jim. I want you to talk to the guards. Find out what they know, what they've been seeing. They can point you toward some prisoners who will cooperate. I'll bet we can get to the bottom of it. It won't take long."

"Sir, it's unlikely that any of the prisoners will talk to us. They know they'll end up like Dreisenmann and Jauch."

"Jesus Christ, Major! We'll protect them if they help us. We'll catch the son-of-a-bitches who are behind this and throw them in the brig. *Then* we'll call in the PM. Let them clean it up from there. We'll look shinier than a half-dollar in a goat's ass. And in the meantime, they won't be screwin' up my camp."

Davenport left the mess hall. Without logic, he'd become the crime investigator. He wasn't surprised. Nothing in the Army surprised him.

"Come on, Sergeant Keller. We only have a half hour of sunlight left," said Schatz. He led Keller and Weber outside Barrack 19 where he'd rigged up an imitation steer, a wheelbarrow with a two-by-four strapped across the front of it. "What do you think Sergeant? We can use it to practice our roping. It'll work great! Don't you think?"

The young man's exuberance was refreshing. Keller played into it. "I don't know Schatzi. That's a fairly ugly cow."

Weber chimed in. "Are you sure it's not a bull, Schatz?" He reached under the back end of the wheelbarrow. "No, we're safe. It's a steer."

Schatz handed Keller the stiff rope he'd brought back from the Jackrabbit-J. "Here sergeant, you rope the horns while I run by."

A small group of POWs gathered to watch the absurd spectacle. Schatz, pushing the wheelbarrow, ran circles around Keller, bellowing wildly while animating the wheelbarrow as if it was a rampaging steer. Keller tossed the lariat at the mighty beast as it passed by. The onlookers laughed at Schatz's antics. After a few minutes, Schatz came to a stop, panting.

"My turn," said Weber grabbing the wheelbarrow. "Be ready. This is no longer Schatz, *the calf*. It is Weber, *the mighty bull*."

The crowd egged him on. Weber wielded the contraption to a distance of about ten meters. Then he began pawing at the earth like a desperate beast in a bull ring. Schatz swung the lariat over his head. Weber snorted and slobbered. Keller backed into the ring of laughing onlookers.

"Muhhhh! Muhhhh!" bellowed Weber-the-bull. He charged toward Schatz. As *El Toro* slashed by at full speed, Schatz threw the lasso. In perfect form, the loop caught the two-by-four and the noose fell over *the head*. The lariat tightened under Weber's thrust. Schatz anchored the end of the rope firmly behind his rear end, just like Hector had taught him when roping calves. The line became rigid. The front of the wheelbarrow whipped into an about-face.

Weber, who was caught between the handles, flipped head-over-heels, bounced, and rolled into a mouthful of powdery dirt.

The crowd roared as Weber stood up, spitting mud. He grabbed his ailing shin and yelled at Schatz, "Are you trying to kill me? You're supposed to let go of the rope, shit-brains!"

Schatz shouted through his laughter, "I couldn't let go. I roped *the mighty bull*." He raised his arms in victory as the rabble applauded their hero. Schatz stepped toward Weber. "Wait until I tell Hector."

Keller put his hand on Schatz's shoulder and worked up an impersonation of Hector, in English, with a Mexican accent. *"That's some damn fine roping, amigo. Now get back to work."* Keller's accent was lacking, but he captured Hector's expressions and cadence. Even Weber started laughing.

"Major Schwering, take a walk with me," said Colonel Hoefer.

The highest ranking POWs stepped outside. As they strolled among the enlisted barracks, German soldiers parted like the Red Sea. Salutes shot skyward. This was the way Hoefer wanted it. No one could eavesdrop.

Hoefer began, "Are we still getting a steady flow of news from the Fatherland?"

"Some, Colonel," said Schwering. "The Americans never cease to amaze me. They censor our mail. Yet, they fail to comprehend that we can easily undermine them with German soldiers working in the mail rooms and at the telephone switchboards."

"Colonel Riley has given me bad news about our fortunes back home. But as you know, I don't take the Americans at their word. I prefer to hear accurate information from our own sources. Tell me what you've heard."

"Unfortunately, Colonel Riley is probably telling you the truth," said Schwering. "The British and Americans are moving through western Germany. Hanover has fallen. The Ruhr will be next. Two days ago, the Canadians crossed the Rhine. The Netherlands is expected to be lost within the week. Perhaps the worst of it, the Russians have surrounded the capital. Berlin won't hold out too long against those bastard Slavs."

"And the *Führer*?"

"No word, sir."

Hoefer was somber. "So the nightmare is playing out. Major, I don't want word of this to spread to our men. I realize they will hear things from the braggart Americans, but we have conditioned them not to believe the Yanks."

"I agree, sir. This news could damage morale and discipline—and *discipline* is what we need most in these times. The men will be warned not to discuss or repeat any of the American propaganda."

"Yes. If we allow the men to wallow in despair, it will spread like a cancer. Now is a dangerous time. We must hang on. Maintain the status quo until the war is over. Then they may know the truth and we can direct their energy toward repatriation and rebuilding the Reich. Discipline, major! That is the key."

"Yes sir. Absolutely."

"How is the program progressing, Major? Any repercussions from dealing with *the red man*?"

"All is in order, sir. Dreisenmann died of a weak heart. Müller staged it well. There is no reason to believe the Americans will investigate his death any further."

"Very good, excellent," said Hoefer. Their walk had taken them to the front of the new barrack. Hoefer stopped. Odd action caught his eye. A small crowd was watching a few soldiers playing a silly game, tossing a rope over a wheelbarrow. "Peculiar," said Hoefer. "What about the new soldiers in this barrack? Do we know anything about them?"

"I still haven't received much on any of them," said Schwering. "Normally, I'm able to get background information quickly. But because of the situation back home, reports are slow in coming."

"Any cause for concern, Major?"

"Only the usual, sir. Every group that arrives here demonstrates less and less Aryan principle. Most of them were recent recruits—trained haphazardly—then thrown into battle. They don't understand why they're fighting or their covenant with the *Reich*. These new men are not dedicated like those of us who fought in Africa. Though the war may end soon, we'll all probably be here a long time after the armistice, perhaps many months. So yes, I am concerned Colonel. I'm concerned that a virus of American Jew-doctrine could sweep this camp."

"Are there any of the new internees that we should keep an eye on?" asked Hoefer.

"A few have been brought to my attention. They are being monitored."

43

Arnhem

Weisner was a seasoned soldier, having fought in Poland, Italy, and now the Netherlands. Like all military men, he'd been schooled in top-down structure. Obey all orders, without question. A soldier is trained to fight, not to think. He understood it. It worked. It was beyond question. *Until today.*

For the past month, Weisner served as Captain Gerber's lackey. That in itself was no surprise. It came with being a corporal. However, he was troubled by the task required of him. He'd been shadowing the Dutch woman for several weeks, delivering steady reports to Gerber. In Gerber's briefings, he told Weisner almost nothing about this woman except she was an enemy of Germany. Weisner's surveillance revealed there was some truth in that, but the more he worked the case, the more he was sure this was about something else. Weisner had come to believe that Gerber's interest in this girl had little to do with military security. This woman was small potatoes. With Gerber, it was something personal. Why hadn't he involved the Gestapo—or at the very least, a Wehrmacht investigation unit? Why did Gerber refuse to tell him any specifics about the girl's crimes? For heaven's sake, that might help with the investigation. It didn't add up. Yet Weisner had accepted it all as his duty. *Until today.*

It's difficult to judge morality in war. Virtue is lost in the haze. But what Weisner witnessed was clear, and it was *wrong*. Whatever crime the Dutch woman may have committed didn't warrant the beating she took—or Gerber's lechery. That was immoral and flew in the face of Weisner's Lutheran faith. As he drove the staff car toward Arnhem, he prayed silently for forgiveness in his part. Captain Gerber was in the back seat with the unconscious Dutch girl. Weisner forced a conversation with his captain in order to keep him occupied. He periodically checked the rear view mirror and caught Gerber's eye—some assurance he wouldn't commit some perversity on the unconscious woman—if he knew he was being watched. For Weisner, as a Christian, it was the right thing to do.

Taatje sat on the stone floor, her back propped against a wall. She was feeling a path back into consciousness. She'd awakened an hour earlier and had only summoned enough strength to sit up. The room was cold. Her right hand was fat and firm as a tomato. Pain kept her from falling back into a stupor. The little finger angled sideways. She pulled at it, trying to realign the bones, but it hurt too much. With her good hand, she felt her face. Swollen and tender. Her cheek was a puffy knob. She wiped at the crust of dried blood.

Grogginess was wearing off. She looked around. Three walls were plaster. The fourth had vertical bars and a grated door, locked to be sure. The only things in the cell were a bench and a bedpan.

She pushed herself off the floor and stood uneasily. Memories flooded back—Willem's corpse and her fight with the two Germans. The demon, Gerber, running his hands over her body. She shuddered. What had he done while she was unconscious? She felt under her skirt. Her underpants were still in place. No foreign wetness. No pain, just a full bladder. All a good sign. She had not been raped, but she had to pee.

She heard no noise, no voices. She slid the bedpan to the middle of the cell and balanced herself on the cold metal. Her stream rang, echoing off the open-beamed ceiling. She leaned forward and peered through the bars. To one side was a short hall with a closed doorway. The other way, the hall was longer and led to a door with a window and sunlight. Though she was in a locked cell, this didn't seem to be a jail. She recalled a jumbled conversation after Gerber's fist knocked her flat. They said something about getting her out of her apartment and taking her somewhere, but she couldn't recall any more than that. She slid the bedpan under the bench and straightened her skirt.

There was conversation outside the building. German voices. Male. The door opened and boots pounded up the hall. Two soldiers looked at her as they walked by her cell. She recognized one of them, the thin one who had been with Gerber, in her flat. *His name? His name?* They went into the room next door. *Weisner. That's his name.* The other soldier, wearing combat gear, emerged from the room and left the building. Weisner appeared again, also helmeted and carrying a rifle. He stopped in front of her and winced as he sized up her battered face. "My God," he mumbled, and then proceeded down the corridor.

"*Herr* Weisner," said Taatje, her voice muffled through a swollen cheek. She called him by the more personal title, *Herr*, rather than his military rank—hoping to appeal to his human side. Weisner hesitated. "*Herr* Weisner, tell me what's happening. Please. Where am I?" Weisner returned to the front of her cell. He didn't answer, but met her eyes. She sensed compassion. Or perhaps it was pity. *"Herr* Weisner, please tell me what's going on. Where am I?" Taatje pleaded.

Weisner balked, as if examining consequences, then answered. "You're in Arnhem, in the Van Sloten Security Building."

"I see." Taatje knew of Van Sloten House. This was where Franz had been stationed, and where he stole the documents and photographs. She prayed they were still safely hidden in her flat.

"We brought you here a few hours ago," said Weisner. "I watched out for your...safety during the journey here." Taatje nodded, understanding. "I really must go," he said. "I shouldn't be speaking with you." He turned away.

Taatje said, "He'll kill me you know. You saw what he did to my friend." Weisner froze. She'd found the human chord. "You see what sort of man he is."

"There's nothing more I can do for you."

"You saw what he did to me. He's not human. That's the reason he came after me. He thinks I have a secret—a secret that will prove what a monster he really is. He'll do anything to get that. But I won't give it to him, no matter what. My friend didn't talk because he didn't know anything—"

"He did talk," said Weisner.

Gerber stepped in front of Uhlemann's desk and saluted. "General, I've located Sergeant Keller."

"Really, Captain? Finally good news?"

"Yes sir. He is in a prisoner of war camp in the United States."

"My, my. We've been looking under the wrong rocks, haven't we?" said Uhlemann. "Did you learn this from the girl?"

"No sir. I *coerced it* from a friend of hers—a partisan also—who showed up at her place while we surveilled it. Surprisingly, it wasn't too difficult to get it out of him. He had a clear dislike for Keller and seemed happy to deliver him up for sacrifice."

"And the girl?"

"Nothing so far. Still no sign of the documents or the photographs. I haven't gotten it out of her. Not yet."

"What exactly does that mean?"

"She's locked in the cell in the security building, next to my office. I'll make her talk."

"Be sure you do," said Uhlemann. "What about her associate? Any chance of getting that information out of him?"

"...No...General," Gerber sputtered. "Things got complicated with him and ..."

"He's dead?"

"Yes, sir. It was necessary to silence him in order to capture the girl."

"How so?"

"We were set to trap her in her flat. If he'd been able to warn her, she may have fled before we could get to her."

"Too bad. Sounds like he might have been of more use—"

"When I got back to Arnhem," Gerber changed the subject, "I made a few calls to the Reich Security Office in Amsterdam and verified the story with a Captain Forsburg. It turns out the dead man was telling the truth. Keller is, in fact, a prisoner of war. He is in the United States at a camp called Barlow."

"Barlow? What do you know about this camp?"

"Not much so far. It's in the middle of an American desert. Our ranking officer there is a Colonel Erich Hoefer, from a cavalry unit in North Africa, captured in 1942."

"Hoefer, eh? *Afrika Korps*? Perhaps if Colonel Hoefer knows how important this matter is to a Wehrmacht general, he will take care of things for us—particularly if he knows Keller is a traitor. Can we get word to him?"

"I've set the wheels in motion, General. I gave Captain Forsburg specific instructions that he was to do exactly that. Forsburg told me, that until recently, it took about two weeks to get information through *spider-lines* to the prisoner camps in America. Apparently, the only reliable method is through the prisoner mail system. Radio communication is nearly impossible because of the distance."

"It's too bad that he's not in a British camp," said Uhlemann.

"That would be easier. Unfortunately, Keller is about as far away from us as he could possibly be. Forsburg also said that because of the current war situation, systems are breaking down, including the spider-lines. It may take longer than usual for our message to reach Colonel Hoefer, if it gets there at all."

Uhlemann stood and looked out the window. "Captain Gerber, please have another message sent to Colonel Hoefer. Forsburg may code it however necessary. It should be clear that, under no circumstances, should Keller return to German soil—alive."

Taatje asked, "Why am in Arnhem?"

"What do you mean?" said Weisner.

"Why did Gerber bring me here? Why didn't he just finish me off?"

"We were called back from Maarburg. Things are starting to happen."

"Is that why you grabbed your rifle?"

He didn't answer. She tried her first question, again. "Why am I here, *Herr* Weisner?"

"Captain Gerber has detained you." Weisner's shame was clear. "That's his office..." He referred to the closed door down the hallway.

"Mr. Weisner, I can see you're a good man. Please let me go."

Weisner looked up as if he was seeking guidance from heaven. Without meeting Taatje's eyes, he said, "I can't do that." He left.

In September, six months earlier, the German military staved off the Allied assault called Operation Market Garden. The proud Wehrmacht held on to the Netherlands, north of the Rhine. Bulletins from Berlin proclaimed this to be the high-water mark for their enemy, the Allies ill-fated attempt to steal Europe was doomed. The insurrection that started on the beaches of Normandy would now be rectified, and the land-grubbing dogs, Britain and America, would soon be brought to their knees. German losses in France, Belgium, and Holland were being regained. Hitler declared Germany would have *lebensraum*—its rightful land. Its destiny.

The long winter of 1944-45 proved Hitler to be a poor prophet. Though the Germans held the Dutch land north of the Rhine, their other conquests crumbled and fell through their fingers. The Russians steamrolled through Poland and eastern Germany. The western allies slashed into Hitler's *Reich* through Italy and Belgium. Heavy bombers of the RAF and US Army Air Force smashed German cities around the clock.

Germany's day of reckoning had arrived.

12 April, 1945. The assault on Arnhem began. South of the Rhine, the British and Canadian forces massed. Their big artillery opened with a ceaseless bombardment. The city was pummeled with blockbusters and incendiary shells. From above, Spitfires and Typhoons teemed like a swarm of hornets. Bombs pounded away, softening German defenses. A full-scale ground invasion would follow. A horde of infantry and armor would storm over pre-fabbed bridges, perforating the once-impossible Rhine boundary. Beleaguered Arnhem, shattered once, was again the centerpiece of war.

The first artillery shells shattered Arnhem. Uhlemann and Gerber rushed to the window. Black plumes billowed upward, around the city. The river, normally in clear view, was covered in a smoke-shroud. Screaming turbine engines whined above. The wings of a Typhoon appeared out of the overcast sky and swooped toward Van Sloten House. The two officers hit the floor as the plane screamed. Two seconds later, a crushing bomb shook the building from a hundred meters away.

Uhlemann scrambled, grabbed his telephone and began barking orders. Gerber turned to go. "Captain, wait!" yelled Uhlemann. Gerber stopped. Uhlemann worked the phone in a rhythm, hollering at one person after another. Sulfurous smoke sifted through the window.

Uhlemann slammed the phone down. *"Reichsführer* Himmler has given orders to defend Arnhem to the last man—to the death!"

"Sir?"

"Himmler is an ass. Why the Führer chose that goddamned chicken farmer is beyond me. Let *him* come here and fight with the meager defenses he's given us."

Gerber stood silent, afraid to speak to the general's traitorous ranting, though he agreed about Himmler.

The siren atop Van Sloten House was howling. Outside everyone was scrambling. Gerber was desperate to leave Uhlemann's office. No doubt, this building was a primary target and the third floor was no place to linger.

Uhlemann continued. "I've just given the order to set the basement with explosives. If we evacuate this building—and I suspect I'll give that order soon—we can't leave the archives behind." He pointed his finger at Gerber. "But you and I also have some unfinished business here, and we have very little time."

"General?"

Explosive thuds wracked the city. "Captain. Our strategy changes." Uhlemann took a familiar envelope out of the top drawer of his desk. He removed the photographs and plopped them in front of Gerber. "We need to cut our losses, Captain. On your way out, drop these in the incinerator."

"Yes sir. Of course, Keller's set is still out there...somewhere," said Gerber.

"I realize that, you fool." Uhlemann grabbed Gerber's lapels and pushed his face to within inches of Gerber's. "They may never emerge. But in case they do, I have made arrangements for my own well-being after the war. I suggest you do the same."

"What do you mean, sir?"

Uhlemann loosened his grip and looked at Gerber as if he was born yesterday. "Damn it, Captain. Certainly, you've considered the possibility that Keller's documents might *appear* someday. If they do, I do *not* intend to be dragged in front of a Dutch tribunal. If I even get a sniff of that happening, they will not find me. There are SS men who have already put together a system to aid patriots, patriots like you and me. They'll provide new identities and passage out of Europe, if necessary. I've made my arrangements. I suggest you do the same."

"Yes sir."

"Right now you must deal with the young lady in your cell. Any information we could get out of her would be useless now. *Conclude* that matter as soon as you've burned the photographs. Now get moving!"

"Yes sir." Gerber scooped the photos from the desk. As he did so, an image jumped off the paper—that of a woman being led into the barn, the woman he'd singled out that day. The one who escaped. The one who broke his nose. The one who destroyed his eye. The woman in the picture was *same woman* that was now locked in his cell!

Gerber pounded out of the general's office and weaved through the frantic building. The siren continued like a banshee. He raged as he ran down the steps. How stupid he was not to have recognized that woman! He slammed photo-after-photo into the incinerator. He would have his vengeance. The girl would pay dearly. And no one would care how he did it.

Gerber grinned as he fed the flames. As the last photo, that of the Hoobinck woman, slid from his fingers, there was a colossal crash, then a *Whhummp!* The building trembled. A ball of flame hurled outward from its core. Van Sloten House was an inferno.

Taatje had never been this helpless—a canary in a cage. Explosions echoed, some far and some quite near. She shook the bars and pounded her fists on the plaster walls, seeking a weakness. None.

An intense light flashed through the hallway, followed by a deafening explosion, just outside. The walls lurched. Plaster chipped from the ceiling. *Is the building on fire?* She didn't know. *Am I the only one here? Am I about to burn to death?* She screamed.

The door to the outside swung open. Boots ran up the hallway. She threw herself against the iron grate. It was Weisner. Taatje reached through the bars and grabbed at him, but he ran past and barged through the door at end of the hall, Gerber's office. A few seconds later, he returned with a key in his hand.

Weisner unlocked the cell. "Let's get out of here. Run!"

She followed him down the corridor and outside the building, halting on the stone pavement. In front of her was the mansion, billowing smoke. Fire leaped from a hole in its roof. People were running everywhere, some escaping the building, others in the street. Weisner pointed to an opening in the fence that had been blown apart by a bomb. "Go that way, and keep running. You're on your own. Go!" Weisner went in the opposite direction. Soldiers were everywhere. German soldiers. Though Taatje was free from the cell, she was still in the belly of the beast. And defenseless. Since she quit Willem's partisans, she stopped carrying her pistol.

She'd regretted that once already. She wouldn't let that happen again.

She ran back into the building, down the hallway to the room next to her cell—the room from which Weisner and the other soldier had grabbed their rifles. It was a bunk room, six beds double-stacked along the walls. The rifle rack was by the door, empty. At the foot of each bunk were foot lockers. *Maybe a pistol?* The first one was locked, as was the second. But the third foot locker's padlock was dangling freely through the latch. She lifted the lid and rummaged through it with her good hand, as quickly as her fingers could move—clothes, magazines, tooth powder, letters, a shaving kit. At the bottom was a knife in a sheath. Not a military knife—she'd seen plenty of those long bladed weapons during her time in the resistance. This was smaller, probably a personal treasure. She took it from its sheath and thumbed the blade with her good hand. It was sharp. She slipped it in her coat pocket.

She hurried down the hallway. She must find a way through the mayhem. If she could get out of this army compound and make it to the Arnhem streets, she stood a chance. A man appeared in the doorway, blocking her only exit. The first thing she saw was *the eye*. Gerber.

44

Barlow

Abbie hated this place, the Cattlemen's Club. She remembered her first time here, right after Hank became owner of the Jackrabbit. On that visit, she never got past the table nearest the door. Her father-in-law, Mason, *politely* told her, "*Wives* don't sit at the bar except on ladies' night. Why don't you have a seat at this table while Hank and I discuss business?" She did as she was told, sentenced to a narrow, Naugahyde chair, while Hank and the men *discussed business* at the sacred bar. That was seven years ago.

Since then Abbie only came to the club when necessary. Today she returned at Mason's request. *Request* was the nice word for it. More accurately, it was a *summons* by the *king of cattle*. She knew how things worked.

Again, she was the only woman in the place. This time, she didn't *politely* sit at the table. She pulled up a stool at the bar. Abbie was a sole ranch owner—had been since Hank's death. No one was going to deny her a rightful place at Barlow's version of the Round Table. She chose a seat at the far end, away from three men who were jabbering about a *four-point muley-buck* that one of them shot up on the Rim. No desire to join that conversation. They wouldn't let her in even if she did. That didn't matter to her. Only one thing did. She'd be damned if she'd be relegated to that hideous Naugahyde chair again.

The bartender set a bottle of A-1 in front of her. Abbie put down two dimes. She didn't drink beer often, but today it would serve as armor. Mason crossed the room toward her. She could tell he wasn't keen on her choice of seats, but he quickly masked it.

"Good to see ya' little lady."

"Mason." Abbie nodded a greeting. By her own choice, she'd quit calling him *Dad* after Hank was gone.

She recoiled slightly as he gave her a peck on the cheek. "How's my grandson? Haven't seen that boy in a while?"

"Will is doing just fine. Looks more like his dad every day."

The mention of Hank stifled the conversation. Hank had always been the bridge. Abbie's husband—Will's father—Mason's son. Since his death, the new triangle didn't work very well.

"We have some business to discuss," said Mason. "Would you be more comfortable if we sat at the table?"

"No, I'm fine right here."

"Suit yourself." Mason took a seat at the bar and motioned to the bartender.

"I'll get right to the point young lady," said Mason. His tone-of-voice changed, shifting from the *kindly grandfather* to his *king-of-all-ranchers* persona.

"Go on," she said, glad to get to the point.

"I know what's happening. Word down at the stockyards is you only brought in seventeen head so far this spring. Am I hearin' things right?"

"Sounds about right," said Abbie. There was no sense telling him otherwise.

"Your ranch is dyin' on the vine, young lady. No sense having a cattle ranch if you can't get your cattle to market."

He was meddling again. Abbie locked eyes on him.

Mason ignored it. "Look, I know you've got Hector helping you, and he's a damn good foreman, but what have you got besides him? …I'll tell you what you've got…Nothin'! You've got one greenhorn Mexican and three Krauts."

One of the muley-buck drunks had been eavesdropping. He chimed in, "Yeah, we been hearin' about your Krauts. How's business at the *Jackboots-J*? Haw! They drawin' little Hitler mustachios on yer steers?" The threesome roared.

Abbie clenched, ignored them, and drove her finger into the bartop. "Get to the point, Mason."

"Awright. You got two Mexicans and three fuckin' Gerries. Honey, that ain't gonna get the job done."

Mason tipped his beer until it was nearly drained and let out a deep waft as he waited for a response from Abbie. She said nothing but took a swig from her beer, angry fire burning brighter.

Mason rolled on. "Look goddamnit, you've got cattle up in the Bosque that gotta get to the rail head. You can't afford to wait until the fall, like the rest of us."

"I suppose that's my business, not yours."

That gave Mason the opening to play his ace. "That's where you're wrong, young lady." Mason cocked his lips in a mock-grin.

"What are you talking about?"

"How closely have you looked at your deed and ownership agreement? A few years back, when Hank and I were first getting ready to buy up the Ol' Jackrabbit, I wanted to make sure we had some security in the deal. So we went down to Harley Penrod's office in Willcox. He's a lawyer who deals with ranch contracts and the like—."

"Yeah. I know who he is," said Abbie.

"Well then, if you know so much, maybe you know that I still own your cattle—fifty percent of 'em anyway."

Abbie bristled. "What are you talking about, Mason?"

"Where do you think your cattle came from? I gave Hank those cattle to get his ranch started. I never intended to take 'em back. Hell, times have been good for both of us. War-time beef contracts have seen to that."

"Those aren't your cattle anymore. The cattle we're runnin' now are the ones Hank and I bred."

"That may be true. But legally, I own fifty percent of 'em. Take a look through your papers. You'll find the Joint Ownership Agreement signed by both Hank and me in 1938."

"What are you saying, Mason?"

"*What I'm sayin'*—if you're *listenin'*—is that I own half your cattle—and I'm sending my cowboys up into the Bosque in May. So *what I'm sayin'* is that any of your stock that are still mixed in with mine are comin' down the hill. When *my men* get them to the stock-yards, I'll walk away with the check. By the time I've paid them out of your half-share—after all, they'll be doing your work—there won't be much anything left for you."

"You can't do that."

"Sure I can. Take a look at the contract."

"Why Mason? Why would you do this? You don't need any income off of my cattle."

"Because if I don't do something pretty soon, you're gonna run that ranch into the ground. There'll be nothin' left but a foreclosure sign."

Abbie couldn't cover the worry on her face.

Mason's persona softened to *father-knows-best*. Abbie hated that one the most. "Listen. You and I have gone round-and-round about this for nearly three years. I'll tell ya' again. Ranching is no business for a woman. We can avoid this whole big mess if you just deed me the Jackrabbit. I'll send my cowboys in there and get the place back on its feet. It'll be the best thing for you and for my grandson. I've told you before that I'll let you and Will live in your house. Hell, Will is named as my beneficiary. Someday it'll all be his. In the mean time, I'll run the ranch the right way, so it'll still be there by the time Will becomes a man. We can go down to Harley Penrod's office and have the formalities done in no time. What do you say?"

Abbie was caught off-guard. She assumed when she came here she'd hear the same old song from Mason, but this was a new tune. Could it be true? She needed to look over the contract.

Mason prodded. "What do ya' say, young lady?"

Abbie downed the beer and smacked the bottle down on the bar. "No." She pushed back the stool and walked out of the club.

45

The Jackrabbit-J

Pay Day responded easily under Keller's reins. This horse was as good as any he'd ridden in the Netherlands. A well-trained *cow pony*, as Hector called him. Pay Day pranced whenever he was ridden into the corral. The horse was like a kid at Christmas. Somehow Pay Day knew this was what he was bred to do—cut cattle. Keller patted the horse's sleek neck and gave his command, "Hyup. Hyup."

Horse and rider moved into the mass of milling cattle. As they did so, the herd parted. One of the white-faces lagged behind, a steer with a red freckle under its eye. This was Keller's test. Control that steer and keep it from rejoining the others. He spurred Pay Day to a position between Freckle-eye and the rest of the mob.

From outside the railing, Hector hollered orders. This was the pattern every afternoon, as Hector's pupils were put through their paces.

"Head down! Keep his head down!" shouted Hector.

Keller reined Pay Day to the right and swiftly cut off the path of Freckle-eye. When the steer stopped, Keller reined back and Pay Day hit the brakes. Perfect.

"Away. Push her away!" ordered Hector.

Keller rolled his spurs along Pay Day's ribs. The horse eased forward toward Freckle-eye. The steer began to run, trying to skirt around the horse and back to the safety of the herd.

"Bring 'em through," yelled Hector, but Keller was ahead of him. He reined left and kicked his horse into a short burst that cut off the steer. He followed immediately by working Pay Day to and fro. Keller coerced Freckle-eye to the far side of the corral, opposite the herd.

"Keep her there! Keep your horse's head down."

Keller had Pay Day in good position. The steer was stymied. No escape. Again, perfect.

"Move the cow this way. Bump! Bump!"

Keller and Pay Day worked the maneuver without a flaw. "Stop her there," said Hector. "Make your horse face-up." Pay Day was again in perfect position, locked on to the steer and anticipating its next move.

Checkmate.

"Alright. Let her go. Nice job, *hombre*!"

Keller tipped his new hat as he released the puzzled steer. He and the others had been given hand-me-down cowboy hats that Hector had picked up in town. Keller's hat was dusty white with a dipped brim. He liked it. It felt like part of him now, like he shouldn't mount a horse without it. They also wore chaps. Not only were they starting to feel like cowboys, they were starting to look like them, too—save for the *PW* stenciled on their backs.

Abbie had joined Hector at the fence rail. She'd been showing up more frequently to watch their progress. Keller tipped his hat toward her. She didn't turn away this time, as she often did when the Germans came near. Keller couldn't be sure, but she seemed to nod in recognition.

"Keller, come here, *amigo*," said Hector. Keller trotted Pay Day to the corral rail. "You're a good rider. We'll make an Arizona cowboy out of you yet."

"Pay Day is *muy bueno*," said Keller. "Your cow ponies are trained darn good, yes?" Keller's accent was thick and sometimes he struggled to make his words known. But his English was coming together. He savored the challenge of learning it, the *Arizona version* of English.

"You bet. They're darn good horses as long as you don't screw 'em up by talking German to 'em," chuckled Hector. It brought a smile from Abbie, the first Keller had seen.

"Perhaps you teach me how to train cow ponies, too?" said Keller.

Hector said, "You've got plenty to do already. I'm counting on you to get those other greenhorns ready to ride herd. Maybe after round-up, if you're still around, you can help me start training the two-year-old filly. She'll be ready. *Entiendes muchacho?*"

"*Si, amigo*, I understand." said Keller.

"Now, you go work on the other guys. If you can get them to cut a steer half as good as you, it'll be a good day."

Before he left, Keller tipped his hat again. Abbie nodded and touched the brim of her own—no doubt about it this time. Keller smiled and rolled his eyes as he turned Pay Day toward the other side of the corral. This was a good day.

Two days later, Will bounded downhill toward the corral rail to join his mother. Deuce saw him coming and raced up the hill. He ambushed Will with a jumping, wet nose. Then he bolted back to the corral where the action was. The Germans were having another of Hector's lessons.

"Mom, can I do it, too? I've been learnin' to cut cattle."

"Hector's working with the new hands, right now. You'd just be in the way."

"Mommm. I'm getting real good. Aren't I Hector? I can saddle-up Daffy, real quick?" Abbie looked toward Hector, who nodded his approval.

"OK, then," she said. "You do exactly as Hector tells you. You need any help with Daffy?"

"No, I can do it, Mom." He was off, high-tailing it to the barn.

Will was glad his mom didn't worry anymore about him being around the Germans. He liked these guys. They were funny sometimes, especially when Schatz played jokes on Weber, just to get him riled up.

Yesterday while they were working in the barn, Schatz put a horse turd in Weber's hat, which he'd just set down outside a stall. Schatz motioned to Will to keep quiet and play along. Will loved it —a partnership in mischief. When Weber lifted his hat, he nearly plopped the turd on his head before he realized it was there. Schatz and Will broke into hysterics while Weber jabbered at both of them with harsh German words. Will didn't know what Weber was hollering, but that made it all the funnier. The practical joke resulted in a wrestling match in which Weber and Schatz tried to push each other into a wheel barrow of manure. Will joined in on the side of Schatz, two against one. The three grappled toward the horse poop. Soon all three were laughing. There were no winners, but the wheelbarrow got knocked over. Schatz called a truce by offering to clean it up. Will grabbed a second shovel and helped him. After all, it was his joke too. And he learned a great new German word, *Scheisse*.

Schatz was Will's favorite of the three Germans. Schatz seemed like he hadn't quite grown up yet. He reminded Will of the high school baseball players he idolized. He imagined Schatz was what a big brother would be like, if he had one. Weber was OK, but a little older and more serious. So Will hung around with Schatz when he could. Sometimes the German even helped him with his own chores. His mom wasn't to know about that. It was their secret.

Abbie watched as the other two Germans took their turn at cutting. The first fellow, Weber, was still pretty rough, though he was a heck of a lot better than he was a week ago. It just didn't come naturally to him. The other one—the young fellow, Schatz, was doing alright. He had the feel of the horse underneath him and was developing a rider's instincts. He was figuring out where to throw his weight, when to rein-in, and how to roll the spur.

Most surprising to Abbie though was the fact that Hector wasn't saying anything. For the past week, she'd watched him as he cussed and pushed the greenhorns into following his orders. Now Hector was quiet as a church mouse. He was letting Keller take over the teaching. Now it was Keller who barked out commands from the back of his horse, mostly in English. She looked over at Hector who stood a rail section away from her. He glanced back with a reassuring wink. Things were going the way he wanted.

It was Will's turn. He'd quickly saddled Daffy, a dapple mare. This was his chance to show off for the Germans. Hector opened the corral gate for him. Will moved Daffy into the bawling group. He selected a cow and then began cutting her away from the others. Deuce worked the far side of the cow. With shoulders low and short bursts into the cow's flank, the dog kept her close to the rail. Will maneuvered Daffy back, forth, and around, keeping control of the small cow. The cow broke into in a run. Deuce barked and dashed to keep up with the runaway. Will leaned forward, flicking Daffy with his boot heels. As Daffy ran parallel to the cow, Will began to list sideways.

Abbie knew immediately what was happening. Will hadn't cinched his saddle—*tight*. The nine-year-old boy had been in such a hurry to get into the ring that he hadn't double-checked the cinch. Horses can be shrewd. Daffy had probably pulled the old horse-trick of inflating her girth when Will cinched her up, then let out the wind for a more comfortable fit. Will's dad had taught him about this. "You always double-check the cinch. If it ain't snug, you need to tighten it again." Will hadn't done it this time, and now his saddle was loose and inching sideways.

Abbie yelled. "Lean up! Grab her mane!" Will was fighting it—trying to stay in the saddle. But Daffy was darting alongside the cow. If Will stayed in the saddle—and it slid under the horse's belly—he'd get trampled.

"Jump!" Abbie screamed. But her son didn't hear her. He was hanging on to the saddle horn for dear life.

"Jump! Jump!" Soon the others were yelling at him. The saddle was parallel to the ground. Will continued to clamp down on the horn.

Keller saw what was happening and spurred Pay Day into action. He galloped from behind and overtook Daffy on Will's side. Anchoring himself to his saddle horn with his left hand, Keller reached with his right and grabbed Will's shirt collar. He pulled hard. Will, frozen in fear, was locked on to his saddle. Keller yelled his name and simultaneously jerked the boy's collar, "Will!" Will glanced quickly at Keller and released his grip. Keller reined Pay Day into a hard left turn, pulling Will away from the bounding Daffy. As soon as Will was free of the horse, Keller let go, lest he would have pulled the boy into Pay Day's churning legs. Will smacked the powdery earth and tumbled like a rag doll until he flopped to a stop, face down in the dirt. It knocked the wind out of him. He sprang to his knees, panicked, until his chest finally heaved a few spasms. Tears spat from his eyes. Then he burst out with heavy sobs. Deuce was the first one to him, wig-wagging and nosing the boy's face. Will pushed Deuce away, yelling, "Deucey, cut it out, doggone it!" He was alright.

Keller was the last out of the barn. He hiked up the beaten path toward the main house. Spring rains had summoned green shoots from the desert soil. Mesquite buds perfumed the cool air. In the short time he'd been at the Jackrabbit he'd come to like it—the ranch work, the horses, and the desert sunshine. When he was at the ranch, he was far-removed from the war. Even Camp Barlow seemed a world away when he was working cattle. He was on his way to join the others at the picnic table, under the sycamores. That was part of the routine now.

He walked over the rise and saw Brooks' truck parked in the gravel. Brooks was early today—still some time before he hauled them back to camp. Brooks had joined Schatz, Weber, and Will in a game of *flies-up*. American baseball was confusing, but *flies-up* was simple enough. If you caught a *pop-fly*, then it was your turn to bat. The four of them were playing on the flat pitch in front of the bunkhouse. Brooks batted the ball, difficult for a man with only one arm, but he managed alright when Will pitched him easy ones. Brooks smacked one through a gap in the outfield and Weber chased the ball into the mesquite. Keller thought he might join the game. But first, he'd wash-up at the pump.

Abbie was talking to Hector at the picnic table. As Keller lathered his hands, he overheard the conversation.

"Is that the contract?" asked Hector, referring to the papers in Abbie's hand.

"Yeah. This is it," said Abbie.

"So Mason was right, *Señora*?"

"I think so. He worked it out so there's really no difference between a Jackrabbit-J brand and a Circle-J brand."

Keller was aware there were two cattle brands on the ranch.

"Why did he do that?" Hector asked Abbie.

Abbie went through her meeting with Mason earlier in the day. "He said he did it so there would be some security when the Jackrabbit-J got started. I think he wanted to keep Hank tied to him and keep control of our ranch. But the main reason Mason helped us buy this place was so there would be a Johnson ranch bordering the Bosque. Cheap grazing rights."

"But he can't take your cattle and sell them, can he?" said Hector. "I've been around here all my life and I've never heard of anything like that."

Keller toweled his face and sat at the far end of the table. He was able to pick up the stream of the conversation. The owner of the Circle-J cattle, Mrs. Johnson's father-in-law, also claimed owner-ship of the Jackrabbit-J cattle.

"According to Mason, he can round 'em up and sell 'em. If anyone asks questions, he'll just show them the contract," said Abbie. "But let's face it, no one around here questions Mason Johnson about anything."

"But he can't do that," said Hector. "Those aren't his cattle."

"According to this contract they are—fifty percent interest. A Jackrabbit brand works the same way as a Circle brand. He can sell them the same way he sells his own." Abbie looked up from the document. "And it looks like there's nothing I can do about it."

Keller spoke up. "Pardon, but you are saying this man… Mason… says he owns your cows, yes?"

"That's right," said Abbie, surprised that Keller had taken an interest.

"Then…you own his cattle, also? Emmm… *beide zusammen…* both own together? *Eine Partnerschaft.*"

"—a partnership?" said Abbie. She looked toward Hector.

"What do you think? Does this contract mean Mason and I have a partnership?"

"I ain't no lawyer, *Señora*, but that's how it looks to me."

Keller said, "You own his cows too?"

Abbie stood up with renewed energy. She paced around the table as she scanned through the language of the contract. Keller and Hector waited.

She came to a stop and leaned against the sycamore. "You know, Keller, just maybe I do. Maybe I do own that son-of-a-bitch's cattle. This thing works both ways, doesn't it?" She looked up from the papers. "When can you two have these men ready to head up to the Bosque?"

46

Arnhem

Gerber blocked the doorway—Taatje's only escape. The mansion, framed behind him, was a blazing holocaust. His glass eye shimmered in the flames. Nearby, artillery explosions pulsed and shook the earth. Taatje was in Hell. The Devil stood between her and a way out.

His hands held no weapon, though a holster hung from his side. He hadn't seen her yet in the dark corridor. This gave her one opportunity. She charged into him, smashing all her weight into his gut. Gerber gasped as they crashed through the door and into the courtyard.

Taatje rolled once. Twice. Again, scrambling to get away. She rose to her feet and ran toward the breach in the fence, the one Weisner had pointed her toward. She felt as if she was in a desperate dream and couldn't run fast enough. Her knees churned.

If she could clear the fence she'd disappear into the bedlam of the city.

In front of her, a bright light flashed from the opposite side of the street. The bomb's concussion walloped her like a giant hand. She somersaulted backward, head-over-heels, before skidding to a stop. Her ears wailed and her body stung. She attempted to right herself but felt a burning on her right side, below her ribs. Her hand slid to the pain and felt a wet slick. Her fingers were coated with a bright, red smear. Something had ripped into her belly.

She pulled herself to her knees. The building across the street, where the bomb had landed, was a tower of flame.

Keep moving. Toward the gap in the fence. Keep moving.

Running was impossible now. Her head throbbed and her side seared like a hot spike. Consciousness wavered. She moved on instinct—one foot under her, then the other, staggering forward, toward the breach.

She was close now. *Keep moving. Toward the gap.* From behind came a stiff jerk on her jacket. She was yanked backward into someone's grasp—*his* grasp. One arm clamped around her. A Luger pistol appeared. The barrel was buried into her neck.

"You're coming with me, you whore."

She had no strength. No fight. The Devil steered her back, inside the security building. He manhandled her down the hallway, past her cell, her feet barely touching the floor. The pistol barrel jabbed into her neck as he pushed her into his office and kicked the door shut. Gerber muscled Taatje across the room and bent her over his desk, face-down. She glimpsed a paper next to the telephone, a blue sheet that had the words *Sgt. Franz Keller* scribbled at the top. Before she could see more, Gerber slammed her face onto the desk and needled the pistol barrel into the back of her head.

She understood. Gerber would rape her. Then, he'd murder her.

Taatje's strength was gone. Tears welled. Her head was spinning and the fiery wound in her belly burned. For that moment, she wished she could just pass out.

The muzzle bit down. Gerber lifted her skirt over her back and pushed her underpants to the floor. With his boot, he kicked her legs apart. She felt him fumbling with his free hand to loosen his belt. The cold metal buckle jangled against her buttocks. The humiliation lit a spark. *I won't let him do this. I will not!* Her anger built. *He may kill me, but I will not let him do this!*

As Gerber fumbled with his trousers, Taatje slid her left hand—her good hand—inside her jacket pocket. *He didn't notice. Too busy with his own prick.* There it was—the knife, still in its sheath.

He rotated his hips against her. Her left hand manipulated awkwardly to release the button-snap on the sheath. Gerber was getting rougher now and nearly erect. *He will not do this! I will die first!* Inside her pocket, the sheath unsnapped. She flicked it away and grasped the knife in her palm. Gerber began to push.

"What's the matter, can't get it up?"

"Shut your mouth, you Dutch whore!"

"Can't get it hard, can you? You don't even know how to fuck a woman, do you?"

He jerked her hair backward so hard it pulled her face off the desk. "I told you to shut your mouth, slut."

"You only fuck animals, I'll bet—"

Gerber smashed her head into the desk top.

Taatje didn't stop. "Is that why you do it from behind, like a dog? That's what you do. You fuck animals, don't you?"

Gerber took a step back and flung her around. She faced him. He back-handed her with the pistol. The steel barrel smashed her cheek and sent a tremor through her body. But the separation gave her the opening she needed.

She thrust the knife upward into Gerber's crotch. The blade plunged in, behind his balls. Buried to the hilt. He went rigid, his eyes frozen. She jerked the knife forward, slicing into his scrotum, then pulled it out. Blood pumped over her hand. Taatje screamed—a primordial cry, summoned from deep within. In simultaneous motion, she bulled Gerber backward while repositioning the blade. Gerber stumbled over his trousers that were around his ankles. He crashed backward, into the wall, as Taatje pitched into him with full force. The blade jammed into Gerber's chest. He flailed. His body spasmed. Taatje buried her full weight into the blade as she pivoted it back-and-forth inside his chest, stirring to find his heart. She pressed against him until he stopped moving. Then, she let go of the knife and backed away.

Gerber was a motionless heap. A dark pool formed between his legs. The knife handle, slick and red, projected from his chest. He still held the Luger in his hand. Afraid to take it, she grabbed a marble bookend from the shelf. With a terrorizing shriek, she smashed the thing downward onto the monster's forearm. The pistol fell away. She kicked it to the wall, retrieved it, and stepped back—pointing the pistol at Gerber's head.

He didn't move. Taatje's heart was pounding. Her mind raced. *Is he dead? Is he dead?* He had to be, though he still glared at her! That wicked face coaxed a loathing she had never known. She charged forward and kicked the head of the lifeless Nazi.

"Aaaiiiee! You fuck! You lousy fuck!" She frantically kicked and kicked—anywhere she could land a blow. Her screams transformed to a shuddering sob. "You lousy fuck!" She kicked until she had nothing left, her cursing reduced to gasping phrases. "You… perverted fuck…you…you…lousy, perverted…fuck."

She stood and sighted the pistol between Gerber's eyes. If he moved, even slightly, she would empty the chamber. Taatje remained in that posture until gradually her heart eased. Sounds of the bedlam outside again registered, though her attention was still devoted to the evil thing in front of her. It didn't move. It was dead. She had killed her devil.

Taatje put the pistol in her pocket. Balance was difficult. As she moved forward her body listed like a torpedoed ship. The bomb's blast had set off a whistle in her ear. Every part of her hurt. The broken hand and battered knees. Her face, swollen once, had been bashed again, by Gerber. *He can rot in Hell.* But it was the gash on her belly that frightened her. It burned hot inside, like an iron. The puncture wasn't large. The red patch on her blouse had only grown to the size of her hand. She gingerly felt along her back. There was no blood—no hole where the thing might have exited. The shrapnel was still inside her.

Taatje turned to Gerber's desk. Her body swayed as she picked up the blue slip of paper. Her vision played havoc and the German's script was difficult to decipher but it clearly had Franz's name at the top. Below were other bits of information.

Franz Keller
Camp Barlow / America
2ⁿᵈ April adm.
Arizona
Cmdt. Erich Hoefer / Africa Corps / 1942

It made little sense. Her head was still spiraling. She stuffed the slip in her pocket and stumbled, but steadied herself against the desk.

Her cognizance was returning, along with the reality of her circumstances. She was still in the heart of the Nazi compound. The main building, only a dozen meters away, was burning. Outside the fences, the streets of Arnhem were under a rain of hellfire from Allied artillery. If she hoped to live, she must run a gauntlet. Gripping the Luger, she staggered down the hallway, leaving Gerber's corpse behind. Forever.

She entered the courtyard to see Van Sloten House, half-consumed in flames. The siren had ceased, probably destroyed by the blaze. People were rushing frantically, evacuating the building. A group of four officers emerged from the back entry, on the opposite side of the courtyard. The man in the middle was being protected by the others—a large man with an ambling gait. *Unmistakable. Uhlemann!* The big general was escorted into a waiting black sedan, the same car Taatje had memorized from the photographs. Uhlemann and the others piled in. It was moving before the doors were closed, speeding for the front gates that now stood open.

Taatje screamed and ran after the car, but her legs wouldn't respond. She paced forward in a dizzy stagger and lost her footing in the rubble. Tumbling forward, she swung the pistol in the direction of the black car that was speeding away. One shot. Another. And another. The bullets blazed wildly. No chance of hitting the car —let alone Uhlemann. The clip was empty.

The blaze was scalding. Taatje dropped the spent pistol and pulled herself to her feet. She staggered from the inferno, toward the gate. The grounds of Van Sloten House had emptied. The surrounding streets were mantled in a dusty firmament. She rounded the front gate and wobbled over smoking debris, past the torn bodies of Germans. One of the corpses was face-up, mouth wide open. It was Weisner. Taatje choked at the sight and fought back a sob. She barely knew him. Yet, there was little doubt, she would have faced worse horrors without him.

She swayed like a drunk as she made her way into the street. Her mind was a muddle. Instinct told her to put distance between herself and the German compound. She plodded down the middle of the road. Her vision fluttered in and out. She negotiated with her consciousness—willing her feet to stay underneath her. She made it two blocks.

Behind her was an ear-splitting explosion. The basement of Van

Sloten House—the records room—had been laced with dynamite. Simultaneous blasts undermined the three-story building.

Taatje turned in horror to witness the giant mansion fall inward on itself, radiating a roiling shroud of dust. The cobblestone pavement rumbled under Taatje's feet. She panicked at the sight and tried to run. That was more than her body and brain could take. By the third step, she tripped and sprawled to the rugged road.

A cloud of dirt swept down the street as if it was a wave dousing a beach. Gray turned to black. Taatje's lungs convulsed in the cloud. She managed to bury her face inside her blouse and filter the air. The fury of diving airplanes and bombs blasting in the distance continued as she struggled to breathe under the black shroud.

It took a half hour for the cloud to thin. Everything underneath was dusted in gray-brown.

Taatje's shoulder was being shaken. There were voices around her. She groggily comprehended that they were speaking Dutch. Dutch, not German!

A woman's voice. "Miss. Are you alright?" A hand was delicately tugging her arm. "Miss?"

Taatje's eyes opened a crack. They stung from grit and she squeezed them closed again.

A man's voice. "Come on. Let's get her inside."

Taatje slit one eye open and coughed violently. A scene was spinning around her. She made out the figures of two or three people. Firm, masculine hands lifted her off the ground. Her head dangled. A woman's face appeared and said, "Let's get you inside, darling. We'll take care of you." Taatje tried to say something, but the woman's face spun madly. Then, Taatje passed out.

47

The Jackrabbit-J

A *shake-down*. It was a term Hector learned in a letter from his son, Manny. Manny was aboard the USS Twining, a Navy destroyer in the middle of the Pacific. Hector figured Manny's ship was probably one of those that bombarded the hell out of Okinawa a couple weeks ago. He hadn't received a letter in a while. When it would finally come—and it would—Manny wouldn't be able to tell his dad exactly where he was, or what he was doing out there. The Navy was strict about that. But Manny could tell his father other things about Navy life. Hector devoured those descriptions about his son's adventures on the other side of the world. In one letter, Manny told Hector about a *shake-down*, when the Navy sent his ship out to sea for a three-day test to see if the sailors and equipment were ready to join the fight—to be sure everything was *ship-shape*.

Today, Hector was holding a shake-down. Over the past few days, they'd rounded-up about fifty head that had wandered down from the Bosque. The cattle were being held in a corral at Jackrabbit Springs Tank, about three miles south. The cattle needed to be moved to the feed lot on the northwest slope of the ranch. The terrain wasn't too difficult, treeless with no steep arroyos. If it all went right—if these new cowboys remembered their jobs—it would take only a few hours. When all was said-and-done, Hector figured he might have a gambler's chance of pulling off a decent round-up with this bunch of greenhorns.

Hector was the drill instructor today. He gave his recruits different jobs—riding point, drag, and flanks. Every half-hour he switched them around so they'd get some experience in each position. Hector rode from cowboy to cowboy, shouting orders, making sure everything was done right. That everything was *ship-shape*. Manny would be proud.

Hector's crew numbered eight. If they were all seasoned vaqueros, eight would be a good number. But this team didn't resemble a normal crew of cowboys. It was made up of three German prisoners, one illegal Mexican, a one-armed American guard, a woman who might weigh a hundred-ten-soaking-wet, her nine-year-old boy…and himself. Hector had his work cut out.

As he rode the herd, he spent most of his time with the weakest riders. Mostly Weber. Weber still didn't have the feel of a horse. Hector worked him over. "Keep your butt planted in the saddle, *amigo*. Toes on the stirrups! Move *with* the horse. You keep bouncing like that and your butt'll catch fire." He doubted Weber could react in the clutch—that he could cut off a bolting cow or ride swiftly to the front of a spooked herd. He shook his head and moved on.

Brooks was the other guy who concerned him. Unlike Weber, Brooks was getting to be pretty good in a saddle, but Hector was still trying to figure out how to deal with the fact that the man had only one arm. Brooks could easily operate the reins, but he didn't have the other arm for balance, something cowboys just take for granted. And he didn't have an off-hand to anchor himself in the saddle if things got dicey. Brooks, more than Weber, posed the greatest risk of falling off his horse—the biggest danger in this line of work.

No second thoughts about the other two. Heck, Keller was one of the best ranch-hands Hector had ever hired. He just needed more experience. And Schatz was a natural. Hector figured he'd hire either one of those two guys if they ever came looking for a job. He laughed at the thought. *What are the chances of a German ever lookin' for a job as a cowboy? This war has turned the world crazy.*

It was an hour into the drive and the cattle were settling in. They were a little jumpy when things started out, but now the cows and the cowboys had lulled into a methodical migration. Hector was on the far side of the herd. His eyes settled on the flank of a calf ambling along next to him. It wore the *Circle-J* brand. About half these cattle had that brand. *Señora* Johnson had told Hector not to cut those cattle out of the herd as they normally would. She didn't say *exactly* why. She was sort of like the Navy in that regard—not telling you more than you need to know. Hector wasn't *exactly* sure what she was planning, but it was obvious she was preparing to fight her own war.

Keller rode Pay Day to the back of the herd. He found Mrs. Johnson back there following the white-face Herefords along their dusty path. She'd spent most of her time riding back there, not working the herd. Keller heard Hector tell her at the onset to "lay back and let the new boys see what they can do." Today, she was merely an observer.

Keller tipped his hat and left some space between them. He thought it was interesting the way she ran her ranch. No doubt, she was the boss. But she let Hector make the decisions that involved ranch work. It connected well to Keller's military experience. The best officers were the ones who listened to their sergeants. The worst ones were the pompous know-it-alls. He'd seen plenty of both types in the *Wehrmacht*.

To his surprise, Abbie rode up beside him. Chief and Pay Day were walking neck-and-neck.

"I never properly thanked you for the other day," she said, "when you saved Will."

"He is a good boy," said Keller, feeling a bit awkward. He'd never had a true conversation with the quiet woman.

"Yes he is, but he made a mistake and learned a lesson by it—luckily without getting himself killed. Thanks to you."

Keller grinned. "He will check for a tight cinch next time, I think."

Abbie said with a mother's smile, "Oh yes, he definitely will."

Keller assumed these formalities had ended the conversation, but Abbie didn't ride away. She kept her horse close as they weaved through some gnarly chaparral.

"You're a good rider, Keller. You must have grown up around horses?" said Abbie.

"When I was a boy, I went to Netherland in summers ... to visit my mother's family. There, I rode horses."

"You must have ridden a lot."

"Yes. I like riding. But it is different there than here."

"How?"

Keller considered the question and how to answer it. His English was holding up well. "Saddles are different. No horn. Riding is different." He demonstrated the up and down cant of a European rider, glad that none of the other men were within sight. "Horses are bigger there also."

"Bigger?"

"Yes, a little."

"Did your family own horses?"

"No. Not family. My *Freundin*…uh…girlfriend."

"Girlfriend? Is she still there? Waiting for you?"

Keller looked away. To Abbie, he probably looked embarrassed. But it wasn't that. He was caught off guard because he didn't know the answer. Two months earlier, when he'd been with Taatje, their love reignited. But would Taatje have an interest in him when the war ended? Or would his soldiers' stripes forever separate them? He didn't know.

"I'm sorry," said Abbie. "It's none of my business."

Keller fought for the words. "I…I…do not know if she will be there…when I return." He looked up at Abbie to see a reassuring smile.

"I'm sure she will be," said Abbie. "What's her name?"

"Taatje."

Abbie repeated it. "Tot-yuh. Tot-yuh. That's a nice name. Tell me about her."

Keller was surprised by Abbie's interest. "She is very smart. Very pretty. Dark… *glänzendes* … ehh .. shine … shining hair. Big, big brown eyes." He smiled when he described her eyes.

"She sounds beautiful," Abbie said. "She'll be there for you, Keller. She'll be there."

Abbie gave Chief a little nudge with her spur and cantered around the left flank of the herd. Keller fixed his gaze on her until her hat disappeared over the slope.

The bunkhouse was cool in the night air. Hector pulled the chain that hung from the lone light bulb. He felt his way gingerly, with bare feet through the darkness, until he reached his bed and eased down on top of the blanket. Bedsprings squeaked under his weight. Umberto was already asleep in his bunk on the opposite side of the room. His gargling snore had taken Hector a while to get used to it, but he was oblivious now. The rest of the beds, a half-dozen, were empty.

This time of year, the *barracón* was normally filled with high-spirited cowboys. Ranch hands came and went with the seasons, and springtime was busy—second only to fall round-up. This time of the year, each bunk would be spoken-for. Hector normally hired about an even number Mexicans and Whites. The fellows were usually young and that kept the place moving. Cussing, poker, drunkenness, farting, practical jokes, fighting—all brought the bunkhouse to life at the end of a day. English and Spanish flew back and forth over each other, sometimes all mixed together. Hector was not only the boss; he was also their *father* and was constantly keeping the young guys in line. "Knock it off. *Duérmanse pendejos!*" He had their respect and they didn't cross him. The few that did found themselves walking down the road with a cut paycheck.

Hector missed the springtime ritual. This year, his hired hands slept in a different bunkhouse, the POW camp. *Strange.* The thought of his German cowboys made him worry. In the past, he always knew his men were good horsemen and could handle what-ever surprises were thrown at them. But today, his new crew had only managed to move a herd of fifty head across an easy stretch of three miles. They still had a lot to learn and a lot of ground to cover.

He lay on his back, staring at the ceiling to the music of Umber-to's guttural symphony. He thought about Manny and wondered what he was doing at this moment in the middle of the Pacific. Manny was one of the best cow hands the Jackrabbit had ever seen.

Hector was sure that he was also one of the best sailors the USS Twining had ever seen. He wished Manny was in Europe fighting the Germans rather than on the other side of the world fighting the Japs. The war against the Germans was almost over. The war against the Japanese might go on forever. He worried about his son. He had a lot to worry about.

48

Camp Barlow

Four weeks ago Keller was herded out of a cattle car and marched to Camp Barlow. He and the other POWs were afraid of what awaited them, vengeance by the Americans. But that was not the case. The rigors and discipline were similar to a German army camp. Food, health, and hygiene were superior here, and the recreational opportunities were better than any they'd experienced.

Camp sports were popular—volleyball, handball, gymnastics, and the favorite, soccer. Intra-camp league standings posted daily. The prisoners had a camp orchestra, choir, and theater troupe. Newspapers were available in German and English, including the camp newspaper, *Der Wachtung—The Watch Tower*. The library held over six thousand volumes, a mix of English and German texts.

The most popular program was education. Courses were taught by prisoners, many of whom were qualified to teach in German schools and universities. One camp building was a dedicated academy, containing eight classrooms—each with a chalkboard, lectern, and pine tables. Prisoners were encouraged to take courses that earned them college credit at several German universities. Classes included German Literature, Mathematics, History, Commerce, and Agriculture of the American Southwest. The most attended course was English Language.

Keller signed up for an English course when he arrived at Camp Barlow. His English skill was beyond the beginners' level, so his professor transferred him to an advanced class. The class met in the evenings, making it accessible to students like Keller, who worked in the labor program during the day.

Keller had been sitting in a metal chair for an hour and a half. His legs were cramping. It had been a long day. His work at the Jackrabbit-J had included fence repairs, a first lesson in branding cattle, and three hours in the saddle. Now he was enduring a lesson in English verb conjugation. He was fighting to stay awake and anxious to get to his bunk for some much-needed sleep. Tomorrow he needed to be rested for whatever tortures Hector had in mind. At 8:30 PM the class finally ended. Students stood to leave when an American officer came through the door. The prisoners snapped to attention.

He addressed the professor. "Lieutenant, I'm looking for Sergeant Franz Keller."

The professor pointed him out.

"Sergeant Keller, you speak English?"

"Yes, sir."

"You're working a labor detail at the Jackrabbit-J Ranch. Correct?"

"Yes sir."

"Stick around. I need to talk to you." The American turned to the teacher. "Lieutenant, you may dismiss the others."

As the other students were leaving, the American major said, "Sergeant Keller, there's been a request for your labor crew to be part of three-day cattle round-up. You're the highest ranking man in that crew. I have some questions." When the others had left the room, the American shut the door.

He said, "Sergeant, have a seat. I'm Major Davenport, the XO here at Camp Barlow."

Keller knew who he was, the number-two man at the camp. "Is there anything wrong with the request, Major?"

"No, Sergeant. There's no problem. Private Brooks will be going with you. That's one guard for three prisoners. No problem there. Your crew will be cleared for the round-up. Wish I could go."

"Sir, but you wish to speak to me. Why?"

"Sergeant, I just used that as an excuse to talk to you in private —without raising suspicion. There's something I need to know about and I don't want anyone else listening."

"Sir?"

"Sergeant Keller, you were posted in the Netherlands when you were captured, correct?

"Heil Hitler!"

"Heil Hitler! At ease Müller. Take a seat," said Schwering.

Schwering had summoned Müller to *Officers' Country*—the German officers' sector at the north end of Compound A. These barracks were set off from the enlisted prisoners. The bunks were more spacious. Each officer had a desk. Hoefer and Schwering had private offices. There was also an officers' BX—a small general store —that carried better items than the larger store used by the enlisted prisoners. Barlow had a cozier standard than most POW camps. Colonel Riley believed if he kept the German officers happy, he wouldn't have many problems to deal with.

The day was warm. A dry breeze carried the perfume of orange blossoms from nearby orchards. Müller sat opposite Schwering at a table in the *beer garden*. A bottle of A-1 and a glass were waiting for him. "It is an honor for you to have invited me here, Major Schwering," said Müller.

The beer garden was the pride of the Germans at Camp Barlow. It was situated in front of the officers' BX—a brick patio, adorned with carved "Black Forest" tables and benches. Each table had a canvas umbrella to ward off the Arizona sun. A dark-stained picket fence lined the area, complete with two colorful Bavarian-style flower boxes on either side of the entry arbor. It had all been built in the prison workshop. Though the beer garden was off limits to the enlisted ranks, it was clearly visible from the quadrangle and was a visual comfort to the homesick soldiers. There was a camp myth about it. If you stood in the center of the quad and stared at the beer garden long enough, you would see mirages of beer hall maidens toting steins of pilsner—and wearing low-cleavage *dirndls.*

"Sergeant Müller, have you heard the latest news?" asked Schwering.

"Yes, Major, I've seen the American newspapers. May I speak freely, sir?"

"Of course, sergeant."

"If we can believe the American journalists, the Allies are squeezing Germany from all sides."

"Unfortunate, but true. Colonel Hoefer and I have heard those reports. They are confirmed by our sources too."

Müller said, "Then the Fatherland is defeated, or nearly so?"

Schwering removed his glasses and dabbed his perspiring brow with a handkerchief. "You use the word *defeat*, Sergeant. To the world, it will appear that Germany is defeated. More accurately, however, this is but a *setback*. It happened to us before, in 1918, but we were resurrected by Adolf Hitler. We will rise again, Sergeant Müller. That is where you and I come in."

"Sir?"

"You haven't touched your beer, Sergeant." Schwering reached across the table and poured Müller's beer into the glass. "The next few years will be dark times for the National Socialist movement, to be sure. But thanks to many forward-thinking party members, the machinery will remain in place. We will rise from these ashes, stronger than ever." Schwering raised his glass. "To the Third Reich."

Müller matched his glass in the toast. "*Prosit.*"

"*Prosit.*" Each man took a lengthy sip. "New leaders will emerge. They will rise through the ranks. Their stature, in the new order, will be determined by their actions and their patriotism during *this* war, this struggle! Sergeant Müller, you and I are two patriots who should be in middle of that rebirth."

"I hope you are right, Major."

Schwering continued. "We will be judged by what we have accomplished here, at this sorry outpost in America. With the war drawing to an end, there is the danger of morale and discipline deteriorating. Sergeant, we may be here for quite a while after the armistice—months, perhaps a year—or more. It will be our duty, yours and mine, to see that a breakdown does not occur. We will keep order and keep the ideals of the Führer alive."

"I agree, Major."

"Yes. Yes indeed," said Schwering. "I have no doubt that the cause of National Socialism will rise again, this time quickly. I don't intend to be watching the parade. My aim is to be in the parade, preferably at the front. Are you with me, Sergeant?"

"Absolutely, sir."

"A toast to the future. *Prosit.*"

"*Prosit.*"

Davenport moved his chair a few feet from Keller. "Sergeant, I'm sure you're familiar with the term *spider lines*, *Spinne Fäden*? I hope I didn't butcher the pronunciation."

Keller was backed in a corner. This was the situation he wanted to avoid. He met Davenport's eyes but gave no response.

"I really didn't expect to get answers, at least not yet." Davenport took a pack of Lucky Strikes from his shirt pocket. "Cigarette, Sergeant?" Keller declined. Davenport lit his own. "Sergeant, the spider lines have been operating ever since we started putting you POWs here in the states. It's a pretty interesting system. Your guys send coded messages to ships off the American shore. The ships radio those messages and the signals are picked up in camps on the East Coast. Then the messages are re-coded and usually sent through the mailrooms to all the POW camps around the country. Since the US Army sees fit to assign prisoners to work in mail-rooms—." Davenport shook his head at the ignorance of Army policy. "—you guys have developed quite a system. And you Germans are damn good at it, miles ahead of the Italians or Japanese."

Keller said. "Major, I do not work in the mailroom."

"No, you don't. Here's the point, Sergeant. Your name popped up in a message that our boys intercepted at Camp Lee in Virginia. The message was being sent here, to Barlow. Sergeant, are you somehow associated with a General named Uhlemann?"

Keller's heart nearly jumped out of his chest. His face flushed.

"I'll take that as a *yes*," said Davenport. "Look, the message said that you were a traitor, that you defied this great general, and that you are still a threat to disclose classified information to the enemy."

"Those are lies," said Keller. "I have no information for you."

Davenport flicked his cigarette ash into the trash can and leaned on the podium. "No, Sergeant Keller, you misunderstand me. I don't want any military secrets from you. Hell, the war over there is damn near over."

"What then do you wish, Major?"

"To protect you, Sergeant. You see, that message also said that you were not to return to Germany—alive."

Keller's worst fears were being realized. He'd hoped to lay low —that his situation in Arnhem wouldn't follow him here. Then he'd return to Europe after the war and help Taatje expose Uhlemann and the massacre. In that scenario, Keller thought he could be vindicated. Now he knew it would never play out that way. With or without a war, the Nazis would eliminate their enemies. And he was one.

Davenport said, "Sergeant, I'm investigating the murders of two German soldiers here at Camp Barlow. Those two men were in the same situation as you. You can help me and help yourself at the same time." He waited for a response, but Keller said nothing. "Look son, we may have intercepted the last message, but they won't stop there. When that message does get through, you'll be next in line."

After a long pause, Keller said, "What do you want from me?"

"You can tell me what you know about a group called *The Circle*. You help me to understand what's going on right here at Barlow— and we'll protect you."

Keller heard about the Circle the first day he arrived. Their presence was made clear at Schwering's *welcome* speech. Rumors about their terror flew around the barracks every day. "How can you help me?" said Keller.

"We can take you into custody. We can move you to another camp, give you a new identity."

Davenport sounded like an officer who knew what he was he was doing. It seemed like an honest proposal, and Davenport might deliver. Keller was tempted, but since his capture he'd observed a general lack of efficiency from the American garrison. If he told Davenport anything about the Circle, there would be no turning back and he'd be placing his neck upon the block if his American protection broke down. He weighed his odds. Who ran a tighter machine… the Americans…or the Circle? Keller put his money on the Circle.

Keller said, "I'm sorry Major, I know nothing. I cannot help you."

49

Outside Arnhem

A ruckus came from another room. Shouting. Gleeful voices. A male momentarily drowned out the others, chortling as if he'd just won a gold medal. Then others picked up a frenzied chant. A booming tenor sang *Het Wilhelmus*, the Netherlands national anthem. The other voices joined in.

William of Nassau, scion
Of a Dutch and ancient line,
I dedicate undying
Faith to this land of mine.

The giddy celebration awakened Taatje. She mouthed the lyrics in a hoarse whisper. *Het Wilhelmus* hadn't been sung openly for five years—not with its true lyrics—though the Nazis had bastardized it with their own. But now Taatje heard the rightful verses—patriotic lyrics. It was beautiful. Her lips moved to the sing-along though her voice had run out.

I've ever tried to live in
The fear of God's command
And therefore I've been driven,
From people, home, and land…

Taatje had been confined to this bed for three weeks. The makeshift hospital was set up in a schoolhouse outside of Arnhem—a building that had survived the battle. Her bed was one of four that occupied a classroom. She heard familiar footsteps clop into the room, Cecile's, the kind woman who had been nursing her through her ordeal.

"I see you are awake," said Cecile. She sat on the side of the bed and held Taatje's hand. "How are you feeling?"

Taatje mouthed the words dryly, "Ceceeel Weeel." She rhymed her friend's name in a playful manner. Her voice was shallow but clear. She pried open her eyes to catch Cecile's grin.

Cecile Wijl wasn't a nurse by vocation. She was a bookkeeper who, like most Dutch, was displaced during the war. Three weeks earlier, the British and Canadian armies liberated Arnhem. The carnage was heavy among the citizens and the military. Cecile helped to organize the little hospital ward in Hoenderloo, a village outside Arnhem. Professional medical help was in short supply. A few Red Cross doctors and nurses came and went from the schoolhouse infirmary, but most of the care was up to volunteers like Cecile.

Cecile was there when Taatje arrived, the day after the battle ended. Taatje was brought to the infirmary by an Arnhem couple who'd found her lying in the street. The couple had kept the unconscious girl in their apartment until the fighting stopped. Then they brought her there. Cecile had never seen such a battered woman—

not one that was still alive. She took a special interest in Taatje and gave her as much attention as she could.

During Taatje's second week, her condition improved. Bouts of unconsciousness had all but disappeared. The savage swelling on her face subsided. Through the yellow and purple bruises, evidence of a beautiful young woman emerged. Taatje's broken finger had been re-set and the hole under her ribs was dressed and sutured. The two women became friends. Cecile stole time to sit at Taatje's bedside. Taatje loved hearing stories about Cecile's eight-year-old daughter, whose grandmother cared for her while Cecile worked in the ward. Though Cecile was a few years older than Taatje, they were close enough in age to share stories about things that happened in their lives before the war—sometimes silly school-girl stories that got both women laughing. How long had it been since Taatje had laughed? She longed for Cecile's visits and those happy conversations.

In her third week, however, Taatje developed a fever and it was getting worse. As the fever climbed she spent more and more time in comatose sleep. Lucid moments were becoming infrequent. Something was taking over her body—something that Cecile, despite regular ministrations, was not able to cure.

"Cecile, why is everyone singing?"

"Wonderful news today, dear Taatje. Hitler is dead!" Taatje's eyes widened. "It's true. The coward killed himself before the Russians got to him."

"…hope he burns in Hell," rasped Taatje.

"Oh, I'm sure he's there already, giving Satan lessons." Cecile wiped Taatje's face with a damp cloth.

Taatje snickered, but the throbbing fever cut to the quick. "What day is it?"

"Wednesday."

"What date?"

"May 2nd. Why?"

"I want to remember the day this damned war ended."

Cecile said, "I guess Hitler's been dead for a few days, though it didn't make the news until today. But the Nazis say they will continue fighting—though who knows how they plan to do it? They don't have a country left to rule. According to the radio, this whole thing should be over very soon. Wonderful news. Eh, luv?" Cecile wrung out the washcloth and draped it over the tin basin.

Taatje's mind was already elsewhere. "Wednesday? The last time I asked you ... it was Monday, wasn't it?" Cecile nodded. "Seems like yesterday. I've been losing time. Where is it going?"

Taatje began coughing—a spasm that came from deep in her lungs. Cecile held her hand until Taatje finally caught her breath. Cecile prepared a syringe of sulfa.

"What about me, Cecile? What's wrong?"

"You'll be fine, luv. Just keep eating and you'll get your strength back in no time. Roll a little the other way, dear."

Taatje rocked to one side and lifted her nightshirt. Cecile inserted the hypodermic.

Taatje winced at the painful needle. "No Cecile, something's wrong. I'm getting worse, aren't I?"

Cecile stuttered. "There's no pulling the wool over your eyes. There was a doctor here yesterday from the Swedish Red Cross. You were in a deep sleep. I stayed with him while he examined you."

"Tell me," said Taatje, rolling back to face her friend.

"That hole in your side has created some problems. The doctor thinks you have sepsis, an infection in your blood. Your blood pressure has dropped down so your blood isn't feeding enough oxygen through your body. Your organs are having a hard time fighting it off."

"Am I going to die?"

"Let's pray not, luv."

50

Hamburg

The document appeared to be authentic, pressed with an official stamp and displaying a convincing signature of authority. The description of the holder was that of a large man, 188 centimeters in height, a weight of 109 kilograms. His birth date was 27 July 1898, making him forty-six years old. His occupation was listed as *Industrial Manager*. His name was typed at the top of the first page, Otto Schröder, from Hamburg.

A fellow with a thin mustache passed the papers to the large man. They both wore business suits. The shorter man said, "These documents should be all you need until you get to Vienna. Once you're there, arrangements will be made to supply you with permanent records—a birth certificate, employment dossiers, and so forth. Is the raincoat satisfactory?"

"Yes, it fits quite well."

"Everything is secure?" Inside the waist lining of the coat were hidden compartments—pockets that held two stacks of equal value, Swiss Francs and American dollars. There was enough cash to purchase a nice Alpine chalet or a small Mediterranean yacht.

The large man nodded his approval and said, "Getting from the North of Germany to Vienna will be difficult, yes?"

"No doubt. Our enemies have taken control of nearly everything. What they don't have yet, they will, within the week. Much of how you get to Vienna will be determined by how the Americans and British control the roads and rail lines. How you get there? —you'll have to invent that as you go."

"Piss on the Brits. Those fucking Americans too," said the large man.

"Just stay to the West as you make your way into Bavaria, then on to Austria. Don't take a short cut by going through the East. The Russians control the East. You want to stay away from those barbaric assholes. You've memorized your contacts in Cologne, Heidelberg, and Munich. Right?"

"Correct."

"Rely on those contacts to help you along the way. It might take a few weeks to work your route to Vienna. Things are unpredictable now."

"Vienna? Is it really necessary to go to Vienna? I never liked the Austrians—a bunch God-forsaken philistines."

"Afraid so. The system goes through Austria now. It has since last year when the Balkans blew up in our faces. The SS put it together and they've already delivered several of our fellow countrymen to safe havens. They're giving priority to officers like you—those that will face criminal charges. They'll take care of you. Probably get you to Spain or Egypt. There are also rumors that a few South American countries will be opening their doors— provide our people with asylum and new identity. Argentina is supposed to be a beautiful place. Lots of Germans there already."

"Good. I don't speak Spanish."

"Vienna is the jumping off point. So, yes, you must get there. Don't worry, it's a big city. You'll be able to get lost in the crowd, General Uhlemann."

"No, no. It's not *General* Uhlemann anymore. The name is *Mister* Otto Schröder.

"Of course. Have a safe journey, Mr. Schröder."

51

Outside Arnhem

Cecile was hopeful. Taatje had been awake for over an hour, her greatest duration in five days. Taatje was a tough, young woman. Maybe she had enough fight in her to beat this horrible infection, though the doctor hadn't been optimistic.

The infirmary had only one wheelchair. At Taatje's insistence, Cecile had taken her to the toilet rather than use the dreadful bedpan. Stubbornness was a good sign, but there were also discouraging omens. Taatje had been unable to urinate and the transfer from wheelchair to toilet, and back, had nearly worn her out.

"Please take me somewhere…where you and I can talk…alone." Taatje's voice was rasping and labored. Her lungs were bubbling.

"No. Let's get you back to bed. We can talk there."

Taatje grabbed Cecile's sweater and pulled it toward her. "Somewhere alone…just you and me…please…*Ceceel Weeel.*"

This was against Cecile's judgment, but there was a heavy

weight on Taatje's mind. "Very well, luv. But only for a few minutes. I know just the place."

Cecile pushed the wheelchair down the main corridor and out the front door of the former school house to the concrete porch. "Here we are," said Cecile. "Let's get some fresh air. We bring patients out here all the time."

It was a warm, spring day. Taatje hadn't felt sunshine in so long. It seemed like a lifetime ago. There was evidence of war in every direction—scarred buildings and burnt trees. But neither woman would see fit to comment on that. That was in the past and done. It seemed better to embrace the sun and the fragrance of hyacinths on the breeze. Cecile blocked the wheelchair and positioned herself closely on the bench, opposite Taatje.

"Now, what is it luv?" said Cecile. "Must be mighty important."

Taatje fumbled in her pocket and pulled out a rumpled piece of blue paper. Cecile had witnessed her taking the paper from her bedside drawer a few minutes earlier as they prepared to make the trip to the toilet. At that time, Cecile said nothing. In the short time she'd known Taatje, she learned this young lady had a private side —a personal story she protected like a fortress. Taatje was about to lower the drawbridge.

"Cecile…if I die…"

"Don't talk that way, darling. I'm sure you'll be up and—"

Taatje leaned forward, grabbed Cecile's wrist and squeezed hard. The message was clear. *Cut the act. You know—and I know—that I'm dying.*

"Of course, luv. Go on."

Taatje's voice gurgled. "If I die …You must do something for me … I need you … to promise." Taatje pushed the blue paper into Cecile's hand.

"I promise," said Cecile. She leaned in, determined not to miss a word.

52

Exhaust billowed from the old Chevy as it chortled through the intersection of Lawton and Center—the only stop sign in Barlow. The truck pulled a low flatbed trailer—empty now, as it rattled behind. Hector, Umberto, and Brooks were squeezed into the cab. The three Germans sat in the truck bed, propped against the wood rails. This was their first venture into town. The ride into the Bosque was three days away and they were here for supplies. Hector circled the truck to a stop in front of Hooper's Feed and Livery.

Gerald Hooper was on the porch, balancing a sign on top of a pile of burlap bags.

OATS 80 lb. BAGS
20% OFF

Hooper recognized Hank Johnson's old pickup. Six men piled out. Hooper greeted the one he knew. "Hector Cruz. How the hell're ya' doin'?"

"Can't complain, Gerry." Hector stepped up to the shaded porch and shook Hooper's hand.

"What's this you got here, Hector? You runnin' a taxi service for Kamp Kraut?"

"Naw. These Krauts are working on the ranch," said Hector. "This is Private Brooks, their guard." Brooks stepped up, extending his left and only hand to Hooper.

Umberto signaled the Germans to hang out by the truck with him—a quick lesson in American culture. Umberto was brown-skinned labor. He knew his place. The Germans needed to follow his lead.

"Yeah, I heard about the *Jackboots-J*. Guess everybody's got to get into the act," said Hooper. "How much longer you going to have 'em? War's gotta be over pretty damn quick now that the Russkis killed that son-of-a-bitch Hitler."

"No idea," said Brooks. "Army ain't telling us much. Might have to keep this camp going until we beat the Japs too."

Hector said, "Here's a list of the stuff we need. These guys will load it up for you."

"You got a check for me, Hector? You know, I still haven't been paid for last month."

"...Mrs. Johnson wondered if you could hold on for another week, until we bring some steers down from the Bosque."

Hooper rubbed the back of his neck. "Yeah, *awright*. I suppose. She's always paid her bills. But I'm gonna need that payment next week."

"Thanks Gerry, Mrs. Johnson will appreciate it."

"OK. Bring your truck around back. I'll meet you there." Hooper disappeared through the store.

Hector said to Brooks, "I'm going to take Keller with me. The other three can load up the trailer."

"Uhh. I'm really not supposed to let any of the prisoners out of my sight while we're in town," said Brooks.

"C'mon *amigo*. You leave these guys alone with me every other day. No one's gonna run away."

"I know that, but..."

"He'll be with me, Brooks. I'll shoot him if he tries to escape." Hector snickered.

"Shit ... How long?"

"You guys can pick us up in an hour and a half. We'll be at Yolanda's. Umberto will show you where it is. Keys are in the truck." Hector called over to Umberto, "*Recoja a nosostros en la Cantina de Yolanda a las 3.*" Umberto chuckled.

Hector said, "Keller, *amigo*. You come with me. Let's take a walk." Hector started in the direction they came. Keller taxed his bad leg to catch up.

They walked along the dirt shoulder of Lawton Road, Barlow's main street. The road was named for Barlow's historic hero, Captain Henry Lawton, who captured Geronimo not far from here. That was in 1886. The local legend proclaimed Lawton's *clearance of the Chiricahua Apaches* made the land *safe* for settlers.

Lawton Road was a widened section of Route 81, the highway that paralleled the railroad. The highway and the rail spur ran south-to-north through town. There was no railroad station in the town of Barlow. The only stopping point for the trains was at the grain silos, four miles south of town, and the stockyards, two miles north.

"Keller, I'm counting on you," said Hector.

"For what?"

"We're heading up into the Bosque in a couple days. You're the best rider I got. That means that you're gonna be riding up at the head of the herd, while I'm circling around—checking on the greenhorns. It'll be your job to keep the herd under control. Keep 'em from getting spooky and runnin' wild. You need to be their brain. Can you do it?"

"Yes. Hell yes, *amigo*. I can do it."

Hector grinned. "You'd better, or there'll be nothin' left of you but a greasy spot on the trail."

They'd walked three blocks to the intersection of Lawton and Center Street, the middle of town. Here the businesses huddled closer together. They clopped along the boardwalk in front of *Johnny P's Bar & Grill*. Johnny P's had no windows, just sun-bleached siding with signs posted at eye level advertising Schlitz, Coors, and A-1 beer. A chalkboard next to the front door enticed customers with today's special—*Hamburgers 19¢.* Another sign was nailed next to it, this one hand-painted.

NO MEXICANS

Keller pointed at the sign and looked to Hector for an explanation.

"That's just the way it is," said Hector.

"Why?" said Keller.

"Cuz it's always been that way, I guess."

"And you? Does this mean *you*? Are you *Mexican*?"

"I suppose the answer is *yes*—and *no*," said Hector. "I was born in my grandmother's house, about a mile from here. So I'm American. Cut me, and I bleed red, white, and blue." Hector laughed. "But I'm a Mexican, too—brown skin, *amigo*. It don't wash off."

Keller stopped and pointed at the door to the bar. "Can you go in there? To Johnny P's? Drink beer?"

"Only if I was *loco*," said Hector, spinning a crazy finger around his ear.

"What would they do?" asked Keller.

"Probably the same thing they'd do to you. Krauts. Mexicans.

All the same in there. C'mon Keller. Keep walkin'. You ask too many stupid questions."

They turned the corner onto Center Street. The railroad tracks were just ahead.

"Where do these rails go?" asked Keller.

"Why, you thinking of becoming a hobo?" laughed Hector. Again, Keller was confused. Hector let it go. "The tracks head down to Willcox. From there they hook up with the Southern Pacific. A *big* railroad. Head west on that, and it goes to California and all the way to the Pacific Ocean. Go east, and you're in New Mexico."

"*New* Mexico?" asked Keller.

"Yeah. *New* Mexico is a state, just like Arizona. It's about 60 miles that way. *Old* Mexico is a country. It's about 60 miles that way. Confused yet?"

A rusted-out truck turned onto Center. Hector recognized it and yelled out. "*Oye Pedro! ¿Nos da un paseo, por favor?*"

The truck stopped. "*Claro Héctor. En la parte trasera.*"

"C'mon. I got us a ride," said Hector.

"Where are we going?"

"To church, *amigo*. I'm taking you to church." Hector laughed, taking pleasure again in confounding the greenhorn.

They climbed into the bed of Pedro's pickup. It sputtered and slowed as it jiggled over the tracks. Hector said to Keller, "Welcome to San Ignacio. The whites call it *Nacho*. This is where the Mexicans live."

"A different town?" asked Keller.

"*Yes…and no,*" said Hector.

Keller rolled his eyes—no straight answers.

Hector said, "Same town. Same mayor. Same sheriff. But if you're white, you live back over there. If you're Mexican, you live over here. Make sense?"

Keller nodded. Pedro's truck kicked up a fantail of dust. Keller looked around. The town changed after they crossed the tracks. The houses were smaller and spread out. Some were old adobes. Most had corrugated metal roofs and were hunched in the shade of sycamores. No picket fences here. No lawns. Barefoot children and dogs buzzed around the neighborhood. The roads weren't paved. The street sign said they were traveling on *San Ignacio Road*, no longer called *Center Street* on this side of the tracks. Keller was beginning to understand.

They came to a cluster of buildings and a church on the right. Hector slapped his hand on the roof of the cab. "*Si Pedro. Nos puedes dejar aquí.*" They climbed out of the truck. In front of them was the church, the tallest building in San Ignacio—the tallest in Barlow. Keller looked skyward at the white mission. A tall steeple and bell tower topped the church with a big cross penetrating the blue sky.

Hector said, "Welcome to the Parish of San Ignacio. I was baptized here, had my First Holy Communion, and was married here. Beautiful, ain't it? C'mon. We're going to pick up something." They walked through the heavy doors. It was cooler inside with a musty smell of age. Beams of light filtered through the high windows, reflecting off massive timber rafters. The altar shined in carved ornaments and bright color. The crucifix was as large as life —the blood and agony of Jesus looked real. The two men walked across the back of the church where votive candles flickered around a statue of Saint Ignacio. A few people were scattered through the pews, kneeling in prayer. "Follow me," whispered Hector.

As they crossed the center of the church, Hector faced the altar, dropped to one knee, and made the *Sign of the Cross*. Then they went through a door to a garden courtyard. Statues of saints lined the cloister. A fountain was at its center, empty of water. They passed a classroom door and entered the next, a storeroom. Hector pulled out some cardboard boxes and lined them up along the brick walkway. "Here you go. Look through these and pick out some blue jeans. Find a pair that'll fit you, then find some for Weber and

Schatz too. You're going to need jeans for the ride into the Bosque. Those prison britches will chap your ass on that long ride."

"We can take them?" asked Keller.

"All these clothes are donated," said Hector. "They've all been worn, but usually you can find some good stuff."

Within a few minutes, Keller had three pairs of old jeans, all with some life left in them.

"You have any money on you?" asked Hector.

Keller grinned at the suggestion. "No money, only camp chits." He pulled out a clip of blue tickets.

Hector thumbed through the canteen coupons. "These look like carnival tickets," he said. He plucked out three 25¢ chits. "Here, we'll put this in the collection box on the way out. Father Mateo will find a way to spend these things."

They left the church and crossed the dusty street. A few businesses dotted the intersection, boxy buildings with low-slung roofs. The name of each shop was painted on the side of the building—*Carnicería ... Mercantil San Ignacio... Pelucaría.* Unlike the businesses on Lawton Road, these stores had no awnings or shed roofs, no boardwalks—just square buildings set on concrete slabs.

Keller hustled to keep up. "Hector, you were married in that church?"

"That's right."

Keller asked delicately, "What happened to your wife? Did she die?"

"No, *amigo.* I'm not that lucky. She's still around. Lives right here in San Ignacio."

"You are divorced?"

"Divorced?" Hector chuckled. "Hell no, I'm not divorced. I'm Catholic. No such thing. I just stay the hell away from her, that's all. If I get too close, she'll scratch out my eyeballs." Hector clawed the air like an angry cat. "No *Señor*, I'm stuck with that woman—forever. Even after I'm dead, she'll follow me into Hell just to make sure the fire is hot enough." Hector winked and slapped Keller's shoulder.

"Do you ever see her?"

"I try not to. Every time I do, I walk away with an empty wallet."

"So you never *go home* to her?" Keller raised an eyebrow.

"*Go home?* If you mean what I think, the answer is *Hell No!* If I tried that, she'd take more than my money. She'd have my *cajones* nailed to the wall. *Hell No.* Home for me is the Jackrabbit. Much safer there."

They arrived at Yolanda's Cantina. The building had once been slathered in turquoise paint, but the once-bright color had long-since faded to a powdery pastel. Hector said, "C'mon. This is my favorite place."

Keller balked at the doorway. "Can I go in? ...a POW?"

"You're with me. It'll be OK," said Hector.

There were about a dozen folks inside the Cantina. Hector walked in ahead of Keller and was greeted by everyone. Spanish flew around the room like a machine gun. Hector was like a long-lost son, returned. But as everyone noticed Keller, the mood dampened. Hector stepped in and explained who Keller was and why he was there. Hector's short speech was in Spanish, laced with a little English. Keller picked out a few phrases—*damn fine vaquero, round-up, bosque.* Hector was singing praise for Keller. The others laughed as Hector impersonated one of Keller's horse commands in the German language. Hector seemed to put them at ease. A few of the men nodded an acknowledgement toward Keller though none extended a handshake.

"Sit down," said Hector, pointing to a table against the far wall.

A woman emerged from the back room. When she saw Hector, she screamed like a parrot and bounded to embrace him. *"Héctor! Guapo! ¿Cómo estás? Te extrañé."* She jumped and squeezed Hector with a hug that squished her wobbling bosom into his chin. Hector wrapped his arms around her as she crowed. His hands slid down her back and rested on her rear end. Gradually, the woman eased her grasp and there was another flurry of rapid-fire Spanish. Hector again explained who Keller was, this time mostly in English. The woman smiled and welcomed him. Keller learned that this was Yolanda, the owner of the bar—inherited from her dead husband. Yolanda and Hector continued to hold each other, arm-in-arm through the introduction. Hector's hand came to rest on Yolanda's hip—maybe a clue as to the fortunes of Hector's marriage.

Yolanda brought them a couple of beers. *"Dos cervesas, señores. On the house."* She put two bottles of A-1 on the table.

"Gracias," said Hector as he stole one more squeeze from Yolanda before she went behind to the bar. He took a swig and turned to Keller. "Arizona beer. You like it?"

"Yes. Very good."

"You know, they changed the name of it a few years ago. Used to be called *Elder Brau*."

"A German name," said Keller.

"Yeah. But they changed the name right after the war started. Nobody wanted anything that sounded German. Hitler made sure everyone hated Germans."

Keller stared at the beer bottle and muttered under his breath, *"Ja. Ohne Zweifel."*

"Drink up. Umberto will be here with the truck pretty soon."

Keller looked at the bottle label. An American eagle was perched on the hyphen separating the *A* and the *1*. He asked, "Is Umberto an American?"

Hector set his beer down, fidgeted sideways in his chair. He looked at Keller—then looked away. Keller had hit a nerve, perhaps wading too deeply into these waters. This was a part of American culture he hadn't been able to get his arms around. At the Jackrabbit, Umberto often separated himself—became scarce, particularly when anyone from town came up to the ranch. He didn't speak much English, except a few curse words, though Keller suspected he understood more than he let on. At the POW camp, about half the guards were brown-skinned. They spoke English to the NCOs but usually spoke Spanish among themselves.

Hector finally turned back toward Keller. "Keller, you're white and there are some things a white person shouldn't ask—unless he's got a badge. But for some goddamn reason, I trust you. So here's the answer. But after that beer is empty, you don't talk about it again. *¿Entiendes muchacho?* Understand?"

Keller nodded.

"Umberto is from Mexico—*Old* Mexico. He came here illegally. No papers. There's lots of people around just like him, *mojados*. Here's the goddamn thing about it. For years, the government said they didn't want no Mexicans coming here, so thousands snuck across the border. Umberto was one of 'em. A couple of years ago, the government decided that there weren't enough Americans left around here to work the fields because they were all off to war. So then the government said it *wanted* Mexicans—started up the *Bracero Program*, so now Mexicans can get legal papers to come here and work. That's also why they've got all you Germans pickin' onions."

"Does Umberto now have legal papers?"

"That's the goddamned thing about it. Because he was already here before the program started, he'd have to go back to Mexico to make an application. Sure, he could get back into Mexico easy enough—anyone can. But if the government changes its mind again … eh … not so easy getting back here. Too much trouble. No guarantees."

"So he can't get papers?"

Hector snickered, then reduced his voice to a whisper. "Oh, he's got papers. He showed them to me. They look real good too. Just like the real thing." Hector winked. "*Señor*, you can get anything as long as you're willing to pay the money."

"Umberto does not fear government police?"

"It's a big game, Keller. Right now, they look the other way. But when the soldiers come home, who knows? The government is like a whore, Keller. She fucks whoever pays the best." He raised his bottle in a sarcastic toast. "To the government whore!"

Keller clinked the bottles. "To the government whores —everywhere!"

53

Outside Arnhem

Cecile Wijl settled for frequent cat-naps since she'd taken on the role of a nurse. Two cots were set up in the basement for nurses to use whenever they got a break.

Cecile's head popped up from the pillow. Her eyes immediately went to the clock on the wall. She'd slept almost three hours, two more than she'd allotted herself when her head nestled into the pillow.

She straightened her skirt and dropped a smock over her head. While skittering up the stairs, she combed her fingers through her hair and fastened a pony tail. She hurried down the corridor to check on her most important patient.

In the three days since Taatje had shared her secret with Cecile, her health unraveled. Taatje was rarely conscious. When she was awake, she was in a dream-like stupor. High fevers led to uncontrollable shaking and she lapsed into convulsions. When Cecile saw her a few hours ago, Taatje's breathing was hollow and feint.

Cecile entered the ward room and went directly to Taatje. She sat on the edge of the mattress as she'd done so many times with her new friend. Before she looked down, she knew—knew she'd failed to be there when the time had come. Cecile took Taatje's hand in her own. No more fever. The hand was cold. Taatje's eyes were planted on the ceiling. Cecile delicately closed her eyelids and ran her hand through Taatje's hair.

"It's alright now, luv. God is holding you now. It's alright, luv."

54

High in the Bosque, Rosado Tank served as the central point of the round-up. On Thursday, Ol' Javier brought Willy and Tojo, the pack mules, into the mountains. They arrived a day ahead of the others —packing in all the food and cookery. He set up his outdoor kitchen under some juniper arches, away from the cattle pens. He would prepare two meals a day for the hungry Jackrabbit-J cowhands.

On Friday the crew arrived. The plan was simple. The cowboys scoured the high country to find the scattered cattle. They brought them back in small groups to the corral at Rosado Tank where they had high hopes of assembling a large herd, destined for market.

Hector divided them into three crews. Abbie, Will, and Schatz covered the rolling hills to the East. Keller and Umberto handled the western—more rugged—terrain. Hector managed the third group, keeping Weber and Brooks with him. Hector's crew served as the jack-of-all-trades—dividing time among gathering, separating, doctoring, and branding.

Now it was late Sunday afternoon. They'd been collecting cattle for two, long days. The sun was settling into the boughs of the piñons and would soon be over the western range. The riders hadn't returned yet. Hector surveyed the ridge. "I hope they get back here soon. Pushin' cattle ain't no fun in the dark."

"Yesterday, they didn't get back until sunset," said Brooks.

"Well, they'd better save some muscle for tomorrow. It's gonna be the toughest day for all of us—cuttin', doctorin', brandin' 'em, fixin' 'em—."

"Fixing them?" asked Weber. "Vass is —?"

Hector laughed. "Cuttin' off their gonads, *amigo*. Their balls. Their *cajones*." Hector made a *grab-and-slice* gesture. "Maybe I'll give that job to one of you!"

Brooks and Weber pointed at the other, laughed, and shook their heads simultaneously in a *not me* motion.

Hector snickered, "Doesn't really matter who does what, because we're all going to be workin' our tails off. We've got to get it all done tomorrow because we're taking this herd down the hill on Tuesday."

Six steers wandered among the chaparral. They were playing hide-and-seek in the thick brush, keeping the horsemen at bay. Abbie coaxed Chief through the bristling thicket, thankful for her leather chaps. She wondered how horses could easily scrape through these thorny bushes—or why a horse loved to lop off the head of a spiny thistle and roll it around on his tongue. *Tough creatures.* Will and

Schatz rode parallel to her, pushing the ornery cattle out of the underbrush. Cows and riders broke into the open at the same time. Immediately, Will went right and Schatz rode left. Abbie held the center. Deuce darted from side to side, lunging at errant steers. In less than a minute, they had this group in a tight pack, plodding toward Rosado Tank. This had been their pattern for two days. They were pretty good at it.

Schatz yelled across to Will. "Vill. Vatch ze big vun zair. He iss spooking."

Will answered. "*Ja, ja*, Schatzi. I got him." Will had picked up a collection of German words and made a game of mixing them into his conversation. He pushed his horse onto the path of the skittish steer and guided it back to the herd. "See. *Nicht* problem. *Wunderbar*! Huh, Schatzi?"

"*Ja*, Vill. *Wunderbar*," laughed Schatz.

"*Wunderbar*! Huh, Mom?"

"Yes, Will," replied Abbie. You're doing a *wunderbar* job."

A month earlier Abbie would have forbidden Will to latch on to anything German, but the presence of the three POWs had softened her. Abbie often worried that Will didn't have many friends, a drawback of living on a ranch. He had a few buddies at school, but none that lived close by. His only fast-friend was Deuce. When the Germans arrived, Will cottoned up to Schatz and vice versa. Their friendship gradually grew into a *big brother-little brother* relationship. She was leery at first, but Abbie let the bond develop. Schatz seemed to be a good-hearted young man—still a big kid in many ways. Gradually, Abbie warmed to the idea. It was good for Will to have an older boy to look up to. She suspected it was equally good for Schatz to have a *little brother* too.

It took a half-hour to drive the new cattle back to Rosado. The large corral was already crowded. By Abbie's guess, it was holding over two hundred head. Schatz rode ahead. By the time Abbie and Will had the little herd up to the corral, Schatz had the barbed wire gate unhooked. Abbie and Will drove the new cattle through the gate. Schatz stretched it back into place. Like clockwork.

Keller and Umberto emerged from the other end of the cienega, driving fifteen head. They'd been working the watercourses along the slope—an area creased in rugged rock and arroyos. As Abbie watched them come up from the draw, she was reminded of the last time she worked cattle in that area—when she crashed into that old juniper tree. The bruises were only now disappearing.

"Will, let's help them. Move back, toward those pines," said Abbie.

Will spurred his horse to the front of a ponderosa stand at the edge of the meadow. Abbie moved Chief where she'd be in position to turn the head of the herd. Deuce darted across the open field as soon as he heard the newcomers. Within seconds, he was at the back of the new steers, nipping at their heels.

Keller saw his helpers up ahead and moved to the back of the procession. Umberto copied Keller's action on the opposite side. They drove the whitefaces toward Will and Abbie, who began whirling their hats—ushering the cattle toward the gate where Schatz stood ready.

"Git up! Hyup!" yelled Abbie as she paced Chief to and fro, filling the space and coaxing the cattle toward the gate.

"Hyaw! Hyaw! *Macht schnell*! Hyaw!" cried Will.

The herd moved perfectly, making a long arc. Pushed from behind by Keller, Umberto, and Deuce, the cattle trotted right through the gate, content to enter a refuge from the irksome cowboys and the devil-dog. Schatz shut the gate.

Hector made his way over from the smaller corral where he'd been working with Weber and Brooks. "Damn, if I didn't know better I'd think you all were *real* cowboys."

Two days earlier, Abbie wasn't sure this crew would be up for the job. But the results spoke for themselves. There were more cattle in the big corral than she'd ever seen there. She smiled at the thought of their success and noticed Keller looking her direction, also reveling in Hector's backhanded compliment. When she caught his eye, she glanced away.

"Did you bring 'em all in?" Hector asked Keller.

"We saw some over that hill, when we were coming in."

"How many?"

"Hard to see in the trees. Maybe five or eight," said Keller.

"We only have about a half-hour of daylight. Should probably leave 'em be. We can get 'em in the Fall." said Hector.

Brooks and Weber joined the others. The entire crew was assembled—some standing, some on horseback. Hector said to Abbie, "*Patrona*, it's time to start cutting cattle. You need to tell me what you want to do."

Normally, the Circle-J cattle would have been cut and released by now. But this year, Abbie instructed Hector to keep *all* the cattle in the corral. No one, not even Hector, could figure out *exactly* what she had in mind. She wasn't saying anything, but it was obvious she was heading for a show-down with Mason Johnson.

In truth, Abbie was wrestling with her decision. The contract Mason had pushed on Hank seemed to open a loophole—one big enough to separate her from Mason's grip forever. But she was no lawyer—and couldn't afford to hire one. She hoped that contract was as simple as it looked. If not, her plan would backfire, and she could lose everything.

All eyes were on her. Everything was riding on this roll of the dice.

She looked at Hector and set her jaw. "After branding, cut the cows and babies loose. Keep all the steers that are old enough to sell. Doesn't matter what brand they've got—*Jackrabbit-J* or *Circle-J*. We're taking them all down the hill."

"*Patrona*, are you sure you want to hang on to the Circle-brands? There'll be trouble. Lots of trouble," said Hector.

"Keep 'em all, Hector."

Hector and Umberto eyeballed each other.

Abbie wasn't finished. "And Hector, I want all the calves branded with our brand. Doesn't matter if their momma is a Jackrabbit or a Circle."

Hector was staggered. "Ma'am. We can't do that!"

"Hector, I have a contract that says I can."

"But ma'am, branding another man's calves—that'll get you locked in jail—might even get you hung."

"They're my cattle, Hector."

"But *Patrona*, these cows have Mason Johnson's brand. *Mason Johnson*, ma'am! He'll never let you do it, no matter what that paper says. Ma'am, you don't want to cross him."

"I'll take my chances."

"*¡A la chingada! ¿Qué estamos haciendo?*" muttered Hector as he turned and gripped both hands on the corral rail, shaking his head as he surveyed the sea of cattle on the other side of the fence.

From her saddle, Abbie scanned her crew. They may not have understood the consequences of her decision, but they all knew Hector understood them—and they sensed his mood. Will looked worried—the others dumfounded. Except Keller. She saw in him an understanding. She'd felt it before. He nodded as if to say *good decision*. She met his eye. This time, she didn't turn away.

Abbie spoke to everyone. "That's how we're going to do it."

Hector turned and said, "You heard the lady. Weber and Brooks, you two get back to work with those calves. Umberto will help you. The rest of you, help me start separating these cattle. Let's get as much done as we can before we lose the daylight. We've got a full day tomorrow."

5 5

Jackrabbit-J Ranch

A new, blue pickup eased along the gravel path and stopped under the shade of the giant sycamore. Mason rarely visited the Jackrabbit-J since his son's death. In one way, he regretted it. He was losing touch with his grandson. That was the fault of his daughter-in-law, Abigail. He'd never seen eye-to-eye with her and doubted he ever would. She was a bull-headed woman. Hank had given her a loose rein—more than a man should ever give his wife. Now Mason was here to try to talk some sense into her. One last time.

He walked up to the house and was surprised when a round, Mexican woman came out the door with two children in tow. He recognized her.

"Good morning, Nana Elvia." said Mason as he touched the brim of his hat. Nana Elvia was Ol' Javier's wife—called Nana, *Grandma*, by all who knew her. She seemed to have more grandchildren than could be numbered which would probably account for the two kids who stood behind her.

"*Buenos dias, Señor* Johnson."

"I was hoping to find my daughter-in-law. Is she around?"

"Oh no, *Señor* Johnson. They are all gone to the Bosque. They leave three days ago. I stay here with my *nietos*. We take care of the animals while they gone."

"Gracias, *Señora*." He tipped his hat.

Mason spun on his heels and stamped back to his truck. His gait was rigid. By the time he got in the cab he was seething and muttering. "Goddamn! Goddamn! I told her to let my crew handle the Bosque. Fucking woman! Goddamn it!" He backed his truck around in a whirl of dust. Tires spun and the truck fantailed as he sped away, spraying gravel in his wake. "Goddamn bitch! She'll fuck up everything. Fucking goddamn woman! Just gotta do things her own fuckin' way. Goddamn bitch!"

56

Barlow

"Look-a-here, Mason, I'm a cattle broker. I got no aim to get in the middle of a squabble between you and the Jackrabbit-J." Augie Cooper closed his ledger and pleaded with the man in his doorway. "Mason. I can't do business like that…"

"I ain't *askin'* you to change the way you run your goddamn business." Mason pointed his finger at Augie. "What I'm *tellin'* you is this. Don't make any offer to my goddamn daughter-in-law until I've had a chance to shake some sense into her. So, when her stock finds its way into your pens, you let me know about it—*right away.* And don't sign nothin' until I've had a chance to get here first. Simple?"

"I can't do that, Mason. I'm sworn to carry on fair commerce. The Jackrabbit-J ain't your ranch."

Mason plopped a leather binder on Augie's desk, opened it, and pointed to a paragraph near the bottom of the second page. "But they *are* my cattle. Read that."

Augie perused the paragraph. Then he thumbed through the entire document. "From the law office of Harley Penrod? Where the hell did you get this? It was signed in '38. Why haven't I seen it before?"

"Because I haven't needed it before, Augie. Now I'm tellin' you, those are *my goddamn cattle* that she'll be bringing in. I've got the right, as owner, to make the deal."

"I don't know, Mason. Abbie's always dealt square with me, before. This just don't seem right."

Mason leaned on the desk and drove his finger into Augie's chest. "Look, Augie. Either you're dealin' *with* me or you're dealin' *against* me. There are brokers in Willcox that would love to have my business—and the business of every other member of the Cattlemen's Association. Do ya' catch my fuckin' drift?"

Augie had been backed into a cave by a rattlesnake. He fidgeted with his fountain pen. "Yeah, Mason. I got it."

Mason's scowl warmed to a frank smile as he retrieved his binder. "Good. It's a pleasure to do business with you, Augie. See ya' soon."

5 7

The Bosque

Monday evening. The sun was down and the breeze took on a chill. Abbie stood in the doorway of the small cabin. She watched the cowboys who were sitting around the fire on fat sections of sawn log. They'd just finished eating their fill of Javier's chili beans. In an hour, or so, they'd spread their bedrolls out around the same ring.

Rosado Tank was Abbie's favorite place. The stars were beginning to appear. Silhouettes of tall pines guarded this grassy swale in the mountains. Cows let out occasional bellows from the pole corral on the other side of the creek. Just enough light was cast from the campfire to make out the shape of a white tail doe that had entered the meadow.

She'd been up here, to the high country, several times since her husband's death. The first few journeys were difficult because the place reminded her so much of Hank. After all, she was here when Hank built it—the corrals, the dam, the cabin. This was her third year without him. It was becoming a little easier. New memories now. Different years—different crews. And this crew might be the most memorable.

The day had been back-breaking. Cutting. Separating. Branding. Castrating. Vaccinating. Keller called it a battle, cowboys versus cows. They had started at sun-up, and only finished when the western range was painted in an orange glow. Abbie's cowboys were victorious. She wondered what drove these men. They worked hard—but all cowboys work hard. The cowboys Hector usually hired did it because it was their calling, because they had a reputation to polish. But what made these guys tick? They were soldiers, not cattlemen. Brooks, the American, spent the better part of the day wrestling heifers to the ground and pinning them. He hardly stopped for lunch—all that with only one arm. And the Germans! They'd be gone before long—back to Germany, probably never to rope another calf. Yet they worked through the day with a fury. Especially Keller. Keller. He would run this round-up by himself if he had to. What pushed these men? Abbie couldn't figure.

She joined them at the campfire.

Keller saw her coming and playfully pushed Will off his stump. Then he offered it to Abbie. "Here you are," he said. "Zis vun is for you."

"Aww. That's my seat," said Will. Abbie took the stump and Will took the ground, propping his back against his mother's knees.

"Don't get your feet too close to the fire," said Abbie.

"I'm too tired to move 'em, Mom."

Schatz said to Will, "Too tired to brand some more cows. Get up. Let us work all night."

"*Nicht lustig*," said Weber, who was already lying on his bedroll behind Schatz.

"He said I am not funny," said Schatz.

"He's right," said Umberto. "I don't stand up. *Todos los músculos mi hacen dolor.*"

Hector sat down. "Those chili beans were excellent, Javier. *Gracias.*" He pulled a bottle out of his jacket. You all worked hard today. I brought something to warm your bellies so you sleep well tonight." He opened the bottle and took a swig. "Ahhh. That's good tequila, my friends. Pass it around."

Schatz took a glug. His eyes lit up. "Whew! *Starkes zeug!* Like Fire!" He turned to the figure lying on the bed roll behind him. "Weber, want a drink?"

"What is it?" said Weber, half asleep.

"Mexican schnapps."

"No thanks. I am dead already."

"I'll take a drink, Schatzi," said Will.

"No you won't, young man," countered Abbie.

Umberto laughed and said to Will. "Not until you grow a beard, *hombrecito.*" He took a swig and passed the bottle to Brooks.

Brooks said, "Well boys—and lady—I think we earned this. This was worse than boot camp." The Germans raucously chimed in agreement.

"*Sergeant* Hector, we will call you," said Keller.

Brooks jumped in. "*Sergeant* Hector Cruz, the meanest *sombitch* in the army!" The toast brought a roar and applause.

"How'd we do today, Sarge?" Brooks asked.

"You guys did real good," said Hector. "You got a job here anytime."

"Even Weber here? He tried to brand ze wrong end of a steer." said Schatz, chiding his friend who was trying to sleep.

"*Halts maul*...Shut up Schatzi, or I vill brand you next time," said Weber.

Keller said, "Hector, was this a good round-up? Did we get enough steers?"

"Oh, I'd say so. We've got a big herd to drive down the hill tomorrow. What do you think ma'am? You've been counting the numbers."

Abbie said, "We've got about 140 head for tomorrow. Next week, we'll find the ones in the low country. If we can pull in another fifty head from down there, we'll be able to pay our bills—for a while anyway."

Brooks said, "What about those Circle-J steers, ma'am. You really gonna sell those too?"

Silence shrouded the campfire. Instead of answering, Abbie reached out to Schatz for the bottle of tequila, wiped the rim with her denim sleeve, took a swig, and stared into the flames.

Keller broke the silence, "In Netherland, we say *'geef hem geen ruimte'*. Don't give your ... enemy any room. As with... How do you say it?" Keller imitated a prize fighter.

"Boxing," said Brooks.

"As with boxing," said Keller. "Do not let ze other man have room to swing his fists."

Abbie took another sip of tequila and said to Keller, "The Netherlands? I thought you were German?"

"I am both," said Keller. He put his hand on Hector's shoulder. "Like Hector, I am from two places."

"Isn't Holland fighting against Germany?" asked Will.

"This is true," said Keller.

"That's gotta be tough," laughed Brooks. "You must wake up fighting with yourself."

"Every day," said Keller in a fading voice. "... every day."

"It's a crazy world," said Abbie. She slipped the bottle into Keller's hand. "How's that saying go again? The one from Holland?"

Keller pronounced it slowly. *"Geef hem geen ruimte."*

Abbie repeated the words. "Kif...hem...keen...room...tuh. Sounds like good advice."

Part Three

Part Three

58

Camp Barlow

"Well, I think a little celebration is in order, Jim." Riley reached to his lowest drawer and took out a bottle. "Kentucky bourbon. Good stuff." He tipped it back and slugged down a gulp. "Paahhh! Here you go."

"No thanks, Colonel. Maybe later," said Davenport.

"Where'd you hear the good news?"

"It just came over the radio." A refrain of whoops could be heard through Riley's office window. The yelling was coming from the enlisted soldiers' mess hall—cheerful hollers and siren-like screams, laced with joyous profanity.

"Sounds like the news is spreading fast. So the goddamn Nazis finally surrendered?" said Riley. "Didn't think they'd last long once that son-of-a bitch Hitler was dead. Cut the head off the snake, y' know. Hey, what's the date today?"

"May 8th, sir."

"May 8th, 1945. Sure to be a day we'll always remember. Another Fourth of July. Here's to the Eighth of May!" Riley toasted the date with another swig. "Haaah…Sure you don't want some, Major?"

"No sir. Not now."

"I think I'm going to make a long distance call to my wife back in Ohio. This is a day to celebrate."

"Indeed it is, sir. I'm sure she'll be happy to hear from you."

"You're sure acting like a wet rag. Got a bee in your bonnet?"

"Colonel, I think you should address the prisoners this afternoon."

"What for? I'm sure they've already heard it. Hell, they get most of the news around here before we do."

"Probably true. But it all changes now. There are some things they're going to need to know about."

"Like what goddamnit?" said Riley. "What the hell can I possibly say? I could tell them that their beloved Hitler fucked up. And how their country has been blown to smithereens. And how there ain't gonna be nothin' left of it when they go home. Is that what I should tell them, Major?"

"We need to keep a lid on things, Colonel. There's no telling how some of the POWs might react, but emotions will run high. I'm sure of that. And there's no telling what the Nazis might do—"

"The Nazis? The goddamn Nazis? Are you still on that jag? What can the goddamn Nazis possibly do now? Hitler's dead! Goebbels is dead! The rest of 'em surrendered today. Why are we still worryin' about the goddamned Nazis?"

"Colonel, I'm concerned about the Nazis in *this camp*. They might see this as a reason to tighten the noose. If that happens—if there's another *incident* here—you won't be able to keep the Provost Marshall off your back."

Riley grimaced as if a cesspool had just flooded the room. "The Provost Marshall? Hell! Gotta keep those pencil-pushing, *sons-a-*

bitches out of my camp. You really think our Nazis might do something stupid, now that the war is over?"

"I don't know what they'll do, Colonel. But they're sure-as-hell not going to sit around and play pinochle," said Davenport.

"Well, what can we tell the POWs that they don't already know?"

"You can tell them what's likely to happen to them now. That's what they want to know."

"Hell, *we don't even know* what will happen to them. Those idiots in Washington have their thumbnails inserted squarely up their assholes."

"You can tell them they will be here for a while—months probably. You can tell them that things won't be changing around here. The daily routines will be the same. The labor program will go on. So will the classes. Tell them they'll be here until our government can figure out the best time and way to get them back home."

"Hell. They aren't gonna want to hear that."

"Actually sir, I think some of them might be glad to hear it. They know how bad things are over there. They're better off here for a while. But one way or another, they'll want the truth. They should hear it from you."

Riley walked over to the window and watched as some raucous GIs spilled out of the mess. "I suppose you've got a point, Jim. Set up a muster on the quad for 1600 today. But I'm not gonna talk to 'em. I hate talking through a goddamn interpreter. I'll let Colonel Hoefer tell 'em. Let 'em hear it from one of their own. Arrange for me to meet with Hoefer an hour before the muster. I'll tell him what he needs to tell his men."

"Are you sure that's the way you want to do it, Colonel?"

"Hell yes, I'm sure. Now get crackin'. And keep a close eye on those goddamn Nazis. Can't afford to have them stirring up any trouble."

"Yes sir."

59

The Jackrabbit-J

Keller swung his leg off the saddle and eased to the ground. His feet felt like they were swimming when they hit the dirt. He'd never been so happy to be off a horse. Keller tied Pay Day to the hitching rail and slipped off his bridle. The horse's ears cocked forward when Keller shook the oat can and scooped a handful of the grain into his palm. Pay Day's lips churned away as Keller gave him a couple of affectionate slaps on his neck.

"Who's more tired boy, you or me?" Keller walked around Pay Day, pivoting his hand on the horse's rump. His legs felt like they were still locked in the round shape of Pay Day's girth, like his legs were permanently bent. He chuckled at his plight. *Great, I not only limp, now I'm bow-legged too.* He unhooked the cinch and pulled off the saddle and blanket. Pay Day's back was a wet slick. Keller carried the saddle into the tack room and returned with a curry brush. "Here you go, boy. This will feel good." Keller ran the brush along the grain of the horse's coat. The horse wriggled as the brush massaged his back.

The other cowboys brought their horses into the stable. All wore weary, hang-dog faces. "Here Brooks, let me help," said Keller. Brooks had proven to be a fine one-armed cowboy while they were in the Bosque. Weber helped Keller with Brooks's horse.

"Thanks fellas," said Brooks. "That was one long day, wasn't it?"

"A long *veek*. I think I shall sleep for three days," said Weber.

"Yes, a bed will feel good," said Keller.

"We got the job done though, didn't we?" said Brooks.

"Ja, hundret and forty head. And we did not lose any cow," said Weber.

"That was some damn fine work, *muchachos*," said Keller, imitating Hector's sing-song accent.

"Damn fine work, *muchachos*," said Umberto, joining in.

An army truck pulled up to the corral. Its headlights lit up the stables. Private Halloran, the driver, yelled toward the cowboys, "Where the hell've you been? I've been driving around this goddamn ranch for two hours."

Brooks yelled back, "Where the hell do you think we've been, Halloran? Took all day to bring those cattle down off the mountain."

"Well, drag your asses over here. I was supposed to have those Krauts back by 1800. We've already missed chow. Be lucky if they've even got any cold meat loaf left for us."

Umberto said, "I finish horses, *amigos*. You go."

Keller looked at Brooks and tugged at the collar of his cotton shirt. "Two minutes? For changing clothes?" Before their journey into the Bosque, the three Germans had left their POW togs in the tack room in favor of their ranching outfits.

Brooks thought about it. "Yeah, you guys had better change. They might frown on me bringing cowboys back into camp." He yelled toward Halloran, "Give us just a couple more minutes."

"Shit," said Halloran.

It took about fifteen minutes for the truck to make its way down the washboard road from the Jackrabbit-J to the pavement of Highway 81. Halloran was driving and Brooks was seated on the passenger side. Keller, Schatz, and Weber rode in the back on the wood benches that ran along the bed of the vehicle. The canvas canopy had been removed when the mild, spring weather hit. Within a mile, Highway 81 turned into Lawton Road. This was their usual route back to camp—through the town, then two miles north to the POW camp. But today, Barlow wasn't a sleepy town. It was alive.

Keller leaned out so he could see around the cab. Up ahead, at the main intersection, dozens of people were out in the middle of the street. Car horns blared and voices peeled above a steady din. The truck slowed as it approached the crowd. From the second story of the hardware store someone had hung a white bed sheet with the words painted on it.

GOD BLESS AMERICA
BRING THE BOYS HOME!

American flags were hanging from the fronts of all the main street businesses. As they got closer to the center of town—the corner of Lawton and Center—they could hear a phonograph that had been hooked up to some loud speakers. It was playing Sousa's *Stars and Stripes Forever*. Some people ran around. Others were dancing. Whiskey bottles were making the rounds.

Keller slapped his hand on the top of the truck cab and yelled to the front, "Brooks, What is happening?"

Brooks leaned his head out the truck window. "The war's over, Keller. Germany surrendered."

"When?"

"Today. Earlier today." said Brooks. "Halloran just told me. We weren't supposed to tell you guys until we got you back to the camp. But it's a little bit hard to hide right now."

Keller, Weber, and Schatz were silent. Their eyes moved back and forth among themselves. This was not unexpected but the unspoken truth had a sting. Keller patted each on the leg. He said, "Not sure where we go from here, my friends. Let's make the best of it."

The truck crept into the intersection, easing through the crowd. A man in a tall Stetson, the apparent master-of-ceremonies, stood on the boardwalk in front of the movie house. He'd rigged up a microphone. When he saw the army vehicle approach, he boomed, "Ladies and gentlemen. Here they come. America's finest. The brave soldiers of the United States Army."

The crowd turned its attention to the transport truck. Everyone cheered. The man in the Stetson moved the phonograph needle to a new selection. The loudspeakers crackled against the microphone. Sousa's *El Capitan* blared. A young woman ran up to the truck and jumped on the running board. She cradled her arms around Brooks's neck and landed a big kiss on his cheek, leaving a ruby smear of lipstick. Others went to the driver's door and grabbed Halloran, nearly dragging him out of the cab. The crowd rallied around the two heroes—each of them pounded with handshakes, backslaps, and pecks on the cheek.

The young lady, who'd started the frenzy, reapplied her lipstick. This time she targeted Halloran. She held his head in a bear hug and landed a lingering, red smooch on his lips.

"I think I just died and went to heaven," Halloran yelled to Brooks.

"If I'm dreaming, I don't want to wake up," replied Brooks, his arm around a young lady who was wearing his head gear.

Brooks and Halloran instantly became the guests-of-honor at the street party. They were ushered up to boardwalk. Brooks found himself facing the crowd with a microphone jammed in his face. The phonograph volume was turned down and the crowd quieted.

Brooks spoke into the microphone. "Thank you all."

"No. Thank you!" came a voice from the crowd, followed by more cheering.

Brooks fidgeted. "I'm not much for giving speeches...but..." He saw a banner hanging on the opposite side of the street and took his cue from it. "God bless America!"

The crowd hollered its approval.

The microphone was then thrust under Halloran's chin. The yelling died down again. Before Halloran could speak, a voice rang out from across the street. "What about those fuckin' Krauts. Who invited them to the party?" The man was standing in front of the door of *Johnny P's Bar and Grill*. He held a bottle in his hand and staggered into the street. The crowd went quiet.

The man in the Stetson took the microphone. "Now Curtis, c'mon. No need to get riled up."

"I ain't gittin' riled up. I'm jus' gittin' started. I'm thinkin' we need to finish off the goddamned Krauts once and for all. Let's start with these three."

Keller motioned to Schatz and Weber to stay still. They sat rigid —statues in the back of the truck.

The man in the Stetson tried again. "C'mon now Curtis. Go back in the bar. Your next drink's on me." Other voices encouraged Curtis to back away.

Curtis was standing next to the truck now, supporting himself against the bedrail. He was directly behind Weber. Weber remained frozen. His eyes darted back and forth from Keller to Schatz, scared as hell.

Curtis said, "I don't need another drink. I got a bottle right here. What I need to do is to kill me a fuckin' Kraut." Curtis swung his whiskey bottle upward and caught Weber with a sideways blow to the back of his head. The bottle shattered against Weber's skull. Broken glass sprayed outward and the aroma of whiskey enveloped the truck. Weber pitched forward onto the floorboards. Schatz huddled over him. Keller stood, ready to take on Curtis, if need be. He could easily break Curtis—kill the drunk with his bare hands—but that would only make the situation worse. Other men ran toward the truck. It wasn't clear if they were out to stop Curtis or to join him. The street became bedlam.

A gunshot rang out.

The crowd froze.

Brooks stepped off the boardwalk and into the middle of the crowd, his pistol pointed in the air. A pathway cleared for him as he walked toward the truck. Halloran followed Brooks and upholstered his pistol too.

Brooks announced. "These here Germans are the property of the United States Army. Private Halloran and I are sworn to protect that property. Stand back from the truck. We need to get these prisoners back to Camp Barlow. Now!"

The man in the Stetson spoke into the microphone. "You all heard the soldier. Give 'em room. Let 'em make their way through."

A circle of folks slowly moved back from the truck, except for two men who held Curtis pinned to the ground with his arms twisted behind his back. Brooks and Halloran pointed their pistols downward, but didn't holster them. They got in the truck and started moving. Halloran kept the truck in low gear until he cleared the intersection. The Germans stayed huddled against the floorboards. When the vehicle accelerated, Brooks shouted to the back, "How's Weber?"

Keller yelled back, "His head is blood...lots of blood."

"OK. We'll get him right to the infirmary and get him stitched up," said Brooks. "Step on it." Halloran stomped down on the accelerator leaving a cloud of diesel smoke hovering over Lawton Road.

60

Barlow

The rail platform at the stockyards reminded Keller of the Rhine docks in Düsseldorf, where he grew up. The system was much the same as on the Düsseldorf quay. River transport—rail lines. Floating barges—rolling stock. Cargo on—cargo off. Commerce.

Keller stood on the planked gangway that connected the cattle ramps. Inclined ramps were used to walk cattle up to the gangway, to the level of the rail cars. Keller's boots were at head-height with the cattle that milled in the pens below him.

It was almost noon and the day had grown hot. The steers huddled around the water troughs, thirsty after the morning's trek from the Jackrabbit. Waves of cow-stink drifted over the stock-yards. Keller was immune to it.

Schatz and Umberto joined him. They looked down over the stock pens—packed with Abbie Johnson's cattle. By afternoon, these steers would be loaded onto stock cars and on their way to transfer yards in Willcox. From there, the Southern Pacific would transport the beeves to markets from Los Angeles and St. Louis.

Keller gave Umberto a friendly slap on the back. "It took six days, but we got them here," he said.

"*Si* Keller. We do good work," said Umberto.

The crew was short a few members. Weber had spent the night in the Camp Barlow infirmary getting his head patched after the *victory* attack. Brooks was back on duty at the Stephenson farm supervising his other POW laborers. And Will was back in school, despite an unsuccessful plea to convince his mother he was needed for the last day of round-up.

About twenty feet down the gangway was Augie Cooper's brokerage office. Abbie, Hector, and Augie stood outside the door discussing business. Keller and the other hands kept their distance. Something wasn't going right. For some reason, the broker was stalling an agreement.

A blue pickup came tearing up the road. A dust-tail slip-streamed behind it as it slid around the long curve. Augie and Abbie paused in conversation. Everyone on the gangway watched as the truck slid to a gravelly halt.

The driver, a stocky man in a tall hat, jumped out and stomped toward the ramp. Although Keller had never seen this man, he'd heard the stories, and knew who it must be. Mason Johnson. Abbie's father-in-law. All eyes were on Mason as he pounded up the steps.

Abbie walked over to Keller, Schatz, and Umberto.

"The life of the party just showed up," she said. "Just stay over here. I'll handle Mason." Although her message was for all three, she looked only at Keller.

Schatz and Umberto nodded. But Keller squared on Abbie's eyes. He sensed fear. "OK," he said, though it was more a question than an affirmation.

"What was that old Dutch saying?" she asked him.

"*Geef hem geen ruimte,*" he replied. "Don't give him room to breath."

"Wish me luck," Abbie said. She returned to Augie and Hector about the same time Mason joined in. Mason bit off a hunk of tobacco and pushed it under his cheek. He ignored Abbie and spoke directly to the broker. "Augie, I'm claiming those cattle to be mine. Every last one of 'em. You can pay me cash or bank credit. Don't care which one, so long as the Circle-J Ranch is paid for them cattle."

Another pickup pulled next to the blue one. This truck had gold lettering stenciled to the door—*SHERIFF.*

"Who the hell called Gene Kirby?" said Mason. "Why in the *sam hell* do we need him here?"

"I called him, right after I called you, Mason," said Augie. "I don't want to get stuck in the middle of this thing."

"Stuck in the middle? You ain't stuck in the middle of nuthin'! I showed you that contract a couple of days ago. It shows that *I own these cattle.*" Mason stepped into Augie, their chins nearly touching. "All you need to do, Augie, is credit the sale of these cattle to the Circle-J Ranch and I'll be on my happy way. What's so tough about that?"

Abbie spoke up. "Those cattle don't belong to the Circle-J."

Mason ignored her. He kept drilling Augie. "Augie, you saw the contract. You know what I'm talkin' about."

Abbie spoke again. "And they don't belong to my ranch, either—."

Mason faced away from Abbie, toward the pens. He was silent for a moment and stepped along the gangway, scrutinizing the cattle below.

Then he whirled on Abbie. "What the hell do you think you're doin'? Half those cattle got my brand! You come here thinkin' you can sell *my* cattle? You got another thing comin', young lady!"

Deputy Kirby entered the fray. "What's goin' on here Mason?" he said.

"I'll tell you what the hell is goin' on! My fuckin' daughter-in-law here thinks she can steal my cattle and sell them right out from under me. Right here, to my own broker." He scoffed, "That's about the stupidest kind of cattle rustlin' I've ever heard of."

Abbie squared her shoulders. "Those cattle don't belong to your ranch—or to mine. They belong to the *Circle-J Cattle Company*. All of them. Doesn't matter which brand."

"You're finally talkin' some sense. The Circle-J is my ranch. So, those are my cattle!"

"The Circle-J *Ranch* is yours alright, but the Circle-J *Cattle Company* isn't," said Abbie. "When you pulled Hank into that contract seven years ago, you formed a partnership with him. You did it so you could run your cattle up in the Bosque."

"Yeah. So?"

"So the contract says that *Circle-J cattle* and *Jackrabbit-J cattle* are *both owned* by the Circle-J Cattle *Company*." She took a step and closed the gap between her and Mason. "And *I'm* your partner now, Mason. I've got the right to sell Jackrabbit-J or Circle-J cattle. I've also got the right to fifty percent of the profit from any cattle I sell—or *you* sell."

"Like hell you do, you goddamn bitch."

His face was only inches away. Spit splattered as he snorted but Abbie didn't back off. *Geef hem geen ruimte.* "Like hell *I do*, Mason. As a matter of fact, if I hire a lawyer, I can probably sue you for half your profits for the last seven years." She stared him down. "Of course, you could sue me for half my profits too. But I guess that you've sold about twenty times as many cattle as I have."

"Now you listen here, you goddamn—"

Gene Kirby stiff-armed Mason the way a referee takes a boxer to a neutral corner. He steered the angry man away from Abbie. "Just hold on Mason. Hold on."

"Git your goddamned hands off me, Gene."

"Not till you settle down."

"Settle down? You heard what she said. Ain't no one ever tried to push me around like that!"

"I'm here to keep the peace, Mason," said Kirby. "And I aim to do it."

"Yeah, and you're here to enforce the law, too. Goddamnit! You gonna let her sell my cattle? *My cattle?!*"

"Settle down Mason and listen to me," said Kirby. "Augie called me two days ago and filled me in on this whole thing. I knew it would lead to trouble. So, yesterday I drove into Bisbee to look through the county records. To find out where this thing stands."

"Ya did, did ya'? And what'd you find?" growled Mason.

"Well, I ain't no lawyer, but I think she's right, Mason. You two have a partnership in the same cattle company. The company owns all the livestock, both ranches. You two are in it together, fifty-fifty."

Mason flung his shoulder upward and threw off Kirby's grip. He walked away from the circle, moving toward Keller, Schatz, and Umberto like a wounded bear. Mason scowled as he faced them. Umberto and Schatz looked away, avoiding his glare. Keller didn't.

"What the hell are you lookin' at, ya' fuckin' Kraut?"

Keller stared back.

Abbie followed behind Mason. "I'll make it easy on you, Mason. I'm not after your money. All I want is to break up this partnership. I'll run my cattle, and you run yours. I'll even have my cowboys cut your steers out of these pens and you can take 'em."

"Your *cowboys*? You mean your fuckin' *Jackboot-J Nazis*, don't ya'?" Mason's eyes were steeled on Keller.

Abbie said, "We can do this right away. I'll meet you at Harley Penrod's office tomorrow if you want. You can be done with me once and for all. Isn't that what you really want anyway, Mason?"

"And what if I say no?"

Abbie said, "I guess we'll end up in the Bisbee Courthouse.

There's a lot of money at stake—your money. Money you've made over the past seven years. I don't reckon I'll have much trouble finding a lawyer in Tucson who'll be willing to take on my case, not with that big of a pay day on the line."

Mason pivoted on Abbie, stepping toe-to-toe. "You bitch! You fucking cunt bitch! Do you really think you can push me around?" More spit flew as he raged. "I'm the biggest rancher in this valley! I tell people what to do, not the other way 'round. Cross me you fucking cunt bitch and I'll break you!"

Abbie's voice wavered, but she stood firm. "There's one more thing Mason. Once the partnership is over, you won't be runnin' your cattle in the Bosque. Grazing rights go with the Jackrabbit-J. That land butts up to my ranch. The federal contract is with my ranch, not yours."

Mason grinned, masking his rage, but his jaw pounded on his tobacco chaw. "You think I'm going to give up my rights to run cattle in the Bosque? Ha! This just gets funnier and funnier. Why in the *sam hell* would I do that?" Brown slaver oozed down his chin.

Abbie fought for a steady voice. "Because Mason…if you don't agree to break up the partnership…and you don't pull your cattle out of the Bosque…I'm going to keep markin' every calf on that land with a Jackrabbit brand." Abbie could feel her hands shaking. She locked her thumbs into her jeans' pockets. "Two days ago…my cowboys branded sixty-three calves with Jackrabbit-J irons…Half their mommas were Circle-J cows. They're runnin' up in the high country right now…with my brand…"

Mason bellowed a low, bullish grunt. He swung his arm in a roundhouse motion and caught Abbie with an open palm across the side of her face. She shrieked as the blow sent her backward into Gene Kirby. It broke Abbie's momentum and she landed hard on the wood planks. Kirby wasn't so lucky. The force knocked him off the gangway and he fell backward into the stock pen. Startled steers jumped and recoiled. Kirby tried to brace himself as he plummeted headfirst. He smashed into the ground, his arm crumpling underneath him. "Dyahhh!" he screamed.

Schatz and Umberto jumped into the pen, pushing and shoving the steers away from Kirby. They wrangled the beasts to the opposite side of the pen.

Keller's move was automatic. He stepped in behind Mason. In one motion, Keller pushed his chest into Mason's back and thrust his arms upward under the shorter man's armpits. Then Keller's hands came together behind Mason's neck. He then constricted his hold in one quick burst. Mason blurted out in agony. His legs flailed, but it was no use against Keller's grasp. The headlock was designed to incapacitate and immobilize an enemy. Keller had practiced it thousands of times in infantry training.

Mason struggled, but his strength and air supply were running out quickly. Keller tightened his grip. Mason cursed in guttural gasps. "Gnaaggh. ...kill you ...Guhhh...fuckin' Nazi." Mason writhed one last time to free himself. But Keller clamped down until Mason had nothing left. His face was scarlet. "Gnnaggggh..."

Schatz and Umberto lifted Gene Kirby off the dung-soil.

Kirby wailed, "My shoulder. Yaaoowww. Watch my shoulder, boys!"

"Vee must get you out of ze corral," said Schatz.

"Away from the cows, *Señor*," said Umberto.

"Yaoow. Shiiitt! That hurts. Watch the shoulder." Umberto and Schatz cradled the anguished deputy. Cows scattered as the men made their way to the gate at the far end of the pen.

Mason's muscles went limp as Keller supported his full weight. He lost his strength—and his spirit. With Mason no more threatening than a sack of potatoes, Keller released him. Mason fell to the planks, gasping for air, but kept muttering in a hoarse whisper, "Fuckin' Nazi. Fuckin' goddamned Nazi." Mason was in a heap, twisted on his side with his cheek buried in the boards, sucking in air. A wet ring soaked his jeans where he'd pissed himself. Between gasps, he repeated, "Fuckin' Nazi...Fuckin' goddamned Nazi." Keller stepped back, ready in case Mason tried to come up for round two, though that was unlikely.

Hector helped Abbie to her feet. A small stream of blood ran from her lip. She wiped wet pools from her eyes. Her body quivered, but she fought it off. She had the upper hand now and she wasn't about to lose it.

"C'mon *Patrona*," said Hector. "Move away from here."

"No," said Abbie. She brushed Hector away. She looked down at her vanquished father-in-law, then looked over at Gene Kirby who was being aided by Schatz and Umberto.

Umberto yelled, *"Creo que se ha roto el hombre."*

Hector said to Abbie, "It looks like the deputy has a busted shoulder."

Abbie yelled back, "Umberto, you drive him to town in his truck. To Doc Butler. *Sabe dónde está?"*

"Si, Señora," said Umberto.

Abbie looked at Keller. "Is he going to be OK?" she said, referring to Mason.

"Yes. Just needs air."

"We need to get you out of here, Keller," said Abbie. "Best if you're not around here long. Schatz too."

The sheriff's truck left, Umberto at the wheel, and Gene Kirby sitting in the passenger seat, his face white as chalk.

Abbie said to Augie, "I've got to get my cowboys back to the ranch. I don't want 'em round here if Mason starts callin' in his cards. I'll be back later today. You're not going to sign away anything on those cattle, right?"

"No ma'am. I ain't gonna do nothin' till someone can tell me what the law says. Ma'am, those cows will be right here where you left 'em."

"Thanks, Augie."

Abbie stepped over to Mason, who was still pitched down on the wood slats, and stood over him. His eyes turned skyward, toward her, but his body didn't budge. She said, "You know my terms Mason, and they ain't going to change."

She walked away.

61

Vienna

"Here are your identity papers, Mr. Schröder. These will be enough for you to get around safely in Vienna."

Uhlemann scanned the credentials. They matched his new identity, Otto Schröder, a businessman from Hamburg.

"And here is the key to your flat," said the Austrian. "The landlord is one of us. No questions will be asked."

Uhlemann surveyed the Spartan apartment, perturbed. "I was led to believe I would not be in here long, that I would be transported to Spain, or perhaps to Egypt. It's not safe for me here in Austria. Not with those invaders prowling about—British, Americans, *Russians*."

"Arrangements for your departure will take some time. Our system has slowed considerably since the occupation. A group of Franciscan priests make the arrangements. They are quite sympathetic to our cause and they've been able to get travel papers for many patriots by using their pull with the Vatican. It is a slower process now that the Allies control all the borders. These priests will fabricate exit documents for you, probably through Italy. But it will take time."

"How much time?"

"Impossible to say. Days. Weeks. Perhaps more. We will keep you informed. Until that time, you must *blend in* with Vienna, Mr. Schröder."

62

Jackrabbit-J Ranch

Abbie waited four days for something to happen. Anything. Mason had her ultimatum. With Mason, nothing came easy.

Abbie knew she could lose Keller, perhaps all three Germans. She was afraid Mason would stir up a hornet's nest after the stockyards incident. He was a self-centered ass and the *fat cat* of the valley. He wouldn't take this lying down. He might take his complaint to Camp Barlow? She imagined him blasting into the commander's office, pounding his fist, "Abbie Johnson's goddamned Nazis need to pay the price! They need to have their goddamned balls cut off!" That was his standard judgment for anyone who crossed him.

But Mason had disappeared. *Very strange.*

Augie Cooper hadn't seen him either. Augie had checked on the legalities of the cattle in his stock pens. No question, Abbie had equal authority to sell the cattle, Jackrabbit-J and Circle-J brands alike. Since Mason made no attempt to the contrary, Augie made the deal with Abbie. The cattle shipped off to Los Angeles yesterday morning.

Augie wrote Abbie a check for the entire amount. She would have cashed it, but she took Keller's advice, and didn't. Keller reasoned that if she accepted payment for cattle with a Circle-J brand, there was nothing to stop Mason from sending his cowboys out to take her cattle. If this turned into a range war, she would lose. Keller was right. The law was on her side but not the manpower. Her strategy was to live by the letter of the contract until Mason agreed to void it. That was what she really wanted—separated from Mason Johnson forever. She took the check back to Augie and tore it up. Then she asked him to write two checks, each for half the total. The second one was mailed to Mason.

Mason would probably explode. She expected to see his truck screaming up to her ranch. It didn't.

She expected to lose her German cowboys. She hadn't.

She waited for Mason to make his move. But he didn't.

63

Camp Barlow

June 12th . Hot! Not like back home in Germany where June is a warming introduction to summer. Not here. The *Arizona Republic* headline read:

PHOENIX HITS 115°

Barlow sits in higher desert than Phoenix. But even in Barlow, the thermometer was predicted to climb to 104°. Most POWs didn't convert the archaic Fahrenheit reading to Celsius, but the sun told them what they needed to know. It was hot.

In the mailroom, a clerk named Staudinger sorted through the day's delivery, mostly letters from hometowns in Germany. The volume of mail had slowed to a trickle in the weeks that led up to the German surrender. But now, a month later, the volume was on the rise.

Staudinger shuffled through the mail, looking for a particular type of envelope. He wasn't interested in its point-of-origin, or names, or addresses. That was irrelevant. He was looking for any envelope that was made of a particular type of paper, a paper that was slightly thicker than the norm and had a grey-white hue. A novice eye would never notice these envelopes as anything extraordinary, but Staudinger had been working the mailroom for two years. He could spot a grey-tint envelope as if it was a flashing beacon.

Staudinger took off his PW shirt and hung it on a hook. His thin undershirt was soaked in sweat. He turned the fan directly on him and dumped another mailbag onto the sorting table. In the mound of letters, one envelope popped out. That unmistakable, light grey. The letter was from Stuttgart and addressed to a corporal in Compound 2—just a smokescreen. Staudinger, a member of the Circle, knew what it really was.

He slit the envelope's rectangular flap with a razor blade. Two thin wafers separated and he removed a slip of onion skin paper with tweezers. *The spider lines are working again. At last.* The slip was a nonsensical message scribbled in light pencil, so as not to be detected through the envelope. He slipped the coded message inside his hat brim and would pass it to Sergeant Müller at the noon meal.

Keller and his bunkmate, Dieter Jung, were in the barracks getting ready for the day's work detail. Jung would go to the Anderson farm, Keller to the Jackrabbit-J.

"Did you hear about those idiots from that camp near Phoenix?" said Jung. "The ones who tried to escape last week?"

"Why would they do that?" said Keller. "The war is over."

"Who knows? By the time we get any news, big pieces are missing. One thing's for sure though, they must have felt a big need to get out that camp! The funny thing is, they got pretty far. All the way to Yuma."

"Where is that?" asked Keller.

Jung reached to his stack of magazines and pulled out a copy of *Life*. On the back cover was an advertisement for Chevrolet with a painting of an automobile superimposed over a map of the United States. Jung pointed to the map. "We're about here. Phoenix is here. Yuma is right about here. Very close to Mexico. Those guys hopped off the train and were going to cross the border there. Probably a good thing they got caught. The desert would've killed them."

Keller studied the map for a moment. "Yes. You wouldn't want to get lost out there this time of year. You'd bake, like in an oven." He handed the magazine back to Jung.

64

Abbie was covered in dirt. As she smacked her jeans, wisps of dust carried into the hot breeze. She was ready for a break. Umberto opened the wire gate and Abbie guided Chief to a water trough under the windmill, just outside the pasture fence. A couple of spindly mesquites had rooted around the man-made oasis. The mesquite didn't offer much shade, but it was better than nothing. Abbie tied the halter to a fence post. She sat in the grass, propped her back against a windmill stanchion and fanned herself with her hat. She watched the cowboys working in the pasture.

On the other side of the barbed wire, Schatz roped a bull calf. Weber wrestled it until he had control and then hoisted it with a quick lift, flopping the beast on its side. Schatz tied three legs. Keller stepped in with a hypodermic. The floundering calf went rigid when Keller pushed the needle into the animal's shoulder. Then, in a soapy bucket, Keller washed a scalpel. Weber pinned the calf's neck under his knee and Schatz held its legs. Keller made an incision into the animal's scrotum. With a practiced hand he pulled a testicle and sliced it from its cord. Deuce sat a few feet away from the cowboys and gave an anxious whine. Keller lobbed the slimy thing to the dog that caught the treat and swallowed it in one gulp, then waited for the next. The surgery complete, Keller brushed a disinfectant salve on the incision. Weber and Schatz then released the calf and it ran back to its mother. Umberto called from the opposite fence. He'd roped another. Weber hurried to lend a hand. Keller grabbed the kit.

Hector was gone. He'd left four days ago to visit his sister's family in Phoenix. He'd be there for another week. While he was away, Keller was in charge—the temporary foreman. Abbie watched him. He didn't have a lifetime of ranching experience, but he might be the most resourceful man she'd ever known. The cattle were in good hands.

Keller washed his hands in a pail of suds and wiped them on the legs of his blue jeans. He noticed Abbie sitting against the windmill, pried apart two strands of barbed wire, slipped through the fence, and walked over to her.

Abbie was glad to see him coming. Since the day Keller took on Mason, she trusted him—something she reserved for few men. She leaned on him for advice too, whether it was about hay storage, water tanks, or legal matters. He was easy to like. Even through his foreign accent, he showed a keen sense of humor. When Keller spoke she knew to listen or one of his quips might slide right past her.

Keller squatted down on a salt block. "That was zee last calf. I think in afternoon we will drive this herd to Foothills Tank for grazing. Lots of fresh grass over there. Do you agree, *Señora* Johnson?"

"*Señora*? Now you're speaking Spanish?" laughed Abbie.

"That is what Hector calls you," said Keller.

"But he speaks Spanish."

"So I shall call you *Frau* Johnson?"

Abbie snickered. "Noooo. That wouldn't go over too big in this town, *Señor* Keller." They both laughed at the unlikely sound of that name. Abbie asked, "What is your first name, Keller? I don't think I've ever heard it."

Keller poorly imitated a western drawl. "Round these parts, ever'one calls me Kraut. Kraut Keller. You kin just call me Kraut, ma'am."

She pushed him playfully and he lost his balance off the salt lick. "No, really. What's your real name?"

He chuckled as he righted himself. "Franz."

Abbie slowly pronounced it. "F-r-o-n-z. F-r-o-n-z. Sort of sounds like France, doesn't it?"

"Or Frank in English."

"I don't think I can call you Frank or F-r-o-n-z. You'll always be Keller to me. Just Keller. Like you only have one name."

"Like Plato—or like Napoleon?"

"Or like Chief," she said, pointing to her horse.

"Very funny," said Keller.

"You'll always be just Keller to me."

"And you vill always be just *Frau* to me."

"Noooo," implored Abbie. She slugged the top of his boot.

"Aiiee," cried Keller in mock pain. "You break my toes and you lose one cowboy."

Abbie's smile faded and her tone became serious. "That's what I'm afraid of. Gene Kirby came out to see me today."

"The deputy? How is he?"

"Got hurt pretty bad. Arm's in a sling. That fall busted up his shoulder, dislocated it." She pantomimed the injury. "He's pretty mad at Mason. Actually I think he never liked him—

just put up with him because he had to. Kirby's sort of looking out for me now after what happened at the stock pens. He told me what Mason's up to. It might involve you."

Keller sat up straight.

Abbie continued. "Mason's been running around everywhere, trying to get this thing stirred up. He called a meeting of the Cattlemen's Board. He even went to the County Recorder's Office in Bisbee trying to find some way to keep control of the Jackrabbit. Good news is I'm legally on solid ground. At least that's what Gene Kirby is hearing from the sheriff in Bisbee."

"This is good, yes?"

"It's not all good. Mason also went to Camp Barlow. Kirby says he's pretty chummy with your commander over there. If Mason starts pushing his weight around, it could come crashing down on you. Maybe Schatz and Weber too. I'm afraid to lose you Keller."

65

Camp Barlow

In the June heat, the officers' beer garden was usually deserted until after sundown. But when Schwering heard that Müller had news, he chose this place to meet. It was out of earshot. They moved their chairs under the shade of an umbrella, careful not to touch the metal fasteners that were as hot as a frying pan.

Schwering's brow beaded with sweat. He wiped his square rimmed glasses with a handkerchief and said, "You have news for me, Sergeant?"

"Yes, Major. The spider lines are finally opening again."

"I knew they would. Go on."

"We received a message from patriots in the fatherland. They tell us we have a traitor among us here."

"A traitor at Camp Barlow? Who?" asked Schwering.

"His name is Keller. Sergeant Franz Keller. He is one of the last arrivals. Been here since March. Compound 4, Barrack 19."

"What do we know about him?"

"The message was short and sketchy. Apparently, Keller deserted his post in Arnhem. He was attempting to steal sensitive Wehrmacht records and pass them on to the enemy. We are to make sure he doesn't return to Europe."

"Then he truly is a traitor. I wish we knew more. Do we know where the message originated?"

"Yes, Major. From a General Martin Uhlemann who ran the Records and Archives Office in Arnhem. Do you know of him?"

"No, never heard of him," said Schwering. "Sounds like a pencil-pusher to me. A desk jockey." They laughed. "I'd like to find out more about this. See what you can do."

"Yes Major," said Müller. "What about Sergeant Keller? Shall we consider him a *red* man?"

"Oh yes. Definitely so. You will organize a surveillance plan. Keep an eye on him for a week or so. Find out his patterns. Then we'll act. Let's have a plan running by tomorrow morning."

"Yes sir."

"Now, let's get out of this damned heat."

66

Jackrabbit-J Ranch

The kitchen table—the *only* table—in Abbie Johnson's house was made of Chiricahua Pine. Hank built it from some old plank floor boards. With saws and hand planes, Hank created a beautiful heirloom that still bore the blackened marks of old cut-nails. It was the young couple's first piece of furniture in their old adobe.

Two army officers sat across from Abbie. They'd shown up unexpectedly and asked to speak to her about a reported complaint.

"This is a fine little house you got here, Mrs. Johnson. Reminds me a little of my own place back in Ohio. Real cozy. Course mine's not made of dirt," chuckled Colonel Riley.

The comment felt like a snub. Abbie said, "The old adobe part of the house, where you're sitting, was built in the 1890's. A homestead. It's one of the oldest ranch houses in the valley. My husband

added the brick—the kitchen and bedroom, about five years ago."
She put on a pot of coffee.

"Real quaint," said Riley. "But doesn't the adobe get things kind
of dusty and dirty?"

"No Mr. Riley, it doesn't—"

"That's *Colonel. Colonel* Riley." He pointed to his insignia.

"No Colonel. I love my adobe house. It's the coolest, cleanest
place you could be on a hot day like this."

The other officer sensed the awkward direction of the conversation. He said, "Mrs. Johnson, the reason we're here is because there
was a complaint against one of your POW laborers. It's important
that we get your side of it."

"Well, it must be important since the top two officers from the
camp came out here to tell me about it, Mr. ... err ..."

"Major Davenport. Please call me Jim." Davenport's smile
seemed genuine. Abbie had a good sense of people. This was the
man to deal with, not the hot-aired colonel.

"What's this about, Jim?"

Riley butted in. "We have a written complaint about one of our
POWs. What's his name Major?"

"Keller, sir."

"Right, Keller. He attacked one of the ranchers in the area.
Caught him off guard, from behind."

"That rancher wouldn't happen to be my father-in-law, Mason
Johnson, would it, Colonel?"

"That's right. Fine man. I've worked with him before. Important
man around here too."

"I see," said Abbie.

"So, we're here to take the POW back to Camp Barlow," said
Riley. "The guards are getting him now. He'll spend some time in
the stockade for what he did."

Abbie said to Davenport, "Jim, did that complaint mention
that Keller was protecting me from my father-in-law who had just

hit me and knocked me to the ground? Did it say that Keller was protecting me by simply holding Mason back, not attacking him?"

"No, Mrs. Johnson. It didn't mention any of those things," said Davenport.

"Whew. Sounds like we got ourselves in the middle of a family squabble," chuckled Riley.

Abbie turned on Riley, "There was nothing funny about it, Colonel."

Riley bit his lip. "So be it, ma'am. We'll take the prisoner back to camp and sort it out there. You don't need to trouble yourself about it anymore."

"You can't have him. I need him here," said Abbie.

"Don't you worry Mrs. Johnson. We'll have a replacement here tomorrow," said Riley.

"I don't need a replacement. I need Keller. He's the best cowboy on this ranch right now." Riley had already dismissed her argument but she had Davenport's attention. She explained to him how Keller had learned the ranch work, how his skill with horses and cattle was irreplaceable, and how he was temporarily in charge until her foreman returned next week.

Davenport said, "I grew up in Montana, ma'am. I know the value of a good cowboy."

Riley interrupted Davenport. "That's all good and fine, Mrs. Johnson, but we can't have a dangerous man—"

"He's not dangerous," interrupted Abbie. "There were other people there who witnessed what happened. You can start with the deputy, Gene Kirby, who got his shoulder broken by Mason. You can also talk to Augie Cooper down at the stockyards. They saw the whole thing."

Riley was shaking his head. Davenport spoke up before the Colonel could say anything. "I'll talk to them, Mrs. Johnson. Today, if possible."

"Come on, Jim," blurted Riley. "We don't have time to turn this into a Supreme Court case."

"But Colonel, I think we owe it to Mrs. Johnson here to get to the bottom of this. If Keller was, in fact, only protecting her then I think she should keep her best cowboy working on this ranch."

Riley was angry. "If that's what you want to do Major, then you go right ahead. I'm not spending any more time with it." Riley stood and grabbed his hat. "But for today, we're taking the prisoner with us." Riley walked out the front door.

"I'm afraid I'll have to take a rain check on that cup of coffee, Mrs. Johnson," said Davenport as he followed in Riley's wake.

Abbie said, "Jim, thank you."

"I'll see what I can do, ma'am." Davenport's expression made it clear that dealing with the thick-headed colonel was an ongoing quest.

Abbie watched from the front door as Davenport hurried to the Jeep where Riley was waiting. In the second vehicle, a transport truck, she could see Keller in the back with a guard next to him. Keller's hands were cuffed behind his back.

Keller was taken back to Camp Barlow. The guards ushered him into the stockade. He'd been given no explanation why he was there but the guards bantered with each other, assuming Keller didn't understand English. One of the guards said, "This dumb Kraut bastard beat up a local cowboy." The other responded, "Even a dumb fucking Kraut should know better than that." Keller had his answer. Mason Johnson had broken his silence. But what was he up to? Why did it take so long? What was in store for Abbie?

He remained in the stockade for three hours. Solitary. Then a guard opened the steel door and a familiar face stepped in.

"You remember me, Sergeant?" It was Davenport.

"Yes Major. Of course," said Keller.

"Trouble seems to follow you around, Sergeant."

"Is this about the rancher, Johnson? Am I charged a crime?"

"You probably would be but I talked to three witnesses who said you did what any man should have done. You protected a woman."

"Then I may go back to work on the ranch?"

"It's not that simple, Sergeant. Even though that rancher is a son-of-a-bitch, he's still screamin' bloody murder. And he has important friends, even in this camp." Davenport raised his eyebrows. "I worked it out so you can go back to the ranch until the foreman returns next week. Then you'll be re-assigned back here, inside the camp."

Keller had been in the Wehrmacht long enough to know that armies didn't pass out justice. Armies were about moving forward and he was just a bump in the road.

Keller said, "Is that all, Major?"

"One more thing. When I talked to you last month, I told you that you might be a target of a group inside the camp. The Circle. Anything to report? Anything I should know about?"

Davenport was in earnest. Keller could tell he truly wanted to put a stop to the Nazis in Camp Barlow. But he also knew that other Americans would be involved. They may not be as sympathetic—or as intelligent. Keller might again become the sacrificial lamb but, in this case, he could pay with his life.

Keller said, "No sir. Nothing to report."

Davenport stared into Keller's eyes, trying to gain some insight. After a long pause he said, "That'll be all Sergeant. You may go."

67

Barlow

It was late afternoon. Abbie sat on a bench in front of the post office, holding a letter. She didn't want to wait to get home to open it. The return address was from Harley Penrod in Willcox. Mason's lawyer.

She opened it. It was a request for her to be present at his office, at 1:00 PM, Thursday. After a month of silence, Mason was making his move.

Abbie felt suddenly inadequate. Lawyers. Contracts. Did she really know what she was doing or was she just kidding herself? Up to this point, she'd been playing penny ante poker. Now they moved to the high stakes table and she'd never played this game before. But Mason had been playing it all his life.

6 8

Camp Barlow

Keller returned to his barracks, took off his shirt and grabbed a towel. An envelope was sitting on his bunk. It was written in a personal hand and addressed to him. This was the first letter he'd received since he'd been at the camp. He'd open it after he washed up.

In the lavatory, he dipped his head under the faucet, working soapy water through his hair. Someone tapped him on the back and whispered, "Keller. Keller."

He sloshed the water out of his eyes and spun around to see Dieter Jung.

Jung continued whispering, "Keller, what the hell have you been up to?"

"What do you mean?" said Keller, toweling his face.

There have been three, *at least three*, people asking about you today."

"What are you talking about?"

"This morning when I came back to my bunk, after taking a shit, a fellow was searching through your things."

"A guard?"

"No. Hell no. Not an American. He was one of those Nazi bastards. Then at lunch, that big fucker, Müller, sat across from me and started asking me questions about the work routines of the sergeants in this barrack. About Luzig, you, and me. The truth, he really didn't care what I said about me or Luzig. He wanted to know about *you*. Another one of those bastards questioned Luzig during a soccer match this afternoon. About *you*. What the hell have you been up to? These guys don't come around because they want to make friends."

Keller said, "Look Jung, I'm sure it's about nothing. Maybe my salute wasn't at a perfect angle, or maybe I don't bark out *Heil Hitler* loud enough. There's nothing to it."

Jung seemed to be buying it.

Keller knew this day might come. He was working on a plan but it wasn't in place. Not quite yet. How long until the Circle was ready to act? That's what he needed to know.

Keller finished shaving, draped the towel over his shoulder and returned to his bunk. He picked up the letter. His name and the original address appeared to be in feminine handwriting. Underneath that, the Camp Barlow address was printed in block letters from another person's hand. The envelope had been rubber-stamped in red from the Canadian Military Postal Service. On the opposite side was an American MPS stamp. The envelope had been cut open—no surprise. He took out the letter. It was written in the feminine handwriting and was in Dutch.

Dear Sgt. Keller,

My name is Cecile Wijl. I am a nurse at a medical infirmary near Arnhem.

It is with deep regret I tell you that your dear cousin, Taatje Hoobinck, has passed away.

His vision blackened for a moment. His head pulsed. *Is it true? Could it be? Why does this nurse refer to Taatje as my cousin? She's not my cousin.*

She was wounded during a bomb blast during the liberation of Arnhem. She fought for her life for three weeks before the Lord took her. During that time, we became fast friends. When she knew her death was inevitable, she told me her last wish was to tell you what had happened. She wants you to have the family photograph album. It was her dearest treasure and she trusts no one else in her family to have it. I am to tell you that it is right where it's always kept, and you are to get it when you return from the war.

Family photograph album—*the massacre pictures and documents.* My God. No one would know this unless Taatje wanted them too. *It's true. She's dead.* Keller's knees went weak. He sat on the bunk. His face tightened and a tear streamed down his cheek.

The Canadian Army controls Arnhem now. They have been very kind to the people of this city. They have promised me that because this matter is about the death of a family member, they will find your whereabouts through the Red Cross and get you this letter.

Taatje was a lovely girl. Though I only knew her for a short time, I miss her greatly. May God protect her.

Cecile Wijl
Arnhem

357

Keller stared at the photograph above his pillow, his only picture. *Taatje.* He gently ran his finger along its edges.

69

Jackrabbit-J Ranch

Abbie found Keller inside the stable. He was sitting on a hay bale and staring blankly into Pay Day's stall. The saddle and blanket were draped over a rail.

Abbie said, "Keller, Major Davenport just left. He told me what's going on. Says you'll only be working here until Hector comes back."

Keller sat, hypnotized.

"We've got to fight this. It's wrong. Mason's pushing his weight around. He's doing it to get at *me*." Keller remained silent. "You already know about this?"

He turned toward Abbie, his face weary. "Yes." His voice cracked.

"What's wrong?"

He shook his head.

Abbie sat next to him, "Tell me, Keller."

He grabbed a deep breath. "You remember I told you about a girl, in Netherland?"

"Yeah. The one with dark hair, and a pretty name—."

"Taatje."

"Yeah. Taatje." Abbie patted his arm. "Bad news? Did you get a dear-john letter? She find someone else?"

Keller looked at Abbie. "She is dead. Killed by a bomb."

"Oh. Oh. I'm sorry. So sorry."

His chest heaved and tears came.

She put her hand on his shoulder and rubbed. It was the first time she had touched a man with any sort of intimacy since Hank died.

He said, "I should not be so weak."

"It's alright, Keller."

He turned toward her. "You are a good person, Mrs. Johnson."

"It's *Abbie*," she said.

He looked up and wryly smiled. "You are a good person— *Frau* Johnson."

"Noooo. Not that name!" She playfully slapped his leg, stood and grabbed an oat can. "Saddle your horse. There's a place I'd like to show you." She walked over to Chief's stall and shook the can. The big gelding hurried toward her and stretched his head over the rail, reaching for a handful of oats. "Ready to go for a ride, boy?"

Abbie and Keller rode side by side. Little was said. His world was falling in on him. Had he done the right thing in Arnhem? If he hadn't stolen those records, or Brill's photographs, would any of this have happened? Would Taatje be alive? The past was catching up with him and he wondered if he would live to return to Maarburg. Could he fulfill her last wish?

"Where are we going?" asked Keller.

"We're riding the wire," said Abbie.

He shrugged, questioning her.

She said, "Riding the perimeter of the ranch—following the barbed wire fence. Hank used to say that if something was going to go wrong it would probably happen out here, on the edge of the property. If a calf gets killed by a mountain lion—if there's a break in the fence—that sort of thing.

"Does that ever happen?"

"Sure. A pack of coyotes killed a calf out here a couple weeks ago. Happens more often than you'd like to think."

"And a break in the fence?"

"It happens. We're constantly replacing these old posts when they rot out. One time, a section blew over and some cows got out. They found their way about a mile over that way to the Mitchell farm." Abbie chuckled. "They were feasting on some young corn chutes until Ol' Man Mitchell caught 'em. Whew! You ever seen a farmer get mad? That one cost me a few bucks."

Keller smiled. "So, ranchers and farmers—not always best friends."

"Let's just say it can be difficult sometimes. Seventy-five years ago, when Hank's family settled in this valley, they didn't need fences. It was open range, just like it still is up in the Bosque. Then the farmers came in. Things changed after that. That's why we're ridin' the wire. Find the trouble before it starts."

Their horses followed the property line to the foothills at the base of the Bosque. On a rounded hilltop was a small cemetery with a black iron fence and shaded by a few young trees. They tethered the horses to a post rail.

She led him through the arched gate.

In front of them were a lone headstone and a rock cairn. The headstone was inscribed.

†

HENRY LEE JOHNSON
1917 – 1942
Beloved Husband and Father

"This was Hank's favorite place on the ranch. The highest ground we own," she said.

The scent of sweet mesquite was on the breeze. The hills rolled downward toward the ranch house about a mile away. From where he stood, Keller could see the entire ranch. "It is beautiful to look from here," he said.

"I'll be buried here too. And who knows, someday maybe Will and his family." She looked down at the headstone. "It caused lots of trouble to put this little graveyard here. Family trouble."

"Why?"

"Hank died in '42. North Africa. Fighting Germans. Did you know that?"

Keller nodded. "Hector told me."

"Mason planned a funeral for him. He wanted Hank's grave to be on *his* ranch, in *his* family plot. I said no. Hank's grave will be here, on *his own* land. That's when I built this little cemetery, Hector and me. We had the funeral service here."

"Did Mason come?"

Abbie pursed her lips. "He came. But he didn't say a word to me. He's hated me ever since." She swallowed hard and wiped away a single tear. "And the funny thing about it—Hank's not even buried under that headstone. He's buried in Tunisia along with other Americans who were killed over there." She laid her hand on Hank's marker. "This is just a headstone."

"Will you bring him back, now … war has ended?"

"I don't know, Keller. I just don't know. The Army tells me it's a very nice cemetery. They brought me a picture of it. Neat white crosses, kept up with green grass and flowers. Maybe that's where he belongs, with other American soldiers. To me, it doesn't really matter where his body is. Ashes to ashes. When I come here, I come to be in this place, his place. I feel close to him here." She wiped away a tear. "Mason still fights me on it. He wants me to promise him that I'll have Hank's body brought back. But I won't make that promise. Not until I can figure out what's right."

Keller stepped away to give her some privacy. She was re-living an old fight. He walked over to the rock cairn. Volcanic stones had been thoughtfully stacked in a four-sided pillar that narrowed at the top. "What is this?" he asked.

"It's a memorial to my mother. My father visited me here a couple of years ago. He and I built it."

Keller shrugged. "I don't understand."

"My mother died when I was a little girl. She's buried back in New Jersey. When we moved out here a couple years later, my father built a cairn like this one behind our house, next to our flower garden. It was his way to remember her. He's a Munro. Thick Scottish blood. That's what they do."

"I have seen pictures of stones in Scotland. Was your mother … Scotland blood, also?"

"No. She was Irish—and German," she said with an awkward hitch. "Sometimes at night, Daddy would sit out by Mom's cairn and just talk to her. Sometimes I did too. It felt like she was really there with me. Then I didn't miss her as much."

"Is it still there? The stone—?"

"The cairn? No. My father sold the house when the war started. He moved to California where the jobs were good. He's in Los Angeles now, building Liberty Ships."

Keller said, "So, this is your mother's new place?"

Abbie nodded. "Now I come *here*. Sometimes I talk to her. Sometimes Hank. Sometimes both." Abbie smiled. "A pretty big conversation, huh? Silly, I know. But I like to come here when I'm sad."

"Not silly," said Keller. "You keep them alive inside you."

Abbie took Keller's hand and led him to the opposite side of the plot. She crouched down on one knee and cleared away a level area in the dirt. "Here Keller. Right here. You should build a stone cairn for Taatje." She reached through the fence and picked up a piece of malapai rock and put it in Keller's hand.

"But—this is *your* place."

"This is God's place," she said. "And he won't mind." She squeezed his hand.

Abbie went outside the fence where there was an abundance of volcanic malapai and shale scattered along the hillside. She picked out the flattest ones and carried them to Keller. He arranged the stones in a circular pattern—testing, fitting and re-fitting each one so the edges stayed even and the circle continued neatly upward, forming a cylinder. He worked in a trance. Abbie didn't speak, letting his mind go where it needed. It took almost an hour to complete the stone column.

The cairn was chest high when he finished. Abbie was on the other side of the iron fence, holding her horse's reins. "It looks just right, Keller. I give you my promise, it will always be here." She mounted her horse. "I'm going to let you be alone now. Come back when you're ready."

70

Camp Barlow

The truck was late returning from the Jackrabbit. When Schatz got to the barracks, others piled out, heading to supper. His shower would have to be quick or he'd be the last one to chow and have to settle for whatever was left.

Schatz washed in rapid motion, skipping the soap bar over his body and scrubbing in quick circles. He rinsed off and stepped over to a urinal, still naked and dripping. He was in front of the urinal when he heard footsteps behind him. He thought nothing of it. Men came in and out of the lavatory all the time.

Then darkness. A sack was thrust over his head and he was pulled backward, still peeing. His piss whipped around like an errant water hose until fear shut it down. Two pairs of hands clamped on him, then jammed him forward. He smashed against the wall, his nose and forehead smacked into the bricks. The assailants pinned him vertically and pressed him hard into the wall. He could barely breathe. One of the hands reached from behind, between his legs, grabbed his balls, and squeezed. The pain was searing. His impulse was to curl up, but he couldn't move. The electric spasm radiated from his testicles until all his muscles loosened in a sickening ache. Warm blood ran from his mashed nose into his mouth.

A voice spoke in a Bavarian accent, pressed behind Schatz's ear. "Now listen you asshole. I'm going to tell you something. If you don't listen carefully, my friend will jerk your nuts off. Understand?"

The grip tightened. He tried to answer but he couldn't summon a voice. His flesh had gone cold.

"Understand?" The grip pulled backward.

Schatz nodded and pushed out the words. "Yes. Understand." The grip eased.

"Good. Then listen. On Friday morning, the day after tomorrow, you are not going to go to work at your cattle ranch. Instead, go to the infirmary. Tell them you had the shits all night long and you're too weak to work. You got it?"

Schatz shook his head.

"That's all you have to do asshole. Don't fuck it up. If you show up at your truck, you'll be as good as dead. Screw with us, tell *anyone* about this, and you'll be buried in the back of this camp next to Jauch and Dreisenmann. But do what I tell you and you'll live to be an old man. Is everything clear now, asshole?"

"Yes," gasped Schatz.

"We're leaving you now," said the voice. "Don't move for two minutes. Are you listening?"

"Yes."

The grip twisted Schatz's testicles one more time as another charge jolted through his body. Then the hands released him and he heaped to the floor, moaning.

POWs were paid 80¢ per day. Those that worked for civilian employers, under the Labor Program, made more. Businesses that used prisoner-labor were required to pay the standard wage, the normal workers' rate. In the San Miguel Valley, farm labor was paid $1.20 per day. Ranch hands made $1.40. Each POW's "paycheck" was credited to his Camp Barlow account. While in camp, he could draw on his money in the form of canteen coupons, never cash. On the day the prisoner was finally sent home, he would be paid the balance. Then, and only then, would he be paid in real currency.

Keller walked out of the Camp Barlow Canteen with two cartons of Lucky Strikes. He made this trip every other day. Each carton cost him a day's pay. He put the cigarettes in a paper bag and walked to the motor pool. Next to the mechanic's grinding wheel was a 55 gallon drum, marked *SCRAP*. Keller dropped the cigarettes into the drum.

Sergeant Freddy Gonzales was the chief mechanic. He was also a black market operator. Gonzales's enterprise was geared on the German's need for American dollars—real cash. The POW laborers could buy things in town that they couldn't get at the canteen, primarily hard liquor and prostitutes. For a few, morphine. These things required hard cash and that's where Gonzales came in. He paid the POWs fifty cents on the dollar for their canteen purchases. When he had a few days leave, he took the loot to Tucson where he fenced it for a nice profit. Cigarettes worked best.

Keller placed the lid on the drum and walked toward Gonzales, whose head was under the hood of a Jeep.

"Watcha got?" asked Gonzales.

"Lucky Strike. Two cartons," said Keller.

Gonzales took a large roll of cash out of his pocket. He unraveled it and gave Keller a dollar bill and some change, $1.34, exactly half of what Keller had paid for the cigarettes. A bad bargain—but it was American cash and that's what Keller needed.

Schwering sat across the Camp Commander's desk. Colonel Riley shuffled through some papers. Standing next to the door was Major Davenport, Riley's XO who'd been snooping around, asking too many questions about the Circle.

Riley found what he was looking for and looked up at Schwering. "Major, it's going to be quite a process getting all you POWs back to Germany. *Repatriation* is what they're calling it. In order to make it look like we're doing something, the American government has decided to send a few Germans back now. They want officers, leaders who can help rebuild your country."

Schwering interrupted, "Excuse me Colonel Riley, but why are you telling zis to *me* and not Colonel Hoefer?"

"Because, Major, you've been selected as one who will be going home. Soon."

Schwering peered at Davenport. He suspected the XO had learned quite a bit from his investigation. Likely it was Davenport who suggested Schwering be among the first sent home, and away from Camp Barlow. Davenport returned Schwering's glare.

Riley continued, "Major, you're the lucky one. Hoefer will be here a while longer with his men. And those damned idiots in Washington will probably keep the enlisted men here until hell freezes over trying to decide what to do with them. France is screaming for us to send all our POWs to them. The goddamned French want you as slave labor to rebuild their country. If you ask me, we should just send all you Germans back home and stop spending money on a war that's over. Then we can stick to kicking the Japs' asses. But that won't happen. Truman is just as bad as Roosevelt—only dumber."

Schwering was amazed that an officer would talk about his government that way. In the German Army that would be grounds for treason. *The Americans are so weak.* Schwering couldn't imagine how they won a war.

Schwering looked at the paper in front of him. After almost three years at Camp Barlow, he was finally going to leave. Departure: June 16th. Saturday. In three days.

Riley said, "Major, I can't say that it's been a pleasure. This is a prison camp after all. But I will say that I know you are responsible, in a big way, for keeping order and discipline with our POWs. And I appreciate it." Riley reached across the desk and offered his hand. Schwering took it. *A civilian handshake instead of a military salute?* He took the hand and tipped his hat toward Davenport, then left Riley's office.

As Schwering was escorted from the American Officers' sector he felt a sway of emotion. He was happy to finally be leaving, to return to Germany. He joined the Wehrmacht in 1933, the year Hitler came to power. Soon he would be a civilian for the first time in twelve years. But his conviction would remain the same, faithful to the Nazi cause. The movement would certainly go underground in Germany—at least for a few years. Schwering pictured himself as one of the leaders of that cause. His new vocation would be the restoration of National Socialism to the Fatherland. It would happen.

Schwering also had misgivings. Camp Barlow had been his project. Since he arrived in 1942, Colonel Hoefer had turned the reins of the Circle over to him. He believed in himself and that he had done a superb job of keeping the Führer's ideals alive in this camp. But he also felt that his job wasn't finished. The captain of the ship should be the last off board. The choice wasn't his. He would put the Circle in Müller's hands. Müller, the Bavarian sergeant whom he'd sculpted. It would be up to Müller to run the Circle until all the soldiers were repatriated.

There was one loose end that Schwering must attend to—before he left.

Mess Hall 4B was filling up. The tables had been stacked outside to make room for benches. About three hundred POWs packed into the room, filling the makeshift auditorium.

Keller's shoulders were crammed for space as another man pushed in from the end of the bench. He saw Schatz come into the room. His nose was red and his cheek bruised. Keller tried to get his attention. Schatz glanced at Keller then looked away.

Keller looked around the hall. Two rows directly behind him, that big fucker, Müller, pushed his way in and commandeered a seat from an enlisted man. Müller glanced at Keller, then at Schatz, then back to Keller.

The Americans had been mum about the purpose of this meeting. Probably more *re-education* as the Americans called it. The Germans called it *Yankee dog shit*. In the evenings, POWs were sometimes required to sit through lectures on topics such as capitalism, democracy, and the American Bill of Rights. They watched American movies too, all with blatant anti-authoritarian plots. The movies were produced in Hollywood however—top quality. Two nights earlier they watched *Confessions of a Nazi Spy* starring Edward G. Robinson. Silly, but quite entertaining. The projector was set up in the center of the hall. Apparently, tonight they'd see another movie. Oddly though, they hadn't been charged the normal 15¢ coupon for this one. And why were they cramming so many men into one hall?

Major Davenport, the American executive officer, worked his way through the crowded room until he stood in front of the white projector screen. The room hushed.

Davenport spoke through a POW interpreter. "Men, as you

know Germany is now occupied and stabilized by American and Allied forces. You are about to watch a collection of film scenes that were taken by the American Army over the past few months. These films were shot as Americans liberated Jewish concentration camps. As you have heard, no doubt, Herr Hitler repeatedly denied that any wrongdoing, anything inhuman, had taken place in these camps. He claimed these camps were for the sole purpose of protecting the Jews until the fighting ended. That was a lie. Watch the film and you'll see the truth."

The lights went out and the projector started with a whirr and flicker. The film had no narration, no sound, only black and white footage. The first scene showed emaciated people in striped pajamas loading dead bodies onto a truck. Close-ups of living persons revealed them to be starving, walking skeletons. A few muttered conversations scattered among the German soldiers in the hall. The awkwardly spliced film then jumped to the next scene, more skeleton-people lying in bunk racks, too weak to stand, flies buzzing about their lips. A close-up showed a woman with sunken eyes and a vacant stare. The next clip panned the crematorium where naked, dead bodies were stacked halfway to the ceiling of a holding room. The camera moved to the ovens where partially charred bones and skulls were still inside an oven door.

Near the back of the hall, a POW began to wretch. He hurried through the doorway just as he vomited. The sound of his heaving became the soundtrack for the continuing scenes, one Jew after another, whose bodies were only loose skin clinging to bones. And many, many corpses.

The projector stopped. Though the room was dark, the profile of a German officer could be seen next to the projector. "This film is a lie," bellowed the officer. His voice and stature were known to all the POWs, Major Schwering. "It was certainly staged by the Russians as they invaded Germany from the east. The victims that you see in this film are not Jews. They are your fellow Germans,

371

now defenseless. Some are soldiers just like you who have become prey of the Red Army."

The lights came up. The crowd's eyes flashed back and forth from Schwering to Davenport. Davenport was clearly confused, not understanding the German tongue or the meaning of Schwering's tirade. Nonetheless, Davenport signaled the American guards to stop Schwering.

As the guards jostled their way through the human mass, Schwering hurried his speech. "The ignorant Americans have been duped by the Russian lie. The corpses in this film are not Jews. They are German people, including our women and children, who have been brutalized by the Russian aggressors."

The American guards reached Schwering who threw up his arms in a gesture of surrender. "Take me away. Throw me in the stockade. But that will not change the truth." He was manhandled by the guards and roughly escorted from the hall.

A murmur washed over the crowd. Keller heard the mutters from men sitting around him. "Yes. The fucking Russians did this." "Major Schwering is right." "Lies. Fucking Russian propaganda." But most POWs weren't saying anything. The quiet ones realized the film told the truth. This *was* the evil work of Hitler and his cronies—the National Socialist movement to which they had all sworn allegiance. The quiet ones were tired of the lies, and burdened with shame. Keller included.

"Atten-shun!" boomed Davenport. The Germans jumped to standing attention. "Shut your goddamned mouths!" Davenport's anger was real. The American guards along the perimeter of the room stood, arms ready. Davenport pushed to the front of the room through the silence. The interpreter started to translate. Davenport wheeled on him. "I don't need a goddamned interpreter. This will be crystal clear." He stood at the front of the room. "You *will* be quiet. You *will* watch the rest of this film. If there are any more goddamn stunts, the person responsible will be thrown into solitary and your whole goddamn barracks will be confined to quarters and on a three-day ration of bread and water. Now, sit your asses down. And shut your goddamn mouths."

The POWs sat. The hall was quiet. The lights went out. The projector flickered back to life.

71

Willcox

Harley Penrod grabbed a folder from his secretary and walked into his office. Three people were waiting. "Mrs. Johnson, before we start it's important for you to understand that I represent Mason here. Deputy Kirby is here at your request but he's not a lawyer. No offense, Deputy."

"None taken. I've just come along to keep the peace," Kirby said, as he tipped his hat with his left hand. His right arm was in a sling. "I'll just wait outside. Holler if you need me."

Penrod said to his secretary, "Mrs. Harris, could you get the deputy a cup of coffee?" Then he shut the door, leaving Mason, Abbie, and himself. "As I was saying, Mrs. Johnson, you don't have a legal representative here but it's your right to have one. If you'd like an attorney, we can put off this meeting another week or two."

"Mr. Penrod, you've been hanging your shingle in this town since I was a girl. Everyone knows you to be an honest man. What I

374

expect from this meeting is pretty simple and I shouldn't need a lawyer." Abbie looked around Harley's office. Behind his desk were several framed awards that had been presented to him by the Cattlemen's Association. There were photographs on the wall— grinning Harley, shaking hands with one rancher after another. She saw Mason in at least two of the pictures. Before the meeting, she assumed Harley Penrod would play the part of a mediator. She hoped she was right about that.

Mason sat to the side of his lawyer's desk. He hadn't spoken a word.

Penrod said, "Then let's proceed. Exactly what *do you* expect to get out of this meeting, Mrs. Johnson?"

"A signed agreement that puts an end to this," she said, holding up the joint ownership agreement. "No more partnership. I want to run *my* cattle on *my* ranch, and Mason to run *his* cattle on *his* ranch. That's all I'm after," said Abbie.

Mason rolled his eyes. He wouldn't look at her, but his glare burnt a hole into his lawyer.

Penrod said, "About a month ago, you told my client you believe you have a right to the profits from the Circle-J Cattle Company."

"I think it's stated pretty clearly in this contract. Mason owes me fifty percent of the profit from every steer that he's sold since 1938." Abbie's foot started to shake. She'd rehearsed this part over and over in her mind but now she had to perform it. It was like facing Mason on the gangway, all over again. She hated this but the contract was her trump card and she had to play it.

Penrod said, "Would you be willing to sign away all rights to those profits if my client agrees to disband the partnership?" Mason swiveled toward Abbie with the resolve of a pacing bull. Her instinct was to turn away from him. She couldn't give him that opening. *Don't back down. Don't give him any room.* She met his glare. *Don't back down.*

She said, "Let me put it this way Mr. Penrod—." Though she was talking to Penrod, her eyes were glued on Mason. "—If we can agree to end this partnership today, I'll sign away my claim to all Circle-J income. But if we can't do that, I *will* go to Tucson and hire a lawyer—and I *will* sue."

Mason stood and turned toward the pictures on the wall. Abbie had known Mason for a long time and had even lived under his roof for two years. She'd never seen him this way. She expected him to be full of threats and bluster. Now he was silent. She'd have felt safer with the screaming and cussing.

Penrod said, "My client and I have discussed this at length. He will be willing to break up the joint ownership as long as you will disavow any claim to his past earnings." Penrod placed two sheets of paper on the desk in front of Abbie. "The first agreement here dissolves the partnership. The second one is a statement that you have no claim to Mason's past earnings. In other words, Mrs. Johnson, you won't bring a lawsuit. Take your time and look over the documents. They're straightforward. Again, if you like, you can have a lawyer take a look at them."

Mason was pretending to study the photographs on the wall, but he was as tense as a wound spring. Penrod gave Abbie a friendly smile and nod. "Take all the time you need, Mrs. Johnson," he said.

Abbie leaned forward and read the papers. It all seemed too simple.

72

Jackrabbit-J Ranch

It was the finest saddle on the racks. The red leather had seasoned over the years into a wine-colored patina. It was fancier too. Broad silver disk-rivets connected the straps. The leather had been tooled into pleasing designs, swirling flowers and pine cones. A Mexican eagle with a snake in its beak was imprinted across the back skirt. This saddle had been made long ago by a skilled artisan.

Keller pushed the envelope deep into the saddle bag. It held eight dollars and fifty cents—his final payment.

Willcox

Abbie read the documents and said to Penrod, "They're written in plain English. That's good. I'll sign, but not until I see Mason's signature go down first."

Penrod said, "There is one more item, Mrs. Johnson."

Abbie raised an eyebrow.

Penrod took another sheet from the folder and placed it in front of her. "This is my client's only condition. Mason's ranch, the Circle-J, will be able to continue running cattle in the Bosque Verde. Federal law allows only base property, land that adjoins federal land, to apply for grazing rights."

Abbie said, "The base property is *my land*, the Jackrabbit-J. There are Grazing Service inspectors checking all the time. You're a lawyer, Harley. You know those guys won't allow Circle-J cattle to run up in the Bosque anymore, not once this partnership is over."

Penrod answered, "In front of you is a new contract that allows the Circle-J to lease the right to run cattle on Jackrabbit-J land. That right would legally extend to federal grazing land. Mason will pay you a dollar fifty per head, per year, for that right. This way, everyone's happy. Mason's happy. The GS inspector is happy, and you'll be happy too, pocketing an extra four to six hundred dollars per year."

Abbie said, "There's not enough grass. The GS will only allow four hundred head on that land. If half of those cattle are Mason's, then my hands are tied and my business can't grow. It's the same old problem. Hank let it happen before. He let his father come first."

Mason spoke for the first time. "I put up the money to buy your ranch—*for my son*. I gave him his first fifty head. All I ever asked in return was grazing rights on the Bosque. Hank was thankful for everything I gave him and was happy to return my favor with those rights."

Abbie felt the noose tighten. Mason used this ploy on Hank many times—obligation through guilt. If she let him do it again, she'd be right back where she started. When she walked into this meeting, she told herself she would accept nothing less than complete separation from Mason Johnson. She pushed the third paper across the desk. "No deal," she said.

Mason turned on Abbie. His face was red and eyes were ready to pop. He slapped down on the papers and slid them back in front of Abbie. *This* was the Mason she recognized.

"Sign the papers, you bitch." He leaned over her, placing his hands on the arms of her chair. She crunched back into her seat. He hovered like a coyote over a cottontail. Grabbing a pen, he said, "Sign the fucking papers. All three." He dropped the pen in her lap, grabbed her chair with both hands and shook it.

Abbie shrieked. He was ready to hit her. He'd done it before. Luckily, on that occasion, Keller had stepped in.

Penrod shouted, "Mason, stop. You're only making things

worse." Mason didn't budge. His face moved in, inches from Abbie's. How she wished she had Hank to stop this. Or Keller.

From the doorway, there was an unmistakable click. "Stand back, Mason. Get away from her." Kirby held his pistol, pointed toward the ceiling.

"You realize who you're talking to, Gene? If I were you, I'd turn around and walk away."

"Back off Mason," demanded Kirby.

Penrod huddled for refuge in the corner.

Mason said, "Gene, let me remind you that the only reason you have any authority around here is because I have a hell of a lot of pull with the Sheriff's Office. Now git out."

Kirby leveled his pistol at Mason. "Things have changed around here, Mason. They ain't like they used to be. And you've got only yourself to blame for that. Now step away from her."

Mason didn't move. Kirby kept the gun to his head. Five seconds. Ten. Fifteen. Mason broke his grip and stood erect. He ignored Kirby's pistol and turned to his cowering lawyer. "Give me a pen, Harley. Show me where to sign. Let's get this goddamn thing over with."

The deputy eased the hammer of his pistol and slid it back into its holster.

Mason signed the first two documents. The third, he pushed away and let it flutter to the floor. Then he stormed out of Penrod's office.

7 4

Jackrabbit-J Ranch

"Schatz. Did they get to you? The Nazis?"

"Go away, Weber," said Schatz. He continued loading the pickup with tools—a pickaxe, a shovel, and baling wire.

"Come on Schatzi. No one else is around. Tell me what happened to your face."

"I fell out of bed."

"You're full of shit. They got to you, didn't they? Tell me. I need to know. One of those Nazi peckers stopped me last night in front of the barracks, asked me questions—mostly about how we get back and forth to the ranch. But he also asked me about Keller. He told me that big asshole, Müller, might be talking to me soon. Are they after us? You and me? What about Keller? Tell me what's going on. They're the ones that did this to you, aren't they?"

Schatz piled in to the driver's seat and slammed the door. He faced Weber who was leaning in the passenger window. "Step down. Let me go."

"You've never acted like this before, Schatzi. Damn you. Tell me what happened."

Schatz started the truck. "Get out of my way. Keller wants the fence fixed today. Umberto's up there waiting for me." He goosed the accelerator and cranked left. Weber skittered along next to the truck until he had to let go.

"Wait. Schatz." He ran to keep up, but he was left in the dust. "Schatz! You fucker! What the hell is going on?"

Abbie found Keller in the barn loft, pulling down hay bales.

"Mind if I come up?" she called. "I've been looking all over for you." Her head popped up over the rafters. "I just saw Schatz. What happened to his face?"

"I don't know. He won't say."

"I have some good news, and you're the first one I get to tell." Abbie pulled two papers out of an envelope and pushed them in front of Keller. Wearing a big smile, she said, "Take a look."

"English is difficult to read," said Keller. "Please, you tell me what this says."

"It says that Mason Johnson no longer has any claim to these cattle, this ranch, or the Bosque Verde. He can't touch my ranch. Ever again." She threw her arms around him and gave him a quick peck on the cheek. "I have you to thank."

Keller was dumbfounded, more by the kiss than by the compliment.

Abbie was vitalized. "Now listen Keller. The next thing we need to do is to get that Colonel to change his mind and let you stay here." Her smile grew. "Keller, I stood up to Mason today—*and I won*. I can get Riley to change his mind too, I'm sure—"

"Stop. Stop. It's not so easy, Mrs. Johnson. There are some things that I've been waiting to tell you. To tell you *today*."

"Sounds serious, Keller. What's going on?" She leaned against a hay bale.

Keller's story flowed as he found relief in finally sharing it. He told Abbie about his leg injury and his desk job in Maarburg. He told her about Taatje and the murders in the barn—about his own cousins and Taatje's parents who were slaughtered simply for the political ambitions of a German general. He described how he stole the documents and photographs from Van Sloten House. About their hiding place in Taatje's flat. He relived his escape from Arnhem and his capture by the American Rangers. He circled back to the story of Taatje—how her death left an obligation on his shoulders. He took a folded piece of paper out of his pocket and handed it to Abbie.

"I've written down the important things. The name of my family and others who were murdered. The name of the murderer, General Martin Uhlemann. And the hiding place of the documents and photos that will prove he is guilty. Here it is, 131 Kuiperstraat in Maarburg. Everything is hidden in the wall behind the stove."

Abbie paced the loft while she looked over the paper. "Why are you giving this to me? You must go back to Holland when the war ends and turn this information over to the authorities. What are you not telling me?"

"You are the only one I can trust. If I don't get to the Netherlands, I need you to get this to the right people. I may not live to return."

"What are you talking about Keller? What's going on?"

Keller told Abbie about the POW camp—the Circle—the Nazis —the spider lines. Abbie sat on the floor planks and propped her back against a post. What had started as a joyous afternoon had become deathly serious. She clung to his tale, trying to fathom the hell inside Camp Barlow. He believed the Circle knew his secret, or they would soon. He explained how Davenport warned him about messages coming through the spider lines, that if the Circle finds out they will kill him.

"Have you said anything to the American guards?" asked Abbie. "They should protect you from this...Circle."

"If I go to the Americans and they do not help, I will be dead. The Nazis know everything inside the camp. If that happens, my secret will die also. That is why you have it now."

"But Keller, there has to be something else you can do."

Keller said, "I am working on a plan. But I need another day, maybe two. Then I might be safe."

"You're not convincing me. What are you going to do?"

"I cannot tell you. It is best that you know nothing about it. *Unwissenheit ist ein Segen.* Not knowing is a ... blessing."

She was angry. "Yeah Keller, we have an expression, too. *Ignorance is bliss.* But I'm not buying it. You tell me all these other things —these murders and this Nazi *circle*. But you won't tell me how you intend to save your own life?"

"You cannot know."

75

Weber was awake all night. The Nazis had left him alone. So far.

Drained, he lumbered toward the mess hall to grab breakfast. Schatz usually went with him, but Schatz had been back and forth to the latrine all night. Must have eaten something bad. At sun-up, Schatz reported to sick bay.

Meals at Camp Barlow weren't as good as they used to be. No more breakfasts of eggs, ham, bread, and fresh Arizona oranges. Now it was creamed beef on dry toast. *Shit-on-a-shingle,* the Americans called it. Since V-E Day, the cordial treatment had deteriorated. The American guards were gruff. Privileges and activities were limited.

Throughout the war, Americans had treated their prisoners well. The aim was to set a high standard for reciprocal treatment of American soldiers in Axis captivity. Now the European war was over and the American POWs had been liberated from the German camps. *Quid pro quo* was no longer needed.

As Weber entered the mess, he was stopped by an American guard.

"You Corporal Weber?" snapped the guard.

"Yes sir."

"Come with me. You've been assigned KP duty."

"*Nein*. A mistake. KP? I haf done nothing wrong."

The guard said, "Look, don't give me any bullshit, buddy. You must have done something to piss somebody off. Here's the yellow slip. Look at it yourself. Now let's get going."

All prisoners tried to avoid the *yellow slip*, an order for disciplinary action. The slip was often issued for fighting, breaking curfew, or insubordination. As they walked, Weber looked at the form. His name and ID number were at the top. The offense was scribbled in as *curfew violation - June 14th*. Last night? Impossible. Weber was in his bunk for lights-out. The yellow slip was authorized by an unfamiliar American Lieutenant named Evans. However, the infraction was referred by Major Horst Schwering. Weber gulped. It was common for German NCO's to refer POWs for discipline. The Americans rubber-stamped them for their own records. But to be referred by Major Schwering! Weber's knees weakened.

Weber was escorted to the trash bins behind one of the mess halls. On the wall above the barrels was a sign:

Mess Hall 2A
Keep Area Clean
Trash Removal, 0845, Daily

Standing among the trash cans was Corporal Andreas Lange. Weber knew him by reputation—one of the Circle.

The American guard said to Lange, "Here's the first guy. I'll be back in a couple of minutes with the other one." The guard left.

This was the nightmare Weber had avoided through his sleepless night. The Circle wanted him. But why?

The back door to the kitchen slapped shut. Sergeant Müller eclipsed the entryway. Weber looked around. No one else in sight. Just the two Nazis, *and him.*

Weber backed away from the behemoths. "Sergeant, what do you want from me?"

"KP duty, Corporal," barked Müller.

"But I didn't do anything wrong."

"Sure you did. The yellow slip doesn't lie. Let's see, curfew violation."

Weber had heard of the Circle's ploys before. He choked out the words, "It isn't true. You're setting me up."

The gorillas didn't acknowledge his plea. Lange stepped closer.

Weber squawked, "I'll go to the Americans. I'll tell them what you've been doing—"

"We need to shut him up," said Müller.

Weber panicked. He turned to run, but Lange tackled him before he could get two steps. He was lifted by his collar. Müller swung him around until they were face-to-face. Lange tied Weber's arms behind his back.

"You fool," said Müller. "All you had to do was play along. Two hours of trash detail and no one would ever bother you again. But you've made it clear you're a liability. A stupid mistake, Corporal." Müller produced a strand of wire from his pocket.

The staging area was a flurry of activity every morning after breakfast. The transport trucks were parked in files waiting for their human cargo, POW crews on their way to the farms and ranches of the San Miguel Valley. The Stephenson farm crew piled into the back of Brooks's truck. Brooks took his clipboard off the hook. It had three extra sheets clipped to it. The top one was from sick bay stating that Private Schatz was ill and would be spending the day there. The other two were carbon copies of yellow slips. One for Weber. The other for Keller. They'd be on KP this morning. Brooks was surprised. *Not like either one of these guys to find trouble.* It didn't say whether he needed to pick them up after their KP detail and take them to the ranch. He'd call from town later. *Easier than walking all the way over to Officers' Country right now.* Also best not to ask, lest they find more work for him to do. After he got the Stephenson crew going, he'd have time to stop at the Route 81 Diner for a cup of coffee. Brooks had a chance to loaf a little since he didn't have to go to the Jackrabbit-J this morning. *Take advantage of it when you can.*

Keller was walking to the staging area when an American guard trotted up behind him.

"You Keller?" asked the American.

"Yes."

"Thought that was you," said the guard. "They told me you had a limp. Wasn't sure I'd catch you before you shipped out." The guard gave him the yellow slip. "Here you go. Follow me. Looks like you're in for a fun morning, cleaning out grease traps."

"What is this? Curfew violation?"

"You too, huh? Listen. Don't ask me," said the guard. "My job is to find you and get you to the mess. You can ask all the fucking questions you want, once you're there."

76

Vienna

Uhlemann grew frustrated. He'd been holed up in Vienna for three weeks. The Russian Army was now in control of most of the city. The fucking Red Army! Slavic barbarians now held this cultural gem in the palms of their hands. There was no logic in the way the moronic Allies divvied up their occupied territories. The Russians given Vienna? Might as well give chimpanzees box seats at the opera. There was a small consolation. A slice of Vienna was designated as a French sector. Although Uhlemann had no love for the French, they were a damn sight better than the neanderthal Bolsheviks. The French sector was on the near side of the Danube and only a few blocks from Uhlemann's flat—his hiding place. When he went out, which was rare, that's where he went.

Vienna was dealt its own hell during the war, American and British bombers. Necessities were now in short supply. Starvation and disease were rampant. What little food the Viennese had came from their Russian occupiers. And that was damn little. Grubbing, begging, and prostitution became standards for survival. Only if one had cash were things available—through a well-oiled black market.

When Uhlemann, alias Otto Schröder, went underground he was provided with the best sort of cash, a currency better than worthless Reichsmarks or even French Francs. He had American dollars. He could buy anything he wanted.

In the French sector, Uhlemann learned quickly where and how to buy his staples—bread, cheese, hard sausage, and beer. He also had a new-found weakness for American cigarettes, Pall Malls. A little fellow named Markus hung out around a green warehouse near a railroad siding on the *Felberstrasse*. Markus took care of him. For a price.

Uhlemann found him standing against the corner. "Markus, is your *store* well-stocked today?"

"That depends Mr. Schröder. What do you have for me?"

"Dollars, of course."

"In that case, Mr. Schröder, I have anything you want. How about fresh bread and veal. I have lots of canned meat too, American Army rations. It's not fucking *caviar*, but it will fill your belly. I'm out of Pall Malls, but I've got Lucky Strikes. That alright?"

"Sure. Anything beats the hell out of those Russian cigarettes."

Uhlemann followed Markus through the door of the bombed-out warehouse.

7 7

Camp Barlow

The guard led Keller through the front doors of Mess Hall 2A. The smell of coffee and burnt toast hung in the air. The hall looked the same as Mess 4B where Keller ate his meals. Strange though, the hall was deserted. Breakfast ended only five minutes ago—the entire camp was on the same schedule—yet there wasn't a kitchen worker to be seen anywhere. From behind the swinging kitchen doors, a POW emerged.

"Here's the second one," said the guard. Then he left.

"Come along," said the POW. "You have some dishes to wash."

Keller stood just inside the mess. He didn't move. He'd seen this fellow before, one of Schwering's goons. Things were falling into place—the bogus yellow slip—the empty mess hall—the Nazi thug. He'd walked into their trap.

Keller turned toward the door but the hulking Müller blocked his way. Müller took advantage of Keller's surprise. Lange swept his leg under Keller and Müller bulled him over. Keller crashed to the floor with Müller's full weight smashing into him. Lange pulled Keller's arms behind his back and hitched them with a strap. Müller bore his full weight on Keller while Lange pulled a neckerchief gag into Keller's mouth like a horse bridle, then tied it off. The two goons hoisted him and ushered him down the aisle, his feet hardly touching the floor. Müller and Lange pushed him headlong through the swinging doors into the kitchen, then into a back room —a storeroom, stacked high with pallets of cans and sacks.

Keller was slammed into a chair. "Don't move," bellowed the Bavarian sergeant who stood over him holding a long kitchen knife against his neck. Lange was behind him, hands bearing on Keller's shoulders. He didn't dare move. Above him, a thick wire was suspended over a brass pipe and tied off somewhere behind him. Directly above, the wire had been fashioned into a hangman's noose.

Above the kitchen doorway was a poster of a fat cartoon pig, with the caption, *"We Want Your Kitchen Scraps. Don't Waste!"* A shorter man came through the doorway wearing unmistakable square-rimmed glasses. Major Schwering.

Schwering surveyed the scene, apparently content. "Sergeant Keller, perhaps you are wondering why you are getting all this attention?" Schwering smirked, "Do you like our little meeting room? This storeroom has served us for some time. We like to think of it as a sort of city hall. You know, a police station, council chamber, and courthouse all wrapped into one. Oh, I admit the décor is lacking, but what it lacks in amenities it makes up for in privacy. You're not the first one to face justice here. Hopefully, you'll be the last."

Schwering paced and nodded approval to his cronies. "Sergeant Keller, I have little time. This will be resolved right now, one way or another. I have some questions regarding your messy situation in the Netherlands. I wish to leave no loose ends. So Sergeant, your only hope for an agreeable conclusion is to be forthcoming with answers. Corporal Lange, please remove the gag from Sergeant Keller's mouth."

As Lange untied the gag, Müller made the knife visible and touched the flat blade to Keller's neck. The strap that tied Keller's hands was a little loose. With effort, he could possibly work his hands free. But what then? This was still checkmate.

Schwering pulled up a stool and sat directly across from Keller. Müller and Lange were flanked on his sides. "Sergeant Keller, do you know why you are here?"

Keller didn't answer. He looked around the room. To Schwering, it might have appeared that Keller was afraid to meet his eye, but Keller was appraising his situation.

"Sergeant Keller, the charges against you are quite serious. You have stolen important documents from the Reich, from a Wehrmacht general, no less. And you are a deserter. Both of these acts constitute treason. Do you have any defense for your actions, Sergeant?"

Keller's eyes were focused on the utensils that hung above the butcher's block. The implements dangled from a horizontal bar that was suspended from a ceiling joist. Spatulas, ladles, and at the far end—knives. Long knives used for slicing meat. If he could work his hands free he might rush toward the knives. But at best, he would get one step, one move. The knives were too far away. The goons would be on him before he could get there. That wouldn't work. To his right side were stacked pallets of flour and potatoes. To his left was a waist-high pile of rice sacks. Behind him were shelves holding large containers of canned fruit and syrup. No potential weapons.

His wrist was working its way through the belt knot. His hand was turned at a tight angle and the pain from his skewered wrist was becoming intense—a pain he could not reveal.

Schwering said, "The information I've received from abroad has been sketchy, but one fact was made clear. The documents you stole from the archive were never retrieved. My sources seem confident that you know their whereabouts. Sergeant Keller, if you have any hope of leaving here alive, I suggest you give me a direct answer. Where are those documents?"

Keller didn't answer. Schwering was lying. His only chance of survival depended on his wits. He twisted his wrist a bit more, and the strap moved another nudge.

Schwering leaned in. "I'm not sure what game you think you're playing with your silence, but you may be sure I mean business. Your friend didn't cooperate with us. All's the pity. Corporal Lange, if you please."

Lange left Keller's side while Müller's knife rocked against his neck. Lange chucked rice sacks toward the back of the storeroom. Something was buried beneath them. Lange hoisted a sack, revealing a boot. He pulled another away—the torso wearing a PW shirt. Lange lifted the last sack and tossed it aside. The body was gray-pale, eyes glazed and fixed. Dead. It was Weber.

78

Jackrabbit-J Ranch

"Pick up your head and eat. The school bus will be here in twenty minutes."

The sleepy boy circled the bowl with his spoon, making no attempt to bring food to his lips.

Abbie pushed the bowl of Farina under Will's nose. "Your breakfast is getting cold. Eat, young man."

Abbie used the term *young man* when she prepared to wage a mother-son battle. This was a battle Will would never win, not even a minor skirmish. He surrendered and shoveled a spoonful of the sticky mush into his mouth.

Through the screen door, Abbie saw Hector and Umberto walking toward the barn. She'd heard Hector return in the middle of the night. A pickup truck had dropped him off at the *barracón*. He wasn't due back until later today. Must have gotten an early ride from Phoenix.

Now that Hector was back, Keller would be gone. This would be his last day on the ranch unless Abbie could figure a way to change the mind of that thick-headed ass, Colonel Riley.

She needed Keller.

79

Camp Barlow

"We never intended this to happen to your friend," said Schwering. "If only he had shut his mouth and done what he was told. An obstinate fellow. It made him a liability." Schwering looked down at Weber's lifeless face. "No matter. His body will be burned beyond recognition in an unfortunate accident." Schwering looked back at Keller. "As will yours, unless you tell me where the Arnhem documents are."

Behind his back, Keller twisted his wrist. The belt slipped. His hands were free and tingled as blood flowed through his veins again. Müller stood behind him, holding his blade under Keller's chin. Keller didn't dare move.

Schwering pulled his seat a couple of feet from Keller and sat again. "Yes, burned," said Schwering. He signaled Lange who produced a wrench, kneeled behind the oven, and loosened a brass fitting. A hiss of gas brayed from the opened pipe. From his pocket,

Lange attached a clock-timer to a small battery pack. He set it on the floor next to the leaking pipe.

"You may start the timer when you wish, Major Schwering," said Lange. "It's set for two minutes. Just connect the terminals."

"Thank you corporal," said Schwering. "I believe it's time for you to get to the infirmary. Keep an eye on Private Schatz. No telling what he might do once this ordeal begins." Lange left.

Schwering continued, "You see Sergeant, the gas is heavy. This room is like a basin and the gas will pool at your feet." The rank odor had already spread across the room. "When the timer sparks, the explosion will be quite powerful. This room will go up in a ball of flame. And the building too, I suspect. If you don't cooperate with me, you'll burn too and be identifiable only by your dog tags."

Lieutenant Evans dropped the papers on Davenport's desk. "Here you go sir. Today's delinquents."

"Got a few yellow slips today, huh?" said Davenport. "Anything I need to know about?"

"Not really, sir. "Three guys snuck off the Robertson Farm yesterday and got a ride into town. We picked them up at Sally's Box Car."

"Sally's Box Car?"

"Yes sir. A whorehouse just down the tracks. It's an old train car that's been...umm...renovated."

"That's a new one on me. What else you got here?" asked Davenport.

"The other two slips were turned in by the Germans. Nailed a couple of their own guys for curfew."

Davenport thumbed through the yellow citations. The whorehouse patrons were given latrine detail for a week. The two curfew violators were assigned KP in Mess Hall 2A. Davenport noticed the name at the top of one of the slips, Sgt. Franz Keller. He jumped to his feet. "When did these come in? The curfew violations?"

"I just signed off on them this morning, sir."

"Shit! Get me some MPs to Hall 2A. Now!" Davenport bolted out the door.

Schwering gave a short nod to Müller. Müller dipped his arm downward and then swung the knife like a scythe toward Keller's neck. At that moment, Keller brought his arm upward, deflecting Müller's. Surprise was on Keller's side. In one motion Keller rose from the chair and turned on Müller. His movement was instinctive and automatic, based on years of army training. Keller drove the heel of his boot into the crook of Müller's foot. The giant gasped and doubled forward in sudden agony. Using Müller's forward motion, Keller grabbed the back of the big man's head and pulled downward, slamming his knee into the behemoth's chin. Müller howled and reeled as he crumpled to the floor, cradling his jaw. Blood gushed from his mouth. His teeth had severed his tongue and it dangled by a thread of flesh. Keller was above Müller. With both hands he clasped a large container from the top pallet, a two-gallon can of peaches, and brought it downward with fury. The can smashed into Müller's skull with a sickening thud.

Müller shuddered violently, his body wracking in rapid spasms. His knife had fallen to the floor and Keller grabbed it. But before he could stand, a cord was dropped over his neck from behind—and pulled tight. Schwering. The noose. The cord was looped on the overhead pipe and was jerked upward. Keller writhed against it. With each movement, the slack was taken up and soon he was standing on tiptoe.

Keller grabbed at the cord with his free hand—to no avail. Schwering had the other end of it. Every time Keller flailed, Schwering cinched the line that was cleated on a wood post. Keller was being gradually hanged. With another lurch, Schwering jerked Keller another inch—nearly off the ground. Only the toes of his boots were in contact with the concrete floor. Schwering looped two quick hitches over the cleat, securing the gallows.

Keller was wrestling for air, but it didn't come. He danced on his toes trying to relieve the tension of the cord. He stumbled and swung. No air. No breath. The noose tightened with each motion. His vision became spotted, red and black blurs. The skin of his neck folded up into his jaw and his cheeks were forced into his eyes. He bobbed and turned in a slow circle. Schwering passed through his field of vision. He was bending over the cleat. He was close— within arm's length. Keller felt the grip of the knife in his hand. He hadn't dropped it. He pushed his body weight forward to keep spinning, pivoting on one boot toe. Around again.

As Keller came around the second time, Schwering stood up. Keller slashed at him. Schwering raised his hand to defend. The knife's keen edge swept across Schwering's palm, cleaving the flesh like a butcher filleting a fish.

Schwering screamed. He cradled his hand and banged against Keller as he careened away from him, wailing as he stared at his hand that was flayed open down to the grey bones. Blood pumped from the wound and swept down his arm.

Schwering was consumed with his injury. Keller had an opening. One chance. With the knife, Keller sawed at the cord above his head. Each movement tightened against his neck. He was desperate for air. His vision was a blurry red. The knife cut the fabric insulation, but the metal strands were another matter. He felt the blade grinding against metal. It wasn't working.

Schwering was in the opposite corner of the room, wrapping his hand in a dish towel. The white cloth was saturated in red.

Keller dropped the useless knife. With both hands he reached above his head and gripped the wire cord. With every bit of strength he could summon, he hoisted upward, lifting himself off the ground until his head reached the height of his hands. His arms shook. Grasping the wire in his left hand, he thrust his right hand upward and grabbed the metal pipe. His muscles screamed. He pulled up with one arm until his head was at the level of the pipe. The cord slackened. With his left hand he worked the noose open. Air swept into his lungs. He looked down. Schwering was still at the butcher's block swaddling his hand and screaming curses over the whistle of the leaking gas.

Keller worked the noose off his head. His right hand slipped off the pipe and he crashed to the floor next to Müller's corpse. The gas was suffocating at this level. The back exit—a flimsy screened door—was about fifteen feet away and slapping at its jamb from an outside breeze. He had to get out. Now.

Keller scrambled to find his footing then moved toward daylight. Out of the corner of his eye he glimpsed Schwering who had staggered to the door that led to the kitchen. Schwering turned toward Keller. One hand was bound in a red rag, the other held a small silver object. Schwering flicked it open. A cigarette lighter. Keller bid his legs to churn faster. Schwering thumbed the striker wheel and a small flame flickered. He tossed the lighter in an arc and disappeared into the kitchen.

Keller zeroed-in on the screen door. He pumped his legs and leaped, arms braced in front of him—his body horizontal. As his hands hit the door he saw the flash and felt the hurtling concussion from behind.

Davenport ran toward the mess hall with four guards in tow. As they rounded a corner the hall came into view, two buildings ahead. Fragmented facts flew through Davenport's mind. He knew about the Nazis—about the Circle. No doubt they were behind the deaths of Jauch and Dreisenmann. Maybe they were on to Keller now. Schwering was the ringleader and Davenport knew the names of some of his henchman. But he wasn't able to prove any of it! He was a soldier, goddamnit. Not an investigator. Riley should have brought in the Provost Marshall right from the start. Let the damned professionals handle it. Now Davenport was afraid he'd screwed up and the Nazis would murder again.

FAWHHUMMP! The rear walls of the mess hall blew outward. Chunks of clapboard and asphalt roofing shot in every direction. Davenport and the MPs hit the ground and covered up.

Flames consumed the back of the building. Men emerged from all directions, guards and prisoners. They yelled and pointed, trying to figure a way to fight the inferno. A few of them ran toward the fire only to be backed away by the impervious heat. The area was bedlam.

The front door of the mess hall crashed open. A single man caromed out of the building, tumbled off the stoop and rolled to the ground. Two POWs rushed to his aid, dragged him to the safety of an adjacent barrack and propped his back against the wall.

Davenport recognized the survivor and ran to him. "Major Schwering. Are there others inside?"

Blood streamed from Schwering's hand. He looked up at Davenport and didn't respond at first. Then choosing his words carefully, he said, "*Ja. Ja.* Yes. There are others."

"What happened in there?" asked Davenport.

Schwering's English was normally quite good. Now it seemed to desert him. "*Ich weiss nicht.* I...know...not. *Wir waren...*We instruct men for KP. *Etwas...*Something explodes. In kitchen. I was...*Glück*...lucky."

Davenport didn't believe a word.

8 0

Jackrabbit-J Ranch

It was only 10 AM and already a hundred degrees. Abbie turned the brim of her hat toward the sun as she walked to the barn. The field grass had been a lush green only a few weeks ago. Since then, it baked into yellow straw.

She found Hector saddling Cherokee. The heat inside the stable was stifling.

"How was Phoenix?" she said. "Get a chance to see your relatives?"

"*Si Señora*. Stayed as long as I could stand it. Couldn't wait to get back here though." He straightened the saddle blanket. "Where are those Germans, anyway?"

"I don't know. They should have been here a couple of hours ago." She wiped a sleeve across her forehead.

Hector hoisted his burgundy saddle onto Cherokee's back and

tightened the cinch. "Well, I hope they show up. Lots of work to be done. I need to talk to Keller too—find out what's happened around here."

"This is Keller's last day."

"What? What are you talking about *Patrona*?"

Abbie explained about Mason's complaint to Camp Barlow, and about the compromise to keep Keller on the ranch only until Hector came back.

"Damn," said Hector. "He's the best cowboy I've got."

Brooks's truck pulled up to the barn.

"It's about time they got here," said Abbie. They walked out to the truck.

Hector said, "Get lost? Where the hell have you been?"

"Where are the other guys, Brooks?" said Abbie. "You're alone."

Brooks's face strained. "There's been an accident...at the camp."

"What happened?" said Hector.

"I don't know much about it. This morning I had some notes on my manifest. Schatz was in sick bay, and Keller and Weber had been assigned to KP this morning. Said they broke curfew last night. Didn't sound right to me. Neither one of those guys ever cause trouble."

"KP?" said Abbie.

"Yeah, Kitchen Patrol. Punishment." Anyway, I called base about a half hour ago—talked to my buddy, Smitty, who runs dispatch—wanted to see if I was supposed to pick them up for an afternoon run." Brooks swallowed hard. "That's when I heard the news—an explosion."

"Explosion?" said Abbie.

"The kitchen they were working in blew up. Big fire. No one knows why yet. But it doesn't look good, Mrs. Johnson. They pulled out some bodies. No one's saying who they were yet, but Keller and Weber are both missing...and that's where they were working." Brooks's eyes welled. He paused to wipe away snot with his handkerchief. "I'm sorry." He choked out the words. "They were Germans and all, but they were good guys. Hell, we rode the Bosque together."

Abbie was staggered. "You sure?"

"All I know is what Smitty told me. He said only one guy survived it—one of the German officers, their Nazi bigwig."

Abbie grabbed Brooks's arm. "Nazi? Is this guy one of those *circle people*?"

"The Circle? How do you know about that?"

"From Keller," said Abbie. "Did you know they were after him?"

"You're kidding," said Brooks. "Shit! Those guys are poison. The guy that survived, Major Schwering, is the one that gave them KP. His name's on their yellow slips."

Abbie didn't have all the pieces of the puzzle, but she had enough. The Nazis had gotten to Keller. Weber too. *Why Weber? My God!*

"What about Schatz?" demanded Abbie. "Brooks, what about Schatz? Is he OK?"

"As far as I know. He was in sick bay this morning. Shouldn't have been anywhere near that explosion."

Abbie clenched harder on Brooks's arm. "These Nazis. This circle thing. Can they get to Schatz?"

Brooks's head twisted. He didn't answer. He didn't have to.

Abbie ran to the passenger door of the truck. "Brooks, take me up to the house, right now."

"Whu...?"

"Just do it," Abbie ordered.

They hopped in the truck and sped the short distance up the hill, stopping in front of the adobe. Abbie bounded through the front door and into her bedroom. She took a folded sheet of paper out of her bureau, then ran back outside. She was back in Brooks's truck before the screen door sprang shut. "Let's go. Now!" she said.

"Where're we going, Mrs. Johnson?"

"To the camp," said Abbie. "As fast as you can get us there."

8 1

Camp Barlow

Most of the POWs who made their way into sick bay only managed an aspirin or a Bromo-Seltzer, but Schatz had been convincing with his feigned stomach pain, enough to be given a bed.

While in the infirmary, Schatz heard the story that found its way to every corner of camp. An explosion in a mess hall. A gas line blew up. The mess hall burned to the ground, but the surrounding buildings survived thanks to the firefighting heroics of everyone working together. At least two people were dead. Maybe more. Major Schwering made it out of the building by some miracle. He was in the next room, getting patched up.

Nurse McCarthy came through an inside door. She guided Major Schwering and sat him on a chair in the corner of the room— Schatz's room. Schwering's hand was wrapped in mounds of white gauze. The nurse said to him, "Here sir, rest your elbow on the arm of the chair and hold your hand upright." Schwering was gaunt.

His response to Nurse McCarthy was an empty expression. She said, "That was a nasty cut. Thirty-two stitches. That laudanum injection should keep the pain down."

Like all POWs, Schatz knew who the Major was. Schatz had already figured it was Schwering's goons that beat him up in the shower. Now he sat only ten feet away from the man. He didn't know whether Schwering recognized him. He turned away and prayed not.

Doc Hawley came into the room and sat next to Schwering. "How good is your English, Major?"

Schwering's voice was wispy. The laudanum was taking its toll. "I understand you ... doctor."

"I was able to stop the bleeding, Major. But that hand is in bad shape. Whatever sliced through your hand cut it up pretty bad. Some important tendons and nerves were cut in two. I called the V.A. hospital in Tucson. They have a surgeon there who specializes in this sort of thing. We'll see if we can arrange to ship you up there, have him take a look at it. Might take a few days before we can cut through the red tape."

"But I am to leave for Germany tomorrow," said Schwering.

"Not likely now. Plans change," said the doctor.

Schwering blankly stared at his bandaged hand. "I cannot move my fingers," he said.

Hawley said, "Maybe that surgeon in Tucson can work a miracle." The doctor patted Schwering's back and left the room, leaving Schatz alone with Schwering.

The Nazi appeared to be in a daze. His eyes rolled around the room, then locked down on Schatz. Schwering said in a half-whisper, "You know who died in the fire, don't you?"

Schatz shook his head vigorously. His eyes reddened.

"No? Then you haven't heard?" Schwering's head swayed as he smirked. "Your cowboy friends, of course. If only you and Corporal Weber had played the game ... Too late now."

Abbie was impressed by Brooks's ability to drive the truck. His arm was amputated just below the elbow, yet he handled the shifter easily.

Abbie said, "I need to see Jim Davenport and it can't wait. How can I do it, Brooks? How can I get to him?"

"We're not supposed to bring civilians into the camp, ma'am. But I won't lie to you. It does happen. Some of the guys sneak women in there, if you know what I mean," said Brooks, a little embarrassed.

The truck approached the front gate.

"Slide over to the middle," said Brooks.

"What are you talking about?"

"Move over here next to me. Make like we're on a date," said Brooks. Abbie was dubious. "Look Mrs. Johnson, if you want to get in the gate, you've gotta play along."

Abbie slid to the center of the seat and nuzzled up to Brooks. Then, overplaying the role, she laid her head on his shoulder. "Can you still shift, soldier boy?"

Brooks sputtered, "Yeah…yeah, no problem."

Brooks slowed the truck to a crawl and eased to the camp gate. He knew the sentry in the guardhouse and pointed a confident finger toward him. The sentry laughed, "Hoo Boy Brooksy. That's some cowgirl. Sure you ain't going to need two hands? Just give me a holler if you need some help. Ha." The truck rolled through the checkpoint. Abbie moved back to the passenger side as Brooks weaved past the motor pool. He parked the truck on the backside of the mechanics shed, away from any activity.

"Here," said Brooks, handing Abbie his clipboard and pencil. "We're walking over to Officers' Country. Stay a foot or two behind me and off to the side. It'll look like I'm escorting you. Write while you're walking. Take notes like you're an official."

"An official what?" said Abbie.

"How the hell would I know," said Brooks. "Just look important, like maybe you're from the Red Cross, or a government
auditor or something."

"Dressed like this?" Abbie tugged at her jeans.

"As long as you look like you know what the hell you're doing,
nobody will ask any questions. Welcome to the Army. Let's go."

Brooks paced quickly. Abbie stayed a step behind, scribbling
nonsense on Brooks's roster. He took her along the dirt roadway
that separated the American garrison from the POWs who were on
the other side of a tall, wire fence. They walked under the shadow
of a guard tower. Abbie looked toward the prison side—row upon
row of barracks—dozens of men in blue PW jerkins. Stringy wisps
of smoke rose from the middle of the compound and a charred
odor was on the breeze. Abbie choked a bit at the thought of Keller
and Weber who'd died under that smoke.

"Once we get to Officers' Country, you're on your own, Mrs.
Johnson. If anyone finds out I helped you get in here, they'll have
my butt on a skewer. You might have to do some fast-talking."

Abbie nodded.

They turned away from the POWs and walked toward the Officers' buildings. Brooks took back his clipboard and escorted Abbie
to the guard shack. "Mrs. Johnson has an appointment to see Major
Davenport," said Brooks. He turned sharply and walked away.
Abbie was deep inside the military camp. A foreign world. She'd
have to rely on her wits.

The guard phoned the admin secretary and told her Colonel
Riley was coming out of the HQ building to meet her. *Colonel Riley!
The one man I want to avoid.* Her plan was unraveling. *I can't trust
him with this information. He'll sweep it under the rug, the same way he
did with my Keller request.* There was too much at stake. She would
only trust Davenport.

Riley came down the steps and met Abbie at the guardhouse.

He tipped his hat. "Mrs. Johnson, it's rare we get visitors here in camp. Exactly, how did you get—?"

Abbie interrupted. "Colonel. I have some things to discuss with Major Davenport."

"Well, Major Davenport's pretty busy this morning—been holed up in his office talking to about every war department you can think of." Riley spoke to her in his familiar, condescending tone. She might as well have been a schoolgirl. "He doesn't have time to talk to you right now. We've had a busy morning around here—."

"I know about your morning. I know about the fire and I have information about it. That's why I'm here. Major Davenport has handled things for me before."

Riley spoke skeptically. "Well, why don't you just tell me what you know, young lady?"

Riley sounded just like Mason and it was all she could stand. "No. I need to speak to Davenport."

"Just a minute," said Riley. He stepped into the booth and picked up the phone. He spoke in a hushed tone, but Abbie heard him. "This is Colonel Riley. I need an escort to the HQ guardhouse. Make it quick." He set down the phone, kept his back to Abbie, and huddled with the guard.

Riley turned around. "Mrs. Johnson, we have no time…" Abbie wasn't where he left her. She was already up the steps of the HQ. Riley yelled, "Mrs. Johnson, you can't go in there." Ignoring him, Abbie hurried through the front door and shut it behind her.

Uniformed clerks sat at various desks. She spoke to the first one in her path. "Major Davenport's office please."

The clerk pointed down the hallway. "Second door on the right ma'am." She wasted no time.

Riley flung open the door to see Abbie's backside moving down the hallway. "Corporal, stop that woman."

"Sir?"

"Stop that woman!"

There was a scramble of khaki uniforms. As Abbie stepped inside Davenport's office, two clerks caught her. If she'd been a man, she'd have been tackled and cuffed. But these soldiers weren't keen on roughing up a small, unarmed woman. They found an unspoken compromise by gripping her arms and holding her against the wall inside Davenport's office.

Davenport dropped the phone receiver. "What the sam hell is going on?"

Riley came through Davenport's door—his face red as a beet. He bellowed at the clerks, "Take this woman, under guard, to the front gate. Call the local sheriff—"

Abbie screamed. "Listen to me! Men were murdered here this morning." She tugged against the soldiers' grasp, but they held tight. "It will happen again if you don't listen to me!" She ignored Riley and implored Davenport. "You have to listen to me, Jim."

8 2

Vienna

The victorious Allies divvied up Europe, carving out zones to rebuild the war-torn land. French, British, Russians, Americans, Canadians, and Australians all pledged to work together—but cooperation was a difficult road. Pride, politics, and bullheadedness blocked the way. Sharing resources and information was deemed a weakness by some, particularly the Russians.

There was an exception to this trend—the search for Nazi criminals. Evidence piled in after the war, showing Nazi atrocities to be numerous and far-reaching. Their inhuman treatment of groups such as Gypsies, Poles, and Russian POWs was catalogued daily. Europe's Jews were dealt an abomination that was beyond imagination. With evidence mounting, the occupying nations were sympathetic toward the victims and therefore willing to cooperate on this score—to catch these bastards before they had a chance to slip through their fingers.

Combined Allied intelligence pinpointed Vienna as a hot spot, a bottleneck for fugitive Nazis. In Vienna's French Zone, agents canvassed the streets looking for leads. They plunged deep into the underside of the city, consorting with hustlers, whores, loan sharks, and every sort of criminal—anyone who was likely to get close to these desperate Nazis.

Markus was approached daily by agents. These men wore civilian clothes but fooled no one. They were military men with cheesy accents. They asked questions, showed photographs, even offered rewards for some of the Nazi ringleaders. He recognized one of the photos, Mr. Schröder, a good customer (and by the photograph, a Wehrmacht general). There was no reward attached to Schröder. Must be small potatoes. Why would Markus finger this man? That would be like taking money out of his own pocket.

8 3

Camp Barlow

Davenport jumped from behind his desk. "Hang on Colonel. Why don't we give Mrs. Johnson a chance to speak her mind?" His voice was calm and mollifying.

Abbie pleaded, "But you have to—"

Riley barked, "You're not in a position to tell anybody what to do, young lady—"

Davenport thrust a palm toward each combatant as if to say *put on the brakes*. Riley and Abbie were still huffing, but both took Davenport's cue and backed off. Davenport nodded to the clerks and they eased their grip on Abbie. He continued in a diplomatic tone, "What do you say Colonel? Shall we hear what Mrs. Johnson has to say?"

"Damn it! Nobody pushes their way by me and does what they goddamn feel like around here." He thrust his finger to within an inch of Abbie's nose. "How the hell did you get in here, and who do you think runs this goddamn camp anyway?"

Abbie and Riley continued their stare-down. She realized there was only one way forward and broke the deadlock. "You do, Colonel. Please accept my apology. I was desperate."

Davenport interjected before Riley could return to his inquisition. "Thank you, Mrs. Johnson. OK by you if we hear her out, Colonel?"

Riley growled, "You've got five minutes. So fill us in. What's so all-fire important?"

Abbie sat opposite the two officers. The clerks were dismissed. She told her story. It took longer than five minutes.

She started with Keller's tale of the massacre of Maarburg and about the German general named Uhlemann. Both American officers listened as she told them about Keller's theft of the records, the photos, about Taatje and her hiding place. She unfolded Keller's notes and pushed them across the desk to Davenport who had been writing down everything.

Abbie needed a moment to gather her wits. The realization of the morning's murders was haunting her. Keller and Weber were good cowboys. They were good men. She stood and paced toward the open window. A warm breeze blew in across her face. She watched the prisoners on the other side of the wire. A dust devil skittered across the dirt pitch where they played soccer. She heard their German voices in playful banter, apparently arguing who had possession of the ball before the dust devil stalled their game. She wondered how such hatred could exist among countrymen over political ideals—enough to kill each other.

Riley broke her trance. "Now Mrs. Johnson, tell me how this all fits in with my little POW Camp—and why you found it necessary to bust in here."

Her jaw clenched at Riley's pig-headedness and his blindness to the horrors going on under his nose. She diced her words calmly. It would be counterproductive to further anger the ignorant man. "Because Colonel, that secret I just told you—Keller's secret—got two of your prisoners murdered this morning. Innocent men!" She choked a little. "And because the killing may not be over yet."

She had Riley's attention now. She told the officers how Keller described a group inside Camp Barlow called the Circle—Nazi maniacs—and how he was afraid they would learn his secret. Keller knew they would kill him for it. Abbie told them about Brooks's account of the morning—about the bogus KP assignments and how it put Keller and Weber at the site of the explosion. No coincidence. She told them she was here because her third German cowhand, Private Schatz, was supposed to be in the camp infirmary—also at the time of the explosion. Again, no coincidence. She was here to save Schatz's life.

Davenport had three pages of notes. He paper-clipped them while saying, "I'll be sure that this information gets into the right hands. Our boys in Europe are scrambling to catch these Nazi murderers. I'll send it up the line to Military Intelligence and the OSS. They'll jump all over it. I'll start making phone calls right away."

Riley nodded his approval.

"Thank you," said Abbie.

Davenport said, "Now to matters here in camp. We need to find Private Schatz. Let's see if he's still in sick bay." He picked up his phone. "Hawkins, get me Betty McCarthy in sick bay. And, is Evans at his desk? Good. Send him in here. Now."

Before the phone connected to the nurse, Evans stepped in. "Sir, you wanted to see me?"

"Yes, Lieutenant. You're taking affidavits from the witnesses to this morning's accident, right?"

"Yes sir."

"Where is Major Schwering now?"

"Still in sick bay, sir."

84

Camp Barlow
Five hours earlier

Keller lunged toward sunshine—parallel to the ground as he clipped the swinging door. At that moment, the kitchen lurched like a battleship being pounded by a torpedo. The concussion walloped him from behind, hurling him like he'd been shot from a cannon. He somersaulted in mid-air before he slugged firm earth and bounded to a sliding stop on the hard packed gravel. His ears rang. His face was scraped and his palms were gashed. Keller instinctively got to his feet and kept churning. It hurt but he was in one piece. Fortunately, he'd been moving away from the blast and it picked him up as if he was a bird in a hurricane.

Bedlam. Men poured toward the inferno from all directions. Keller's head was spinning, but his gut told him to gather his wits. This ordeal wasn't over.

One thing was clear—he had to get out of the camp. The Circle wouldn't stop if they knew he was alive. His ticket outside the wire had always been Brooks's truck—no longer plausible. The Americans would tie him to the scene of the explosion. They'd keep him in camp for the inquiry and the Nazis would circle like sharks. He'd have to hide until he could devise an escape. If he could get out, the rest of his plan was already in place.

By design, there are few places to hide in a prisoner-of-war camp—no nooks, closets, or attics. His best bet was to hide in plain sight. Every POW wore the same blue outfit. An odd camouflage, but it could work. He joined a makeshift water bucket brigade—fifty *blue* POWs in a long line. Keller pushed into the middle of the queue, kept his head down and passed bucket after bucket.

It took almost two hours to put the fire out. The mess hall had burned to the ground. The flames were dead but smoke and steam rose from the ruins. An MP jeep rolled around the site with its megaphone blaring, instructing all POWs to muster at their barracks for a headcount. The men trudged away from the blackened hulk. Keller was moving with the herd when he saw Dieter Jung, his bunkmate, up ahead. Jung was the ranking NCO—the "mother" of Barrack 19. All the labor orders went through him. He would also be taking the headcount. Keller hurried to catch him.

Keller was absent from roll call. He went into the latrine and stayed there until muster was over. It was Jung's idea. Jung would give the roster to the Americans, noting Keller's absence. Between the roll call and KP duty, it wouldn't take long for the Americans to place Keller at the scene of the explosion. All the better. Let them think he was among the ashes.

When roll call dispersed, Keller went into the barrack. He rummaged through the bottom of his footlocker, rolled up a couple of items of clothing and cinched them with a belt.

Jung found Keller at his bunk. He had a young POW in tow. "Keller, you know Private Gerhardt, here? I told him what to do. You'll get on his truck with his farm crew. You have your labor pass?"

"It expires today. But it's for a different vehicle."

Gerhardt said, "The guards hardly look at the passes anymore, haven't since the war ended. Just hold it up so they can see you have one, Sergeant."

"Good," said Jung. "Keep your head down. One other thing. Can you hide that limp until you get to the trucks?"

Keller nodded. "I did it once before. I can do it again."

"Good luck, Keller."

Before he left, Keller unpinned Taatje's photograph from the wall and slid it into his clothing roll. He tucked the roll under his shirt and followed Gerhardt.

The staging area was a mass of prisoners, zigzagging to get to their transports. The fire had put them all behind schedule. Now they were being pushed to hurry to make up for the lost morning.

Keller stayed on Gerhardt's shoulder and followed him toward the back of one of the large, canopied trucks. They both flashed their passes at the American driver and hopped into the back. Gerhardt told Keller to lie under the bench. As other POWs piled in they noticed the newcomer but Gerhardt signaled them to silence. Keller was soon hidden by boots and haversacks. The American driver appeared at the back of the truck, glanced at his clipboard and took a headcount. "Eighteen. Good to go." A few moments later the diesel engine chugged to life and the truck rambled out the front gate.

When they were on the move, Keller crawled out of hiding place. He pulled off his prison clothes. The other POWs watched him strip to his underwear. Gerhardt was the only person who knew what was going on, but there was an understanding—they were helping a fellow German beat the Americans' system. That made it good.

Keller unraveled his clothes roll, a beat-up pair of blue jeans and a threadbare western shirt. They didn't fit him—too big around the girth—Hector's throwaways. Keller tightened his belt as if he was cinching up Pay Day.

Gerhardt motioned him to the back of the truck. "Sergeant, after we go over the railroad tracks, wait five seconds, then drop and move right. This truck doesn't have a mirror on the right side, so the driver won't see you. There's an irrigation ditch that runs along the downside of the tracks. Hide in it."

Keller slapped Gerhardt's shoulder. "Thanks, Private."

Gerhardt said, "I don't know what you have in mind, Sergeant, but the trains move slowly through here. If you run fast, maybe you can hop on a flatcar."

Keller made his way to the back of the truck and crouched on the rear bumper. The truck slowed and bumped over the tracks. Keller hunched. As the truck began to accelerate he dropped to the ground and rolled—the second time today he'd gotten a mouthful of dirt. This time the earth was friendlier.

Camp Barlow

Schatz was more afraid now than the day he was captured in the Ardennes. Schwering sat in a chair only a few feet away. Schatz lay frozen on his cot and stared at the rafters—afraid to glance at the wicked major but also afraid to turn his back. There was no doubt Schwering was behind the murder of his friends or that he master-minded the *Circle*. Would he send his jackals after Schatz next? Of course he would.

The infirmary was thick with the aroma of medicines and cleaning fluid. Nurse McCarthy entered the room. She moved a rolling tray table next to Schwering and placed a hypodermic syringe on it. "I have an injection for you, Major. Something to fight off infection."

Three Americans barged into the room, Major Davenport followed by two MPs. It took a moment for Davenport to catch his breath. "Betty, Major Schwering is to come with me."

"We're not finished with him yet, Jim. He has a nasty gash. Doc Hawley wants us to watch him for another hour or two—doesn't want to let him go until we know the bleeding has stopped. Doc's stepped out for a couple minutes. I don't have the authority to let him go."

"What's this all about, Major Davenport?" said Schwering, his English now improved.

Davenport ignored Schwering. He turned to the young man who was now sitting up on his cot. "What's your name, soldier?"

"Schatz, sir. Private Elias Schatz."

Davenport turned to Betty. "Is there another room where we can take Major Schwering? I want him isolated. We'll be posting a guard."

"I suppose we can move him back into the examination room," said the nurse.

Schwering became animated. "I demand to know what this is about, Major Davenport. Are you placing me under arrest? If so, I am entitled to know the charge."

"We can do this the easy way or the hard way," said Davenport. The two guards positioned themselves on each side of Schwering.

Schwering stood grudgingly and allowed the guards to escort him from the room.

"I'll find Doc Hawley," said Betty.

Schatz was alone in the room. Schwering was gone. Thank God for that. The nurse's tray was in front of him. On the tray was the hypodermic syringe intended for Major Schwering. Schatz surveyed the austere space—another cot, a chair, and a sink over a small white cabinet. He looked back at the syringe.

Nurse McCarthy returned to Schatz's room. He was sitting on his cot with his back propped against the wall.

"You look like you're feeling better," she said.

Schatz nodded.

"The doc will be back in just a minute. He'll take a look at you and probably let you go."

Betty picked up the tray with the hypodermic syringe and took it to the next room. Schatz's eyes followed her until she disappeared from view but he could hear her voice, "Here you go Major. Let's roll up your sleeve."

A few seconds later came a piercing scream. "Aaiiieee." It sounded like the gates of Hell had opened. "Aaaahhhh. God in heaven! Aaaiiieee."

Two orderlies and a nurse emerged from the ward and bolted by Schatz's cot. They followed the screams into the examination room.

Schwering's rants grew in intensity. "I'm burning. My arm is on fire. Aaiieeee. God help me. My chest. Aaiieeeee."

Doc Hawley ran past. Schatz didn't understand the frantic exchange in the next room, but it was clear no one knew what was happening to Major Schwering. Sick Bay was a clamoring din. Above it all were the agonizing screams of Major Schwering. Schatz remained still, sitting on his cot.

The screaming stopped. The chattering dissolved.

A young nurse stood in the doorway between rooms. She said softly, "Is he dead?" She answered her own question. "My God, he is."

Schatz leaned over and opened the white cabinet door underneath the sink. He checked to be certain the bottle of bleach was exactly in the position he'd found it.

Maarburg

Davenport's phone call was given immediate attention by the men in military intelligence. The OSS was soon involved. Because the Canadian Military was in charge of the Dutch Zone along the upper-Rhine, the Canadian Intelligence Corps was also in league. In less than two days, a team was in Maarburg to find Keller's documents—lightning speed for military bureaucracy—but the circumstances were distinct. Capture of Nazi war criminals was a high priority for Canadians and Americans alike.

A mish-mash group stood at the door of 131 Kuiperstraat in Maarburg, a little apartment building with a red flower box above the sidewalk. A Canadian IC investigator was nominally in charge, but the American OSS man was calling the shots. The door was flanked by two Canadian MPs. The newly elected mayor of Maarburg, the first non-Nazi appointment in five years, showed up too.

For the mayor this was a political opportunity but he had no delusion of authority.

As the landlady turned the key to Taatje's flat she told the mayor, "When the Germans took that poor young woman away, everyone knew she wouldn't be coming back. So I'm afraid there's not much left in here. Burglars broke in and took her things. Even the furniture was taken—for firewood."

The door and lock were still intact. No signs of burglary. The mayor gave the landlady a quizzical look. He might have assumed she was the thief.

The mayor was the translator. He asked the landlady, "How long ago did the Germans take Miss Hoobinck?"

"Perhaps three months."

The group entered the flat. The landlady was told to wait outside. Indeed, the apartment appeared to have been ransacked. The bed was flipped over. All that remained of it was a mattress and metal frame. Clothes were scattered on the floor. No sign of a wardrobe or bureau. No table or chairs. The doors of the kitchen cabinet were gone. Nothing left there but a few dishrags.

There was a wide, dark smear on the plank floor, surrounded by spatter marks.

"Blood?" said the OSS man.

"Certainly looks that way," replied the investigator.

The OSS man fiddled with the stonework behind the stove. One of the capstones lifted away. "Here we go, right where they said it would be."

He dipped his hand into the void and rummaged around. He pulled out some papers and a tattered envelope. He perused them and handed them to the Canadian agent. The documents were written in German. Neither man was up to the translation, but they could decipher enough to know that the documents originated from the office of General Martin Uhlemann. This was what they were looking for. The CIC office in Amsterdam would make quick work of these.

The OSS man perused the envelope. On the outside was a single sentence in Dutch language. He guessed it to be in a feminine hand. He asked the mayor to translate.

These photographs were taken from the dark room of Wehrmacht Corporal Oskar Brill at Van Sloten House in Arnhem. Brill is the photographic journalist of General Martin Uhlemann.

The OSS man took the photos out of the envelope. He looked at each one then passed them to the next man. Gruesome pictures of a slaughter—civilians shot point-blank by German soldiers including a captain and a general. On the back of each photograph were inscriptions in the same handwriting. Again the mayor was asked to translate. He thumbed through the photos. His brow beaded as he paled at the grotesque scenes. He explained. "At the top, these are the names and addresses of the victims. Miss Hoobinck was very thorough. For instance, this one says the name of the victim was *Regiena Hoobinck*. My God, this is the young lady's mother, isn't it?" He turned over the photo to reveal a picture of a middle-aged woman, Taatje's mother, being shot in the head by General Uhlemann.

The OSS man came back to one picture, that of a little girl at the moment she'd been shot, her mother rushing to her side as a German soldier aimed at the mother. On the back of the photo was the name of the little girl, Jana de Zoute, and her mother, Malena. The OSS agent's upper lip tightened as he looked again at the mother's eyes witnessing her little girl's murder. He compared those names to the ones in his dossier. He said to the Canadian, "The German soldier who supplied this information...This is his niece, and his aunt."

One week later

Cecile Wijl continued her duty at the Arnhem infirmary. Though the war had ended nearly six weeks ago, there was no shortage of patients—townsfolk who hadn't escaped the last onslaught. She'd just come off her nightly rounds and sat on the front stoop enjoying a cup of tea and a hard roll. Cecile reminisced about the last time she sat in this spot with her friend, Taatje. She wished Taatje could be with her now. Things were getting better. Food wasn't so scarce. The Canadians were seeing to that. Yet the wheels of recovery were slow. Half of Arnhem was in ruins. She wondered if her city could ever rise from the ashes.

It was a sunny morning. A wispy scent of flowers was on the breeze. Flowers—a symbol of the nation—and one that had gone missing for a long time. As Cecile sipped her tea, she thumbed through a Dutch news sheet, a small circular. Dutch newspapers weren't up-and-running yet, but small pamphlets like this provided Netherlanders with something they'd been missing—truth. A free press. Not Nazi propaganda. Her people were finally free from the German tyrants.

The headline article was titled *The Butcher of Maarburg*. It detailed a mass murder that was carried out in a barn in the Maarburg countryside. For the Dutch who had just endured the worst time in their history—the *hunger winter*—the news of a Nazi atrocity wasn't a surprise. One item in this story caught Cecile's eye, the name of *the butcher*, the murderous German general—*Uhlemann*. A peculiar name and one she remembered from Taatje's tale. She read on. The story was unique in that it held an element that most stories did not—proof. Photographs. Cecile turned to the inside pictures—heinous and abominable. These were the photographs she'd been told about. Taatje's photographs.

Cecile closed the pamphlet and wondered how these pictures had made it into the public eye. She couldn't be certain, but she assumed the letter she'd sent to Taatje's German soldier, the prisoner-of-war, had somehow liberated these pictures and brought out the truth—the truth that Taatje had so desperately sought. Maybe, from her grave, Taatje would have justice.

8 7

Camp Barlow

After the fire, a team of investigators came to Camp Barlow. They interviewed everyone who'd been connected to the tragedies that day. This included Private Schatz, who sat through several sessions of questioning over a five-day period. When they were satisfied he could shed no further light, they released him from further obligation. The next day, he was back to work at the Jackrabbit. That was a week ago. Schatz was a cowboy again.

Today he'd put in a full workday at the ranch, then Brooks brought him back to the camp. He finished his supper in the mess and walked outside where he was met with a hot breeze. Mid-July, and it was still _hot as hell_ even though the sun had just settled behind the western range. Schatz had a little time so he wandered to the back of the prison compound.

Behind the pump house was a small cemetery. It was little more than a flat, dirt courtyard. The graveyard was outlined by a short picket fence. Off to the side was a small shrine that consisted of a statue of Jesus and a bench. The placard read—

DONATED BY THE CALVARY CHURCH OF COCHISE COUNTY

The cemetery was in clear view of a guard tower so POWs were free to visit. Schatz hadn't been there before, but on this evening he felt a weight. Dusk still afforded him a bit of light. There were nine graves, each with a wooden head marker in the shape of a German cross. Three of the markers were weathered. Schatz had heard the stories of their deaths—a burst appendix, consumption, and a weak heart. But the newer graves were another matter. Schatz, like all POWs, knew about these men and how they'd fallen under the boot heel of the Circle. *Jauch. Dreisenmann.* He stepped to the new markers. *Corporal Niklas Weber.* His friend. There wasn't anything left of poor Weber to bury. Only his dog tags were found in the ashes. Weber's plot wasn't really a grave, only a marker. Next to Weber was another—*Sergeant Franz Keller.* The best man Schatz had ever known. They'd found nothing of Keller among the burnt wreckage, not even his dog tags. Nevertheless, the investigators concluded that Keller died in the blaze. Schatz tried muttering a prayer, but he couldn't remember many of the words from his youth. Instead, he sat on the Calvary bench and spoke to God in improvised verse. He asked Him to accept his friends into heaven, that they were both good men. Schatz felt wrong, felt guilty, that he couldn't show his sadness, but it wasn't in him. He was nineteen years old. He'd been in the war less than a year and had seen so much. Too much. Tears weren't possible.

Schatz walked to the last two graves. Again, one was only a marker—that of Sergeant Müller. The last was a full grave, a fresh mound on the officer's side of the pathway. The marker was engraved.

RIDING THE WIRE

Major Horst Schwering
1903 – 1945

Schatz spat on it.

88

Vienna

The *Felberstrasse* parallels Vienna's rail lines through a tough part of town. Uhlemann paced along the sidewalk on his daily trek. His palate was set on smoked ham and Markus had promised him one today. The black market was burgeoning. Yesterday's cognac was an unexpected windfall. The little pleasures made Uhlemann's existence bearable. He'd expected to be spirited out of Vienna weeks ago—with a new identity. To Egypt, Greece, Argentina... It didn't matter as long as he got away from these damned Allied invaders, especially the fucking Russians. He was chafing at the bit. He had the money and possessed the business acumen. With connections through Nazi channels, he could make it to the top again. No doubt.

As he walked, a train rumbled beside him. The green warehouse came into view. There was Markus, leaning against the lamp post as usual.

Uhlemann's pace quickened. When he got to within fifty meters, he yelled to Markus, "Good day my friend. Did the ham arrive?"

Markus didn't answer, but turned his back. Uhlemann heard footsteps coming on him from behind. He turned. Two men in suits, overtaking him. He tried to run, but they were on him instantly and tackled him face down into the cobblestones. Before he could move, his wrists were shackled behind his back. Two uniformed French soldiers appeared behind the men in suits and stood over Uhlemann. Their rifles were pointed at his head.

One of the suits drove his knee into Uhlemann's neck. He spoke with a broken accent. "General Uhlemann, we are taking you into custody. You will answer for your crimes."

"You are mistaken. My name is Schröder. I'm a businessman."

The second suit jerked Uhlemann onto his back and pushed a handbill in front of his face—a wanted poster—titled *War Criminals at Large*. It featured nine photographs of Germans, including himself. Uhlemann's photo was twice the size of the others and centered prominently at the top of the poster—the big prize. Underneath each photo were the fugitive's names and rewards in Swiss Francs. The talking suit said, "No general, we have the right man. We had no idea where you were until this handbill came out yesterday. Offer a little blood money and the rats come out of the woodwork."

Uhlemann looked closely at the flyer. The photo of him was clear. The reward was 2000 Swiss Francs, twice that of the others. His face became pale. There was no way out.

The suit said, "There are prosecutors waiting for you in the Netherlands. If you ask me, a trial's too good for you. If they'd let me, I'd just a put a bullet behind your ear right now. Save everyone the trouble." The agent's finger prodded the back of Uhlemann's skull, pretending it to be a pistol.

A French army truck pulled up to the curb. Uhlemann was

jerked to his feet and pushed toward the truck. He glanced sideways to see the second suit at the lamp post handing Markus a roll of cash. Markus tipped his cap and walked back to the green warehouse. Uhlemann was muscled into the vehicle and it sped off.

89

Camp Barlow

Bottle rockets spiraled into the desert night and burst into colorful streams. Sparklers crackled in a ring around the platform. Strings of firecrackers sputtered as a cloud of sulphur drifted across the quad. While the fireworks dazzled, a brass band played an up-tempo medley of Sousa tunes, *El Capitan—Liberty Bell March*—and the grand finale, *Stars and Stripes Forever*.

The *Fourth of July* at Camp Barlow. This was the third one since the camp opened. The first two years had seen small celebrations inside the American garrison's compound. This was different. The POWs had offered to host America's Independence Day by staging it on the quad. The festivities began when the sun went down. The POW glee club, *Brise Wüste* (Desert Breeze), began with a half-hour performance. The men's voices rang with beautiful harmonies. All songs were German except for the last—a specially prepared rendition of *America the Beautiful*. Then it was the drama troupe's turn to

436

take the stage. They presented a variety show that tripped between German and broken English. The emphasis was on comedy and the slapstick needed no translation. The crowd roared when Private Heinrich Hägermann, a two-hundred-fifty pound colossus, appeared on stage. He was a character, a renowned camp jokester. The ape-like Hägermann was dressed in a sparkling gown. He lounged on the apron of the stage in a sensuous pose, exposing a hairy leg through a long slit in his dress, and sang *Nur Nicht Aus Liebe Weinen*, a popular love song. His *sultry* cabaret baritone evoked hoots from the crowd. Spectators feigned infatuation with the burly diva. He enticed his paramours with winks and blown kisses. Even the Americans joined in, howling like wolves.

Major Davenport was the guest of honor and was provided a folding chair, front and center, to watch the *Liberty Fest*. He was the acting CO of Camp Barlow now. Colonel Riley had been *reassigned* after the Provost Marshall's investigation. Davenport would hold down the fort until the army assigned another commander to take the reins. He guessed they'd probably find a *full bird* returning from Europe, a Colonel nearing retirement.

Davenport brought a surprise. As the fireworks show was wrapping up, he signaled a commissary truck to drive onto the quad. In the back of the truck were dozens of cases of beer. American guards popped off the bottle caps. Cold beers were passed into the throng of raucous Germans. They were delighted and danced away to the band, swinging their bottles and pounding the desert floor with well-worn boots.

A POW delivered a bottle of A-1 to the American major. "*Danke sehn*," said Davenport, and tipped the beer.

There was a sense that this was an *independence day* for the prisoners too. They would be returning to Europe soon. Transportation was set to begin in September. If everything went according to plan, they would all be on their way home by year's end.

The atmosphere in the camp was relaxed for the first time. The accord was due, in part, to the prospect of their homecoming. But Davenport credited something else too. The Circle had been muzzled. Though there were some diehard Nazis remaining in the camp, their threat had withered with the deaths of Schwering and Müller. Davenport was still investigating those events, but he realized he would probably never know how it all played out—the Germans were damn good at keeping secrets. He figured the three German *cowboys* were behind the demise of the Circle—he just didn't know *how*. And maybe he didn't want to.

Davenport leaned back in his chair, his throne. He listened to the band and watched the jubilant men. The beer tasted damn good.

90

Northbound train

Uhlemann was imprisoned for nine days in a French Army stockade outside Vienna. Then he was put on a train that rumbled north. His berth was a prison cell. No window. A single light bulb. Two guards were posted at his door. The first day on the train he insisted on being allowed to walk to the WC. Instead, a guard tossed a bedpan into the cell. It hadn't been removed yet—and it stank.

He was provided three spartan meals a day. The first supper had the tang of urine in the gravy. Uhlemann stopped eating after that.

The steel door slid open. A military officer, wearing the uniform of the Dutch army, stepped in. Uhlemann hadn't seen that uniform in years.

The officer barked, "Do you speak Dutch?" Uhlemann balked. The officer yelled, "Do you speak my language?"

Uhlemann answered, "A little."

"Good. Because I'm sure as hell not going to speak yours."

Uhlemann shrugged. "Where are you taking me?"

"Back to the Netherlands, of course. The site of your crimes." The officer held up a newspaper, *The London Times*. "You've become famous. They've given you a nickname." The officer pointed to the lead article's title, *Butcher of Maarburg Captured*. "Do you understand the meaning?" Uhlemann only shrugged. "Butcher of Maarburg? *Schlächter von Maarburg*? You son-of-a-bitch." The officer threw the newspaper in Uhlemann's face.

Uhlemann remained stoic. "I shall have a just trial. I am a Wehrmacht officer."

"You'll have your trial alright, in front of the Dutch Military Court in Rotterdam."

9 1

Jackrabbit-J Ranch

Abbie balanced a cup of hot coffee in one hand and her boots in the other. She backed through the screen door and stepped like a tight-rope walker over to the picnic table, taking care not to spill a drop. Under the shade of the sycamores, she pulled on her boots and sipped through a cup of coffee. This was her morning ritual—her peaceful time. It wasn't hot yet. The morning sun wouldn't peak over the Bosque for another half hour. A breeze came up from the south this morning. It passed over the valley farms and carried a sweet hint of fresh-cut alfalfa. The coffee was good.

Hector walked up from the stables. "Morning *Patrona*. You and Will have a good time in Willcox?"

"Good morning Hector. It was fine I suppose. Same old Fourth of July—fireworks at the high school. Will had a good time. What about you?"

"I went to the fiesta down in San Ignacio. Sort of special this year, with the war in Europe being over."

"I suppose so," said Abbie. Her voice was tinged with melancholy. "Any word from Manny?"

"No ma'am, not for a couple weeks now. He's out in the Pacific Ocean somewhere. Givin' the Japs hell."

"The war sure changed everything. Turned our lives upside down. That's for sure."

"Yes ma'am. That it did. It surely did."

"How are Richter and Schmid doing?" she asked.

After the funeral for Keller and Weber, two new POWs were assigned to work at the Jackrabbit-J. Schatz became their trainer, taking on the responsibilities that were formerly Keller's.

"They're doing OK I guess. But by the time we make cowboys out of them, they'll be gone."

"I know. Jim Davenport came by yesterday—checking up. He told me these guys would be shipped back to Germany in September, maybe October. Schatz too. I'll miss him. So will Will." She looked up at Hector. "How's he doing anyway?"

"Schatz? Hard to say. He don't talk as much as he used to. Become real quiet—except around Will. He still treats your boy like his little brother—watches out for him all the time."

"Will thinks he walks on water."

"Yeah, Schatz has been good to have around. I guess it's been real hard on him, losing his friends the way he did." Hector sat down at the picnic table across from Abbie. He leaned in and whispered to her, though no one else was within a stone's throw. "*Patrona*, don't you think we should tell him?"

Abbie shook her head. "We can't Hector. We just can't."

9 2

The Netherlands

Uhlemann awakened to the slowing tempo of the train. The air brakes gushed as it came to a stop. His cell door slid open. The Dutch officer appeared.

"Are we in Rotterdam?" asked Uhlemann.

"No," replied the officer. "The rail lines are still torn up. We're transferring you to a truck convoy. Don't get any ideas. The truck will have iron bars just like these."

Uhlemann was escorted, under guard, down the aisle of the rail car. This was the first time in three days he'd been allowed to look out a window. He saw the rail station sign—*Arnhem*. "Arnhem?" he exclaimed.

The officer said, "That's right. Arnhem. It's no coincidence." Uhlemann could hear a clamor of voices building as he moved through the train.

"What do you mean?" said Uhlemann.

"We could have quietly transferred you to a truck escort anywhere along the rail line, but my commander thought there might be merit in bringing you back through Arnhem. Let the people who lived in your bloody grip see you in handcuffs. Let them see justice."

Word had spread that *the Butcher* would be brought back into the Netherlands through Arnhem. Rage swept the city like floodwater.

Cecile Wijl stood in the crowd that surrounded the rail platform. She felt compelled to be there—for Taatje's sake. She stood toward the back of the throng. As the train came into view, people began shouting—rabid curses and profane rumbling. Fists pumped. The crowd milled forward. The Arnhem police formed a human chain and pushed back at the crowd. It was all they could do to keep the furious mass from rushing the platform.

A large figure, flanked by soldiers, could be seen moving by the windows inside the rail car. The crowd erupted. "There he is!" "The Butcher!" "The fucking butcher." "Go straight to Hell, you fucking Nazi!" The crowd was a pot gone to boil.

Two military guards came out of the rail car first, followed by Uhlemann, then another pair of guards.

"That's him, the Butcher!" The horde exploded and surged forward. Policemen were losing ground as the mob undulated at its bounds. The military guards shouted for everyone to stand back, but their voices were lost in the fracas.

Some men broke through the police line and surged toward Uhlemann. The guards were armed but they did not lower their rifles. These were Dutch soldiers. They would not fire at their own people—certainly not for the sake of a Nazi murderer—and the crowd sensed it. Instead, the guards attempted feebly to push back with rifle stocks. Within seconds they were overrun and separated from their prisoner. Both guards and police squeezed out of the frantic mass, leaving Uhlemann on his own against dozens.

Cecile backed away from the frenzy but her eyes remained riveted on the platform where the villain, screaming, fell under a whirlpool of fists and feet. Some of the men produced bludgeons and battered furiously downward into the Butcher. Cheers erupted. The mob frothed.

The horror was dreadful but Cecile couldn't look away. Finally the crowd parted. Men dragged a bloody, limp body out of the melee, off the platform, and into the street in front of the station. People shouted with angry delight. From the back of a truck, one of the men lifted chains and baling hooks. A few women yelled at the men to stop—the general was already dead and that was enough. They were ignored. Many cheered as the hooks were driven into Uhlemann's legs. Chains were clasped to the hooks and hitched to the truck's bumper. Men crammed into the truck, front and back. The driver yelled, "All ready? Let's drag this bastard all the way to Maarburg!" The truck made a victory circle then sped eastward toward Maarburg with Uhlemann's carcass skittering behind.

Cecile wondered if their blood lust would persist for the twenty kilometer parade to Maarburg. Not that it mattered. The Butcher was dead.

93

Jackrabbit-J Ranch

In early August, monsoon clouds build up every afternoon over the mountains east of Barlow. Sometimes they stay in the high country. Other days, the thunderheads roll into the San Miguel Valley. When the rains come, they come hard.

Abbie pushed open the barn door and watched it come down. Hail bulleted the ground and bounced around like popcorn. The metal roof made a monstrous roar. A Jeep slipped and bounced up the road, steering away from deepening puddles and churning up muddy chunks. Abbie waved and hollered, "Over here, Jim. In the barn." He couldn't hear her voice over the clamor, but he saw her waving and wrenched the Jeep toward the barn. It drifted in a smear of muck and stopped in front of the door.

Davenport hopped out of the Jeep and hustled inside. He was quickly soaked. "Doggone! Storm came out of nowhere," he said. A bolt of lightning crashed nearby and the building shuddered.

"Storms don't usually last too long," said Abbie. "Just stay in here until it passes. Hang on a second." She went into the tack room, returned with a towel, and threw it to Davenport. "Here, it's mostly clean."

"Much obliged," he said, blotting his face.

"You looking for the Germans? They went over to Coyote Tank with Hector. Patching up that old windmill with new timbers. Bet they're wetter than you right now."

"Actually I came to see you, Mrs. Johnson." Davenport pulled a newspaper from under his shirt. It was a bit wet, but still intact. He unfolded it and pointed to an article. "Here, read this."

The article was titled, *Nazi Butcher Killed by Angry Crowd*. It was short, only two paragraphs. Abbie said, "This is our guy, isn't it?"

"Yeah, it sure is, Mrs. Johnson. One less bad guy in the world. Thanks to you, they caught him."

"No, not me. It was Keller. I was only the messenger."

"Him too. Too bad he didn't live to see this day."

"May I keep this newspaper, Jim?"

"Sure. Be my guest."

The next morning at sunrise, Abbie walked down to the stables. Will followed behind. Deuce herded the sleepy boy onward. Hector was already there, outfitting some horses. Deuce wiggle-danced and flopped over as Hector greeted him with an affectionate belly rub.

Hector said, "Here you go, *Patrona*. Everything is ready." Chief was saddled and hitched to the rail. Abbie took a few things out of a paper sack and put them in the saddle bags.

"Is the mule packed? Got everything?" Tethered to Chief's saddle was Tojo, the mule, carrying waterproof canvas bags lashed to a pack frame.

"Everything's there ma'am. I double-checked it," said Hector. "You sure you don't want me to go instead?"

"No Hector. It's time I went."

Hector handed Abbie a leather pouch.

"What is it?" said Abbie.

"Not for me to say. You'll find out when you deliver it."

Abbie nodded and tucked the pouch in a saddlebag. She turned to Will and said, "I'll be back in a few days. You listen to Nana Elvia. Be a good boy while I'm gone."

"Yes Mom." She hugged her son and kissed his forehead. He squeezed back.

"Now hang on to Deuce. Don't let him follow me." Abbie led Chief out of the stables with Tojo trailing behind.

94

The Bosque Verde

Abbie rolled her spurs, nudging Chief uphill. Tojo followed the lead. The breeze was stronger up here along the crest of the foothills. Abbie welcomed it. Just ahead were the switchbacks that climbed into the Bosque, but first she had a detour to make.

At the little cemetery, she hitched the animals. To her surprise the graveyard was tidy. Weeds and piñon needles had been cleaned out. The earth around Hank's grave was clear and had been swept with a pine bough. A wilted bouquet of goldpoppies sat atop Taatje's cairn.

Wind rustled through the junipers. She took off her hat and set it on Hank's headstone. She closed her eyes and lifted her hair, letting the refreshing breeze course over her neck. Her mind cleared. Abbie found peace here unlike anywhere else.

Tojo snorted and startled a magpie that shuffled to flight. Abbie opened her eyes. Puffy clouds hovered over the Bosque peaks. Her meditation broken, she plopped her hat back on her head. "C'mon Chief. Let's get moving. Got to get up there before the thunderheads."

She shut the iron gate. Tojo was head-down in a patch of wild rye. She tugged his tether. "Time to go, boy." They started toward the switchbacks.

The flats surrounding Rosado Cienega were mushy and green thanks to the summer storms. The corralled cattle—all now with the Jackrabbit-J brand—wandered in and out of the marsh satisfying their hunger on the sweet, wild grass. The creek was swollen and the tank was full to the brim of the earthen dam. A gushing waterfall formed over the spillway, as the downhill stream began its course into the San Miguel Valley. The sun was high. Scattered dark clouds were moving overhead—a daily ritual. The afternoon rain would probably come early today.

Pay Day was in the corral. Thirsty from the morning ride, he dipped his snout into the cool water, taking a long, noisy slurp. Then he wallowed on his back, blissfully working the dust over his sweaty pelt.

Keller draped his saddle over the fence rail and worked saddle soap into the leather. He laughed as he watched Pay Day, his lone companion of the past six weeks, rocking upside down like a bug trying to set itself right.

Rosado Cienega had become Keller's home. The cabin was small, but he kept it clean and dry. He'd invented a daub made of pine pitch and crushed cinders that did a fair job of sealing gaps in the log walls. It kept most creatures out, save an occasional black beetle.

Hector rode up to Rosado every week. He brought Keller needed supplies—canned food, soap, matches, and books, mostly tattered Zane Grey novels. Keller's plan to master English included reading Grey's westerns—some of them set in the Arizona Mountains. Hector had also given Keller a pistol. Said he might need it. But Keller hadn't used it, and didn't want to. The sound of a gunshot could be heard for miles. He had to lay low, be invisible, and remain in the high country as long as necessary. His kit was meager but he felt like a king. He had all he needed. This mountain was his realm and the cattle gave him plenty of work to do. Best of all, for the first time in six years, he was away from the war. Things that haunted him—French battlefields—Van Sloten House—the Circle—were now distant.

A flash of lightning. Two seconds later, a thunderclap rumbled through the cienega. The rain wouldn't be long.

Pay Day jumped and turned toward the trail, his ears probing like periscopes. Keller heard it too, hooves clopping up the rocky track. Maybe Hector came up a few days early? The figures were obscured through a thicket of young pines. A rider leading a pack mule. They tromped into the glade. Not Hector. Abbie.

Keller's heart quickened. His mind often drifted toward her. Warm thoughts. At times he remembered their conversations about little things—riding, raising Will, or joking around the campfire. He especially reminisced about the time she helped him through the death of Taatje. He even allowed his imagination to run wild, envisioning a romance with the enigmatic *Patrona*. In the days leading up to the explosion, he thought he'd felt a spark between them. He tried to dismiss those notions. *Just folly. Probably.*

He hadn't expected to see her until he came down from the mountain. But here she was. She had come to him.

Abbie rode up to Keller. She said nothing. Her cat-ate-the-canary grin said it for her.

He searched for the right words. All he could come up with was, "Good day, Mrs. Johnson." *Aargh. Stupid.* He helped her off her horse but didn't pull back once she was on the ground. His hand stayed on her waist for a moment. She didn't step away. Her eyes met his. Her smile widened.

"That's some beard you got goin' there," she said.

"I thought best to change my, em ..."

"Appearance? Makes sense you wouldn't want to be recognized, although I doubt you'll run into anybody looking for you up here."

"You like it? My beard?"

"Hmm. You're lookin' a little scraggly, more like a prospector than a cowboy," she chuckled. "If we can find some scissors, I'll trim it for you."

He smoothed his hand along his whiskers and nodded approval.

"I brought something to show you," she said, pulling a newspaper out of her saddlebag and pointing to an article. "Can you make it out? The English I mean? Want me to read it?"

"No. No. I can understand it." He pieced through the article. "Uhlemann is dead?"

"Not exactly the way you planned it. Murdered by a crowd of people."

Keller said, "Hector told me what you did, running into Davenport's office. Very brave."

"Or very stupid," laughed Abbie. "But it worked. Now you're safe, Keller. So is Schatz. And the general is dead. You can go back to Germany."

"No. I will never go back. Uhlemann is dead ... but there are other Nazis who will know my name. To them I am a traitor. They would find me."

Abbie shook her head. "Then what will you do?"

"I have a plan. I started making it soon after I came to your ranch. Hector helped me."

"Hector helped you? Now you're scaring me. What plan?"

"I will change who I am. When Hector went to Phoenix, he was to see someone who makes false identification papers for Mexicans."

Abbie said, "Oh my gosh, that must be what he gave me." She dug into her saddle and produced the pouch. "Hector asked me to give this to you. Is this it?" She laughed, "You think it'll work? You don't look like much of a Mexican to me."

Keller took the papers out of the pouch and scanned over them. "No Abbie, not a Mexican—"

She beamed. He couldn't tell if it was because she was still amused at the thought of him being Mexican or if she liked him using her first name. "Let me see," she said.

He pointed to the first lines on the immigration visa.

Name *Frank de Zoute*
Country of Origin *The Netherlands*

"The Netherlands? So now you're a Dutchman?"

"I think I always have been."

"Frank de Zoute? Where did you get that name?"

"De Zoute was my mother's name. It is Dutch. Hector says Americans can't tell the difference between a German and a Hollander. *Frank*...it sounds American, don't you think? People around here will call me *Frank*."

"People around here would probably just call you *The Dutchman*. Definitely better than *The German*, though." She paused to consider his declaration. "You plan on staying around here then?"

"Yes. Here is everything I wish." Large rain drops began thwacking the ground in a slow rhythm. "The Jackrabbit needs ranch hands. I'm a good cowboy, yes?"

"Next to Hector, you're the best cowboy this ranch has ever seen." She paused. "You really want to do this, Keller?"

"Not *Keller*. You call me *Frank*."

"Do you really want to do this … Frank? You sure?"

"I think about it every day. I love the Jackrabbit. I want to help *you*. Yes. I am sure."

Abbie cocked her head and ambled away from him, thinking it over. Keller gave her space. There was much for her to consider. Hiding him up here in the mountains was one thing, but keeping him on at the Jackrabbit had bigger implications. She leaned against a ponderosa, stared downward, and kicked up loose dirt with the toe of her boot. Raindrops increasingly pattered into the red dust. Finally, she turned to him, "If you're sure, then so am I. But you can't come down off this mountain yet. You'll have to stay up here another month, probably two. Once the POWs start shipping back home, the army will quit coming around. Then you should come down out of the Bosque. In time for fall round-up maybe. This'll give us time to figure out some of the other stuff. Ain't going to be easy."

"Then you want me?" he said.

She looked him square in the eye. "Hell yes, I want you."

The skies opened up. Fierce raindrops peppered them.

"Come on," he said. "Let's get inside."

As they ran to the cabin he held her close, shielding her from the rain.

AUTHOR'S NOTE

I've been asked several times where I got the idea for this story. I suspect my response would resonate with most fiction writers—lots of places.

I grew up about a mile from the remnants of Camp Papago Park, a World War II POW camp nestled in the buttes between Scottsdale and Phoenix. There wasn't much of it remaining when I was a kid. We heard the story about the ill-fated escape from Papago Park, but there wasn't much else about the camp's lore that I recall. The indoor shooting range, a Quonset hut, was still in use. When I was twelve years old, I took a weekly rifle class at that facility from an Arizona legend, Ben Avery.

Another building to escape demolition was the American officers' club. In the early 1960s it became an Elks Lodge. (It still is today, though renovated.) I attended a wedding reception there in 1976. I believe that lodge is the last standing remnant of the camp.

Kids, growing up in the early '60s, couldn't flip the TV channel without landing on a show about World War II. We ate it up. When we played outside, we often chose a game we simply called *guns*.

"Let's play guns. We'll be the Americans. You guys be the *Gerries*." (Yes, racial slurs, aimed at America's former enemies, were still in full swing two decades after the war.) We shot each other thousands of times with our plastic rifles. We were experts at creating our own sound effects—gunshots, ricochets, and the *coup de grâce*, the dying grunt.

Between the ages of nine and thirteen, I spent my summers in Lincoln, Montana with my friends, the McClellands. Thomas, Martha, William and I were close in age. Our moms oversaw our exuberance—along with other members of the McClelland clan. We lived on Granny Mayger's (their granny) ten acre property in the pines. Spring Creek cut through it. Kid heaven! Fishing, worm-digging, fort-building, swimming, raft-building, and anything else we could invent. Best of all—we had horses.

Grandpa Mayger, who had passed away before my days in Lincoln, had been a horseman. He'd built a barn, corral, and pasture. In summer, our mothers rented horses from a nearby rancher and we kept them on Granny's property. They were our horses for the summer. We rode almost every day. Of course, we also took care of them. Chores! We learned well. Their mom, Mary Louise, was an expert on horseback. She taught us right. My mother, Anne, was pretty good too, though she had learned in New York on English saddle and sometimes reverted to that "bobbing" style of riding—good for a laugh.

One summer, when I was fifteen, I worked on a small cattle ranch outside of Mayer, Arizona. A dollar a day. The cowboy-crew consisted of a foreman and five teenage boys. I was the rookie. Our first weekend afforded some free time. The ranch owner brought us to the corral for some fun—calf roping. The other guys had done it. I hadn't. My second time out of the chute, I roped the calf, jumped from my saddle, and tied the critter's legs! All this, while my horse kept the rope taut. I'd earned instant credit. My Montana days paid off. That cow pony was certainly more skilled than me. But hey, I roped the dang calf.

These childhood experiences served as some of the inspiration for this novel. Heck, I swiped some names, human and animal, from those memories. (For instance, the name of that cow pony that helped me rope that calf—*Pay Day*.) A few other names and places were a tip-of-the-hat to some folks in my life.

In my twenties, I became a history teacher and would continue in that proud role for thirty years. Any of my students will tell you that World War II was my favorite unit to teach. (It was also their favorite unit. *Funny how that works.*) As we progressed through the war, I lectured about prisoners-of-war and the inconsistent treatment from one country to another. The Japanese were brutal to their prisoners, the Germans draconian. In contrast, the Americans were humane and generous to their POWs. Those prisoners were fed better in the American camps than they'd been by their own armies. They had a surprising amount of freedom inside the camps. They could even earn a modest wage (in camp chits) for supervised labor on local farms—or wherever manpower was scarce. A few POWs actually returned after the war and settled in the American community near their former camps! *There was a story there.*

In 2010, I began the research for this book. The ideas mentioned above were reinforced. I was also absorbed by a connecting theme. The most ardent, ideological Nazi prisoners (the SS, for example) were detained in a few high security camps around the country. But *all* camps had some of these zealots. In some cases, they made life a living nightmare for the other German prisoners. *There was a story in that too.*

Back to those kids in my classroom. Students are the primary source of any good teacher's inspiration. The more they want to know, the more they deserve good answers. As my students learned about the war, these questions were inevitable. "Mr.

Dudley, did all the Germans believe in Hitler?" "Why didn't anybody stop him?" "What happened to Germans who weren't Nazis?" Great questions. Complex answers. *I had my story.*

Ford Dudley
May, 2021

ACKNOWLEDGMENTS

Writing is a lonely exercise. That being said, I was fortunate to receive superior help in constructing this novel.

I had several beta-readers, friends who read my work and provided feedback along the way. No one was asked to read the first draft, nor should they have been. First drafts are ugly creatures. I had two readers help me with the second draft. (It was still quite rough.) Olivia Tejeda and I met at a writers' workshop and started a critique group. A few other writers tested the waters, but Olivia and I were the only ones to stay with it. We worked through each other's chapters. Her laptop highlighter worked overtime. She implored me to use an active voice rather than a passive one. It took a while, but I finally started to get it. Noreen Swan also critiqued the second draft. I emailed her one chapter at a time. She called me after she'd read it and we'd go over her notes. Olivia and Noreen, in different ways, coaxed me to lay off so much backstory and "explaining". That rubbed against the nature of this history teacher. *The readers need to know the background, don't they? No Ford, they don't. They want the story.* They were right. It would require three more edits before I rooted out the superfluous stuff. Noreen gave me the best, single piece of advice. *Dirty it up!*

Peggy, my wife, and Lisa, my daughter, read the third draft. They were kind in their appraisal but found the same issues as Olivia and Noreen—just not as many. Todd Mitchell and my daughter-in-law, Jessica, plodded through the fourth draft. They found more errors in punctuation and less in prose. Probably a good sign.

Jackie Davies was my editor. I thought I was fairly good with punctuation and sentence construction until Jackie gave my manuscript a good shake-up. Who would've thought commas were so tricky?

Dawn Cottini is a writer and editor. Two weeks before this book was ready to publish she asked if she could read it. *Well, Yeah!* Through her magnifying glass, some final pests were discovered and exterminated. Thanks to Jackie and Dawn, I have a clean manuscript.

Military life is present throughout this novel. I needed someone to help me sort through that. Fortunately, my friend Dennis Chambers was available. Dennis served for thirty-six years in three branches of the U.S. military: the Marines, the Air Force, and the Army. He started out as an enlisted man and retired as a lieutenant colonel. Who better?

A few elements of the plot involve medical conditions. I leaned on my friend, Dr.Michelina Stazzone, for details. Micky provided me with *colorful* descriptions of complications related to leg wounds, sepsis, and poisoning.

There have been hundreds of websites that have provided answers to my research questions. The following book is an excellent read and resource. It served as my bible when I built the world around Camp Barlow.

Krammer, Arnold *Nazi Prisoners of War in America*
Scarborough House Latham, MD 1992

There are four languages used in this book. I'm fluent in one, English. I can muddle through German. Jan Vonk, my friend in Zwolle, Netherlands, helped me with the Dutch phrases. There turned out to be more Spanish in the text than I'd originally imagined. To compound the challenge, I wanted a realistic, Arizona version of the language. Four friends helped me with that; Chris Young, Esmeralda "Dusty" Amaral, Roman DeAnda, and Todd Mitchell.

My son, Alex, advised me on the technical preparation needed to get this novel ready to publish.

Peggy is my wife and my rock. Eleven years ago, when I told her I wanted to write a book, she was surprised. She realized it was a giant commitment but she never questioned my decision (though I did, several times …). She gave me all the support I could have asked for. That's a gift. Without that, I can't imagine completing this book.